I scrabbled at  possible? It had no keyhole, just two thin lines like the halves had been snapped together and the ring for his leash.

I started hyperventilating.

"Pet…" The sing-song whisper almost made me piss myself it was so close. I jammed my fist in my mouth, keeping still. A twig snapped to my right, and I screwed my eyes shut.

A massive crash followed it, and I took off. In retrospect, that was my first mistake. I mean, my first mistake since I'd tried to knee him in the nuts. I was racking them up like student loans otherwise.

The forest floor quickly smoothed out and become easier to navigate, but the trees here were spiky, twisty things crowded close together. They didn't look, I don't know, earthly. I had a bad feeling that I'd somehow wandered into Fae.

Flame & Shadow

by

AK Nevermore

Book One of The Dae Diaries

Flame & Shadow

Cover Art by *Lisa Dawn MacDonald*

The Wild Rose Press, Inc.
PO Box 708
Adams Basin, NY 14410-0708
Visit us at www.thewildrosepress.com

Publishing History
First Edition, 2023
Trade Paperback ISBN 978-1-5092-5181-0
Digital ISBN 978-1-5092-5182-7

Book One of The Dae Diaries
Published in the United States of America

Dedication

Welcome to my literary temper tantrum, born out of frustration and the desire to prove all the naysayers wrong. Mission accomplished, and insert raspberry here.

To my tribe, I love you guys. I can't tell you how much your support means to me. Mom, you're at the top of the list. Don't let it go to your head. To my husband and the ravens, you have my undying gratitude for putting up with me when I'm stuck in a manuscript. Your unwavering faith in my crazy is what keeps me going. Group 3—ladies, you're amazing and saw me through my darkest days. To all my betas, and especially my favorite introvert, thank you for making me and my work better. Thank you to TWRP for taking a chance on my book, and to the RWA's RAMP program for making that possible. And finally, thank you to my editor, Jon Oliver, who pulled me out of the self-doubt abyss and gave me the courage to keep submitting. None of my stuff would be out there without your kind words.

Before

While God created Adam, who was alone, He said, "It is not good for man to be alone" (Genesis 2:18). He also created a woman, from the earth, as He had created Adam himself, and called her Lilith.

Adam and Lilith immediately began to fight.

She said, "I will not lie below," and he said, "I will not lie beneath you, but only on top. For you are fit only to be in the bottom position, while I am to be the superior one."

Lilith responded, "We are equal to each other inasmuch as we were both created from the earth." But they would not listen to one another. When Lilith saw this, she pronounced the Ineffable Name and flew away into the air.

Adam stood in prayer before his Creator: "Sovereign of the universe!" he said, "the woman you gave me has run away."

-Excerpt from Ben Sira's *Alphabet*

Well, duh…

30 Days

Names hold power, so I won't tell you mine. What I will tell you, is that it was June first, the sun was going down, and I was sitting on the Priory's roof, hating my life more than usual.

And I needed a drink.

Don't get it twisted—I wasn't suicidal or anything, and I'm not an alcoholic. What I was, was destined to die at the end of the month. Me, and every other half-elemental that'd hit twenty this year. See, you'd want a drink too. If I had one, I'd pour some out for the fallen.

Hah. No, I wouldn't. I'd down that shit. I probably was an alcoholic, but whatever. I wouldn't be around long enough for cirrhosis to set in.

I closed my eyes, trying to enjoy the last few rays of sun. I'd spent the past hour lamenting my fate and the way my nail polish clashed with my bikini. You know, multitasking. And in weighing my options, such as they were, I kept coming up with snake eyes.

It was bullshit.

I pulled my knees in and sighed, looking out past the crew installing razor wire on top of the compound's tall adobe walls. The desert stretched out towards Vel in the distance. There weren't any better answers there, but I knew people, and one of them owed me a beer. My eyes flicked to the highway running past the Priory, a straight shot into the city.

I could use one of those, too. Preferably tequila.

The sun dipped behind the mountains, and I shivered, shrugging into the scratchy novice robes I'd been sitting on. I padded across the roof and swung onto the ladder. Halfway down, I could pick out Sister Reticence waiting for me in the shadows. I didn't bother saying anything. She never did. I just followed the nun's withered backside to my mother's office, a funeral dirge shuffling through my head. Time to receive my proverbial flogging. I tried to focus on the positives. At least I wouldn't have to sit through many more of these.

My mother had been a showgirl. A good one, headlining her own extravaganza at the biggest casino in Vegas. As I came into the room, it was hard to see past the wimple and remember her raven hair caught up with rhinestones and feathers. Calista Starr had smiled back then. Now Sister Contrition's plumped lips pruned at me. Collagen injections were taking a lot longer to fade than the lipstick had.

"Sit down, Envy."

Hmm? Oh, not my name, but I answered to it. I plunked onto the crappy straight-backed chair in front of the desk. It looked like it had grown up from the floor, then been squished down by the adobe walls pressing in around us. The light coming through the thin scarlet windowpanes painted the top in long, bloody gashes.

What? I was feeling melodramatic.

I picked at a flake of nail polish, also red, and, like roof access, also not allowed.

"Sister Reticence saw you going up to the roof, and I asked her to collect you."

I shrugged, feeling the miserable bitch's eyes on my back. Sister Reticence should mind her own goddamned business.

My mother frowned at me for a moment longer, then shook her head. "Why do you insist on being so difficult?"

I swallowed the lump that'd materialized in my throat. Ever since she'd signed on to become a dedicate of Our Lady of the Blessed Inferno, everything was more than "difficult."

It straight-up fucking sucked.

That's saying something. It wasn't exactly peaches and cream before.

She sighed, stretching out her long fingers in front of her. They looked naked without her rings. I hoped she missed them. I used to imagine the Prioress squeezing them over her bloated knuckles to watch them sparkle. Now I knew better. Nothing in the convent sparkled. Not even Tiffany diamonds.

"Envy—"

"Yes, Sister Contrition?"

Her mouth pinched into a white slit as she glared at me, then took a slow breath.

I liked to watch her nostrils flare out.

"The roof is strictly off-limits."

"So is the quad, the city, the—"

"For one month. Lady forbid the press gets pictures of you up there flaunting yourself."

That coming from the Queen of Burlesque? I laughed.

Bad idea.

She picked up a pen, clicking the end. It was her tell. I was pressing my luck. My gaze drifted from hers

4

to the sunburst on the otherwise bare wall behind her. The Great Lady herself, surrounded by flames. Seemed like a sweet gig.

"The choice is almost upon you. Have you given any more thought to our conversation?"

I bit back another laugh, meeting her eyes again. They'd teared up like some daytime Telemundo star's. She blinked the emotion away so quickly I questioned it ever being there—No. That wasn't fair. I knew she cared. Just not about me. It was the threat to her celebrity.

Wimple or diamonds, my mother was an attention whore and commanded it. She was beautiful, with the voice of an angel. She'd used it to weasel up the convent's hierarchy until she sat just below the Prioress herself. The perfect frontwoman for the Lady's sect, a siren luring other fallen women into the fold. So very contrite after succumbing to the wicked wiles of a daemon.

Well, that she'd gotten caught.

That was on me. My stigmata flaring into being with puberty had fucked the both of us, and she'd never let me forget it. I shifted my shoulders against the severe angle of the chair. They'd stopped itching years ago, but it was a mental thing. My tell. Sugar Daddy might've forgiven her for cuckolding him with a human, but getting knocked up by a dae then passing off his spawn as a normal for a decade crossed the line. He'd dumped us on the streets without a backward glance.

She frowned again, watching me. I rolled my eyes and looked away.

"I'll be late for vespers."

Her gaze rose with me. "Three days of contemplation as penance, starting now. Sister Reticence will see you to your room."

Of course she would. My jaw tightened, but I didn't argue. I followed the miserable nun from the office, through the warren of close, burrowing halls, to the cell I'd been allocated for the past nine years. It wasn't home. It was a place for me to die a little every day.

A hard cot, small chest at its foot, desk, and chair. A hook for my robes. Those were on the floor as soon as the door thudded shut. I missed the click of a real doorknob latching. Hearing the slide bolt engage wasn't nearly as comforting. On the far wall was a high, thin window. I'd broken out the red glass enough times they'd stopped replacing it. Bars lined the gap, but in fairness, they were on all the windows at this level of the dorms. Strictly for the safety of us vestal virgins, I'm told. I could almost believe it with the way tensions were picking up again. That razor wire was no joke.

I sat on the cot in my bikini, staring at my toes. She hadn't made me take the polish off them, and the red made my skin look even paler. Not even the desert sun could give me some color, but I didn't go up on the roof for a tan.

I craved the heat. Half or not, all dae did.

That was the worst part of penance, and she knew it. Everything on the north side of the compound lay in shadow. Only a sliver of sunlight hit my wall for a lousy sixteen minutes in the late afternoon. It was torturous.

I laughed. Had I given more thought to our conversation? I didn't have to. I wasn't sputtering, and I sure as hell wasn't doing it live-stream like they'd been advertising. If I had to die, it was gonna be in a blaze as I surrendered to my elemental half. I wasn't a freaking PR op; I was leaving, this time for good. It was sooner than I'd planned, but locking me up again had torn it, and I wanted that drink.

I wriggled into a pair of jeans and pulled on a tee. Ironically, it was of the Ramones, and I was trying to avoid sedation. The bells had rung for vespers. Everyone would be at chapel. I licked at my lips, pretty sure I could pull this off without tripping the smoke alarms. And if I couldn't?

Yeah, I wasn't gonna think about that.

I focused on the tiny gap between the door and the jamb, calling flame. It wasn't easy. I mean, calling flame was easy, like, I can manifest plasma when I'm desperate, but controlling it? Not so much. I kind of sucked at that, especially when I was nervous. I had to fumble around a bit before I tasted the bite of metal, but once I did, I placed my finger on the point, and let it rip.

I should explain. All daemons can call and control fire. It's our element. We're one of four under the fae umbrella. You know, Air is sylphs, Earth gnomes, Water's undines...but the others, especially undines, aren't nearly as cool.

The stigmata on my back crazed light through my tee and around the room. Stupid nerves. I tried to tamp it down. Last thing I needed were wings of flame bursting out and incinerating everything within a ten-foot radius. No lie. That shit happens.

The gap had started to smolder and blacken up the frame. The slow pulse of the smoke detector's little green light was freaking me out. Once they knew I could mess with metal, they'd keep me drugged. Not an experience I wanted to repeat, and that pen click...my mother was already thinking hypodermic.

All at once, the taste of metal was out of my mouth. I wiped my sweaty hands on my thighs and opened the door. The slide bolt glowed white-hot, and a low ribbon of smoke hung in the hall. Crap. I needed to move.

No way the latch would pass close inspection, but I'd be long gone by then. At least, that was the plan. I mean, I kind of had a plan. Once I got to the undercity, it would be a whole 'nother can of worms, but hey, horse before the cart, people. Berk would let me stay with him, probably.

I ghosted up to the fourth floor on the east side. My mother and the other sisters' rooms were on this level of the dorm. It was a lot posher than below, with a communal sitting room. A lamp was kept burning in the center of a table, the flame leaning toward me as I passed, licking up the scarlet globe containing it. Stupid nerves.

No bars were on the windows up here, and in a heavily curtained alcove at the end, one opened to a narrow ledge. From there, I could get onto the chapel roof. Then freedom was only a drainpipe away.

"...after which, I'll be back to collect them."

A man's rumbling voice stopped me cold as I went to throw the latch. Pressing myself deeper into the shadows, my heart pounded, aching beneath my scar. I rubbed at the stupid thing. What was a man doing in the Priory?

Sounds a moment later cleared that up.

"It won't be an issue..."

Shit, it was my mother. I snuck a peek through a gap in the curtains. The man was tall, with coal-black hair, streaked gray at his temples. Her hand was halfway down his impressively tailored pants.

"No, it won't. I've taken steps to ensure that." He pushed back her wimple, the lamp's flicker glinting off his heavy gold ring. They moved up against a wall, and the lamp flared, then snuffed out.

I fell back with my fist shoved into my mouth to keep from crying out.

Not a man. A daemon.

My father? The possibility floored me.

Her door opened and closed, unmistakable noises coming from behind it. I swallowed my shock and got my ass on that ledge. The moon hadn't risen yet, and it was barrel-bottom dark. I crept across the rooftops and out of the compound, numb.

The first car that came along once my thumb was up, stopped. I thanked the little blue-haired ladies and hopped into the backseat. Must be bingo night. Hitching a ride into the city had never been a problem, even though most of the jerks that picked me up wanted their dick sucked for the privilege. Plenty of pervs drive this stretch. They all rethink their life choices when I call flame. Works better than a brake line on a bus.

As the lights of the Priory dwindled into the distance, the shock of what I'd just seen turned giddy. I was never going back. I laughed. I was never going back, and my mother was screwing a daemon. I wondered if good ol' Sister Contrition would stand up at the next Fae-A meeting and cop to relapsing. I laughed again.

Why did I find this so funny?

My mother was screwing a daemon in the founding church of a religion dedicated to expunging the sin of screwing fae. Their entire bullshit dogma revolved around a supposed vision some patrician asshole had of the world engulfed in flames. Cue finger quotes around their whole "Retribution." Apparently, it's brought on by the aforementioned carnal sin.

Spoiler, half-elementals—halflings—are to blame for their apocalypse, specifically a half-dae, like me.

That's why those bitches at the Priory were so hot to stream my "Redemption" live at the end of the month. Some marketing firm they'd hired to revamp their image said it'd tested better with the focus group than going all jihad on us. All they needed was some impressionable half-dae to sputter, giving up the elemental half of their soul to become fully human, then wax poetic about how wonderful it is.

Getting a better idea of why they were so tickled my mother signed on?

Yeah. Except fuck them, I'd rather go out in a blaze.

Literally.

They hadn't gotten the memo. Otherwise, I'd be strapped to a gurney in a semi-comatose state for the next month. No way I was spending my last days on earth as a vegetable.

I'm sure the biddies that'd picked me up thought I was on something with all the giggling I was doing. I wished I was, because regardless of what hypocritical fuckery my mother was up to, it didn't change the fact that come July first, I'd be dead.

And yes, I know that's not traditional Midsummer. Fae have different rules and halflings have to play by them. I wasn't complaining about an extra nine days.

Whatever. My impending death sobered me up pretty quick. I called a trickle of flame to thread between my fingers and steady myself.

It flared. Stupid nerves.

The car screeched to the side of the road. Told ya. Why does that work so well? To put it mildly, halflings aren't well-liked, though some are tolerated more than others. Half-dae don't make that list. Refer back to the above end of the world stuff. Kind of sours other halflings on us, too. The whole one bad apple thing.

I didn't care. Them booting me gave me a chance to run, and the desert at night? Man, you've never seen stars like that. Being out there was one of the things I missed being under lock and key. Well, behind slide and bolt. You needed a doorknob for the other.

I sprinted the last mile to the subway and rode it into the undercity.

The pub was hopping and tense as hell. The hopping part was only to be expected this close to Midsummer's Eve. June was one giant send-off. Like I said, I wasn't the only one under a sentence of impending doom. Kyle was on stage at the back of the low-lit room. Half the women in the place were breathless as he sang. The other half were breathless because he wasn't wearing a shirt. Sylphs in general have issues with clothes. I have zero issues with their issues.

Before I get ahead of myself, you should know I have a thing for men. I like them. A lot. They like me too, but here's where it gets tricky. Remember I mentioned that whole lack-of-control problem? Yeah, it's not just nerves that make me lose it. Believe me when I tell you, there's nothing worse than incinerating someone just when things are about to get interesting.

Normals are out. Totally.

Halflings are a close call. Like, close enough to scare the crap out of us both before the deed. If there was another half-dae in the city, I'd be all over that, but none in their right mind is hanging out anywhere near the Priory. Before the sisters decided to go all Redemption, it was open season. It left me in a less than satisfied situation, but I did like to look.

God, I liked to look.

I grabbed a beer and leaned back against the bar, my tee sticking to its worn edge as I checked out the crowd. Vel City didn't have a huge halfling population, thanks to the proximity of the Priory, but the community it did have was pretty tight, and most tolerated me. I knew almost all of them by sight, if not by name, though there were new faces replacing the regulars who'd gone missing. That wasn't surprising. As a rule, we're pretty transient.

And we got offed a lot, by both sides. Statistically, maybe a quarter of all halflings make it to the final countdown. The majority are picked off by normals, but fae snagged us too. I'd been talking to a guy once, and then I hadn't been. Like, poof, he was gone. Classic fae move. It was a lot rarer than death by normal, but it happened. As to why, your guess was good as mine, but my money was on dinner or sex.

I should be so lucky.

Berk waved at me from the pool tables. Like that's what I needed to pick out seven-and-a-half feet of bulging brown muscle from the crowd. I pushed through the room of people, and he gave me a hug, his movements more ponderous than usual. He looked like shit. Berk shrugged at my expression, his voice gravelly.

"Working triple shifts. I'll not sputter and see the others safe before I fade."

I looked away, and he tipped up my chin, trapping my eyes with his. I didn't see any turmoil about his fate in their mossy depths, just acceptance. I was nowhere near as sanguine about giving up my mortal form and having my consciousness snuffed.

Being a halfling was a raw fucking deal.

Shut up. I didn't cry.

"Can I crash on your couch?"

His lips twitched. "If you can play nice with Morgana."

That would be a no. I can't stand undines. Especially that undine. "Why's she there?"

"Normals raided the culverts."

My stigmata flared, and he hugged me to him. I couldn't fault Berk, but I didn't have to like it, either. Don't get me wrong. I was mad about the raid, not him taking in the fish. If we didn't look out for each other, no one else would. Most of us were abandoned as soon as our stigmata came in, and once twenty hit, whoever was left was forced to choose: fade into the element of our affinity, or give it up and sputter, becoming human. That would buy you maybe a handful of years before you suicided. I'd never heard of a halfling older than twenty-three. What was the point once your spark was gone?

Whatever. I'd have to look for another place to crash.

The crowd clapped, and I turned to do the same,

wiping my eyes. Stupid allergies. Kyle bounded off the stage, heading right to me, moth to flame. Enter candidate number two.

"Hey, Snow," he said, kissing me. God, I hated that. The nickname, not the kiss.

His breath mingled with mine, and the fire at my core jumped. Sylphs have that effect on daemons, half or no. The whole Air/Fire affinity thing. He thinks it's hysterical. The nickname and my response to him…and most everything else. His white-blond curls stirred in their own private breeze as he pulled away, laughing. Jerk plucked the beer out of my hand and finished it.

"I'll grab another round." Blue eyes twinkling, he went to the bar.

I leaned against the pool table, watching the flickering azure of his stigmata play across his lats. They spread over his back like wings. I wanted to follow them with my fingers and lick them down past—

"Cool it, Vy."

Berk's voice snapped me back. I jumped up, the felt of the table singed beneath me. I swept a hand across my rear. Crap. My jeans were crispy. Berk grunted at me with a look and took his shot. He was playing against a blonde I didn't recognize. She was a few years younger than us, trying to pull off sexy-grunge with her kohl-lined eyes and midriff concert tee. The brunette she was sharing a beer with kept looking at me like she was trying to figure out where she'd seen me before.

I sighed, waiting for it. A or B?

A: As much as I hate to cop to it, I look like a certain will-not-be-mentioned fae-tale princess. Skin white as snow, blood-red lips, ebony hair minus the bob. Yeah, her. No lie. I'm gorgeous, and my mother's just as pissy about being supplanted in the looks department. Enough so that I stay away from apples on principle.

Kyle came back with the beers and handed me one.

"Didn't think you were coming tonight." He flipped his hair out of his eyes, and I swear to God one of the teenyboppers next to us swooned.

"Decided to bail early. She assigned me contemplation again."

Kyle laughed. "For what now?"

"Sunbathing."

"Yeah?" He pulled me close. "Naked?" I rolled my eyes and let him kiss me. My arms felt good around his neck. His hands felt better on my back. He gave a deep chuckle. "You're all fired up tonight. I got the second half of my set, then you wanna get out of here?"

I looked at him like he was an idiot, and he raised an eyebrow at the singed ass-print I'd left on the felt. He might like playing with fire, but third-degree burns sucked.

"I'll be fine after a few more of these," I said, taking a long pull of my beer. It was true, to a point. Getting drunk tamped down my ability, but it also made me more likely to slip. Drunk or sober, I was a living, breathing game of Russian roulette. Good thing for me sylphs were adrenaline junkies. Especially Kyle. Seeing how close he could get was like some kind of fetish. I wasn't complaining.

"Then drink up, babe, my tab." Kyle laughed, chugging his. He kissed me again and went back up on stage. Damn, he was fine. With an opportunity like that, the fact that I was going to die a virgin was definitely my biggest regret.

"I know who you are." The brunette had come up beside me.

I sipped my beer and ignored her, my gaze running over Kyle's chest. The brunette popped her gum, and my eyes flicked to hers in annoyance.

"Yeah?" I already didn't like her.

"Yeah. You were on the Faith Hour."

Shit. It was B. They must've rebroadcast that episode recently. Her friend had stopped to listen, pumping her cue stick like a dick in time to the music. I met Berk's eyes over her shoulder. He licked his lips, knowing this could go bad fast.

I mentioned earlier things have sucked since my mother became a dedicate of the church. Cult. Whatever. You get the idea. I've also mentioned she's an attention whore and isn't particularly fond of me. Unfortunately for both of us, she needs me around to maintain a certain level of gravitas. Having never been the maternal type, (I got cigarettes and a garter in my stocking when I was seven) and unable to guilt me into anything, she tried bribing me for a while. When that lost its luster, the natural progression of incentives became death threats.

Oh no, not from her. Violence takes effort, and God forbid she breaks a nail. She's much too clever to get her hands dirty, but manipulating the rest of the populace into doing it for her…

All it took was one appearance on Our Lady of the Blessed Inferno's internationally syndicated Faith Hour. After sitting between my mother and the Prioress as they discussed the evils of a halfling's nature, they turned to me, and asked a single, damning question.

"Don't you wish you had a soul?"

I won't get into semantics. Suffice to say, they're contentious, and there was no good answer. I've paid for the one I gave. Repeatedly. Glancing at the density of the crowd forming around us, tonight was shaping up to be another installment. I sighed, wishing I hadn't worn my favorite jeans. Whatever. They were already crispy.

"Lay off," Berk growled, taking his shot. The three ball slammed into the side pocket where the brunette was standing, making her jump. I bit back a smile as the crowd wavered. No one wanted to be around when Berk got pissed, especially below ground with his earth affinity.

Unless you were a slightly tipsy, very stupid brunette.

She laughed too loud. "So what, you gonna shepherd the local Fae-A chapter when you sputter?"

My hands were around her throat before she'd taken her next breath. My stigmata burst out from my back into great wings of flame, dripping down, searing molten holes into everything below me.

I think I mentioned I was having a problem with control.

Screams and hissing clouds of steam filled the air as the sprinklers went off. The girl's face darkened, and her neck hardened to stone beneath my fingers.

What the—

Her fist cracked against my skull, and I was thrown to the side, dazed.

She came at me swinging, and I rolled, the concrete floor blackening beneath me. Behind us, the pub had erupted into mayhem, people fighting to get out. This much commotion, the cops would be here in no time. I needed to disappear, fast.

Not the easiest proposition when I was trying to dodge this bitch.

Flames licked up the walls, and I pulled them to me, condensing them into a burst of plasma. The shot took off her arm at the elbow. It dropped to the floor and turned to dull gray stone.

What the hell!

Shock made my stigmata go dark. I scrambled under the pool table as she came at me again, undeterred. Christ, she wasn't a halfling; she was a golem. Why would a golem be here? My mouth went dry. There wasn't an answer to that question that didn't end with me being in deep—

A hand clamped around my arm, pulling me back out. Startled, I looked up into the eyes of a daemon.

The pool table hit the far wall, and he frowned, flicking a burst of flame from his hand. The golem disintegrated into a pile of scree, and a smile flickered over his lips. I blushed, trying to cover my nakedness. I might be fireproof, but my stigmata are hard on textiles.

His storm-gray eyes went completely black, glamouring me. None of it mattered anymore. The pub was silent, and for all I knew, we were the only two people in the world. He raised me to my feet, then cupped my chin, his midnight gaze holding mine. The fingers of his other hand trailed down my breastbone, following the long scar on my sternum. It burned, the tips of my breasts tightening.

He smiled, and the pub was gone.

29 Days

I awoke in a very soft bed, in a room made of sunlight and glass. My hair smelled like jasmine, and my jaw ached less than I'd expected where that thing had clocked me.

Shit! That thing had clocked me—I pushed back against the headboard, heart pounding with its stupid double thump. I rubbed at my scar, trying to catch my breath.

A golem. What had a golem been doing in the pub? Only one of the Lords of Earth could breathe life into a working like that—

Oh, sorry. Lords are the highest echelon of elemental, and the only ones to have a form that can pass for human. There are lords of Air, Fire, and Water, too, but they don't do stone people. If you really want to piss them off, call them a fairy. It's basically like the worst slur ever. Calling them fae or an elemental is considered politically correct.

My father's one. A fairy. Yeah, I said it. So is every other halfling's.

I digress, but I was freaked out. I was also still a virgin, if you're wondering. I know! Considering I was naked in some daemon's bed, it shocked the shit out of me, too.

I sat up, pulling the airy duvet around me, then dangled a foot to the floor. It landed on the softest

19

sheepskin rug you could imagine. I scrunched my toes in it, staring through the window to the blue-green water spreading out to the horizon. I sure wasn't in Vel City anymore.

Taking the duvet with me, I crossed the gold-striated marble floor. There was a door that led to a wide, white, stuccoed balcony with clusters of big, leafy plants in turquoise pots. I was surprised to find it unlocked. Sad, huh? Outside, it was just water and sky. The sun was magic on my skin, and I raised my face to it, soaking it in with my eyes closed.

It was a balmy, wet heat. The kind that makes you feel like you've got a steamed towel wrapped around you. That, the blistering sun above... I dropped the duvet and gave a huge sigh, letting it beat down on me. The steady breeze flicked my hair against my backside, and I smiled, wondering at my luck waking up in paradise.

"And I'd thought that view couldn't be improved."

I spun at the cultured European drawl, scrabbling up the duvet and clutching it to my chest. My heart was going gangbusters, and I'd flushed scarlet. The daemon that'd taken me sat at a small breakfast table tucked amidst that potted jungle of greenery. No wonder I hadn't seen him. Asshole could've let me know he was there before I'd dropped trou.

His ankle was crossed over his knee, and he was reading the paper. He wore charcoal slacks and a crisp white shirt, the sleeves rolled up and the collar open. A large gold watch was on his left wrist. There was no trace of gray in his jet hair. The top was long, and it'd been slicked back. He was clean-shaven, and let me just say, holy freaking drool. I swallowed, and he grinned an impossibly white smile.

"Good morning, Lovely. Come, sit. Have something to eat." I didn't move, and he slid out the seat next to him with an oxford-shod foot. "Please, I promise not to bite."

His smile said something totally different.

Jerk was playing with me, and my temper jumped. The dimple in his cheek deepened, and the last thing I felt like doing was eating, but you don't just tell a fae to piss off and expect to walk away. They had a thing for manners. I sat, trying to dig mine out, and a small woman in a uniform came over with a plate of crepes. She set it in front of me. I stared at her pebbly skin. Her smile had too many teeth, and they were super pointy.

Not a woman, an imp.

"Uh...thank you?"

She nodded curtly and left, toe talons tapping. I paused before picking up my fork. Taking anything from a fae was dicey—

"You have my word that nothing offered in my home will indebt you to me."

I made myself meet his eyes. "Is this your home, and will it indebt me to anyone else?"

"Clever girl...it is, and no debts will be claimed by any other. I offer no promises beyond that...unless you'd care to bargain for more?"

"No."

"Pity." He snapped his paper back up, and proceeded to ignore me while I ate.

I tried to study him from beneath my lashes as I did. He was too young to be the one I'd seen with my mother, but what were either of them doing? Fae in general were high rollers, living the lifestyle of the rich and famous. They didn't slink around Priories and in undercity pubs. I could write off my mother with one given her past, but me? I was a nobody. It didn't make sense. Neither did the golem. I started to feel weepy, and that made me mad. So did the daemon's eyes crinkling at me over the edge of the paper as my stigmata flared with my temper.

I stabbed a stupid crepe, trying not to think about Kyle and Berk back in Vel. I was sure they were okay. I just wasn't sure I'd ever see them again. Who was I kidding? They, and everyone else in the pub, would've written me off, and they'd be right to. I told you, getting snagged by a fae had a survival rate of zero. At least, nobody I'd ever heard of had come back to tell the tale.

Despite my cheery thoughts, I won't lie, the crepes were just about the best thing I'd ever eaten. I figured I could die happy with them in my stomach. The imp seemed pleased when I said so and asked for seconds. As soon as I'd finished, the daemon tucked away his paper and lit a long, gold-filtered cigarette. The imp came back with espresso. I was feeling fancy and had mine with a twist.

"Thanks for that with the golem... I mean, it was a golem...?"

He blew out a long stream of smoke. It was a gross habit, but he made it look worth taking up. "Yes, and you're welcome."

"Uh, any idea why it was there?"

"For you, otherwise it wouldn't have revealed itself."

He didn't seem particularly concerned, but my mouth went dry. Had he been watching me? Did he have anything to do with the dae Calista had been screwing? And more importantly:

"Are you going to eat me?"

He took another drag and raised a gorgeous eyebrow at me. "Would you like me to?"

Yeah, I just about died. That totally wasn't what I meant.

I went scarlet, my heart pounding in my ears. Here I'd been praying for someone I wouldn't immolate, and I was the one who was going to be tied up and burnt at the hypothetical stake. Maybe it wouldn't be hypothetical. I'd heard fae could be into some seriously kinky shit, but did I really want to go back? Priory, hot daemon. Priory, hot daemon. Pretty sure I knew which one was winning that throw down.

Sorry, I was terrified, and he just watched me with that smirk, smoking his cigarette and sipping espresso while I panicked. Asshole.

"So, what am I supposed to call you?" It wasn't what I really wanted to know, but you don't ask a fae their motives, or their true name, and you sure as hell don't tell them yours. Like I said, names hold power, and they already have enough of an edge. The imp started bussing the table.

"I'm called Brennan, and you're Vy. Short and sweet for Envy." His eyes roamed over me, and I pulled the duvet closer to my throat. He leaned forward and cupped my chin like he had last night, tucking my hair behind my ear. His thumb grazed over my cheek, and I shivered. "I've healed as much of the damage from the golem as I can. It's not my forte, but the bruising should be gone in a few more days. You're a resilient little thing."

I bristled at that last bit, but it was of some comfort

to hear I'd be around for that long. He smiled at my annoyance, and I couldn't hold his gaze. "Why were you there?"

His fingers lingered for a moment longer before he sat back and took up his cigarette again. "Business. I've been contracted to prepare you for your introduction into fae society. Specifically, the Midsummer's Ball at the end of the month, though depending on how quickly you progress, there may be other opportunities to mingle." Brennan flicked his cigarette, his eyes laughing at me. "Jaw, Lovely."

Face burning, it snapped shut.

"Karen's taken your measurements, and there should be something for you to wear in the dressing room."

"Karen?" He waved a hand at the imp from earlier standing in the doorway. Karen. "I don't understand, Midsummer's—"

He stood, putting on a pair of gold-rimmed aviators. "I've things to attend to. Feel free to make yourself at home. I'll be back to join you for lunch."

And poof—he vanished.

My jaw was hanging open again, and I snapped it closed. When I finally came to grips with the fact that he really was gone, I went back inside.

When I'd said the place was made of sunlight and glass, I meant it. I mean, the floors were all that swanky marble, but the walls were glass. From the bedroom, I could see across the hall into a room with an infinity pool. It looked like it dropped right off into the horizon.

A couple of walls were tinted this teal-y color instead of clear. One was for the bathroom, which by now I needed desperately, and the other a dressing

24

room. The right side was filled with suits, all in tones of gray and black, and had a line of neatly placed oxfords beneath them.

I flipped through his drawers the same way I had his medicine cabinet. What? Like you wouldn't. He had an impressive collection of dental floss and wore boxer briefs, in case you were wondering. He didn't have anything I would consider casual wear.

The other side of the dressing room held three sheath dresses. One red, one black, and one a dove gray. I'd never worn anything like them in my life, nor the coordinating four-inch heels below. He had to be kidding. I'd break my neck. A drawer had some lacy underthings and just about the teeniest bikini I'd ever seen. It was black with nary a polka-dot in sight.

That was it. No sweats, tees…

I stood there with the duvet clutched around me, fuming at my options.

Fuck him. I went for his business casual.

When I finally emerged, Karen was waiting for me. She snickered and led me back into the bathroom, then had me sit at the marble-topped vanity.

"Knots." She'd picked up a brush and started fiddling with my hair. It was really tangled, but I flinched away from her, my eyes darting around for scissors.

Look, my hair has always been a source of contention between my mother and me. Granted, one of many. She'd always been keen to cash in on my mouse-based pop-culture princess-esque appeal and bob it. Me? Not so much, and after a brief period of playing "snip when Vy's not looking," and me walking around looking like a badly trimmed hedge, we came to an uneasy detente. As a result, it was long, falling in waves way past the middle of my back. I don't like people touching it. But I had to admit, having it brushed felt good, and after a while, I relaxed. The absence of scissors helped.

"Karen, why am I here?"

She seemed surprised I'd spoken to her and shrugged. "Daemon games."

I laughed and saw her wide lips quirk up in the mirror. If you've never met an imp, they're waist high and not what you'd consider attractive. Daemons use them as servants, minions, whatever. I told you their skin is pebbly. It's also like a weird, fleshy gray. Their features are exaggerated. Long earlobes, noses, and chins. What they did have, is beautiful auburn hair. She'd fixed hers up high and there was a seashell comb in it.

"Would you do mine like that? Your hair, I mean. It's really pretty."

Her sunken cheeks colored, and she gave one of those curt nods. While she was piling and fixing it, I took in all the cosmetics, little bottles, and jars in front of the mirror. Someone liked makeup. I picked up one and sniffed it. Yuck. Way floral.

"You no like?"

"Uh, it's ok."

"Boss say get you what you want. What you like?"

English was not her first language. I wondered what was. Impese? I didn't know how to answer her. Perfume had been one of those bones of contention I hadn't won.

Karen finished and reached for the eyeliner. I stood, the plush crimson stool almost tipping over before I grabbed and righted it.

"Th-thanks, but I'm all set." The hair thing had already thrown me off balance. Getting primped by an imp was too much. What the hell was going on? I couldn't get out of the bathroom fast enough. The hall ended at a door set into another wall of that teal-y glass. I padded toward it, taking in the other rooms as I passed.

There was that one with the pool I told you about, a dining room with a long chrome and wood table, high-backed chairs. Across the hall from that was a room with a baby grand up on a dais, and deep leather couches. I took note of the well-stocked wet bar, and then I was at that door. It was slightly ajar, and I pushed it open, peeking around the edge.

It was an office, and shocking after the stark perfection of the rest of the flat. A big desk dominated the room and the top of it looked like a library had thrown up over it. Books were stacked, flipped open, and studded with sticky notes. Papers were everywhere. They spilled onto the floor, and wadded up balls littered the Oriental carpet. The only thing in the garbage was an empty bottle of cognac and a couple pounds of gold-filtered cigarette butts. From the looks of the ashtray on the corner of the desk, it was due to receive another deposit.

I could maybe make out three words between the books and the papers. Most of it wasn't in English, and the handwriting was so awful I couldn't tell if the notes were or not. The pictures were a bunch of biblical-looking pen and ink-type crap, all Garden of Eden-y. The dude playing Adam looked like a dick. I've never understood why Eve didn't tell them to piss off.

Yeah, I said it. Him and God. Must've been the rib cloning thing.

The desk drawers were locked. Sighing, I swept my eyes around the rest of the room. Three of the walls were lined with bookcases. The fourth behind the desk was a single, massive pane of glass overlooking the water.

Where was I? It was like this place was on a rock in the middle of nowhere. Just me, the horizon, and the surf pounding against the cliffs. I did see a small beach below. The sand was very white. I wondered if there were shells.

Instead of more of what was on the desk, the bookcases were mostly filled with ridiculously boring tomes on musical theory and other edifying texts that sounded just as dull. Lucky me, those were in English. Then some glass sculpture-y stuff and an old record player. I flipped through the vinyl. Classical, classical, jazz, classical, Les Mis— I walked away with that pain in my chest, breathing hard.

Fuck Broadway.

I made for the wet bar.

The couch was the kind you could just melt into, and I did, with one of those fancy imported beers you were supposed to drink warm. I stared up at the cathedral ceiling, watching the fan spin, wishing there was a TV. Maybe he had a laptop under all that junk on the desk, but I wasn't going back in there.

Karen came in halfway through my second beer. "Boss say come to office."

Guess I was going back in there.

I chugged the beer and followed her into that damn room, avoiding looking at the records. The mess I'd seen before was gone, and Brennan was speaking to another imp in what I assumed was Impese. Huh. It sounded prettier than I would've thought. He glanced up, then sat back as I walked in. I couldn't read the look on his face, but I didn't get the impression he was pleased.

"Do you have on my briefs as well?"

I flushed, not answering. I didn't, but he could go pound sand before I'd tell him.

"For future reference, your clothes are on the left side. I suggest you wear them, especially with your penchant for immolating garments. I'm quite fond of those trousers. Take them off."

I stood there stewing, but it hadn't been a request. My hand shook as I undid the belt, and that pissed me off more. His pants pooled around my ankles. I stepped out and slammed them onto the desk. His eyes went from me to them at the clunk of the buckle. I crossed my arms over my chest in nothing but one of his white button-downs, hoping he was happy. What an asshole.

Brennan's eyebrows furrowed, and he made a low growl. His form wavered like heat off hot pavement. "Did you put another hole in my Armani belt?"

What little courage I had went poof. I swallowed, looking away. Crap.

"Left side is yours."

I nodded. Left side. I peeked over to see him smooth his hair back with a funny look on his face. Like he was mad but had just found a twenty in his pocket. Make that a hundred. He wore Armani.

"Right." His "T" was super crisp, and I winced. Nope, just mad. He motioned to the seat in front of the desk. Why did I always end up feeling like I was in the principal's office? The imp delivered him a highball. Brennan went to take a sip, then paused, collecting himself.

I have that effect on people.

"Can Peter get you a drink?" The imp beside the desk stood a little straighter.

"Sure…uh, I mean, please." I tucked my bare feet up under me. Brennan stared at me like I was a problem until a bright green martini was set in front of me.

Goddamn it.

I hate appletinis. I know, I know. The whole She-Who-Will-Not-Be-Named princess thing. People get off on giving them to me. The joke was old and not that funny to begin with. They usually ended up down the front of the smug asshole who tried to buy me one. That didn't strike me as wise in this instance. I choked down half a sip to be polite, and set it back on his desk, trying not to gag. Brennan's eyes were still on me.

"Not to your liking?"

"I don't care for apple anything."

That smile flickered across his lips. "Beer?" At my nod, he gestured to Peter, and a moment later, he brought me a bottle. I downed it, trying to get the sickeningly sweet taste from my mouth.

"Wearing my clothes, chugging beer. How am I to make you a fae lady, Vy?"

I bit back a belch and a rude comment right before they tripped off my tongue. His eyes were laughing at me again. I glared back. "Why would you want to?"

"My employer has a vested interest in you attending the Midsummer's Ball. Only details pertinent to my task have been disclosed. Motive wasn't one of them."

I still tasted apples. "Can you guess?"

He flashed his too-white teeth at me. "I could."

"But you won't."

"Would you care to bargain for it?"

"No." His grin got wider. I crossed my arms under my boobs, perking them up. He noticed, which was the point. "If you won't tell me what I want to know, what's there to talk about?" I took the second bottle Peter offered me, and downed half of it just to be spiteful. And yes, I was catching one hell of a buzz. It's probably why my mouth kept going without waiting for my brain. "Why bother with any of it? I mean, I'm going to be dead at the end of the month. I've got better things to do than hang around here with your imps, drinking shitty martinis."

He laughed, then bit at his bottom lip. It looked very kissable. I wet my own and set the stupid beer down. I needed to cool it. My control was starting to feel slippery.

"It really is appalling how uneducated those on this side of the veil are. Tell me, Vy, haven't you ever wondered why none of you halflings have fae mothers?"

I hadn't, but mothers weren't a subject I was real keen on exploring. "They're on the pill?"

He sucked in his cheeks, and I winced. Stupid beers. I shrugged, but the fact that I could make an asshole remark like that meant the name he'd used had no power over me. Made sense, since it wasn't the one I'd been born with.

"It's a woman's duty to raise her child, be they fae, or human."

I took another swig of beer, wondering if he really

believed that, or if he'd said it just to piss me off. Those eyes of his... I couldn't figure out if he was messing with me. For his sake, I hoped he was. "How progressive of you. And what, pray tell, is a man's duty?"

The asshole just smirked, all smoldering. God, he was a dick, and it was freaking hot. I wanted to make him say sorry, and I wanted to do it with my tongue.

Brennan flicked his ash. "Halflings across the veil don't fade, Lovely. They become. Those born on your side deemed acceptable are brought over a short time before the choice is upon them. Midsummer is when you're now slated to gain the rest of your elemental soul and become a full daemon. That's why I've been hired to prepare you."

What? My stomach cramped, and heat seared up through me like a boulder had been dropped down a well shaft. It wasn't, couldn't be true. And if it was, the idea that so many halflings were left to live truncated lives and die—Deemed acceptable? What kind of fucking bullshit was that!

My stigmata flared before I could stop them, and I didn't care. I was so pissed; I didn't give a shit if the whole place went up.

Brennan was abruptly in front of me. He grabbed me by the shoulders, snuffing them. Black pools where his eyes should've been trapped mine. The world became muted, and I went limp, something taken from me by his glamour. He scooped me up, cradling me against his chest as he carried me through the flat.

He laid me on the bed, his fingers grazing my scar again. I'd had open-heart surgery when I was a kid. Whatever they'd done hadn't worked, hence the double thump. I trembled at his touch, feeling it flutter now. He pulled the sheets over me and tucked me in.

I slept until sunset.

When I woke, the first thing I saw was his silhouette at the railing, looking out over the water as he smoked. I didn't want what he'd said to be true. I thought of how many of us that'd died, been hated, been preyed on by normals…why me and why now? If I was so special, why put me through all of it? Why put any of us through it?

I cried. A lot.

At some point, I felt his weight settle on the bed. His hand on my shoulder. I did and didn't want to shrug it off.

"Shhh…calm yourself. I've only told you the truth. My father was from this side of the veil, my mother dae. I was chosen for this because it was thought I'd be able to relate to your…unique position better than most. Very few half-dae are brought over." His fingers moved to stroke the hair back from my temple.

"What you call fading, we call becoming," he said softly. "Beyond the veil, on Midsummer's Eve, there's a grand ball upon the mesa where the four realms of Fae meet. At the moon's apex, Fire will come, cleansing away your humanity and filling you. It's like being reborn." I stiffened as he worked the pins from my hair and ran his fingers through it.

"You make humanity sound like an affliction."

His mouth tightened. "To the fae, it is. For most after they become, the memory of it fades like a dream. They choose to forget, though I never have."

For all my bitching about not wanting to be me, when faced with the opportunity, I balked. Big time.

Don't get me wrong, there was plenty of shit I wanted to forget, but all of that made me, me. If it went away, what was left? A fantastic pair of tits and a chippy manicure. It didn't sound much better than sputtering. Forget about that bell curve of options, I was stuck in a bell jar, and the air was running out.

"So instead of dying, fae halflings get a lobotomy."

The asshole laughed, and I turned my back to him. "Yes, it's like that for some. You, I think not."

"It sounds like a shitty system."

"It's not of my design."

I suspected that was true, but his ambivalence pissed me off.

"But you're fine with it. Just leaving your kids to die."

"I've yet to have any, but I can't imagine abandoning them as some do, no."

Pretty sure I saw the back of my skull as my eyes rolled. "As some do. Try all of them—" I bit my lip just before I called him an asshole. From the smirk on his face when I sat up, he knew it, too. He'd been threading a lock of my hair through his fingers, like I did with flame. I yanked it from them.

"You'd be surprised. Just because you can't see us doesn't mean we're not there."

Well, that was super creepy. It must've shown on my face.

He made an exasperated little growl, like I wasn't getting what he was saying. More like he knew anything he said was going to make him sound worse than he already did. "The current political climate on your side of the veil has necessitated in Fae taking a greater interest in its affairs. Halfling persecution is something we're keenly aware of, however, our Proscriptions only allow for limited contact—"

I laughed. He sounded like a politician. "You call screwing us limited contact?"

Brennan wet his lips. I stared at them, abruptly aware that I'd gotten way too close, and the flimsy sheet I was wrapped in had ridden up over my hip. He was too. His hand moved like he wanted to touch me. I was on the fence as to whether that would be a bad thing.

"It refers to limiting one's involvement socially. Physical contact is encouraged." His fingers curled up into a fist, and his knuckles went white. My eyes jumped to his, and I can't even explain what I saw there.

But if I'd been wearing panties, they would've been ash.

He shook himself and moved a little away from me. "We, ah…we can only do so much, but I'd expect that will change. The recent uptick in attacks on the halfling community has the Council concerned."

I wasn't. Concerned that is. I was looking at his lips, his jawline. I wanted to know what it tasted like. I reached out and traced it with a finger. His Adam's apple bobbed, and the pulse beside it sped up.

"How do you get so close a shave?"

"St—" He cleared his throat. "Peter uses a straight razor." Pointedly not looking at me, he pulled out a cigarette.

I sat back at the sight of it. "Why me?"

"Ah, there are several factors taken into consideration, but only one is really important."

"So let's hear it. Are you seriously going to light

that nasty thing in here?"

"Does it bother you?"

"Yeah."

Brennan met my eyes again and lit the freaking thing.

"I'd say you were chosen for your fire, Lovely." He ran his gaze over me, exhaling a stream of smoke to the side as he stood. "If you're hungry, Karen will bring you whatever you wish. We'll talk tomorrow."

Poof. He was gone.

I sat there, feeling very alone as I thought about what he'd said. Could it be true? If it was, it made the whole raw deal even worse. My shithead father hadn't just abandoned me, he'd sentenced me to twenty years of unnecessary misery and impending doom just because he couldn't bother to pull out, then sat back and watched the entire train wreck that was my life. And now, to be offered the opportunity to become a creature just like him?

I'd rather be dead in a month.

28 Days

I hadn't slept well.

I mean, I don't usually, but this was different. It wasn't the dreams that got me; it was everything that Brennan had said. That, and I kept jerking awake at the slightest sound, wondering if he was going to suddenly appear. It hadn't been lost on me that there wasn't a second bedroom, and his clothes were right in there beside mine. I'll spare you the scenarios that played out in my head, but more than one ended all *bow-chika-bow-wow*. The rest pinged off the sides of that damn bell jar.

It made for a shitty night.

The first of the sun's glow was just blushing the horizon. I lay in bed, thinking I was going to be really late for matins. I giggled and scrubbed at my face. Stupid.

Anyways, I'm one of those people that once I'm up, I'm up, so I got up. Everything was dark and silent, the door to Brennan's office closed. He didn't have a couch in there, but I suspected he could poof out to some posh hotel if he'd wanted to. Maybe he was bedding down with the imps. I giggled again.

Yeah, I was starting to lose it, and needed something to distract me. I hadn't seen a laptop on the desk. How could he not have a TV?

My stomach rumbled, and I kind of wished Karen

or Peter would show up. I hadn't eaten anything last night and was starving. There wasn't even a fruit bowl on the table. I wasn't quite desperate enough to eat the olives out of the wet bar. Yet. I sat on the edge of the bed and kicked my feet, getting angry.

Back when I was a kid, Calista had one of those yappy little rat-fuck dogs. You know, with the big ears? A papillon. If she left it alone in a room, it would tear everything to pieces and shit all over the place. I was feeling a kinship.

My eyes landed on the pool.

It's a common misconception that dae don't like water. I mean, we don't like Water elementals, undines are assholes, but in general, we have no problem with the actual substance. Personally, I loved swimming, and hadn't gotten to do it in way too long. Like since the casino long.

I put on the bikini and wondered if Karen knew how to wax. Grabbing a towel, I laughed all the way into the other room, just about dying at the thought of an imp giving me a Brazilian.

It was a really nice pool, heated don'tcha know. I dove in and started doing laps.

It was glorious, and I didn't see Brennan until the tips of his oxfords were right in front of me. I wiped the water from my eyes, treading. He'd crouched down at the edge with that crooked smile of his.

"Good morning, Lovely. Been up for some time, have you?"

"I didn't sleep well."

"Mmm. You didn't have dinner, either. Anything tickle your fancy this morning?"

"Those crepes." Popped out before I'd even

thought about it. He gave me another smile and went out to the balcony. I toweled off and joined him in a fluffy white bathrobe that'd appeared. I wished some sweatpants would.

"Too much on your mind last night?" he asked. I shrugged. "Today will give you more to mull over, I'm afraid. We've a great deal to cover, and not a lot of time."

"Where do you and the imps sleep?"

His gaze burnt.

"I—There's no other bedrooms or a kitchen, and I just wondered, I mean, I wanted a banana or something, but…" God, I sounded stupid. I gave Karen a huge smile as she delivered my plate, rescuing me. I thanked her and stuffed a bite into my mouth. He was carefully slicing into a couple of poached eggs and asparagus, all pensive.

"Are there shells on the beach?"

"Possibly."

I laughed. "How can you not know if you live here?"

"I don't care for sand."

Well, excuse me. That pretty much killed conversation.

When he was finished, he took a cigarette out of a fancy gold case, running his eyes over me. They lingered on my chippy pedicure. I curled my toes toward the floor, and he failed to hide a smile. "Perhaps you'd enjoy a spa day. Karen's highly skilled, I'm sure she can see to your needs."

I thought about my bikini line and laughed.

He gave me an indulgent look. "Afterward, your control is abhorrent and needs to be addressed. My compensation package doesn't cover the cost of redecorating my flat."

I refrained from sticking my tongue out at him. Barely. He wasn't telling me anything I didn't know, but he didn't have to be such a dick about it. It's not like they had fae-school. The tip of his cigarette sparked crimson as he called flame to light it. Showoff. He looked at his watch and frowned, pulling out those aviators.

"I've an engagement this morning, and I'm not sure how long I'll be detained. Until then, try not to incinerate anything else."

Poof.

I spent the day being plucked, slathered, and rubbed down by an imp, thinking it must be how a chicken feels. A super spoiled one. Karen's foot massages were to die for. She didn't talk much but put up with my rambling. I didn't get any information out of her, though trust me, I tried.

Brennan didn't get back until sunset, or at least, that's when he summoned me.

I wore the gray sheath.

He frowned at my bare feet, even though my pedicure was on point. I flopped down into the straight-backed chair that'd replaced the one I'd fried earlier. The plush Oriental carpet was gone, too. Whoops. I avoided his eyes. They were harder than I'd seen them before, and he had a set to his jaw that made me nervous. I sat up straighter and put my knees together. Guess his engagement hadn't gone so good. He made a concerted effort to smile, then laid into me.

"That you're able to manifest plasma with such ease, yet are unable to shield flame boggles the mind. A real imp in the emporium, aren't you." I didn't get the reference, but I went scarlet at his tone. And his gaze. It was intense enough to make my mouth go dry. "Most dae are unable to do either without instruction. Even tutored, it took me several years to manifest plasma. Shielding should be as easy as breathing for you. Shall we try an experiment?"

He forced another smile at my chagrined nod.

"Splendid. Come here."

I didn't want to but joined him by the window. He held out his hand to me, and I shied from him, not liking the vibe he was giving off.

"For the love of—come over here!"

He wasn't asking. I did, and he stood very close. The top of my head was level with his chin, and I stared at the divot between his collarbones.

"Watch. I'm going to push my aura out."

He held his arm between us so that the dying sunlight hit it, then blew out a slow stream of smoke over the top. As I watched, it was pushed upward by some invisible force. What the hell? I started to reach out, then pulled my hand back.

"Go ahead, I want you to touch it." I went scarlet again, much to his amusement. Jerk. "Ready?" He repeated the process a few times. It was bizarre, but I could feel something push out from him, like armor, or a carapace.

"Is it always hard?" I almost died as soon as the words left my mouth. Worse, when I looked up, I was abruptly aware that he'd reeled me in like a fish. I took a step back and stumbled. He caught me up against the long, lean length of him.

"Careful, Lovely." His lips were very close to

mine, and his hand skated down my back as I got my balance. "No, not always. With practice, you can change the density to achieve different results. Ready to try? Close your eyes." He scowled at my expression, and I swallowed a nervous giggle. "Just do it." His exasperation made him sound a lot younger, that cultured inflection softening. How old was he? He didn't look much older than me, but that meant spit as far as fae were concerned.

I closed my eyes. After a moment, the whisper of his fingertips were against my cheek. My breath caught, and I wanted to bolt.

"Shhh, relax."

Yeah, right. My eyes popped open, and I flinched back.

His jaw clenched. "Forget it. Just—stay out of my clothes." He flipped open a gold case and pulled out a cigarette. The tip flared as he lit it. "Damn it."

I ran from the room, through the flat. I ended up out on the balcony, as far from him as I could get, my face streaked with angry tears. Why was I here? I couldn't understand what anyone wanted with me. I mean, seriously, a vested interest I went to some ball? To become a fae lady, he'd said. I didn't even know how to be a normal lady…though I suppose that didn't matter if I was just going to get lobotomized. What was I saying? It was all pointless. I'd fade, and that'd be it.

I was out there for a good ten minutes before Brennan cleared his throat behind me. I dashed an arm across my face and turned, sure I looked like a raccoon. He'd lounged back against the doorframe with his cigarette and offered me the cocktail in his hand. The breeze ruffled his hair. He looked like a GQ model.

"Here, a peace offering. I'm sorry. I've had a trying day. I know that's a bit tricky and shouldn't have been so short with you."

I laughed. A daemon was apologizing to me. He put the drink on the table, and then came over to lean on the railing, looking out over the ocean. His skin was golden beside mine. That perfect shade of sun-kissed I used to dream about when I was little.

"If you close your eyes, can you feel me beside you?"

I glanced at him, but he wasn't looking at me as he smoked. It made it easier to relax. I closed my eyes, and after a moment I could. My sense of him grew stronger until it felt like his arm was pressed up against mine. I opened my eyes and frowned. He hadn't moved.

"Like that. You try."

Licking my lips, I closed my eyes again, and reached for him.

It was easier and harder than I'd thought it would be. Once I figured out the trick to it, pushing out my aura wasn't the problem. Reining it in was. It kind of swept over him, and I felt a whole lot more of him than was polite. Yeah. That control thing again. Whoops.

And sorry, but I was so not sorry. I might have, uh, lingered.

His eyes flew wide, and he made a strangled grunt, then vanished.

I laughed and grabbed that drink he'd left. Daemon or not, he was still a man. Maybe I would have some entertainment. I stayed out there, practicing with my aura until the sun began to set, and Karen came to the door. She had a funny smile on her face, but on an imp, most smiles are.

"Boss say shoes at dinner."

I wanted to hit him as I clomped into the dining room with a stride a Clydesdale would've been proud of.

"I'll admit, you were much more graceful without." I glared at him, and he laughed, placing his napkin on his lap. "Perhaps kitten heels would be more appropriate to start. I had no idea you were so naïve, considering."

My jaw tensed at the allusion to my mother. I knew for a fact she could run for a touchdown in stilettos without breaking a sweat. Or an ankle.

A couple of imps came in with covered platters and started serving us. How much did he know about me? It irked that I knew zero about him.

"Don't slouch."

"I'm not slouching."

He raised an eyebrow at me, and I pulled my shoulders back. His gaze dropped to my breasts. "Yes, that's much better."

I scowled. The rest of the meal was a long list of curtly delivered directives and innuendo that was seriously messing with my head. I don't know if you've ever spent time with a dae (I don't recommend it), but they're ridiculously adept at manipulation.

I don't mean glamour, that's, well, you saw what that's like. It makes you go all soupy but can't make you do things. To compel you, they need to trick you into wearing a fae-band, but he didn't need one. By the end, I was trying to anticipate what he wanted me to do as much to please him as to shut him up.

The food was some kind of fancy nouveau like they'd served at the casino. I took petty pleasure in his surprise that I knew how to use a snail tong and fork. What? I'm not a goddamned savage. My mother had liked to show me off. In the beginning, at least.

Everything was delicious. I drank more wine than was probably wise and had an excessively healthy buzz by the time he suggested we "retire to the den." God, he was so pretentious I couldn't stand it.

No, I'll be honest, I couldn't stand, period. I wanted those damn heels off.

They had thin little straps that buckled crisscross around my ankles, so I couldn't just kick them into the corner. Or at him. I must've fumbled with them for too long because Brennan came over and kneeled down. He took one foot, and then the other, nimbly unbuckling the clasps and sliding them off. His fingers skated along my instep, and I was horrified when I giggled.

"Are you ticklish, or just that drunk?"

"I'm not drunk!" I was pretty drunk.

His fingers trailed back along my foot, and I giggled again, jerking it away. He smiled, and there was that little dimple in his right cheek. I looked away as soon as I realized I'd been staring. I seriously needed to start working on my sobriety.

Brennan stood, holding out a hand to help me rise. I took it, stumbling against him. He was rock-solid beneath his white button-down and smelled really good. Like, well, heat. The fact that he was a daemon, and I was essentially his captive, didn't seem very important anymore. I was twenty, a virgin, and had less than a month to live.

And right then, I wanted him, bad.

I stretched up against him like a cat and put my arms around his neck. His eyes had little wiggly ribbons of blue threading through the gray. I watched his pupils expand and contract as he looked down, focusing on me. He brushed his knuckles against my temple. My eyes closed, leaning into them.

"You're very drunk."

"Mmm."

"What am I to do with you, Lovely?"

"Take me to bed."

I think I mentioned I was very drunk.

He scooped me up like I was eiderdown and started through the flat. He wore some kind of light, spicy cologne, and I could tell he'd shaved for dinner. My lips found his jawline, and I kissed up under it. His fingers tightened where he held me.

The bed had been turned down, and he slid me between the sheets. I pulled him to me, his lips soft against mine. He tasted of cognac and the vanilla ice cream from dessert. The heat in me leapt, and I felt something in him respond in kind. God, this was going to be hot.

Literally.

My stigmata began painting the room with a crimson glow. He pulled away from me and groaned, blocking my fingers from his belt. His breath was coming as fast and heavy as mine.

"Good night."

Poof.

"You son of a bitch! That's not what I meant!"

And I swear to God, I heard him fucking laugh.

27 Days

I woke up with a hangover. Not the throbbing head-achy hangover from too many beers I was used to, though one of those was rockin' through my skull; this was a rot-gut hangover. And yes, there are distinct degrees of hangovers. I was kind of an expert. Look, I already said I needed to work on my sobriety. At any rate, this hangover was bad enough that I was finding it difficult to function. Karen just clucked her tongue and delivered a mug of something that smelled like feet.

"You drink."

I scowled at her, but drank, then hid back under the duvet, feeling like I was going to hurl. Weren't there any curtains in this place? It was too goddamned bright. I heard Brennan's shoes tread loudly across the marble, and I held my breath, hoping he wouldn't say anything and keep going.

No dice.

"Rise and shine, Lovely. We've work to do." The balcony door opened and closed.

Fuck my life. Like it wasn't bad enough I only had twenty-seven days left. The proposition of spending them at charm school with Mr. Dae-licious held zero appeal at the moment. I couldn't believe I'd thrown myself at him like that.

Yeah, all right, I totally could.

What I couldn't believe, was that he hadn't taken

me up on it. What the hell?

Not for nothing, but guys' tongues usually roll out of their mouths like cartoon characters when I batt my eyelashes. I wasn't kidding about being gorgeous. I'm pretty much pin-up perfect. I mean, there was the incredibly remote possibility he was just that honorable. It wasn't what dae were known for, but I'd been pretty drunk. There'd been proof positive he wanted me. I bit my lip and smiled, remembering that. Mmm.

Anywho, the fact that I'd wandered off into some interesting scenarios was a testament to Karen's nasty little mug of feet. I got up, not feeling like I was going to puke at the motion. I actually wanted something in my stomach, like a big, greasy sausage and egg drive-through concoction. A pair of wide-legged lounge pants and a tunic had appeared in the dressing room. I pulled them on and took my walk of shame outside to the table.

Brennan raised an eyebrow at me over the paper. It irked that he looked so damn good while I sat there feeling like chewed shoe leather.

"A bit rumpled this morning?"

I glared at him beneath my brows and stole a piece of toast off his plate. Peter came over with a bowl of sausages and what looked like mashed potatoes. Brennan was way too amused at my condition.

"Bangers and mash. Surefire hangover cure. Trust me, it works." He snapped his paper back up and ignored me, just like yesterday.

I didn't trust him, but it did work. I was feeling almost like myself when I'd finished and wanted some answers. I was definitely feeling well enough to be a pain in the ass.

"Why would a golem want to kill me? I mean, who would send one?"

"A gnome, I'd imagine."

No shit, Sherlock. I was glaring at him again. He flipped to the next page of his paper, and I could totally tell he was getting off on irritating me. Peter brought over an espresso and a Bloody Mary. I crunched into the celery. Loudly.

Brennan lit a cigarette. He met my glare with a smile. "Did you enjoy your breakfast?"

"Why would someone send a golem to kill me?"

"Better question. Would you bargain for the answer?" He blew out a long stream of smoke, his eyes intent.

In case you didn't know, all fae are inherently gamblers, especially among themselves. Betting, bargains, and wagers, you name it, they can't resist. Everything I knew about them stemmed from watching them around the tables at the casino, and believe me when I tell you, they're cutthroat. They didn't give away anything for free, and almost always got the better end of the deal. It was that "almost" that made it so damned tempting to try your luck.

Screw it. I said the ritual words.

"What do you desire?"

His face lit up, and he set his paper aside. Crap.

"I'll answer your question, exactly as posed, in exchange for you allowing Karen to dress and style you while you remain under my care."

"Fine, but nobody's cutting my hair, and I want a better answer than 'so I would be dead.' I want to know the motive, or your best guess at one."

Brennan actually rubbed his hands together. I'd

started to sweat. "If you fail to allow her to perform her duties, the only drink you'll be allowed are appletinis."

Son of a—he laughed as my mouth screwed up.

"Then I get to ask a follow-up question, and you have to answer without evasions."

He took a long drag. "And if I don't?"

"You don't smoke in the flat."

"Agreed. I don't believe it was sent to kill you, though its attentions most certainly would've resulted in that." He grinned from behind his cigarette, tonguing the tip of a canine and waiting for my next question.

And this was why you don't bargain with fae.

I'd thought I'd been slick getting a follow-up question out of him, but after that, I needed like fifty. What the hell would a golem—no, a gnome, want from me that would—

I didn't have an epiphany on that front, but something clicked on another.

I think I mentioned the pub had been tense. The last couple times I'd made it out, people had been talking about some seriously grisly halfling murders in other cities. I mean, nothing that would make mainstream news, but someone had been going around ripping the hearts out of half-dae. Rumor had it Earth was responsible, but I hadn't given that much credence, since they were pretty tight with Fire. Shows how much I knew. Maybe it hadn't been after me specifically. As I said, we weren't well-liked as a rule. I rubbed at my scar. It fit a bit too neatly, though what the hell was it doing if not trying to kill us? Whatever. The matter at hand was more important.

"Why does your employer want me to become fully dae?"

Surprise flickered across Brennan's face for all of half a second. "As I said, motives weren't discussed…" He drew out the silence, playing with me again until my temper spiked. "But if I had to guess, I'd say it was because they wanted something from you. Now, off you go. Your hair is dreadful." He'd picked his paper back up, just freaking tickled with himself. "Jaw, Lovely."

I snapped it shut and went inside. I'll say it again—that was why you don't bargain with a fae.

Being primped by Karen wasn't so bad, but the end results kind of were. Don't get me wrong, I looked good…too good. Like Calista Starr good. It made my stomach churn again.

When I went out, Brennan was in the pool. He climbed out when he saw me, and a quick flash of flame dried him off. Well, that was a neat trick, but not what had my attention as he came over. Dae-licious. Mmm. He was seriously cut, and the rest of him was as smooth as his face. What? Oh, trunks. If he'd been in a speedo, I don't know what I would've done.

His hair fell over his eyes, and he looked decidedly roguish. He'd definitely benefit from skipping a shave or three. He stepped close and tilted up my chin. "Yes, that's what we're going for. You'll fit right in."

I wet my lips and peeked up at him through my lashes. Maybe he was one of those guys who preferred women to be coy. "You like it?"

"Very much."

My hand had come up, and I ran a finger down his chest to his waistband, slipping my first two knuckles in, and giving it a little tug. He smiled. That dimple was there again.

"Let me change, and I'll be right with you."

He walked past me to the dressing room and closed the door.

What the hell? Karen caught my eye leaving the room and shrugged. Great. Even the imps didn't know what his problem was. At least it wasn't just me. I needed a different strategy.

Let me back up a bit. You might be wondering what in God's name I was doing. I mean, he'd shut me down hard last night, and again just now. At this point, most women would say, oh well, he's just not interested. Others that he was a dick, and they were better off. Me? I wouldn't disagree with either rationale, but no way in hell was I letting him win at whatever game he was playing. I was doubling down.

I know, petty, stupid, and vindictive. That's me in a nutshell. I also don't know when to quit and am competitive to a fault. Whatever, it's not my only one. Just ask my mother.

I was in the piano room with a beer, plotting his seduction, when he found me and frowned. Granted, I wasn't in the most dignified position, lying down with my feet propped up on the back of the couch, but we weren't at afternoon tea.

Peter came in behind him with afternoon tea, and I laughed. Brennan's frown deepened.

"As marvelous as your legs are, they belong pointing at the ground."

I met his gaze, daring him to do something about it, and took another pull off my beer.

He sat beside me, his lips pursed. Batting my eyelashes at him, I dropped my legs into his lap. He made that angry-but-I-found-a-Franklin expression again, then he kind of rolled, and the next thing I knew, he was above me, between them. He took my beer and set it on the table.

My heart was beating very fast as he turned back.

"Shall we try and be friends?" His nose brushed against mine, and I could only nod. He raised my hands up over my head, his fingers lacing through my own. I closed my eyes as his lips skated to my ear. He inhaled against my skin, and I let out a little cry. I could tell he liked that. "Mmm. Can you be a very good girl for me? I need you to cooperate and do as you're told."

I nodded again, swallowing as his weight pressed down. My hips shifted to meet it, and I hooked a leg around his, drawing him closer. His breath was very hot against my throat.

"Say it, Lovely. Tell me you'll behave."

"I'll be good." God, he had me panting, and I had to make a concerted effort to push my aura out so my stigmata didn't brand the leather on his couch. He smiled, noticing.

"Very, very good. Now. I'm going to let you up, and you're going to sit like a lady and have some tea."

"But—"

"Shhh." He held a finger to my lips. "No arguments."

He released my other hand and sat up. I followed suit, pulling my stupid skirt down and glowering at him while he lit a cigarette. The tip flared, and he swore, adjusting himself. He ran a hand through his hair, and his hand had a tremor. Goddamn it, it better have a tremor.

"Right, then. You can look the part; now to act it. Fae society is a great deal more formal than what you're used to…"

I retrieved my beer and chugged the rest. What I wasn't used to was being told no, and I didn't like it. The whole dynamic was pissing me off.

I made it through tea. It was tense, and he was lucky it didn't end up in his lap. Him patronizing me through the entire wretched experience didn't help. I knew how; I just didn't care. As soon as I could, I ripped off those stupid heels and stalked back into the bedroom. I threw them into the closet and pulled down a couple of his suits for good measure. I might've stomped on them. Asshole.

Karen came in, and I felt bad. I kneeled down and helped her hang them back up.

"What's his problem? Does he have a girlfriend, a wife?"

She paused but shook her head with one of those shrugs. "Daemon games."

Great. I was a fucking game. I made a point of only playing ones I could actually win. I didn't even know the rules to this one, but it was obvious he was ahead. It was stupid, but I'd become determined it wouldn't stay that way. I hadn't started this, but I damn well was going to finish it.

Yeah, I know how that sounds. Here I was being held captive, and I'd decided I was going to bang my captor, come hell or high water. Refer back to my twenty-year-old-virgin-about-to-die spiel. That, and it was the principle of the thing. Guys didn't tell me no; I told them no. Who the hell did he think he was?

I didn't see him until dinner. Karen had pulled out a board game, and she and Peter trounced me between his hotels on Park Place, and her railroad empire. She picked out a different dress for me that put my cleavage on display, and he suggested something amber-y for my pulse points. I had to laugh at them trying to pimp me out but appreciated having co-conspirators and lower heels.

Brennan chewed on his bottom lip when I walked in, cigarette already burning. Dinner was lamb, which I hate. Bloody meat makes me ill. I concentrated on the salad. He mostly concentrated on his cognac and my boobs.

"Did you go out after tea?"

He pushed his plate away as the imps brought in bowls of gelato. "Yes, I had some business to attend to."

I dandled my spoon in the gelato, then sucked it off slowly. Yeah, I know how that sounds. It was exactly what I was going for. "What do you do? I mean, other than babysit wayward halflings."

"I…" His eyes lingered on my lips, and then he shook himself. "I'm sure it wouldn't interest you. Clan matters." He picked up his own spoon and began eating. "You?"

"Board games with the imps." Brennan grunted, not really listening. "So, what's next on your list? It's a ball, right? Do I need to know how to dance?"

"Yes. Waltzing is something we need to cover, but surely you know—"

"Nope." I did. It's amazing the skills you pick up living in a casino.

He kept his attention on his gelato and ate the rest very slowly. The moment his spoon rattled into his bowl, music started. Haha. Imps for the win. Brennan's eyes briefly closed.

"Well, no time like the present, I suppose."

I smiled at his false cheer, and then proceeded to act like I had no idea what I was doing.

We were out on the balcony with the doors open. The night was balmy, and the sky—

Look, it was all something right out of one of those crappy romance novels Calista used to burn through. Long-haired dude on the cover holding some quavering chick, love-is-in-the-air type bullshit.

I just wanted to get laid.

After the fourth or fifth time I stepped on his foot while pretending to concentrate fiercely on them, he pulled me in close against him.

"Come now, Lovely. Back straight. Eyes on me. It's really very simple. One, two, three, one, two, three."

"Like this?" I pushed my butt and boobs out and allowed myself to marginally improve.

"Y-yes, brilliant." We got to a turn, and I stumbled. Whoops. I fell against him with a little gasp, and he caught me. "Are you all right?"

I looked up at him with as much wide-eyed innocence as I could muster. "I-I think so…it's these heels…" I reached down, pretending to adjust my shoe, face wavering at groin level. His hand trailed up my spine to the back of my head. I took my time straightening up, lightly brushing against the front of him as I did. His hand moved with me, coming to rest an inch shy of cupping my rear. I threaded my arms around his neck.

He looked down at me, and I did my best impression of wholesome, looking back up at him. I thought he was going to say something, but then he dipped his head, and kissed me.

It was a good kiss, slow and deep. His other hand had come up under my hair, and I melted against him. When it ended, his lips dropped to my throat, and the fire at my core jumped. My stigmata flared, and little flames began to lick across my skin.

Brennan made a kind of pained rumble, and I gripped his shirt.

"Please…"

He pulled me against him, this time crushing my lips as he kissed me. The heat coming off him… Then he shook his head and stepped back.

Poof.

I collapsed, looking out over the ocean.

And then I cried.

26 Days

My attempt at sobriety hadn't lasted the night, and the next morning, I wasn't in the mood for his bullshit. I had done a lot of thinking, and granted, most of that was muddled, but one salient point had surfaced and stuck with me.

If he had a contract to deliver me at the end of the month, he wasn't going to hurt, kill, or otherwise damage me, no matter how much I pissed him off. Hell, he wasn't even going to follow through with all that innuendo and sleep with me. Why was this important? It gave me an open license to behave badly.

What? I told you, I don't like to lose.

I mean, within reason. I wasn't a total bitch, but I had been raised by one. I knew the ropes and was pretty sure I knew how far I could push him. Maybe it would've been different if there was TV kicking around somewhere, but there was nada to distract me from my goal. Or my humiliation. Jerk kept one-upping me.

You might be thinking that this was a bad idea. I mean, he was a freaking daemon, and you'd probably be right, but come on. What else did I have to do? Twenty-six days to Midsummer, and this cat-and-mouse thing was already old. If he thought he was going to keep playing with me, he had another thing coming.

Oh, all right, fine. His rejection had stung. A lot. I

wanted to hurt him back.

I put on some frilly halter thing that'd appeared in the closet. I hated the way it pushed my boobs up, but it fit the persona I was going for. I could also walk in the matching wee heels. Karen must've been vibing off me, because she fixed my hair into a messy updo and gave me a fierce cat-eye. I looked like one of those rich party girls I used to make fun of.

Brennan was on the balcony with his paper and espresso. He watched me warily as I glided over to the table with my mother's megawatt smile plastered on my face. His Adam's apple bobbed, and there were shadows under his eyes. Good.

"Ah, feeling well this morning, Lovely?"

"Peaches and cream. You sleep okay?"

"Not particularly. Vy—"

"You really should've told me you weren't into women."

The look on his face was priceless.

"I'm n—"

"It would've saved us both some embarrassment. I mean, stupid me, why else would you be hired to teach me how to act like a fae lady?" I laughed. "Really, it's my fault. I should've read between the lines after you were so upset about your clothes and the carpet. Thank you, Karen." I beamed at her as she placed my crepes in front of me. She snickered.

Brennan looked like he was having trouble forming words as I cut dainty bites and ate them with relish. He raked a hand through his hair and pulled out a cigarette, swearing as it incinerated between his lips. Hello, tell. Vy - 1, Dameon - 0. I gave him a sympathetic moue.

"Sorry, should I not have said anything? I thought

59

that kind of thing was pretty common for fae, but if it makes you uncomfortable—"

"It doesn't make me uncomfortable in the least, but I'm—"

I grimaced and raised a finger, then dropped it with a wince. "Aww. I hear they make pills for that." He was fuming. I reached over and patted his arm. God, I hated it when my mother did—

His hand snaked out and grabbed my wrist hard enough to hear it crack. I gave a little scream, and he swore, releasing me. I cradled it against my chest, cowering back.

Yeah, antagonizing him had been stupid.

My heart was beating very fast, that double thump pounding in my ears. I'd been wrong about how far I could push him. He'd seemed like a decent guy, but he was still a daemon. He raked a hand over his face before throwing his napkin down and kneeling beside me. "Bloody hell. I'm sorry. Here, let me?"

I didn't say anything, and he looked pained. "Please?"

"Why am I here?" My eyes were hot, and I bit the inside of my cheek to keep from crying.

"I've told you what I can per my contract. I'd tell you more, but there's…consequences."

"For me, or you?"

Brennan didn't answer. His eyes had scrunched shut, and the muscles in his jaw were super tense. I shivered and glanced up. It'd gotten abruptly cooler, like a cloud had passed over the sun, though the sky was bright blue. He let out a long breath and held out his hand for mine.

"I can't talk about it. Please, Vy."

I glared at him but let him have it. He gently took it, and warmth coursed up my arm. "You know very well I'm not gay, and I don't have issues."

He said it almost apologetically, and I laughed, waiting for the "you're just not my type." When he didn't elaborate, I got angry. Fuck him. I wanted out of there so bad the Priory sounded good.

"Take me home."

He laughed, and I slapped him.

Brennan let me go. He knew there wasn't anywhere to go. I'd already gone through every room, thrown open all the doors. There was no way out except over the balcony railing and onto the rocks below.

Over the next few days, I considered it. I spent a lot of time looking down at them. Karen shadowed me. I refused to be in the same room as him. When he did corner me, I ignored him, hiding my face. I wouldn't let him glamour my compliance. The shadows under his eyes got darker, and I never saw him without a cigarette. I wanted out. I stopped eating, bathing, not caring about that stupid bargain I'd made. It would all be over soon anyway. Why bother?

On the third or fourth day, Karen woke me and put a finger to her lips, beckoning me to follow. Halfway down the hall, I could hear raised voices in Brennan's office. She mimed listening, and I joined her crouched by the door.

Brennan was laughing in response to something, and he sounded manic. "She's a bloody succubus! I never would've agreed—"

"Devil's in the details, now, isn't it? We have a contract. If bending the little slut over is what it takes to get the job done, then do it. Sure you don't have issues?"

I knew that voice and felt like I was going to be sick. It was the daemon from the Priory. I bit my fist, and Karen gave me a warning look. He wasn't just an asshole; my father was pimping me out and, from that comment, watching the play-by-play.

"My God, Silas, it's not the wanting or my ability that's the issue. Amelda—"

"Is well apprised of the situation, in its entirety. Did you think she wouldn't be?"

"Knowing and sanctioning are two very different things."

"She'll allow it. Last chance, Brennan. Else Mica will relieve you in the morning, and I can assure you, he's champing at the bit."

"Mica! He'll—"

"I'll take that chance. Everything else is on target; this needs to be as well. There are other ways to garner compliance. You, of all people, should know that."

The weight of a presence beyond the door was abruptly gone.

I heard Brennan collapse bonelessly into his chair. He swore, and I bet he'd incinerated his cigarette. Karen took my hand and pulled me into the piano room. My mind whirled as she sat me on the couch. He'd been hired by my father? I hated to admit it, but that prick was right. As far as garnering compliance, willing or no, my mother could run circles around Brennan in those aforementioned stilettos. Holding on to a soft touch like him in lieu of whatever Mica turned out to be was a no-brainer. Forget the details; better the devil I knew than the one I didn't. I was startled from my thoughts by a noise at the door.

Brennan stood there with an empty bottle, the reek of chain-smoking on his rumpled clothes reaching me from across the room. His eyes were glassy, and it didn't look like he'd shaved in a while. I laughed, liking the look of him all disreputable. He turned to leave.

"No, don't go, please. Sit with me?"

He wavered, then traded his empty bottle for a full one from the wet bar. He took a long pull off it, then offered it to me as he sat. I took it.

"I like your scruff."

He raised a hand and scratched at his jaw. "Itches."

"Who's Amelda?"

Glancing over in surprise, he sighed, his shoulders collapsing. "Clan Malten's queen. I'm sorry you had to hear that, Lovely."

"So am I... Silas, he's my father, isn't he?"

"He's a lot of things. Most of them are disagreeable."

"Will Mica hurt me?"

Brennan pursed his lips and nodded, taking the bottle back. "Yes."

"Will they hurt you?"

He tipped it back and didn't answer.

I leaned up against him, and after a moment, he put his arm around me. "You really think I'm a succubus?" I knew there were different kinds of dae, but that one wasn't particularly common. He looked me up and down with a little snort. Guess that was a yes.

We drank. A lot. Finished the cognac, and part of another bottle, the both of us silently lamenting our shitty situations. After a while, he pulled out a deck of cards and was trying to teach me how to play poker. I had a hard time keeping a straight face and suggested the strip part. What? Like I was gonna quit now. I had him on the ropes.

I'd gotten him down to his briefs and the view was glorious.

"S'what's wrong with me?" I was tired of dancing around. I wanted to know.

He laughed past his cigarette. "Not a fuckin' thing, Lovely. Your bet."

"I'll raise you an answer."

"I'd rather your top." I stuck out my tongue at him, and he acquiesced with another laugh. "Very well, as long as it doesn't—"

"Break your contract, blah, blah, blah." I trounced his pair with a straight. "Why don't you want to sleep with me?"

"Sleep is the last thing I want to do with you."

"Fine. You won't bang me. Why not?"

He blew out a stream of smoke. "S'another answer."

"I'll throw in my bra." He bit at his lips as I slid a strap from my shoulder.

"I won't because you want me to."

"Asshole." I chucked my cards at him, and he laughed until I started putting my bra back on.

"Hey! Nah! I'm serious. You're untouched, s'like a gift. It indebts—" I dropped my bra, and his chest rumbled. "Mmm…there you are. Damn."

I'd piled my hair up on top of my head, giving him the pin-up pose. "Fae rules are so stupid. I've been plenty touched."

"Not like that you haven't."

I crawled over to him on the other side of the coffee table. "Yeah? What makes you so sure?" I straddled his lap, determined I wasn't going to wake up that way.

Brennan stubbed out his cigarette. His fingers skated up my back, and I drew in a tight breath as my stigmata flared in their wake. "Doesn't do that after, unless you will it."

"Maybe I did." One of his hands had slid up from my thigh to cup my breast. He pinched me lightly, and I gasped, small flames dancing over my skin.

"I think not." His other thumb made a slow circle over my panties, his gaze locked on mine. God, I wanted him. He wanted me, too. I ground myself against the evidence, and his eyes closed. "You're drunk."

"So are you." I kissed him, and this time he didn't pull away. He exhaled raggedly when I did. "What if I release you from all obligation?"

"Then you're just stupid." He laughed when I smacked him, and then tried to be all serious. "And it's not possible. A debt is made, a debt must be paid." His face clouded, that pretension of his creeping back in.

Like hell it was.

"Wanna bargain for it?"

He went very still, and I knew I had him. "What d'you desire?"

"Have sex with me, and I'll do whatever's on your to-do list, as it stands right now, to get ready for that ball."

His eyes skated down my body, and he bit at his lip again. "Yeah?"

"Yeah."

"If you don't, the obligation I incur from taking your virginity equates to one dollar, which you shall

65

take as payment, all debts satisfied."

"Agreed."

He looked at me for half a second more, then his lips were on mine, and we were in bed. They trailed down my body, and my eyes rolled up into the back of my head, fingers tangled in his hair. It took very little time for me to make the acquaintance of God. Brennan worked his way back up, my skin on fire beneath his. It was a good thing he'd pushed out his aura to save the sheets, because my control was nonexistent. He smoldered down at me, slicking himself against the cleft of my legs, and I panted for him.

"Are you very sure? You're not afraid?" he murmured between kisses.

Kind of, but I wanted him more. "I'm sure." I reached down and guided him to me.

"Then as agreed." His eyes held mine as he gave a little growl, then proceeded to defile me seven ways to Sunday, and in the morning when I woke, he was still beside me. His hand smoothed across my bare stomach, and he kissed behind my ear.

"Things have just become very complicated, Lovely. Will you trust me to keep you safe?"

I laughed and rolled over to kiss him. "Of course, you're obligated to now."

He smiled and proceeded to deepen his debt.

Things were good after that.

Well. Not like good, good. I mean, easier between us. I was still stuck there but figured I knew enough of the why to go with it. He started spoiling the crap out of me, and after living in a nunnery and in my mother's shadow, I lapped it up. That line about his compensation package? Bullshit. Well, unless he was planning to return everything after I died. I mean, it'd still be within the thirty-day window.

Don't get me wrong; it's not like I asked for gifts. What the hell do I need with diamonds? You know, that whole can't take it with you thing? But he genuinely seemed to take pleasure in it. What's a girl to do? I let him. I liked to watch his face when he did, and being a kept woman wasn't so bad. Hell, my mother had done it for years. I did as Brennan asked, listened to what he wanted to teach me. Like how to walk in those stupid shoes, and a whole lot of how not to piss people off.

That was some seriously random shit. Like, leaving during a meal without express permission by the highest ranking fae was a punishable offense. Just so we're clear, I'm talking a drawn and quartered kind of punishable. What if you had to pee? They were totally stupid.

As far as I was concerned, the only really useful thing I learned was how to control my stigmata. I basically ignored all of the socio-political crap he was trying to drill into me. CliffsNotes, he was at the bottom of the top of the hierarchy, the bastard son of one of the great five dae clans.

If you don't know the basics of that, it's pretty simple. Think of a big family led by a matriarch. She's more or less their queen and runs the show. She's also dangerous as hell. The only thing above a queen is an ancient, which is an old queen. I got the impression that retirement wasn't a thing in general, but our clan, Malten, was one of the exceptions. The Dowager was old with a capital O, and way reclusive. He didn't elaborate, and I didn't ask.

I didn't care about any of it. I was gonna die,

remember?

Anyways, little by little he started to loosen up, and I'd catch glimpses of the guy under all those formal manners, and Brennan…whatever, I don't know how to explain it.

Look, I just liked hanging out with him.

The moon was massive when he woke me.

"Come on; I want to show you something."

I rubbed the sleep from my eyes and sat up. He handed me a loose sundress, and I shrugged into it. He had that look on his face that meant he was going to surprise me. I couldn't help but smile back. He got so excited, like he was going to visit a chocolate factory and had a golden ticket.

He pulled me to my feet, and we poofed.

Then stood in wet sand. It spread out in all directions from a cluster of jagged cliffs. I could see the moonlight glinting off a window far above. His hand buried itself in my hair, and he pulled me close.

"It's neap tide, the lowest it gets. Shall we find your shells?"

I laughed at his grin, then kissed him, and ran.

It felt so good.

For a while, he just watched me, trailing after with a bucket. There were shells and tide pools full of weird fish, their colors rendered out by the moon. I dug starfish out of their shallow holes, teasing their tentacles with my fingers, then tossed them back into the water. It lapped against my ankles, warm in the shallows.

When I turned to see him again, he sat in a folding chair, smoking. And yes, he was in trousers and a button-down. What else? I was filthy, my hair knotted, and my dress wet. Somehow, it didn't seem fair.

I threw a handful of mucky sand at him.

He moved a lot quicker than I'd expected.

I screamed and laughed with him after me, slinging mud, and getting pelted in return.

When he caught me and bore me to the ground, he was a different man. Lighter. A wave came up and drenched us. I laughed at him again as he sputtered, wiping water from his face. Then he laughed, too. I could feel his joy.

Taste it when he kissed me.

His stigmata flared. Great wings of crimson and carmine, fading to candlelight. I'd never seen them before. He closed his eyes as I teased my fingers across them. They were beautiful, much more substantial than mine. Fire made flesh. He groaned as I stroked them. It was such a mixture of longing and release. My own flared, fragile and fierce beneath his, painting the sand scarlet.

When he looked at me again... I'd never had anyone look at me the way he did then.

Brennan's wings cupped around us. Our clothes began to steam, and then incinerated. I laughed, and he pressed his brow to mine.

"What am I to do with you, Lovely?"

I didn't know how to answer him. I kissed him instead.

Maybe I hadn't needed to say anything.

Shorts and T-shirts appeared on his side of the closet, and a pair of worn, army green Chucks slipped in between his oxfords. We went to the beach often after that. He just smiled at the piles of shells and sand the imps were forever cleaning up. I didn't get any more diamonds. I didn't care. I hadn't wanted them in the first place.

My lessons progressed.

Surprisingly, I found I could act the part he wanted me to play, though it burnt my ass that it was pretty much just channeling my mother.

And I was good at it. She'd be so proud. Hah. As if.

It was still a shock when he told me over breakfast we were going out. His cigarette flared when he lit it. It hadn't done that in a long time.

"Where?"

"A luncheon. My stepfather wants to meet you."

I laughed. "What, like to see who you're dating?"

"Are we dating?"

"Would you rather I said fucking?"

Brennan looked away, his cigarette crackling as he drew on it. "The ball's at the end of next week. He wants to assess your progress." I snorted and won a smile from him. "That will definitely single you out for special attention. Trust me, you don't want it. Wear that new gray dress, and have Karen do something a bit extra, won't you?"

I hadn't noticed a new gray dress, but I nodded. My side of the closet had filled up to rival his, though I didn't see the point. My time breathing was rapidly coming to a close. We didn't talk about it, but I still wasn't convinced I wanted to give up my humanity. I didn't want to give up the rest of me either. I think he knew and focused on his to-do list, staying away from that subject, and anything else personal.

It wasn't as difficult as you might think. We had a lot of sex. That was beyond good, good. And no, he wasn't into any seriously kinky shit, though he did like to talk dirty.

Brennan wasn't… Being with him wasn't what I thought being with a daemon would be like. He wasn't what I thought a daemon would be like. I mean, he could vaporize me if he wanted to, but after that whole thing with the wrist, he hadn't even tried to glamour me, not even when I was being a total shit. I was glad, and a little disappointed, truth be told. I knew that fucking comment bothered him, because we didn't. He was always gentle with me, loving even. It sounds really stupid, but it's true. He just…felt. Made me feel. I kind of hated him for that. Sorry, I don't mean to laugh, but how can you hate someone for making you happy?

Whatever. Look, I'd spent all my life in terrified awe of daemons, and he was turning out to be a nice guy. A super intense nice guy, but still, a nice guy. He was kind. Affectionate. Stupid hot. And the fire between us…it made me think maybe giving up my humanity wouldn't be so bad if he stuck around.

Stop. I didn't love him. Sometimes I didn't even like him very much. I hated that he smoked, but I could do a hell of a lot worse as far as captors went. And it was just the two of us, locked up with no entertainment but each other. You do the math.

Maybe I had Stockholm syndrome, but if it came with an orgasm like the one he'd given me this morning, I was cool with it. The thought made me climb into his lap, and he smiled.

"As much as I hate to, I'm afraid I'm going to have to take a rain check. We need to leave sooner than not. Go get dressed." He gave my rear a slap, and I stuck my tongue out at him. He laughed as I went inside.

Karen had set out the new gray dress. It was a halter with a knee length pencil skirt. The back dipped way far down. Brennan had a thing for backs, well, for mine at least. I put it on, and Karen pulled my hair into an elaborate up-sweep with seed pearl combs. She went with a heavy smokey-eye. I didn't argue. I'd gotten pretty good at being passively dressed like a doll.

Brennan was waiting for me in the bedroom. His suit was a darker shade of gray than my dress, and he was wearing a tie. He held out a wide flat box. I stopped short seeing it. He hadn't given me anything like that in weeks. Inside were pearl earrings, a wide matching wrist cuff, and a ring. He held that back until I'd put the rest on. Pearls were an odd choice I associated more with undines. Daemons typically preferred the fire of diamonds. He'd never gifted me with anything but.

"Pearls?"

He flushed. "I know diamonds are more traditional, but given your fondness for the beach, I—you don't hate them, do you?"

My eyes got hot, and I fanned at them with a laugh, then shook my head, all choked up. No one had ever—

His hand was trembling as he ran it over his jaw.

"What's the matter?"

"Ah…business matters, I'm afraid."

I wasn't liking his tone. "What are you asking me to do?"

He got on one knee and offered me the ring. "Trust me."

The expression on my face must've been something else because he looked ill.

"Is that a no?" His voice was thick and a sick certainty washed over me.

"It's a fae-band, isn't it."

Brennan's eyes closed, and when they opened, they were glassy. "I would give you what protection I can offer before I take you into the realms. While you wear it, no other will be able to glamour you, nor take you for their own. I swear I'll let you go, should you ask it thrice, and won't compel you otherwise. I…I won't compel you at all, Envy, please. This is important."

My temper jumped, and he winced. He'd made it so easy to forget he was a daemon, to forget I was a captive here…to forget I was an assignment—

His expression pleaded with me, and my chest hurt seeing it.

I didn't love him.

I held out my hand, not trusting myself. He slid the ring onto my finger, and it tightened, just shy of painful. Don't let the whole on one knee thing fool you—a fae-band's not like an engagement ring. There was zero romance in this. I'd just allowed him to tag me as his property. Forget about glamouring me stupid; he could compel me to slit my own throat, and I'd do it cheerfully. God, what was wrong with me?

It had to be Stockholm syndrome.

Brennan got to his feet and wrapped me up in his arms. "I am sorry for this," he murmured into my hair. I could only nod. He stepped back after a moment. "Ready?"

I wasn't. I was terrified and felt violated. I looked out over the balcony rail to the ocean, then down at the pearl on my finger. I was also completely at his mercy and felt bad for him about it. I definitely had Stockholm syndrome.

Nothing about the past few weeks had been real. God, I was so stupid.

"Yea—yes." He gave me a sharp look, and I squared my shoulders. "Yes, of course," I said airily, slapping Calista's stupid smile onto my face. He breathed a sigh of relief, and the room vanished.

We stood in a garden of obsidian beneath an aubergine sky. I flinched into him at a sudden effusion of flame at my side. To our right, clinging to the stone fretwork, a rosebush proliferated glowing buds of violet, bursting into violent, crimson blooms of flame. Other flowers flickered into being on either side of the meandering path. A pair of winged goblins no bigger than bread slices stopped to stare at us, then chased each other around a corner. Others flitted about foliage made up of every shade of decay. Brennan took my hand in his, and it shook. He kissed my knuckles with a forced smile.

"Welcome to the daemon realm."

9 Days

He set off at a dogged pace, not giving me much time to take things in. I was sure I looked like a tourist, but I'd never even heard this place described, which made it even weirder that it felt familiar. We'd entered a maze of thorns. They threaded through bones like fence wattling, and bloomed fire as we passed, leaving a trail of flickering luminescence in our wake. The path widened, and we passed a gap in the hedge. Brennan's steps sped up. I caught a glimpse of a necropolis in the distance, covering the low hills. Clouds had gathered, and jagged streaks of tangerine light seared down from above it. He pulled me around another corner, and I cried out, stumbling on an uneven paver.

Swearing, he led me over to a dry fountain of bone, its lip a low wall of blackened skulls. He took my ankle between his hands and warmth spread up my leg. "Sorry, I'm a bit on edge, and not keen to tarry here." His eyes were behind me, where a hissing sigh had begun, something viscous burbling in the depths. A low growl rumbled in his throat.

Brennan helped me to my feet, looping my arm through his. I faltered as he tried to lead me away. Lights like will-o'-the-wisps had populated the eye sockets in the base of the fountain. My skin prickled, very sure some kind of sentience stared after us.

"Come, lest I carry you." I started at the snap in his

75

voice but did as he said. Those lights creeped me the hell out, and they were definitely looking at us.

We reached a dense thorn hedge. It was long and curved, with archways of stone set into it. He made for one, and we stepped through it into a dusky restaurant. His jaw was tense as we parted the layers of smoke drifting between close-set cafe tables. There was a low murmur of discussion and eyes on us as we passed.

Two sets in particular set my teeth on edge. A couple of dae females were way too interested in Brennan. Like, on the menu interested.

Oblivious, he headed toward an empty horseshoe-shaped booth of tufted green leather in the back and motioned for me to slide in. He followed, taking my hands in his, and rubbing his thumb over the band.

"Forgive me for all of it, Lovely. You've no idea how much I wish our circumstances differed, but there's no other—"

"You owe me."

He laughed. "Very well, what do you desire?"

"Kiss me."

"Is that all?"

"Mmm, for now. I'm sure I'll think of more later."

My terms must've been agreeable, because when he leaned in, it wasn't a peck. It was hungry. I hoped those bitches got an eyeful. His fingers trailed down my back, and the heat in my core built. When it ended, I was breathless, my fists crushing his lapels. I pulled him back to me, wanting more. That lack of control thing again.

"Definitely succubus."

I jumped at the nightmare voice. A massive daemon with a midnight jerry curl sat beside me. My cheeks went scarlet, and he grinned around his cigar showing prominent, age-yellowed canines. It wasn't like an amused grin. It was more like how big cats bare their teeth before they rip out your throat. His pecs were at eye level, and he was in a suit so crisp if I'd brushed against it I would bleed. The look in his eyes made me think he'd enjoy that. They were black on white and slit vertically. This was the kind of daemon I'd grown up fearing.

He ran a thumb and forefinger down either side of his pencil-thin mustache. "Don't stop on my account. In fact, I think you'd enjoy taking us both together. Shall we see?"

And he was a fucking creep. Brennan's arm tightened around me. He was so angry the muscles beneath his shirt rippled subtly as his form wavered. Not for the first time, I wondered what his daemon self looked like.

Oh, sorry. When a fae fully gives into the elemental side of their natures, their forms, I don't know, morph. With dae, think badass winged pro-wrestlers. This happens incrementally as they age, with their features gradually changing. A fang here, talon there… Brennan's stepfather had definitely hit the mid-point slide, whereas Brennan was about as close to a normal as a dae could get. It lent credence to my theory he was pretty young, for a fae at least.

Anyways, the exception to the morphing rule is when they get really pissed. Then it all bursts out. Brennan was toeing that line, and his stepfather was loving it.

"Throwing your hat in the ring, little man?"

"Not at all. I'm a neutral party, as per my contract."

"Her effect on the dead gardens would say otherwise."

"You can't be surprised after Amelda allowed it."

"Did she?"

Brennan ghosted whiter than me at his stepfather's question.

Chuckling, the daemon plucked the cigar from his lips and flicked his ash onto the floor. He held up a thick finger signaling our waiter. He ordered drinks and food without input from either of us. When an appletini was placed in front of me, I drank it. Brennan did the same with his scotch. Three gold-filtered cigarette butts studded his bread plate. Every one had flared as he lit it.

"She's willing to overlook your indiscretion, provided the rest falls in her favor," the daemon said when our meal and the second round of drinks arrived. I felt sick from the first. I placed my napkin on my lap and focused on the food. Carpaccio, tartare, oysters. Everything was raw. I sipped at my martini, stomach churning. It was marginally more appetizing than the meal.

Brennan stubbed out cigarette number four. "That puts me in a rather difficult position, now, doesn't it?" His voice was hollow.

The daemon grinned, breaking the egg yolk over his mountain of ground gore. "I believe that was her intent in giving you enough rope to hang yourself."

"No doubt." Brennan made up a small plate of the carpaccio and passed it to me. It was mostly the bed of greens it'd rested on, and he gave me a flicker of a smile. The daemon caught it, and I could see him filing it away. His eyes went to my ring. I didn't much like the expression that followed and was abruptly, stupidly glad I'd been banded.

"She also said something about the desire to see you lead the vanguard when the Council gives its blessing." He said it as an afterthought, but that was bullshit. Brennan's knuckles went white, and the daemon was waiting for it. I think he savored the reaction more than the meal.

Brennan snorted like it wasn't a big deal. Also bullshit. "Decreed herself warlord already, has she? Bit premature before another Cleansing is declared, and even when it is, she's made very certain I've lost my taste for battle, along with everything else. Unless she's finally ready to put me out of my misery?"

His stepfather gave a disappointed sigh and slurped down one of the oysters. "That would be my preference, but no. I've advised against it, but your mother's inclined to allow you a bit more freedom, should you deliver."

Brennan went very still at his stepfather's words. "Forgive me if I'd prefer to hear that from her lips directly."

"Learning your lessons quicker these days, are you? Pity. I was rather looking forward to taking away your pet as a punishment." His thick lips split into a nasty grin, and he leered at me. "I'd be sure to give her plenty of exercise."

"You look like you could use some. Too bad Amelda won't allow it."

For a moment, I thought the big dae was going to hit him. Then he grunted, and they began to talk about people and places completely foreign to me. I picked at my meal, eating what I hoped was just enough not to cause offense. I'd finished the second martini, praying it would calm my nerves, but it just made me more keyed up. I looked around the dim room. It wasn't easy to see past the circle of light cast from the dangling shade above. That and the ribbons of smoke striating through the air made everything hazy. Did all daemons smoke?

The cafe was full of them, and there was an intermittent, but regular flow past our booth. A frosted door to the right labeled *Powder Room* explained the foot traffic.

As soon as I read the words, I had to go.

I didn't want to go.

I bit back a giggle at the thought of asking Brennan to take me. Stupid martinis. He shot me a look, and I dabbed at my lips with my napkin.

"I need to use the powder room."

A look of panic flashed through his eyes, but he slid out of the booth so I could rise. As I did, he pulled me close.

"Accept no gifts."

I smiled at him. What the hell would someone try to give me in the bathroom?

I kept my shoulders very straight as I pushed through the doors and found an empty stall. I bit back another giggle, never having envisioned fae toilets. In case you're wondering, they were exactly the same as human ones, and I had to wipe off the seat before I sat. The door opened and closed, two sets of heels clicking in. The door to the stall next to me banged, and there was the snick of a compact being opened by the sink.

I finished up and went out. One of the daes that'd been looking at Brennan was standing by the sink, and let me tell you, she was gorgeous. Maroon-black hair, boobs out to here, and a fanny you could bounce a quarter off. She was staring at me like someone had given her a present. I avoided her eyes and went to the other sink, washing my hands.

"You're Brennan's pet."

I stiffened, but smiled, focusing on her lips in the mirror. They were very lush and the color of ripe plums. "I came with Brennan, yes."

"Has he told you his name yet?" I flinched at the voice over my shoulder. The other daemon had materialized behind me. She wasn't as pretty as the first, but as she ran a long black nail down the side of my throat, I knew she was the more dangerous of the two.

Which was kind of like saying an asp wasn't as bad as a cobra.

I was glad I'd emptied my bladder already.

"She is appealing."

"Mmm, all fresh and innocent, just like—what's that story? You know, the one where they cut her heart out and put it in a box?" Fingernails skated up my spine, and I gasped. They laughed. Backing away, I shook the water off my hands looking for a towel. The dae by the sink held one out to me.

I stopped just shy of taking it and ran my hands down my skirt, leaving dark streaks.

"Thank you, but no." Their laughter followed me through the door. Cut it out? It felt like my heart was going to explode from my chest and save them the trouble.

Brennan looked like he'd been arguing. He stood as soon as he saw me, his jaw tight. I slid back into the booth and rubbed my arms. I wanted to go home.

Home. I bit back a sob. The two females sauntered past, still laughing, and I sat there like a post, trying not to let them see how badly they'd rattled me. My temper flared, and Brennan's hand tightened on my knee in warning. The daemon in our booth had settled back with a cocktail and a big, black cigar the size of a banana. It looked reasonable between his fingers. He stared at my fae-band intently, and I shivered from the heat in his gaze.

"Did they speak to you?"

It was the first time he'd addressed me, and my eyes flicked up to his I was so surprised. I quickly dropped them to focus on the cleft in his chin.

"Yes, sir."

"Expound."

Jump! How high? I didn't ask. I just did. Verbatim.

He grunted and blew a smoke ring wide enough for me to hula-hoop with. He didn't seem particularly satisfied with my recitation, but then he didn't strike me as the type that was particularly satisfiable.

"Tomorrow night, at the club. Your mother's having a party, and your attendance is required." The daemon stood, towering over the table. I'd be lucky if I came up to his breastbone. "We'll send over something appropriate. Free of obligation, of course." Pursing his lips at me, he disappeared.

This time Brennan's cigarette did incinerate as he tried to light it. He swore and pulled out another.

"What do you call him?"

He shot me a look, frowning. "In polite company? Horatio. You want dessert?"

I laughed, and he finished his drink in two long swallows.

"Let's go."

We went. As in one second I was sitting there, and the next I was on the couch at the flat. I choked down the bile in my throat. Materializing tipsy sucks.

Brennan ripped off his jacket and flopped back against the cushions. His tie followed, cigarette crackling. I could tell he didn't want me to ask questions. How could I not? I had a bajillion, starting with the garden, and ending with what the hell Horatio thought was appropriate. The longer I sat there, the more I had.

Glancing at me askance, Brennan blew out a long plume of smoke and sighed.

"Three, Lovely, and I want three answers from you in return."

It felt like my birthday.

"What did he mean about throwing your hat in the ring?"

Brennan pulled a bottle over from the table beside him and spun off the cap. "It was a bad joke. Clan Malten's internal politics are delicate. Female fae are dominant, but our clan has precious few capable of leading thanks to infighting. Silas was acting liege, as proxy for the Dowager. He was forced to relinquish his position when Horatio wed my mother. She has not been wise with the power he'd amassed and has made enemies. This contract…its outcome is much more far reaching than you attending a ball." He seemed pretty bitter about it, and took a long pull from the bottle, grimacing.

"Is that why you were talking about all that battle stuff?"

"No. That's a separate matter that's coming to a

head. I told you Fae was concerned with halfling persecution. There's talk of going to war to stop it."

My brow furrowed, watching him drop the bottle into his lap, thumb rubbing at its neck.

"What does the garden have to do with any of it?"

He threw one leg up on the couch and leaned back against the arm. "It bloomed."

I glared at him, and his eyes laughed back at me. Asshole.

"It rubbed Amelda's nose in your fertility, and can be taken as a very public challenge to her position, which would be bad for both of us."

I wasn't even going to try to unpack all that. "Then why did we go through there?"

Brennan shrugged. "It's where I always materialize into the dae realm."

He was so full of shit. I grabbed the bottle from him, hating fae doublespeak and half answers. I was also kind of pissed I hadn't paid more attention to all of that socio-political crap he'd been so keen to impart. I mean, I knew we were in the same clan, though not related by blood. His stepfather and my father were brothers, which made Horatio my uncle. Yeah, double creep, right? Amelda was from pretty far down the totem pole, and I vaguely recalled Brennan saying that hadn't sat well. Wrong side of the tracks type thing.

Look, if you were pretty certain you were going to be dead in a couple weeks, would you be paying attention to who was pissed at whom when you didn't know them from sliced cheese? I was much more interested Brennan's dick, catching a buzz, and as many blueberry crepes as I could eat, in that order. Whatever fae bullshit I'd wandered into made no never mind.

When that moon hit its apex, I was done, especially after being banded.

The moment of gratitude I'd felt for it with Horatio aside, it really pissed me off.

Brennan was silently brooding with another cigarette. That pissed me off, too. All he did was smoke and read the paper. Well, when he wasn't banging me, but still, what the hell did fae even do all day? It was like they just sat around and thought up ways to screw with each other.

"Do you have a job, like, an actual marketable skill, other than just looking good?"

"Several. Of most note, I'm a classically trained pianist." He smirked, and I didn't take the bait.

"You never play."

"Not in some time, no." The ice in his voice warned me to leave it alone. And this was why we didn't talk. Fine. I was out of questions anyways.

"Aren't you going to ask me anything?" What? That didn't count.

He tipped up the bottle and smacked his lips as it came down. "So eager to share. All right then, tell me, have you ever been in love?"

I stared at him. "Define love." I didn't think he was asking about the crush I'd had on the casino's bellboy when I was eight. Why would he ask me that? When he didn't answer, I went on the offensive. "You?"

"You've already used more than your three. Are you bargaining for more?" He snorted at my expression. "Those dae in the powder room. Serena and I grew up together. At one point I thought…" He shrugged. "I was wrong."

"Was she the one with the bubble-butt?"

He choked a little on his mouthful. "No. That's Meredith. Serena's the nastier of the two."

"You told her your name?"

"Enough. She made things very difficult before Amelda put a stop to it." Brennan ran his thumb over his watch. "You did well today, but need to know the club will be worse. My mother's parties…" He grabbed another cigarette.

"You smoke too much."

He raised an eyebrow and lit it, smiling. "And you ask too many questions."

At least they wouldn't give me lung cancer. I crawled over so I could lie against him, listening to the smooth, slow beat of his heart. Mine was running like a cylinder misfiring, but nothing new there. My eyes gravitated to the piano squatting in the corner on its dais. It was one of those polished black baby-grand jobs you could see yourself in. I had an abrupt desire to hear "Chopsticks."

He'd plucked the pins from my hair so he could run his fingers through it. I'd gotten to like that. A lot. I closed my eyes, enjoying his touch.

"Would you play for me?"

"Would you sing if I did?"

My eyes snapped open, and I froze. Like, wave of anxiety strong enough to close up my throat until my vision began graying out. Brennan sat me up and shook me to get me to inhale. That kind of froze. When I did take a heaving breath, I pushed up off the couch, feeling like I was going to puke. I fled across the flat to the bathroom and ran the cold water, splashing it over my face and hyperventilating.

Super extreme response to an innocent question,

right?

Hah. You'd be wrong.

Remember when I told you my mother had her own Vegas extravaganza? Mmm. She was the casino's headliner, but nothing drew the over-sixty crowd like a little girl dressed as a fae-tale princess trilling to captive woodland creatures. Especially when that little girl really could sing.

Like, I mean, Sing.

It's a fact that all fae have a love of music that borders on obsessive. My mother's beauty was only half the honey trap for daddy dae. I'm sure her voice sealed the deal. I'd inherited her talent and then some. I'd also be damned if I ever uttered another note.

Look, I'll just lay it out.

For years, my mother tricked me out as a pedophile's wet dream in the city of sin. Law of averages, people. What do you think was bound to happen? That I'd be cornered in a dressing room and instructed to perform while some perv ripped open my shirt? That my stigmata would flare into being and fry the man mid "I Dreamed a Dream," just as Sugar Daddy walked past with a group of Japanese tourists? If that was your guess, you'd be spot on. Give that reader a pony.

I don't sing.

I don't even think about singing.

I do have the tendency to lose my shit at the mere suggestion, as illustrated by me essentially wedging myself between the toilet and the tub, knees to chest, rocking. In fairness, it doesn't always hit me that hard, but the whole fae-band thing had messed me up bad, and I'd been due for a mental break.

Brennan was freaked out. The dilated pupils didn't help. They never do. This is where my mother would jam a tranquilizer down my throat early on, then later inject me with some fucked-up sedative cocktail. He glamoured me after a half hour of trying to coax me back into the land of the living. Whatever works I'm game, as long as it shoves the ugliness back down to where I don't have to look at it.

But that always left dreams in its wake.

I told you, I don't sleep well. It wasn't that I had the dreams every night, but for a long time, I was terrified to sleep on the off chance I would. A shrink said something about it being PTSD resulting from that operation I had. That's bullshit, but the Thorazine helped. Captain Morgan did too.

Even with all that, sometimes they still snuck through, especially after a panic attack, and when I was sedated, I couldn't wake myself up. It was like they waited for that shit to happen, and then I was stuck in someone else's head, living their life, and it was progressively awful.

There was always the same man, and I loved him.

That made all of it so much worse, especially since I knew how it ended.

He was one of those rugged guys who belongs in flannel. The kind that make you feel small and just, I don't know, protected. His eyes were liquid brown, and when he laughed…it was big-throated and didn't care about anything but filling up the space and melting all over everything.

In the beginning, the dreams were, I don't know, idyllic. I mean, we were in a garden and everything. There was an innocence to all of it. We weren't kids, but we grew up together. I don't even know if that makes any sense. Anyways, for a long time it was PG, but it didn't stay like that. Then, when it changed, so did he. All of a sudden he was boss. Took without giving, then without consent. We fought. He struck me when I wouldn't submit, and I ran. Before I knew it, I'd been replaced.

She was all boobs and no brains.

I wasn't just pissed that they were deliriously happy. Bimbos make me twitch, and I can't stand ignorance. God, how can guys go for that?

Whatever. The last two times Brennan had glamoured me I got to experience all of the above, so it didn't surprise me that this time I was dropped into the next installment.

It was the one where I gave her an education, took my snake, and left.

How'd ya like them apples, bitch?

8 Days

I wasn't in the best place when I went off autopilot and rejoined reality. Neither was Brennan. He was using a fancy Zippo to light his cigarettes. We'd gotten to his mother's party late, and I swear he'd had half a pack just waiting in line at the door. It wasn't moving, and we were way far back, which I was pretty sure was by design. He seemed content to keep leaning up against the graffitied brick wall, smoking.

I should explain. This shindig wasn't tea and crumpets in some snooty garden. We were in the equivalent of a gentrified portion of Dae-Vegas waiting to go into a nightclub. A massive bouncer in a dark suit was checking names off a clipboard, every so often stopping to listen to whatever was chirping at him through his earpiece. He bent over a little when he did, like that helped the reception or something. When he straightened up after the fourth or fifth time, he made a point to pick us out of the line and make that "come hither" gesture.

Brennan swore but started walking. The bouncer ignored him as we approached, leering at me. Horatio's idea of something appropriate was black, slinky, and semi-opaque. The whiteness of my skin didn't help with that. The dress's front was cut as low as the back, and God forbid I had to bend over. It looked like something my mother would've worn on stage. I could totally rock it, but it was basically lingerie.

I fit right in. This place was skank-central.

It pissed Brennan off. Like, enough for his form to waver. He couldn't look at me without grinding his teeth and reaching for his Zippo. He'd had Karen leave my hair loose. I'm sure it was so he didn't have to see me all slutted out. I was glad to have something to hide behind. He didn't have the same luxury, but man, could he fill out a pair of leather pants.

The bouncer pulled him aside as we went past. "She says, stop fucking around, and go right up." Brennan shrugged out of his grip, and I swear his form bulked when he did.

Inside was like every pseudo-swanky techno club I'd ever snuck into, which was more than a few. At the back, a neon-lit bar mirrored the little pools of pretension clustered on and around well-oiled barstools. They laughed too loud and smiled too wide, their eyes fevered with drink and whatever else they were on.

The seedier element clung to the corners.

A dae in ass-less chaps snorted a line of green crystals off an imp's backside as we passed a table. He straightened up, his eyes hungry black voids. Brennan's hand tightened on my hip, and the dae grinned, his teeth elongating.

Between the two, people throbbed, and it was hot. Like slipping into a sweltering womb of seething, shifting flesh, hot. The air was fogged and flavored with the musk of bodies undulating to the pounding bass beating up through the floor. Hands tripped across my skin, inviting and teasing me to join them. I would've if it weren't for Brennan's solid presence behind me, steering me toward a back-lit stair. It snaked up to a balcony overlooking the churning sea of wanton abandon. As we ascended, a wash of cool air prickled across my slickened skin. Goosebumps sprang up in its wake, and Brennan slid a hand over my bare shoulder. I licked the sweat from my upper lip. It had a funny, acrid-sweet tang.

"You okay?"

I gave a little nod, whatever that was tingling on my tongue.

The balcony was lit by tall columns of black flame writhing up through tubes of iridescent glass, running floor to ceiling. It gave everything a weird, dreamlike flicker. Maybe a dozen dae sat around in scattered groups of overstuffed chairs. The few women I saw were nothing like the two in the bathroom. In the quick glance I got, they were either old or seemed, I don't know how to describe it…flat, I guess. None of them were particularly impressed with me, either.

But the men were.

Brennan scowled as he led me over to the largest of the sitting areas.

Horatio was sprawled out on a couch of oxblood leather, dwarfing one side. His eyes drank me in. A blonde woman lounging at the other end smiled ferally at us. She didn't look old, and she wasn't flat. She was way pregnant. Her strapless snakeskin sheath made her look like she was digesting a gopher.

I swallowed a giggle, and her eyes flicked to me, smile widening. I didn't like it, or her. I could see her roots below the bottled-blonde as we got closer. She held out a long golden arm, her pointed manicure an obnoxious shade of fuchsia I associated with high-cut leotards and annoying personalities.

"Brennan! You're so naughty dawdling outside." The set of his shoulders tightened as he went to her. She pulled him down, kissing him like a lover. I blinked—a lot. When she released him, he grabbed a cocktail napkin from the table in front of them and spat something into it. He shot her a dirty look, wiping off the lipstick smeared over his mouth. She laughed. His cheeks flushed, and he wouldn't look at me as he fumbled for a cigarette. Her hand skated up his hip, and she began to pet him, her nails progressively digging into his side as he remained silent.

He winced and blew out a shaky cloud of smoke.

"Mother, this is Vy. Vy, my mother, Amelda."

To my credit, my jaw was clenched way too hard to drop. What the fuck was with that kiss? Remember when I assumed that daemon all over my mother was my father? Brennen's irritation with Horatio picking out my outfit? Putting aside the massive skeeve factor of what'd just gone down, dae have a tendency to be territorial, and this bitch was pissing where I ate.

Her lollipop lips quirked up. She knew exactly what she was doing.

"Charmed." I gritted out.

Horatio snorted and called for a round of drinks. He had on a blue satin shirt that was open to his cummerbund. I had to make a concerted effort not to stare at the mound of thick, black hair curling over his chest. A silver nipple ring glinted to one side. The opening bars of "Just a Gigolo" ran through my head. Before I could snicker, Amelda crooked a finger at me and patted the couch between the two of them.

"Come, sit."

After glancing at Brennan I did, on the very edge.

The hem of my skirt rose up to kiss my panties. Horatio's eyes went with it, and Brennan's form wavered. His stepfather grinned around his cigar. He knew what he was doing, too.

It was going to be a fun night.

Drinks were delivered. I started to sigh at the appletini as it was set in front of me, then jumped. Amelda had sat up and was playing with my hair. She looped it around her fist before I could squirm away.

"You'd look so much more fetching with this pinned up. Such a long, white throat." Her nail followed my jugular, and I could feel her breath on my shoulder. The heat in me quickened. She called to someone, and a moment later began twisting it into an updo. I tried not to think about the way her hands felt. I was enjoying them way too much. Brennan watched us, smoking like a rib joint during playoffs. "There, isn't that better?"

A thick finger traced down my spine and slid between my cheeks with a rumble of approval. I bit back a moan, and Brennan pulled me from between them. The room darkened. His mother laughed, watching him glare at Horatio. She clapped her hands together like a child.

I rested my forehead against Brennan's chest, trying to catch my breath. What was wrong with me? My gums had gone numb, and I licked my lips again, tasting that acrid-sweetness with the sinking realization I'd been drugged.

"As always, it was lovely to see you, Mother—"

"Lies." She seemed rather pleased about it. "Sit down. I'm not done with either of you."

Her eyes had gone hard. He led me to a chair at the end of the coffee table and pulled me into his lap, glaring at her. I watched the pulse at his throat. It was very quick. I wanted to eat it.

"You should kiss her, Brennan. Can't you see she how badly she wants it?"

The balcony had gone quiet, the rhythmic pounding from below filling the void. His throat bobbed.

"Go on, show me how you feel about her."

"Don't do this."

"Go, on."

"Silas said—"

"Show me." This time when she said it, her words sent a tremor thorough him, and there was no hesitation. He tipped up my chin and teased my lips with his, like he did after sex when we were both muzzy, but not yet sated, still wanting to touch and be touched, but without the urgency…that in-between time when I pretended maybe it was more.

Did he do that too?

The kiss deepened, and the fire in my core jumped. His hands were on me—

"Gah, enough."

Brennan quavered again and broke away, breathless. My lips found his throat, licking across the quickness of his pulse. He made a pained sound and moved my fingers from his pants, adjusting himself. I bit his lobe. He lit a cigarette and the snick of his Zippo so close startled me from him. Flicking it again, he handed it to me like a bauble to keep a baby busy.

It worked.

"Succubi have such a low tolerance for Bacchanal fog…How are you feeling, Brennan, darling…other than being so obviously frustrated?"

"Say what you have to, Mother. She can't stay here."

"No. She can't." Something about her tone momentarily sobered me up. I caught a glimpse of her face I don't think she meant for me to see. She wasn't pissing on my territory. I was pissing on hers. My eyes dropped down to her baby bump, and I swallowed.

"Have a drink, Lovely." Brennan pressed his scotch into my hands, and I obeyed, Zippo forgotten.

"Mica will be joining us momentarily. They've retrieved the last anathema," Horatio rumbled from the couch. His eyes had never left me.

"Bully for him," Brennan muttered around his cigarette. How many did that case hold? I took it from him and slid down onto the floor, taking them out and laying them on the table in a crisp row of twenty. I closed it, then popped it back open, but nothing happened. There had to be some trick...

I don't know how long I fiddled with it, but when I looked up again, there with two more dae with us. One sat between Amelda and Horatio, clearly their son by his size and the twist to his lips. The other sat in the chair opposite Brennan, watching me. He wore a neat suit, and his midnight hair was streaked with gray. The hand he stroked his jaw with had a large, gold ring.

My father.

I mean, I was ninety-nine percent sure he was my father. It'd been him, back at—Brennan reached forward and took a cigarette from the line I'd made. Another replaced it as soon as he did. How...

They'd been speaking over me, their words tinny and far away. I tried to focus, but everything kept slipping by and only snippets registered. I leaned against Brennan's knee, my skin slick and my head spinning. My heart was thumping double-time, enough to hear the thud of it in my ears. I closed my eyes, wanting to leave.

"Looks like it's past someone's bedtime. Perhaps you should kennel her, so the adults can play." Amelda's syrupy moue pierced my drug-induced fog, or rather, my anger at what she'd said did.

"I'll tuck her in."

Brennan growled, and the room got darker again.

"There's my boy." Amelda had that angry-Franklin thing going on in her voice. He tensed, and his hand came to rest on the nape of my neck. She laughed and now it was just angry. "You've become quite attached, haven't you? I strongly suggest you distance yourself, lest your pet get put down."

"Yes, pass it over here, I've a bone for her."

Excuse me?

My eyes snapped open. Rage fueled my clarity, and the effects of whatever was in my system dissipated beneath it. Brennan's hand slid to my shoulder, stopping me from rising. The man between his mother and step-father was grinning ear to ear. I wanted to put my fist through his stupid teeth. He laughed at me and lounged back against the cushions, grabbing an impressive handful of crotch.

"Come, on then. I promise a rougher ride than he's been giving you."

"You'll not touch her." Brennan had leaned past me, and his form wavered again. A chill cut through the heaviness in the air, metallic and sharp. The man sat forward, still grinning, his eyes eager. His pupils were slit, like a serpent's.

"Who's going to stop me, little brother?"

"Enough, Mica. There's no sport in baiting a caged beast." Horatio flicked his ash onto the floor. "You can wait a few more days for your turn."

My temper spiked again, and I was stone sober. How dare they jostle for position like fluffers at a gang bang! I shrugged off Brennan's hand and stood, pulling that goddamned dress down from around my waist, and stomping off to the other side of the balcony. That bitch laughed, and Mica barked at me as I went. My skin crackled with flames I was so pissed.

Assholes.

Standing at the rail looking down, my eyes were hot. I just wanted...Jesus. I just wanted not to be me, for fuck's sake.

Someone came up behind me and I gritted my teeth. If Brennan was here to tell me how fucking sorry he was—

"You forgot your drink."

It was the dae with the ring. I looked at him askance as he handed it to me. I could see myself in his features, same cheekbones, brow. My hair was his exact shade of ebony, but I'll be damned if I knew where my pallor had come from. He was as bronzed as Brennan. I threw what little caution I possessed to the wind.

"Hi, Dad."

He frowned. "I prefer Silas."

I took a sip and made a face. God, I hated these things. "So, what do you want to clue me in on first? Why I've suddenly been deemed worthy enough to live, or why you hired Brennan to hold me hostage instead of doing it yourself?"

"My responsibilities preclude babysitting, and I

don't care for children. You're being cosseted for your protection. Some rather nasty fae are looking for you. I would've thought the golem made that apparent." His lips rose up in a smirk. "And I was under the impression you've been more than satisfied with the arrangement. Several times a day, if I'm not mistaken."

Asshole. "Enjoying the show?"

"More than you can possibly imagine. You remind me a great deal of Calista. She was exceptional in her prime. It's been rather enjoyable seeing her form with my appetites." I was torn between being offended and vomiting. "How much has Brennan told you?"

"I'm sure you know."

He searched my face rather smugly, then grunted, moving on to the rest of me. It was creepy, but there wasn't a chance I was moving an inch. He took my hand in his, pursing his lips at the fae-band. His fingers were baby-soft iron, and I couldn't read his expression.

"The stipulation of silence is due to Amelda's influence I'm afraid. She's not pleased with the prospect of the boy slipping her thrall. Have you any idea why Midsummer's Eve is so poignant this year?"

I glared at him. "Oh, I don't know, my death?"

"Hardly. It's because the anathema are in play."

He said it like I was supposed to know what he was talking about. The look on my face must've cleared that up. "Skipping the minutia, there are four, one for each element, and once a millennium, they need to be reconsecrated on the summer solstice. Savvy?"

I didn't, but whatever. Nodding, I took another sip of my drink. It was preferable to the acrid-sweetness cloying my mouth which should tell you something.

"During the intervening years, it's become…" He

waved a hand in the air like he was searching for a word. "Traditional, I suppose, to try and discover where the other elementals' are being safeguarded, and capture them. The goal is to withhold them during the ceremony. Doing so results in their element's diminishment for the next thousand years."

"How so?"

His mouth twisted. "That great biblical flood? Water trounced the rest of us. I'm embarrassed to say we've been on a losing streak since."

So they were playing an epic game of capture the flag. I didn't care. Silas didn't notice.

"This millennium has been clan Malten's turn to hide Fire's anathema, the ember, and coordinate the hunt. Amelda's soiree tonight is in celebration of our retrieving the last of them, which was no mean feat. Each is different, a pebble, hummingbird's feather. Water's is a droplet. All of them were hidden someplace exceedingly clever, and the battle for them fierce." He seemed to relish that. I was having trouble wrapping my head around looking for something that ridiculously small. I mean, a freaking droplet? Despite myself, I was intrigued.

"How did you find them?"

"They each give off a distinct, low pulse." He thudded on the rail slow and regular, offbeat from the music pumping up from below. Sounded familiar.

His eyes caught mine. Way too familiar.

My stomach dropped, and my hand rose up. It trembled as I touched my scar. I could feel that double thump even now, that fucked-up thing that symbolized everything that was broken about me. Everything that couldn't be fixed.

"Careful, Envy. Wouldn't want to give the game away. Not every dae is a friend."

I snorted. No dae was a friend, and I had a—Jesus Christ! "You—"

"Yes, and in doing so, made you a very important piece on the board. Though you've a bargain with Brennan, you need to be very clear that your ultimate allegiance is to me. At the ball, you'll be required to name a Guardian as you choose to become. I suggest you speak mine, if you want to keep breathing afterwards."

My breath was coming fast enough now to make me dizzy. I thought about every time Brennan had traced my scar...God, that first night...I glanced past Silas to where he sat in a cloud of smoke, looking everywhere but at us. I could see the tremor in his hand from here.

"Can you get it out?"

"Mmm. Well, that's the trick, now, isn't it? I'm reasonably confident—"

"Reasonably confident!" My voice was shrill even to my own ears.

"Enough." The command paralyzed me. "Its placement is somewhat controversial, but circumstances being what they are, I had little choice. If it's any consolation, your survival is the preferred outcome."

I couldn't even process what the prick was saying. How much power did he have for a word to affect me like that? It'd scattered my thoughts like billiards after a clean English break. I laughed, racking them back together. Preferred. Yeah, for me, too.

Ugh. What difference did any of it make? Nothing had changed. I was still going to die in eight days.

No. I was full of shit. Something had changed. I glanced at Brennan.

Shut up.

"Why couldn't he—"

"Part of the game. We do try to spice it up, and Amelda…" He laughed, and I didn't just not like him, I hated him. "Between us, we've put the boy in an untenable position, and the outcome is eagerly anticipated. A side wager, if you will. Which way will he break? His neutrality can't possibly last, and your influence on him has made things rather more exciting. The bookies have been having a field day." His expression turned to a gleeful kind of pity at my confusion. "Haven't you figured out by now that the boy loves you?"

I put a hand on the railing to steady myself. No. I— it wasn't real. He'd banded me for Christ's sake, he—

Silas laughed, shaking his head. I gave him a withering glare and stalked across the balcony, down to the dance floor. No one stopped me. It was a party, right? I slid into the throng of thumping, churning bodies and tried to lose myself. While I'd been upstairs, that fog had become thicker, and my skin tingled with it. Abandon swept over me as I joined the dancers. Their movements had become even more capricious and lustful, the embraces closer, questing hands more brazen. I spun and writhed with them, and then he was there.

Brennan.

I was torn between kicking him in the nuts and needing to feel him. My indecision was fleeting. The heat of the crowd caught me up, and I breathed it in, wanting the oblivion of earlier, moving against him, my skin sliding against his. His hands skated over me, the music thumping up around us, and bodies closed in tight. He licked a long line from my shoulder to my ear, and I moaned. His voice was ragged when he spoke.

"Forgive me, Lovely. All is not as it seems."

My eyes closed, and my arms were around his neck. I didn't care. His mouth was on mine, and I bit at his lips. I didn't want his apologies or excuses. I wanted him to hurt. I needed to be hurt, to feel pain somewhere other than in my chest.

He obliged. Somewhere in one of those dark corners we ended up against the wall, my panties thrust to the side, gasping and crying out together. He wasn't gentle, and I didn't want him to be. When it was over, he pressed his forehead to mine, his breath heavy and tinged with whatever Amelda had slipped into his mouth along with her tongue.

"Please, Vy, trust me. Let me love you."

I kissed him desperately, my lips bruised and tender. I wanted to say yes, to make it real. To feel what other people did. Instead I laughed, my cheeks wet, too terrified that this was all one big mind-fuck. I didn't love him. His eyes burnt into mine, and he kissed me like he had on the sand, his thumbs wiping my tears away. A smile tipped up his lips.

"What's that for?"

"You didn't say no."

He zipped up, and I fixed my dress. Taking my hand in his, he led me to the bar. He had a goofy smile on his face as he ordered drinks. I sat on an empty stool, and he stood close, bending to kiss me again.

"Quite the performance, little brother. Hell bent on antagonizing her, aren't you?"

"Since when do you care?" Brennan's face closed up as he turned to Mica. He was huge, though not as massive as Horatio. I felt a pang, missing Berk.

"Just an observation." Mica looked down at me and licked his lips. Brennan gave a low growl, and his brother grinned, the red neon from the bar bouncing off his canines. They were pronounced, and wickedly sharp. "No worries, Pet. I've a bed for you when she pulls his leash tight. Should be any moment now."

"You'll leave her alone." Brennan's form wavered, his stigmata flaring as he leaned over me toward him. I put a hand on his chest and glared at Mica, perfectly capable of dealing with him myself. He wasn't going to touch me, not after what Silas had said. I had open license to be a bitch until this damned thing was out of my chest, and I sure as hell was going to use it.

Yeah, I know, that logic worked so well for me before.

"Fuck off, dick."

I hadn't noticed how quiet it'd gotten around us. The two of them had gained an audience, and my voice was very loud. Someone laughed, and Mica's face purpled, but my luck, such as it was, held. The back of the chair he was gripping, not so much. The wood crackled and incinerated beneath his meaty fingers.

His other hand snaked out and grabbed a passing imp, swinging it around and breaking its back across his knee like a bundle of kindling. He tossed it away and leaned in close. "Enjoy him while you can, Pet. The clock's ticking toward Midsummer, and after it strikes, he'll be back under Amelda's skirts. Then it'll be my turn to play with you."

He kicked the imp as he left, walking away with a

nasty smile on his face. The poor creature lay there, not even able to whimper. Brennan crouched down, and the imp said something to him. Brennan answered, then snapped its neck with brutal efficiency. No one blinked. The bartender came out and dragged the mangled thing behind the bar and through a doorway, like it was just another Thursday night. I sipped at my drink, nauseous.

"Though well-deserved, that was not wise," Brennan said, draining his own glass. He ordered up two more and lit a cigarette.

"You just—"

"Put Roald out of his misery? Yes. Those lessons weren't just to protect you, Lovely. I suggest you implement what we've discussed."

Yeah, I felt terrible.

He sighed and pulled me against his chest, kissing the top of my head.

"What Mica said—"

"Won't happen."

I went to say something, but the steel in Brennan's eyes stopped me. His hand rose up to my cheek, and I pressed against it, trusting him, and cursing myself as I did. A little voice inside me screamed, S*tupid! Stupid! Stupid!* Over and over again, and I fought to squash it. Maybe it was wrong this time, maybe—

The house lights flashed, and the music dropped off. Brennan tensed, moving closer to my side. Everyone's attention went to the balcony. Amelda stood there looking out over all of her subjects, like an evil trailer-park queen. As her eyes lit on us, it was clear we were out of favor. Brennan's cigarette crackled beside me at her smile. He had to take after his father.

"Tonight we celebrate! The final anathema has

been won!"

The mood flipped like a politician's stance, and the place erupted with elated cheers. Christ, you'd think they'd just won a big match. I laughed. Daemons were high-fiving, and fist bumping, shooting gouts of flame into the air—it was surreal. Then a loud click echoed through the room, and Brennan swore. I had the distinct impression that leash Mica had been talking about had just been yanked. Silas moved up beside us from the crowd.

"I'll stay with her."

Brennan's head hung, and he nodded.

The largest piano I'd ever seen was rising up through the floor. It was beautiful, a deep burnished maple with an elaborate gold filigree set into the top board. He walked out to meet it, stepping onto the platform before it'd stopped rising. Slinking down onto the bench, he took his time finishing his cigarette, then flicked it away.

The anticipation in the room weighed down on me, like something momentous was about to happen. Amelda leaned against the rail above, a satisfied smirk on her face. I had no doubt she was punishing him. Brennan's finger hit a key, his eyes closing as the note resonated.

Then the world exploded.

The mirror behind the bar shattered, and I was thrown forward onto the floor, my ears ringing from a massive blast. Something heavy was against my back, pinning me to the ground. I struggled to rise, and a hand clamped down on my shoulder. Silas. His lips moved, but I couldn't hear him. Dust and debris clouded the air, and I coughed, wiping at the slick wetness in my eyes.

My hand came away scarlet, and my vision swam.

He pulled me up by my arm, and I staggered, kicking off a shoe. I'd lost the other when I fell. Another explosion peppered us with debris. Dark shadows ran through the haze, and there were bursts of flame. I cried out at the glass slicing into my feet as I was dragged along. Silas threw me over his shoulder like a sack. Why wasn't he poofing out of here? Behind him, a creature the size of a small bus resolved from the mayhem and reached for me. I screamed, and Silas whipped around. My stomach rebelled at the motion, and I puked. It vaporized before it hit the floor, his stigmata flaring. Huge searing wings sprang from his back, and his skin roughened, becoming the color of over-ripe cherries.

He dumped me unceremoniously backward, and my arms hit the ground a second before my face smashed into it. Dazed, I scrabbled up at the muted roar behind me, afraid to look. Staggering away as quickly as I could, shapes flitted past me, knocking me off balance. I coughed, limping through the rubble. A great gout of flame shot up behind me, then another on my left. Something exploded up out of the ground, and I ducked, covering my head as stones rained down.

I felt, more than heard, a deep bellow roll through the room. It twisted my insides, and I pissed myself. Whatever that belonged to, I did not want it finding me. The floor shook, and I fell to my knees, the haze shifting and parting with the force of the tremor.

The stairs to the balcony were maybe a hundred yards in front of me. I struggled to my feet with a sob. I'd gotten turned around and was heading in the wrong direction. The steps were in flames. Muck-colored humanoid shapes with bizarrely distended features loped through them. A daemon with great wings of dark fire reached out, tearing the creatures apart as they darted close. Amelda lay at its feet, cradling her belly, her face twisted with pain and rage.

I spun around to where the piano had been, but I couldn't see through the smoke. Where was Brennan? My heart thudded wildly in my chest, like it was trying to smash its way out. Pressing at my scar, I hunched over, every part of me hurting regardless of the adrenaline coursing through my veins. Something clipped my shoulder hard, and I skidded back, slamming into an overturned table.

I fought to stay conscious.

Forget about eight days. If I didn't get out of here, I was dead now.

The realization got me onto my feet, and I staggered off the direction I thought the exit was in. I heard a hiss a moment before one of those things was on me. Its gravelly hands bore me down to the ground, and I screamed again. It wrenched my shoulder over, flipping me onto my back. The thing weighed a ton, and I couldn't get it off me. My stigmata flared, and I pumped plasma at it. It grabbed a stone dagger from its belt and slammed it down toward my chest.

Everything went white.

6 Days

I was in the rain.

My cheek rested on smooth stone, and I felt like I'd been dragged to it and left to die. I lay there, categorizing all of my aches and pains, for a good chunk of time before I attempted to move. When I did, I was sorry. I rolled onto my back and opened my mouth, catching the rain on my tongue. It tasted like sulfur. Above me, clouds streaked with tangerine bursts of light roiled. How was I still alive? I pawed weakly at my chest, surprised there wasn't a blackened, bloody hole.

It was the only part of me that wasn't mangled, and I was cold. The marble slab I was lying on wasn't doing me any favors in that department. Above me, a stone effigy of a woman towered. She looked incredibly sympathetic to my plight, and I gave a gasping laugh. At least somebody gave a shit.

I managed to drag myself beside her, where there was some shelter, and took stock again. My dress was in tatters, a large gash at my hairline and several on my feet bled freely, most of me looked like it had a bad case of road burn, and I was lost in what I was pretty sure was that necropolis on the hill. I wasn't even going to begin to tackle how the hell I'd gotten here. Oh, and I was being hunted. My head lolled back against the wall, and I tried to breathe normally.

At least I didn't have to pee.

I laughed, and the sound that came out that time scared me. Blackness ate at my vision. I closed my eyes, thumb worrying against the fae-band on my finger. Brennan would find me. The warmth and surety of that thought surprised me, but I didn't love—

I blacked out before I could finish lying to myself.

I've no idea how long I slept.

The crashing boom of thunder woke me, followed by torrents of rain. That didn't bother me so much. My mouth felt like something had died in it, and I was more than happy to lap up the moisture. The thunder was an issue. My head was absolutely pounding, so much so, I couldn't think straight, and I was like ice. I huddled beneath the overhang and closed my eyes, wishing I wasn't me.

When I opened them again, the storm was gone, and the pavement dry. I felt like absolute shit. I just kind of lay there, listening to my tinnitus in the silence, until I drifted away on it again.

I dreamed I heard Brennan's voice. That he held me, was kissing my face. Then it wasn't his voice, it was Silas's, and they were arguing. I wished they would shut up so I could die.

Next it was warmer, and there were other sounds. The slam of a screen door, and the static buzz of an AM radio. Smells too. Other than me. A hand on my forehead. I made a noise.

"Shh, easy now, Lovely. I've got you."

It was too much effort to open my eyes. I whimpered when his hand left, but then his weight settled behind me, holding me close.

I slept like I'd had three pain killers and a fifth of

gin.

When I woke up again, he was gone. I was lying on a crappy green plaid couch, in an army-surplus sleeping bag. The room was teensy and narrow with pumpkin shag carpet.

I sat up and clutched my head, trying to figure out if the thudding I was hearing was me, or something else. Someone had bandaged the gash at my hairline, and I was wearing clothes. I pulled the faded concert tee away from myself, blinking. It was so big the neck hole slid over my shoulder. I fell back against the cushions, watching a puff of dust come up and drift through the sunlight. It filtered in through a high, single-paned window. Where was I? It looked like the inside of a trailer.

I hoped to hell it had a bathroom. It took me way longer to get my legs out of that stupid sleeping bag than it should've. Whoever had owned the T-shirt must've donated the sweatpants. I could've fit in one leg but wasn't up for a sack race. I probably shouldn't have been up at all.

Cursing my bodily functions, I hiked the sweatpants to my chest and held on as I stood, biting back a cry. One of the bandages on my foot bloomed red as I put weight on it. Shit. I limped to the doorway at the far end of the couch. Silas was sitting at a cracked formica table with a Styrofoam cup of coffee. His eyebrow rose when he saw me leaning against the doorframe..

"Where's Brennan?"

"You're up rather sooner than expected. He's getting supplies and assessing what's been compromised. He suggested…" Silas wafted a hand.

111

I leaned against one of the rusted chrome chairs. "Where's the bathroom?"

"A bucket out back, I believe."

"Are you serious?"

"As a heart attack." I shot him a dirty look and started for the door. He hurried to take my elbow. "You don't look capable of navigating the stairs. Your balance afterwards is on you."

Well, wasn't that just tits.

He helped me down the rickety pressure-treated steps. We had been in a trailer. It was up on cinderblocks in the middle of an overgrown field of thigh-high, crispy brown weeds. The land around us was perfectly flat, and the air searingly hot. Oil wells thudded around us, and the sun sat a hand's breath above the horizon in the east. I found the bucket and did what I had to do.

My insides felt hollow. The kind of empty you get when you don't eat for days and have cried for twice that. How long had I been gone? I sat on the bottom step, next to my father. It was weird.

"What happened? I mean, after you dropped me on my face."

Silas rubbed his hands together and chuckled. Asshole. "A magnificent brawl. I can't remember the last time Earth's come at us like that. We sent them packing, but it took a while. Brennan felt you were still in the realm through the band. It's a lucky thing. I'd figured they'd taken you. How did you get into the necropolis?"

I shrugged. "One of them tried to kill me. I woke up there."

"Mmm."

"Everyone else have as much fun as you?" I asked, hoping to distract him. I didn't like the way he was looking at me. I had a feeling I should've left it at the shrug.

"Presumably, though I believe Amelda's busy whelping her next spawn as a result. No one of importance took injury."

The blood from my foot had started dripping off the step to the ground below. Gee, thanks, asshole. I lifted my face to the sun and closed my eyes, enjoying the heat, since I wasn't enjoying the company. The cold from that place had settled into my bones. Psh. More likely it was the chill from Silas watching me. Man, he was creepy.

"You're a great deal more clever than people give you credit for, aren't you? Certainly more capable. Plasma, cleansing your system, materializing from a shielded room… It must have to do with carrying the anathema for so long. My other get was rather disappointing in retrospect."

Whoa, what? "Other get?"

"Mmm." I stared at him, and he laughed. "Did you think you were the only one? Humanity's one redeeming quality is their ability to reproduce like rats. At one point, there were several dozen of you scurrying about, though half-dae have been having a rough go of late. Unfortunate, but necessary. You owe me a debt for gifting you with the ember. As of two days ago, you're the last of my spawn living."

Like hell I did. "Any chance they'd all had their hearts torn out?"

Silas grinned at me, not particularly broken up about it. "As I said, a great deal more clever."

I sat there speechless, in large part at the very idea I'd had siblings. The rest of me couldn't believe he was such a heartless douche. I mean, seriously? I was still in shock when Brennan poofed into view. He was dressed as a laborer. Oddly, it suited him. He had a bundle in his arms and a bag over his shoulder.

Silas got to his feet. "How do things stand?"

"I've put feelers out as a precaution, but as far as I can tell it's just the club that was compromised. I'll plan on returning to the flat in the morning."

"Amelda?"

"I thought it wise to keep my distance."

Silas grunted. "Fair enough. I've arrangements to make."

Poof.

"You're awake." Brennan crouched down in front of me with a broad smile, dropping his bags, and hugging me tight. "You all right? You look like you've had a shock."

"I had siblings?"

He winced. "That's why I was contracted to watch you. Someone other than Amelda was picking them off."

"Looking for the anathema."

"It's likely."

What a bizarre feeling to lose them before I'd even known they'd existed. Brennan's eyes were full of concern, and there wasn't doubt how he felt. All I could think of was the way his mother had kissed him. I didn't want to know what I had to know.

"At the club—"

"I'm sorry, Lovely, I was pinned down by that damn rock troll—"

"No, I—What did Mica mean about you being back under Amelda's skirts?" My voice crackled at the end.

"Ah." Brennan sat on the ground in front of me, his expression hard. He took my bloody foot in his lap, and warmth spread at his touch. I waited for him to speak. After a while, he pulled out a cigarette and tapped it on his knee.

"You have to understand...fae see halflings as a necessary evil, and as such, we're not particularly fancied. Growing up on the other side of the veil's not so bad as you all have it, but it certainly isn't what I'd consider easy. Our existence creates loopholes in the Proscriptions, ah, your stupid fae rules, allowing for our exploitation. I think perhaps that's why most are so vicious after they become. It was different for me, at least, I thought it was. When I was a child, Amelda cosseted me. I worshipped her in return." He laughed at my expression and lit his cigarette.

"She was different then...or maybe I was just very young and stupid. When all that with Serena happened, I was desperate and made a very bad bargain for Amelda to intervene. She banded me." He tapped his heavy gold watch, then leaned back on his elbows. "I was unprepared for the consequences of that. Our arrangement has become increasingly constrictive. I want it to end. She does not. Silas gave me a way out, and I jumped at it." His mouth curdled. "It's put me in a tenuous position I can't get into."

"That kiss..."

"It's...complicated, and I'm sure that was solely for your benefit." Brennan's expression was pained. "Amelda is...capricious, cruel. She takes whatever I find a modicum of joy in and ruins it, because I won't give her what she wants. What's your earliest memory?"

"Being in the hospital." And all I could smell was fried eggs. I know, weird, right? Who fries eggs in a hospital?

"Do you remember how you felt? What color the walls were? What you were wearing?"

"I was alone and terrified. They made me wear boy's pajamas, and it pissed me off…they were blue, or white, maybe. I've no idea about the rest, but I do remember that." Thinking about those stupid pajamas still made me mad.

"All fae feed off emotion. Without doing so, we end up in the necropolis sooner than not. Things that can trigger the depth of emotion like that first memory of yours are coveted. It's why fae love music." He ran a finger over his watchband. "For a large portion of my life, Amelda basked in my adoration and my playing. Then she banded me, and it wasn't enough."

"Her baby…"

He looked confused, and then like he was going to be sick.

"Her—oh, God, no. I haven't—Even if she— Horatio would never stand for it. He barely tolerates me as it is—I swear to you, that line hasn't been crossed."

I wondered how many others had as I watched him smoke, the sun beating down on us, and the crows screaming through the thumping of the wells.

"What about you? I mean, what do you feed off?"

Brennan shrugged. "Battle, then my music. She's cut me off from both. I've been living this kind of half-life… She won't allow me to play for myself or any

116

other but her. I refuse to. Each time she compels me, the music suffers, as do I. She's long since lost my adoration, and what's left I don't believe she much likes the taste or sound of, but she's hell bent on draining me of it. The less I feel, the less she has to feast on. Losing myself was preferable to being her thrall. Then Silas offered me his bargain… I'm sorry about the club. I never would've kissed you like that in front of them if she hadn't compelled me."

"And downstairs?"

He laughed. "Christ, you were bloody irresistible. No, that was all me." He took a deep drag, his smile fading. "You're a feast in and of yourself, Lovely. You've made me feel again, and she hates you for it."

I took a deep breath. "What you said to me—"

"That I loved you?" I winced as he stubbed out his butt and flicked it into the grass. "Since that night on the beach. I know it's unreciprocated." He stood and gathered the bags back up. "As I said, I wish our circumstances differed. Shall we?"

I sat there looking up at him, the sun picking up the blue undertones in his hair, feeling very small and very, very foolish. I held the door for him. He'd brought me clothes that fit, and the fixings for peanut butter and jelly. It felt good to be in leggings and a tee. I laughed as he sprinkled red-hots over his sandwich before smashing the sides together.

"That's disgusting."

He took a huge bite. "Mmm. Not as good as I remembered. Peter's mother used to make them like this."

"What's the deal with the imps?" I asked, glad for a change of subject.

"The deal? They work for daemons. Daemons treat them like shit."

"You don't."

He shrugged. "They've always been kind to me. Others were not. They like you, you know. I never have time to play with them. Board games are their passion, strategy in particular. I'd advise you not to let Peter talk you into Risk—he's rather adept at world domination. Did you really tell Karen her hair was pretty?" I nodded. "It made quite an impression, and I can assure you, there are worse friends to have."

"She woke me that night Silas came."

He laughed. "And Peter was noticeably absent when I needed a new bottle. See, strategy."

"Will they be okay?"

"Hmm? Oh, yes…imps are extremely resourceful, and most daemons can't tell them apart. They know a great deal more about our affairs than people think." He met my gaze and took another bite. Was he telling me what I thought he was telling me? His eyes flicked about the room in warning.

I looked away, twisting at the band on my finger. Karen and I needed to have a chat.

"I'm not sorry I banded you, Envy. I did it to keep you safe. I know intimately what it means, but while you wear it, no one else can glamour you or put you in their thrall. If you wish to be released, you have but to ask. Without it, we never would've found you."

My hand brushed my chest. "Not even by its pulse?"

"The Neither bleeds into the daemon realm where the necropolis stands, deadening everything. It's where we go to die. I'm even not sure the anathema would persist there, given enough time."

I shivered remembering the creeping chill of marble against my skin.

"Do you think Silas can get it out?"

"I don't know, but...you're of importance."

"How so?"

Brennan took another bite, and I could tell he was trying to choose his words carefully. "I had a half-sister, well, more than one, but Genevieve was the last. Since her untimely death several months ago, Amelda's rule has been openly questioned. Some seek to challenge her by proxy, using a younger female of my clan. They've become remarkably scarce. So much so, only a single candidate remains with all the necessary qualities." His expression didn't leave much guess work as to whom that might be. "This candidate will need to name a Guardian as she becomes. Whomever that is will enjoy a certain...status for the duration of their investiture."

He dropped his eyes from mine, and I watched him chew, fitting that together with what else I knew. It came down to him being contracted to prepare me for this fae crap as a neutral party, but both Silas and Amelda wanted him to tip the scales in their favor. Well, Silas wanted me to name him. I mean, he'd said as much, but Amelda...

"What does your mother want?"

"To keep her seat, but the anathema needs to be reconsecrated for her to do it."

Great. So I was in the center of a clan power struggle, and the only thing keeping me alive was the thing that was probably going to kill me at the end of the week. I laughed.

Fuck my life.

I ate my sandwich. The six pack of beer Brennan had brought was warm, and we drank it anyways. The silence crept in between us, and he chucked his empty can in the corner. I was so stupid. All that stuff about being out of options and the rest of it, I couldn't let him go on thinking I didn't care. It made me feel like I was going to puke, but I couldn't keep lying to myself about it either.

"What you said, I—"

"Don't. Please…allow me my fantasy, if only for a few more days."

I went to him and straddled his lap. His chin was stubbly beneath my fingertips, and there was faint bruising over his cheekbone. I kissed across it. "What if it's not?"

"Not what?" His voice was ragged as I put my forehead to his.

"A fantasy."

He smiled softly. "Well, then, that is the fantasy."

His lips were on mine, slow and languorous. If I'd thought he'd been making love to me before, I'd been wrong. Way wrong.

This was…more.

He loved me, and I…I was an idiot. I loved him back and said the words. His face…joy…I felt it too.

It was real.

After, we slept curled together on that crappy couch, and it was pretty much the most perfect moment I'd ever had.

So you know it didn't last.

It wasn't even light out when Silas arrived in a burst of flame.

"Get dressed. We need to move."

Brennan sat up and scratched at his stubble. "What? Why?"

"Amelda's spawn is dead, and she's in a bad way... Our detente is over. This is no longer a game." Silas's expression made me question if it ever had been.

Brennan ghosted white. "She'll be coming for Vy...has she called the clan?"

"They're already assembled. We need to go as quickly as possible. I have to stop and secure the last of the anathema."

Brennan started jamming his legs into his pants, and I followed suit.

We materialized in a large domed room. I stood behind them, so I couldn't see a lot of it, but what I did reminded me of one of those beehives, you know, a skep, the way it was ridged with concentric rings all the way up. Would've sucked for the bees, though, because it was on fire. Flames ran up the walls in a sheet, the smoke disappearing through a small grate in the center of the ceiling. Directly below it was a prayer bench. Silas walked across the glossy black floor and put something into a small box on its shelf. He smiled as he turned, dusting off his hands. Everything about him said job well done.

Behind him was an effigy of the Lady in flames.

I got a really bad feeling in the pit of my stomach. I didn't like the way he was looking at me. I liked it even less when I felt the hypodermic stab into my rear. Bewildered, Brennan caught me as I fell.

My mother just looked satisfied.

5 Days

I had a dream. Hah. No, nothing like that.

It wasn't like the ones I told you about, either. This was an old dream, from before all those other ones started. I'd forgotten about it until I was in it again, then it all rushed back. Kind of like a tendril of scent can evoke a time and place you hadn't thought about in years, then it'll make you smile, and remember the way something tasted.

This was that kind of a dream.

I ghosted through a wasteland of flame and shadow. Ash fell from dark clouds, slowly coating monoliths of stone like papier mâché. The path was lined with shards of obsidian. Their blackness ate the fire and spat it back out as frenetic points of light as I passed. My footfalls were silent; everything was in this place. As close and quiet as a funeral shroud.

My breath caught when I threaded through the last of the standing stones and saw her. She sat beneath a stunted tree, its branches gnarled and bare. Only her long ebony hair and the slate-colored serpent coiled in her lap clothed her nakedness. She hadn't changed at all, but as I sat on the stone by her side, my perception sure as hell had. Now I knew her.

She was me, right down to the chippy peach polish.

"You found your way back through the labyrinth. I've been waiting for you."

My brow furrowed. The path had run straight. "I…didn't know you'd still be here."

"Where else would I be, but at the heart?"

I had no answer for that, and she smiled.

"It's not your fault you've been delayed. Forgive them, Lord, they know not what they do." She held out a half-eaten apple, laughing at my expression. "I've kept it for you. It needs to be finished."

I took it from her, remembering. The bite marks of a child had gnawed away one side. I grimaced and raised it to my lips. Bitterness flooded my mouth, and I gagged. God, I hated apples.

"Eat. There won't be another chance."

I shot her a dirty look but believed her. I can't tell you why it was important, but I knew it was. I forced the entire thing down, my lips puckering, then she plucked the seeds from the core and fed them to me. The last of it burst into flame, and the ash blew away.

The serpent in her lap stirred at the flare of heat and raised its head. It was the same color as my eyes and the pearl on my finger. I reached out to stroke its coils, and its tongue flicked out across it.

"You love him."

I shrugged, my cheeks warm. She sounded sad.

"One way or another, that's a kind of fire, too. You'll need all of it for what's coming. Burning through that sedative they're pumping you full of is just the first step."

Seda—what?

It all rushed back. I'd sure as hell hit the lotto for shitty parents. That prick had set me up, and Calista… No doubt I was back at the Priory strapped to a goddamned gurney—

Brennan.

My stigmata flared, wings unfurling from my back. I was going to kill them.

"Look how glorious you are. Don't worry. You'll get your chance."

Had I said that aloud? I brought my wings forward, cupping them around me, then stretching them out. They'd become an ombre of reds, almost black at the top, then bleeding down to a dripping scarlet edge of flame. It was so easy here. I felt like I'd been un-hobbled. Her smile widened, then she leaned over, and kissed me.

Something wouldn't stop clanging, and it was bugging the shit out of me.

I pried a gooey eye open, my nose crinkling at the reek of antiseptic. Everything was out of focus and my mouth had an awful bitter, metallic taste. My head pounded with the kind of still-drunk hangover that only comes with mescal and sedatives. I was all fucked-up over shitty with a side of tremors. I tried to roll over for the glass water on the bedside.

And was pulled up short by the restraints on my wrists and ankles.

I lay there blinking, slowly recognizing a brown water stain that looked like a shoe on one of the ceiling tiles. Well, hello, there, old friend. Park Place. Mmmm, no, wrong game. I'd played this one before. Let's see... Envy, in the Priory's infirmary, strapped to a gurney, with an IV of oblivion. That sure as hell trumped anything Colonel Mustard could come up with in the conservatory.

The grid of tiles wavered in and out as my vision fuzzed. Fuck my life. I turned my head, nauseous. IV bags making up the cocktail my mother had mixed hung from a metal pole beside me. It looked like they'd just been changed out, but one of them wasn't hooked up right, and nothing was dripping. Whatever was in the others made me feel really drunk.

I laughed. Like that'd ever been a deterrent.

The memory of my dream came back, and with it, what'd happened prior to. Where was Brennan? Crap. I needed to go, like, now. From the light coming in the windows, that clanging had been the bells for matins, but they'd be back. Sister Reticence's knitting bag across the room guaranteed it, and then it'd be lights out. As it was, the cocktail was weighing me down, each drip like another stone on my chest. The room spun, dragging my eyes with it. I scrunched them shut and felt tight bandages pull against my brow. I was gonna puke.

It was stupid, but the next thing that hit me was the certainty that they'd cut my hair.

I know, I've got messed up priorities, but the flare of anger at the thought gave me more clarity, just like at the club. The ceiling stayed put and firmed up. I reached for my fire, and ever so slowly, it came, trickling through my veins, picking up momentum as it flowed. It seared through the rest of the sedatives, and as my body came back to life, my muscles prickled and ticked with fury.

I was going to kill them.

I incinerated the port they'd installed in my arm, so pissed imagining myself with a bob I felt like I was on some kind of upper. My restraints disintegrated with a thought.

I reached up, and my face crumpled.

125

They'd hacked all of it off. Beneath the bandages, my hair was smashed down around my face at chin length. I tore off the gauze, and it foofed out. I had to make a serious effort not to torch the building as I sat there and cried, looking like some kind of mushroom.

That fucking bitch!

Bitches, I amended, wiping my eyes, sure Sister Reticence had handed my mother the scissors while the Prioress watched. I tried to calm myself. They'd get theirs as soon as I got Brennan. My clothes were in the closet. They hadn't bothered to lock the door. I twisted the fae-band on my finger, knowing I should do the smart thing and leave while I had the chance.

I couldn't.

Love's gotta be a mental illness.

He had found me through the band; could I find him? I brought it up to my lips. Maybe, but it was so faint—

I left the room, not wanting to know what that might mean.

One thing I had going for me was that the Priory was my home turf. I'd been sneaking around these halls for years and knew the layout. More importantly, I knew their weird schedule. Outside, the sun was just starting to rise. Everyone would be at service. I briefly wondered what day it was, but really didn't care. All that mattered was I wasn't dead yet.

The infirmary was a small building next to the dorms, and the faint thread of what I was sensing led me through both, toward the chapel. Of the entire compound, it was the building I'd skulked around the least. I mean, it's not like I believe there's really anything to their bullshit religion, but it's never particularly wise to thumb your nose at a deity. You know, just in case. Especially not one that's planning on deep frying the planet.

The chapel was also the building where everyone had congregated for service, but matins were wrapping up. I could hear the Prioress start the final homily as I passed beneath the crimson windows depicting the inferno.

I'd filched a novice's robes from the dorms. I wasn't going to kid myself that it would make me inconspicuous, but it was better than nothing. I headed around the back of the building. The thread was definitely stronger there. Brennan was close. A minute stream of plasma kept the fire door's alarm from going off, then I snuck into the chorus room. They'd started the closing hymn, and I cringed. God, they sucked.

I hid behind the ceremonial robes not a moment too soon. Footsteps came down from the choir loft, and there was a solid fifteen minutes of whiney bitches complaining about the organist, who in fairness, didn't know a flat from a sharp.

I waited until the gouty sister assigned garbage came in to clean up and turn off the lights. It seemed like forever before I heard her hard, flat shoes clop down the aisle, and the clunking echo of the main doors closing. All clear, I edged out into the empty hall. The thread took me toward the altar, but he felt, I don't know, lower. They must have him in the catacombs.

I swore, but it made sense. Men weren't allowed on the Priory grounds, never mind daemons. Outside of yours truly, halflings were also verboten. We've already covered the whys and wherefores of that.

The entrance to the sub-basement was through a

supply room off the hall. I went to melt the lock, but it was open. I wiped my palms on that stupid robe. Crap. Someone must already be down there.

It was right around this point that I started questioning the merits of my plan. Or lack of plan, rather. Brennan had looked surprised, but had he been? Yeah, I was being pretty cynical, especially since I was supposed to be in love and all that, but considering everything that'd happened? A girl's got to have some instinct for self-preservation.

Mine was screaming at me to turn right the hell around and not look back.

My stupid feet didn't listen.

I crept down the stairs. One of those retracting gates was at the bottom, but it wasn't locked, either. I was and wasn't relieved. Not that I couldn't get past it, but every time I did, I was basically leaving a neon sign announcing I'd been there. All anyone had to do to find me was follow the melted metal.

The naked bulbs hanging from the rafters were on, and the room was packed with shit. You know, like stacked chairs and pageant crap. Other stuff was under dusty old tarps, and the air was thick with dry rot. Opposite the steps was a steel fire door, held open by one of the slide bolts used to lock it. There were three of them, and they were as big around as my wrist. Seemed excessive.

Beyond it were the catacombs.

I use that term loosely. There weren't like miles of spooky tunnels lined with the bones of plague victims. The Priory, and Vel City itself, had been built on top of an expansive natural cave system. It riddled beneath the desert and was shady as hell. Locals called them catacombs because unless you had an Earth affinity, you were more than likely gonna end up dead if you went exploring.

Buoyed by that uplifting thought, I started across the room, and heard voices. Crap! I wedged myself behind a scale representation of the Lady, hoping I hadn't kicked up too much dust. The place was filthy. My mouth was dry with it, and my heart thudded—

My heart thudded.

I put a hand to my scar, not feeling its echo. What the hell…? Had Silas taken the ember? Somehow, I didn't think so, it was more like it'd sync'd up… Jesus Christ, like I didn't have enough on my plate, and the next serving was pushing through that fire door. I smooshed myself farther into the shadows.

I couldn't make out what was being said yet, but there was no doubt one of them was my mother. I'd know that smarmy, ingratiating tone anywhere. She had a tendency to use it when she was trying to convince someone that something was really their idea, and that they were brilliant for coming up with it.

She used it a lot with the Prioress.

"His necessity isn't up for debate," the flabby bag of gas wheezed. "What is, are the details of the ceremony itself. In particular, Envy's performance."

"I'm well aware, your Excellency. She'll do as she's told."

"So you've said before."

Hah. She had her there.

"If she wants her defiler to continue breathing, she'll cooperate."

My nails bit into my palms, wanting to wrap them around her smug neck and twist. I heard the door close, and the rasp of metal on metal as she slid the heavy bolts home.

The Prioress spat a great glob of something onto the floor. "Vile creature."

"As you say, she's a necessary evil, but not for much longer. Here, let me help you up the steps. They're steep."

My blood was boiling, and I had difficulty tamping down my temper as I crouched there, listening to them take their sweet-ass time locking the gate and shuffling up the steps. What the hell was going on? I tried to make sense of it as my mother hauled the decrepit old biddy up the narrow flight.

Why the hell was I sitting ass-deep in dust in the Priory's sub-basement when all Silas had to do was wait a few more days, and he'd get what he wanted? He'd screwed up his whole plan by delivering me to my mother, whose goal was the exact opposite of his...except they were somehow in cahoots, as evidenced by the track marks in my arm, and the whole banging thing at the beginning of this mess.

The lights clicked off, and there was the faint sound of the door closing above. My head pounded, the residual from the cocktail creeping back as my anger waned to anxiety. I crawled out from my hidey-hole and crossed to the door leading to the catacombs.

I'm not even gonna lie. At this point, I was freaked and just wanted it all to stop. With that door open, I could feel Brennan. Like really feel him. I knew he was close, and I knew they'd messed him up. Whatever my progenitors were up to scared the crap out of me. So did the single steady beat in my chest. It felt wrong without its chaser.

Hell, everything right about now felt wrong, including the tunnel I was in. I'm not claustrophobic or anything, but the sandstone around me just felt, I don't know, off. I called a small trickle of flame to weave through my fingers, more for the comfort of it than to light my way. Farther down, a glow flickered past where the tunnel jagged.

From that point, the walls were smoothed, like a planned thing, instead of a random passage. Deep crevices still intermittently branched off, but it was obvious what the main path was. I figured I must be somewhere under the Priory's quad, but who the hell knew. Ahead, an oil lamp had been bolted into the rock wall. More lined the way, with large patches of murky black between them.

The tunnel widened, and to one side it'd been tricked out as a sleeping area. A cot, trunk, pegs jammed into the stone…it was way too reminiscent of my prior accommodations. The glass of water at the bedside didn't bode well. Who else was down here?

I came to the first cell after that. It was empty. Just bars across a domed space so cramped Karen wouldn't have been able to stand up. A low shelf was cut into the back, and there was a bucket in the far corner. My stigmata flared as I went past, unable to tamp down my anger at the thought of Brennan crammed into one of those things, hurt.

He was, and I wasn't ready for how badly.

If I hadn't been able to feel him, I never would've picked him out from the shadows. He was in the corner of a pitch-black cell between lamps, in the fetal position. I sliced through the lock and crouched in to touch his shoulder. He flinched, crying out at the movement. What had they—

Oh, God. It was bad.

The light of my flame revealed horrific weeping wounds on his back. They'd tried to carve out his stigmata. I bit back a sob and pushed his hair from his eyes. His pupils were oblong and dilated into slits as he focused on me.

"Lovely…"

"Can you get up? Why aren't you healing?"

Brennan laughed, and it became a raw cough. "S'too much. Go while you can. He's coming back. They mean for me to—"

"Save it. Come on, let's get you up."

I was going to fucking kill Silas. How could he do this? Brennan struggled to uncurl himself, and I did what I could to help. It wasn't much. His face hadn't been touched but the rest of him…

His head hung down, and he panted from the effort to get upright. I didn't have a lot of faith he could walk. Neither did he. He looked up at me through messy strands of his sweat-soaked hair, and I didn't care. I wasn't leaving him there.

"Shut up and move."

He almost smiled.

It took forever, but I got him out of there and onto his feet. We lurched down the hall. He was a lot heavier than he looked and was super weak. It was slow going.

We'd come to an unspoken agreement and kept moving deeper into the tunnels. Trying to get him out through the Priory wasn't happening. Sometimes the catacombs opened out on a random hillside or basement… Maybe one of those offshoots would be big enough for us to get through and find a way out.

Yeah, I know, but I was desperate for a miracle, and Brennan was really freaking heavy.

"Any chance you can poof us out of here?"

"S'a good idea. Wonder why I didn't think of it."

I shot him a look, but it stood to reason that if he couldn't heal, he couldn't poof. We struggled along in silence for a time, his breathing becoming more labored. I stopped so he could rest for a bit.

"How do you do it? Poof, I mean."

"Ah, it's…willing yourself not to be, then imagining you're elsewhere."

I laughed. "If it was that easy, I'd have been on a beach somewhere years ago." That won me another almost smile.

"You've got to kind of throw your aura out, follow it, then suck it back in. No idea how you managed to dematerialize from the club. Takes ages to learn… Silas wasn't happy." He grimaced, glancing at my hair.

I jammed it behind my ears. "Is that why he brought us here?" I kind of had a history of sneaking off. Maybe he didn't want to take the chance I'd bail and find that beach.

"No, I—Lately we've been at odds over how much to disclose to you, among other things."

"He told me that was Amelda's influence."

Brennan gave a wry laugh. "Maybe, but not her doing."

God, I hated fae doublespeak. We started walking again, our pace slowing to a crawl. Brennan wasn't going to be able to go much farther, but there was an opening coming up on our right. I was praying the footsteps I heard in that direction meant it was a way out. I propped Brennan up against the wall and crept forward to investigate.

It was that fiery room of doom we'd been shanghaied in. Chastity, one of the girls I'd been in the dorm with was, I don't know, dusting, or some kind of bullshit house-wifery...tending the flames, I guess.

I snickered. Who knew that vestal virgin quip I'd made was spot on. I mean, I'd heard rumors, and the other girls were always smug as shit about something. They really did have a sacred flame. Guess I hadn't been vestal enough to be initiated into their little sorority. Though I knew for a fact Chastity was a huge whore. With a name like that, go figure. You're just begging for VD.

She turned at the sound and saw me. I didn't stop to think, I bum-rushed her. There wasn't any place to hide in that room, and no door but the one I'd come through. She made a kind of meeping noise and dropped to her knees, praying fervently right before I took a swing. My fist went through the air where she'd been standing, and I sprawled after it, my legs taking her down with me.

A sickening crack echoed through the room, and pain crazed up through my knee. I rolled onto my back groaning and clutching at it. She didn't move at all. I scrambled up, and if I'd had anything in my stomach, it would've been on the floor with her. I'd definitely dislocated her jaw, and she was out cold. I'm gonna say that was for the best.

I limped over to the prayer bench. The box Silas had put the anathema in was still on its little shelf, and as I got closer, I could hear the pulses, matching the beat of my heart.

It was freaking creepy, but I wasn't leaving them,

either. The box was heavy, like lined with lead heavy. I flipped open the lid, not even entertaining the idea of carrying it and Brennan. Inside were the three other anathema. I think I cursed my lack of pockets for maybe half a second.

Then I jammed them into my mouth and swallowed.

What? I already had one of the damn things in me. They'd be fine.

I probably should've been thinking a little more about how I was going to be.

The pebble sat in my stomach, well, like a rock. The feather stuck at the back of my throat, and I started coughing. I downed the droplet, hoping for the best—

It wasn't what I got.

It was like I'd dumped a bathtub of water into a forge.

I tore back out across the room and plowed into Brennan, exploding into a cloud of steam, and taking him with me as I poofed.

What? Yeah, fine, it was kind of cheating, but it's super easy to imagine yourself not being as you're blown apart from the inside. It's not like I planned it. Whatever works, right? Look, all that mattered was that I'd dematerialized. Sucking us back together was a lot easier. Kind of like all your pieces are magnetic and numbered.

So where did we go? The one place I was pretty sure Silas didn't know anything about, that shallow cave in the desert Kyle camped out in.

And we were there.

I was barfing my guts out, and Kyle was staring at me from a nest of sleeping bags with some sleek-looking chippy at his side. Brennan was curled up again, groaning.

The droplet shot out of my mouth, as eager to be out of me as I was to get rid of it. I glared at it, sparkling like a jewel on the ground and spat, wiping my mouth on those miserable robes I'd lifted.

"Snow?"

"You got anything to drink?" I coughed, pulling them off. Stupid feather.

One thing I'll say for sylphs, they're very good at taking things in stride. He rooted around behind him and tossed over a bottle of vodka. While I was shooting it back, he'd gotten up and was looking at Brennan.

"Yo, no shit, that's the dae that nabbed you. Damn, somebody fucked him up royal."

"Yeah." My eyes were on the girl, and hers on me. Remember when I told you I knew most of the halflings in Vel City by sight if not name? Morgana was half-undine. She was also one of the ones that didn't tolerate me. The feeling was mutual, but at the moment, she was exactly who I needed. Or rather, she was who Brennan needed.

"Can you heal him?"

She tossed her lank hair over her shoulder. "What's in it for me? I don't need any trouble. Helping you's aiding and abetting."

"What?"

Kyle scratched the back of his head. "Uh, yeah. It's all over how you torched the pub. Building above went up, most of the block, too. Cops are doing sweeps. Somebody got one hell of a shot with you and the dae." He grinned. "Don't worry. It was your good side."

"It was all her sides," Morgana grumbled.

136

"Yeah, and they all looked good."

Brennan growled at him, and Kyle took a step back.

"Psh. Only if you're into the Corpse Bride."

Bitch. I palmed the droplet. We didn't have time for this. "Help me, and you'll live through Midsummer."

All right, maybe I oversimplified it, but that got both their attentions.

Brennan went a long way toward convincing them I wasn't full of shit. Like I said, once a fae takes you, you're done. Not that he could explain it outright. Those stupid rules prevented him from spilling the story, but sitting there beat to shit looking guilty worked while I sketched it out.

Once I'd convinced them, Morgana became remarkably cooperative. I hacked up the feather for Kyle. He wanted in, too, obviously. Then I made him to go find Berk while Morgana did whatever it was undines do.

They're pretty much useless in my opinion. Well, except for the whole healing thing. Other elementals can do that to a degree, but undines' abilities fall into the miraculous category. I sat there watching Brennan's wounds slowly close beneath her fingers, trying not to lunge at her for touching him. Though in her defense, she looked like she'd rather be picking up dog shit bare-handed.

If you haven't figured it out by now, some elementals play nicer together than others. I've got no problem hanging with Earth or Air, but Fire and Water don't mix. Like, at all, and Morgana and I had a history. Specifically, Kyle.

She was pissy because he liked me better, but I mean, come on, who wouldn't?

He and Berk on the other hand, had their own issues. Not like that—Berk is way gay. Kyle and he just rubbed each other wrong. Ok, that sounds bad, but trust me, it was just an Earth/Air thing.

So, you might be thinking I was an idiot for handing out the anathema like candy, and you could be right. My judgment isn't always stellar. Shocking, I know. But I'd noticed two things while I was on my knees heaving.

One, there was no way I could keep those things inside me, and two, while they were, I couldn't hear the damned things pulse. That included my double thump. Through all of this, it hadn't come back. In fact, I couldn't remember hearing it since I'd kissed naked-snakey dream me. Why it'd chosen now to sync up I hadn't a clue, but there you had it. There was just a single staccato beat in my chest, and when Kyle and Morgana shot back theirs, same deal, which meant Silas couldn't find them by their pulses.

I wasn't delusional enough to think we were in the clear, but I hoped it made things a little less complicated—

Yeah, all right. What I really hoped was that it fucked with whatever he had planned. That whole vindictive thing I was telling you about. He was a full daemon and old, which meant powerful. I was under no illusions that I could actually kill him, as much as I wanted to. Messing up his plans on the other hand... I was kind of an expert at being a pain in the ass.

Anyways, I was pretty sure Morgana thought I was full of shit even as she swallowed the droplet, but that hadn't lasted. I have to tell you, it was weird when they ate the anathema. It, I don't know, changed them. They both went really still for a breath, then became more vivid, like a Technicolor moment. It gave the rest of what I had to tell them credibility, and I needed it. Dae aren't particularly known for being forthcoming, and honestly, it sounded batshit.

They were as pissed about the whole left to die unnecessarily thing as I was. For a solid five seconds, Morgana and I hated someone else more than each other. Don't get it twisted; there wasn't a chance she and I were going to be besties, but we could probably be in the same room.

Maybe.

Brennan was still really pale, like almost as pale as me. Morgana had healed all the superficial stuff, but she hadn't been able to fix what Silas had done to his stigmata. The wounds were raw and oozed molten. No way to sugar coat it, they were gross. I'd say Morgana thought the same from the expression on her face, but she always looked like she smelled a fart.

"That's as good as it's going to get. I've blocked his pain receptors, but it won't last long."

"It's more than I'd expected. Thank you," Brennan said briskly, edging away from her. He hadn't been real big on her pawing at him either. When he held his arms out to me, I went to him and buried my face in his neck. No way I'd let that bitch see me cry. Morgana sniffed and left, taking whatever she'd smelled with her. I pulled back and wiped my eyes.

"How do we fix you?"

He grimaced, fingering his watch. "We don't. Silas was rather thorough, and Amelda—I'm afraid I made things worse by provoking her at the club. No one else can undo the damage. My neutrality has been called into question, and rightly so. I don't know that she'd relent."

My stomach cramped around that freaking pebble. "But you haven't tried to get me to pick either of them... She would let you die?"

Brennan made a noncommittal noise, and the range of emotion playing across his face... I wanted to kill her just for that.

"I don't understand, how could she—"

"I broke my oath, and flaying's the traditional punishment. Depending on her mood, she may see it as apropos, or as a challenge to her position. Even odds there. Damn, I need a cigarette."

"What oath?"

Brennan wet his lips and looked away. "To remain celibate. I told you, that line was never crossed. It was part of the price for her to intervene with Serena. She thought it an appropriate punishment for 'thinking with my dick.' In the beginning of this, she was quite pleased to see you torment me so exquisitely."

My mind flashed back to the conversation I'd overheard. "But she said she'd allow—"

"No, Silas said that she would. I heard what I wanted to, not what he said."

It was my fault that this had happened.

I stared at him, horrified. He'd been mutilated because I couldn't take no for an answer. His face crumbled watching mine, and he kissed my brow. "Oh, no, no, Lovely. She would've forgiven me the deed. It's the emotion she won't excuse, and that's all on me."

He held me as I cried, neither of us mentioning the

140

elephant in the room. Regardless of Morgana healing the rest of him, if his stigmata weren't repaired, we were all in deep shit.

You gotta know normals had tried "curing" halflings by cutting out their stigmata. Surgery, lasers, cryo, you name it. It all ends the same. The patient dies, taking out a massive swath of whatever's around them via their element. Firestorms, geysers, tornados, earthquakes... I didn't even want to think about the devastation Brennan would cause. Maybe those bitches back at the Priory were on to something.

He was chewing on his lip, probably thinking the same thing.

Morgana came back with Kyle, and Berk lumbered in behind them. He looked exhausted. I jammed my finger down my throat and brought up the last anathema.

Kyle must've filled him in because his fingers shook when he took it from mine. He opened up his shirt and held it to his bare chest. The pebble just melted into him, and he bloomed a deep loam brown. He smiled, and his chest expanded like it was the first real breath he'd ever taken.

"Thank you."

I just gave a little nod. We still had to get into the Fae realms if we wanted to live, and they were all looking at me like I had a plan.

Spoiler, I didn't.

4 Days

Berk did.

I'm not saying it was a great plan, but it was more than anyone else had. He'd just gotten takeout and wanted to watch some game that was streaming. I'm not gonna lie. Pizza and wings sounded pretty good right about then. Anyways, he suggested we all go back to his place in the undercity.

I should probably explain that a little bit better, though it's pretty much exactly what it sounds like. Normals lived up above in Vel City itself. They got the apartments, the swanky shops, restaurants. A couple parks, and the zoo, public schools, oh, and a museum. You know, culture.

We got what basically equated to the sewers and the subway tunnels that'd been abandoned when they put in the new line. Oh, and the catacombs. I told you, they were all over the place.

Berk's digs were in an old cistern. It was pretty cozy, for a hole in the ground. Couch, chair. Running water. He even had electricity and a television. Big flat-screen number that must've cost a fortune. If it'd been any other halfling, I would've said it'd fallen off the back of a truck. Not that I was passing judgment, but knowing Berk, he'd probably paid full price for the damn thing. Gnomes are pedantic about things like that.

When we came in, the game was blaring into the

empty room, and a bunch of tailgate food was on the table. Kyle started helping himself.

Morgana started bitching, or rather, continued bitching, just did it more loudly so we could hear her over the TV.

"I'm just questioning the logic of carting a bomb around with us, and he's a daemon for Christ's sake!"

That was it. I opened my mouth to lay into her, but Brennan beat me to it. He spun around and got in her face.

"He's right here, and trust me, fish, if I go, there's no place far enough for you to run." He growled at her and lunged, holding himself back from throttling her at the last moment. I knew the feeling and couldn't help but smirk as she screamed, flinching back against Kyle.

We all stared at Brennan, even me. Well, they stared. I drooled. I'd never heard him sound…I don't know, like a daemon. Beat to shit or not, it was scary, and way hot. His eyes flicked from Morgana, and he flipped over a milk crate so he could sit. As soon as he looked away, she ran out of the room. Kyle chased after her. I went and kneeled in front of Brennan.

"Were you serious?"

He nodded, pulling me close. "Things are going to become problematic sooner than not, and we can't count on Amelda's help…even if she'd give it, the price would be too high. You need to get me to the Neither, or a great many people are going to be hurt." He glanced over at Berk, back in his chair chowing wings, and leaned in close. "As in balefire hurt."

Let me explain.

Think of a match. That's regular fire. It burns at roughly 800 degrees Centigrade, tops. An acetylene torch burns closer to 3,400 degrees Centigrade. That's a daemon's fire. Plasma's, well, plasma. 22,000 degrees Centigrade. Balefire…

Balefire's hotter than the center of the sun, 15,000,000 degrees Centigrade, in case you were wondering.

In layman's terms, he was telling me he was a nuclear bomb.

I met his eyes. "Silas meant for you to…"

Brennan gave an aggrieved nod.

I was having trouble breathing. Jesus Christ. Silas had offered him up for my mother to bring on her bullshit apocalypse.

"Fae's been planning something like this for some time. They need a tipping point, and waiting for another Cleansing is taking too long. I have no doubt my death will be attributed to those vile sisters of the Blessed Inferno, and Fae will have its reason to go to war."

What? This was Fae's doing? But I'd thought… Christ, I don't know what I'd thought, and didn't give a shit about any of it. I felt sick, then laughed. His brow furrowed at me.

"Sorry, just enjoying the irony of my boyfriend bringing on the end of days."

"Am I your boyfriend?"

My stomach flipped at what was in his eyes, and I kissed him. He was definitely my boyfriend.

He winced and pushed me back. "I'm sorry, Lovely, but whatever the fish did is fading, and I doubt she's going to be amenable to doing it again."

"Like hell she's not."

She wasn't.

"No. He can wait," she said, flipping her lank hair

over her shoulder. I think she was trying to pout, but her lips just pruned up like an asshole.

"Fine, so can you. I'm thinking sometime in July."

I don't think it was possible for her to roll her eyes any harder. It definitely wasn't possible for me to contain my temper. The next thing I knew, Berk was holding me back, and she was on the ground, looking like one of those scream queens when they trip in the woods, and the slasher's right there. Undines were such pussies.

"No! You don't understand. It only works for so long, and the more I push the pain out, the harder it's going to rebound on him. I've given him a window, but it's not going to last. He's already so far gone, he's got a handful of hours before he'll be catatonic. Every time I delay it, that window gets shorter."

I stopped trying to lunge at her, the blood draining from my face. Jesus. Why the hell couldn't she have just said that?

"Lovely, a word?" Berk let me go, and I went to Brennan. He looked awful, his face slick with sweat. "As much as I hate to agree with the fish, she's right about the price. What she's done has only delayed payment. We need to use this opportunity to work on dematerializing, when I say I need to go to the Neither, do you know what I mean?"

I kneeled in front of him with a kind of a shrugging nod. I did, but I didn't. The Neither was supposed to be the realm between us and Fae. Kind of like that gross onion skin that's not really a layer. It made up the veil between our two planes of existence but was more than that. I didn't even know how to dematerialize. How could I do it to some place I'd never even seen, never

145

mind understand? Brennan took my hand in his, his thumb skating over my fae-band.

"Envision the inside of a pearl. A misty gray iridescence…dank and forever twilight. No way to tell direction—" He grimaced, folding at the waist and panting.

"I'll get—"

"No…listen. Everything there's muted, just like the necropolis. If I go, it will be absorbed there, but I cannot stay here, or in the realms. Come sit against me and close your eyes."

I did, edging back against the milk crate between his legs. I swear, I tried for what seemed like forever. Halftime came and went, and Brennan's chest dipped closer and closer to his thighs. I had Berk help me lower him flat onto the ground. His back looked like that tartare Horatio had gobbled up, raw egg included.

Morgana chose that moment to walk back into the room. She made a face, putting my hackles up before she'd even opened her mouth. The entire way here, she'd been hanging all over Kyle, not that I cared, and looking at Brennan and me like we were something on the bottom of her shoe. "You got a problem?"

Morgana laughed. "Yeah. I got a problem."

I take back what I said about being in the same room with her. Kyle popped his head in and settled himself against the wall with a bag of chips to watch. He's such a dick sometimes.

Berk got between us. "Stop. Vy's offered us a second chance. If getting him square is what it's going to take, you need to suck it up. Can you do anything for him?"

"You should've waited until they got each other on

the ground. That would've been hot," Kyle said from the doorway. Berk glared at him, his knuckles cracking.

We were just one big, happy, halfling family.

Morgana's face pruned up, but she sank down and looked like she was concentrating. Or taking a dump. It resulted in the same thing. We got shit.

"He's too far gone. I blocked what I can, but pretty soon it won't matter. It's like his element is dammed up, and he's cracking under the pressure. You need to get him to the Neither, and you said we've got to be across the veil for Midsummer's Eve. How do you propose we do either if he can't use his powers to get us there?" She'd crossed her arms beneath her sad little boobs and thrust out a boney hip. I waited for her foot to start tapping. God, she was such a bitch.

I kneeled next to Brennan. He was breathing easier, but that wasn't saying much. I had a very bad feeling that problematic was setting in, and I had no idea how to get him anywhere. Blowing myself to shit had been a one-off. Although tempting, reaching down Morgana's throat to rip out the droplet to try again probably wasn't going to work.

But I hadn't needed it in the club. How the hell had I done it?

"Hellooo…"

I glowered up at her, and my stigmata flared. "Chill the fuck out. I'm thinking." She snorted and went to go watch TV with Kyle. He'd snagged Berk's chair and was surfing channels, chowing chips, and downing a beer. Damn, that looked good. Berk must've read my mind because he came over with one.

"You okay?"

I laughed. "No."

147

I told him about the club, ending up in the necropolis. Waking up in the Priory. Berk's a good listener. He's always grounded me. No pun intended.

"Sounds like you do it when you think you're about to die."

"Let me know if you need help with that," Morgana offered sweetly.

"How? You going to waft your twat at me?"

Kyle lost it laughing, and she lunged. Berk caught her around the waist and took her out of the room.

"You just need to relax. Have a couple more beers and chill out. I mean, you're wound pretty tight, Snow," Kyle said, crunching on his chips.

"What? I am not."

He laughed. "Psh, you're like, the most intense chick I know. Nice massage would help with that." He waggled his eyebrows at me, and I frowned when Brennan just lay there. Crap. That wasn't a good sign. I needed to think.

"Just give me a minute alone with him, will you?"

Kyle chugged the last of his beer and headed off toward wherever Berk had taken Morgana. I put my hand on Brennan's cheek. He was so cold.

The way I saw it, I actually had more than a few problems. How to dematerialize was a big one, but assuming I was able to do that, ending up in the Neither was another. The third was that I didn't want to take him to the Neither. I wanted Amelda to fix him.

I raked back my hair. Silas had said she was in a bad way. How bad was bad? I mean, she'd just lost her baby, and Brennan said his sister had died recently. Would she suffer to lose another kid? I was willing to gamble with my own life that the answer was no.

And I would be gambling with my own life—she hated my guts. Granted, he'd also said she needed the ember reconsecrated, but she didn't strike me as the most rational woman I'd ever met.

Then there was problem number four: Silas wasn't stupid. With both Brennan and me gone, he'd figure that was where we were headed, and would be waiting. I had no illusions about how pissed he'd be to discover us and the other anathema gone.

But it did bring a smile to my face. Suck on that, asshole.

My satisfaction was short lived. Brennan's eyes were open and pain-wracked as he looked up at me. I brushed back the hair from his brow.

"How am I going to do this?" I choked back a sob at his grimace.

"The ember…use it. Your aura, like when you pushed it out to me? That, but to the Neither. Please, Lovely, you need to hurry. God, it hurts…"

I closed my eyes, feeling sick and trying to envision a gray nothingness. Relax. Hah.

CliffsNotes, it took a long time for me to calm myself. Then Morgana came back into the room and shot that to shit. Kyle got his cat fight, and they dragged her out sobbing, her left eye swollen shut.

I paced the room with another one of Berk's beers muttering to myself, my adrenaline up and blood pressure through the roof. Relax. How was I supposed to relax? I hadn't been relaxed at the club. In fact, I'd been keyed up just as much, if not more than I was now.

I stopped pacing. Brennan had told me to use the ember, but it kind of felt like that one time it'd used me.

I sure as hell hadn't consciously done anything.

I didn't know what to do. Or rather, I didn't know how to do it.

I went back over and lay down beside him. He was muttering like he was delirious. Probably because he was. I wrapped my arms around his bicep, then did something I never do.

I prayed.

Like, full on "Please God, grant my selfish desires, and I promise to be a better person, stop swearing, and only drink on the weekends" kind of praying. He must not've bought it because we were still lying there.

At least, we were until the floor exploded upward, and there was a great hulking creature bearing down on me. I just about pissed myself, and then dematerializing was easy. Afterward, Berk apologized and likened it to scaring the hiccups out of someone. He really could be a shit, but I'll admit, it was kind of awesome.

Look, whatever. It worked. For Brennan and me at least. I'd suss out the mechanics later.

So, the worst part of having to figure out stuff on the fly is making stupid mistakes. The kind that those more knowledgeable on the subject look at you and say, "You did what?" then laugh at you for being an idiot and wonder why you're not dead. Brennan had told me to think of a gray nothing.

I thought of his mother, which was problematic in itself. Her wicked, smiling face leering down at me filled my mind, and I hoped to hell I was doing the right thing. It never occurred to me that there's a larger issue with using people as a focus, versus a place. You never can tell exactly what people are doing at any given moment. Eating dinner. Painting the living room.

Watching porn… And objects are worse. God forbid you're thinking of an earring that got flushed. It's much safer to focus on a neutral location, which is why Brennan had materialized in the dead gardens both times we'd visited the daemon realm.

For all these reasons and more, focusing on Amelda was not wise.

We materialized in a gouged-up field, in front of a charging line of cavalry. Amelda was at the apex of their formation, flaming sword in hand. She was close enough for me to see her eyes narrow at our appearance. I threw myself over Brennan and heard her scream something. Hooves thundered around and over us. Clods of turf peppered me like buckshot. Then they were past, and there was a mighty confluence of screaming horses, and the snicking clash of metal.

Velvet quested at my shoulder, and I raised my head at a whinny. Amelda glowered down at me over the horse's neck, tightening the reins. She was in full armor the color of old ivory, helmet tied to her pommel. Her hair had been dyed woad blue, and three lines of the same slashed vertically across her brow and bled down her right cheek.

"Who has done this to my child?"

Her expression was fucking scary, and I knew there was only one thing that would get her to save him.

"I would bargain."

Her face tightened, but she gave a curt nod. The horse danced beneath her. She bared her teeth, and it leapt forward, leaving us in the muck.

We didn't stay there long. A couple of imps brought out a stretcher and hauled Brennan back to the camp that'd been set up. Amelda had a pavilion that put most places I'd been with solid walls to shame.

The canopy bed Brennan ended up face down on was a massive four-poster deal, complete with curtains and its own raised dais. An English king had probably died in it. The imps yammered to themselves over him, looking grim. I mean, they always looked grim, but super so now.

One of them came in with a clear crystal and placed it at the base of Brennan's spine. He groaned when it touched his skin, but then seemed to rest easier. They stripped him down and bathed him as he lay there unconscious and shivering. I sat on the floor at the edge of the bed where his arm hung off, hugging it to me. None of them said anything, and they didn't seem to care I was dripping muck all over the carpets. I can't say I did either.

It sounds stupid, but as soon as they left, I just started talking to him. Telling him stuff… like you would a priest, or a coma patient, I guess. Saying goodbye. Even if Amelda didn't kill me, I had no illusions that I'd ever see Brennan again. I don't know. Maybe I just wanted someone to know who I was. No one else did, and this late in the game, no one else was going to.

After all this? In three-and-a-half days, I was fading.

What? You honestly think that after being slapped upside the head with what being a dae was really like, I'd sign on to that? I mean, it's not like the choice was so radical, I'd pretty much already made it before I'd gotten snagged from the pub. That, and I could give two shits about the anathema. I hope it went out when I did. That'd really fuck with them.

Anyways, that's how Amelda found us. She walked in, her ivory armor streaked and spattered red, a blackened gouge across her breastplate. She pulled off her gauntlets and handed them to an imp, along with her sheathed sword. I watched her warily as she approached, expecting something horrible. She took in Brennan's condition with a sweeping glance.

"Who?"

I think I had some vague intention of bartering that information. Her expression nipped it in the bud. "Silas."

Her lips tightened, and then she proceeded to divest herself of the rest of her armor. The clothes beneath followed, and she lowered herself into a copper tub the imps had filled. A trio of them came to bathe her.

I'll spare you all that. In the end, it reminded me of Venus emerging from the sea and being clothed by snaggle-toothed cherubs. When they were done, she lounged back in a plush chair with a glass of wine, watching me. She'd been silent for so long, I jumped when she spoke.

"Do you know what we reserve that punishment for, Pet?"

I turned, kneeling before her. "Yes, ma'am."

Shut up. You just had to be there. I didn't like it, but I knew how to be contrite. Hah. It seemed appropriate.

Anyways, Amelda pursed her lips, her eyes boring into mine. "I have to wonder what message my brother-in-law is sending me with this. I doubt it was done for my benefit, despite what you've stolen from me."

I lowered my gaze so she wouldn't see how much I hated her. I don't know why I bothered. The air between us crackled with it. For the life of me, I couldn't understand why she didn't just strike me down and rip the ember from my chest. I mean, not that I was complaining, but get on with it already.

She stood, and the abrupt motion made me flinch, gripping Brennan's arm.

"So dedicated to your master. He's done his job well."

I bit my tongue as she came over in her short satin robe to trail her fingers alongside the damage. Brennan whimpered. "But I've made him so easy to love...this is very bad. Silas must've been in a rage." Her lips tipped up into a soft smile. She reached out to stroke Brennan's hair back from his brow. "Such a beautiful boy on the outside. Shall I remove his constraints and leave you with him to see the rest?"

She laughed at the look on my face. What the hell was she talking about? I wasn't about to give her the satisfaction of asking.

"Tell me, Pet, what do you desire of me?"

"His stigmata repaired. His life. Save him, please." It came out a lot more plaintively than I'd meant it to.

She smirked, running her fingers down past Brennan's waist, to his hip and thigh where the last of his stigmata had curved. "I could. What would you offer in return?"

You had to expect that coming. She had me over a barrel and knew it. I sat back on my heels.

"What do you desire?"

"A great many things, but first and foremost, to be rid of you." Her vehemence made me cringe. She dipped her finger into one of the lines of weeping gore, slowly drawing it down, his stigmata reforming in its wake. As it did, color leached back into him.

"I find your existence tiresome. I would have you disappear until the ball, and then after, offer me up that long, white throat of yours to slit. Your life for his."

"You're more than welcome to take payment now."

She laughed. "Would that I could. No, it's better that you share in his anguish, and do penance. It's unfortunate for you that I don't trust you to be pious on your own." Something snicked tight around my neck. A wave of nausea followed, and I fell forward wanting to puke. Her eyes burned into mine. "Now, are you very clear on what you're agreeing to?"

Mica was behind me, the satisfaction on his face adding to my nausea. My hand raised up, knowing what I'd find. The asshole had collared me. It was gritty and sharp against my skin, rust flaking off the metal where it dug in to my throat and collar bones. A ring dangled from the front.

And it had totally cut off any sense I had of Brennan.

He moaned, and Amelda's face rippled, hinting at something terrifying beneath. My God, what had I done? Mica grabbed me roughly by the arm and hauled me to my feet. He leered down at me, and I just felt hollow.

"You'll obey Mica, or Brennan will suffer. Your life for his." She paused in her work to stare at me, waiting for my agreement to her terms. Mica's grip dug into my flesh, and he gave me a little shake.

Full disclosure: Yes, I was out of my mind. Yes, I already knew Amelda had rigged it for me to lose. Yes, I was about to have as many unspeakable things done to me as Mica could come up with. By his expression, he'd already been working on an extensive list.

I didn't care. I just didn't want Brennan to die.

Or that fiery maelstrom thing.

It was only three and a half days.

"Agreed."

A smile tipped up her lips. "Do not doubt that if you disobey, he will end up in the Neither."

As Mica dematerialized us from the room, I was positive that if she kept her word, Brennan was going to hate me. I was also positive that if it saved him, I'd do it again.

3 Days, 12 hours

I've read that a person's home says a lot about them.

Taking in all the taxidermy heads staring down at me from the walls of Mica's hunting lodge, I'd tend to agree with them. He jacked up my arm until I was nose to nose with him, and grinned, his sour breath washing over me.

"Attempt to call flame at any time, for any reason, and I'll remove your fingers, knuckle by knuckle." He released me, and I fell hard onto the flagstones. "Clean her up."

Two imps hurried forward and hauled me off between them. Their idea of cleaning me up was more like a delousing than a bath. The soap was totally lye. By the time they'd finished, my skin was red and burning. A simple linen shift was thrust at me, and I was left barefoot in a frigid little room, with a pallet on the floor.

There were no blankets. No windows. Light came from around the door they'd slammed shut and freezing air poured in through the gaps in the rough log walls. I huddled on the pallet, my back in the corner, lamenting my fate.

It was my go to.

In my defense, I had valid reasons. Not being able to unsee Brennan lying there in Amelda's bed was a big one. I wished it wasn't the last image I had of him. I twisted at my fae-band, feeling nothing. It still wouldn't come off, not that I tried very hard, but I figured that meant she was keeping her word and healing him. He'd be fine—well, he'd live.

Me on the other hand…

I didn't want to think about what was going to happen to me once that door opened. For all I knew, Mica would haul me to the ball pieced together in a suitcase after he had his fun, which was probably preferable to what was going to happen if Silas got his hands on me. Small bright spot: even if by some miracle I survived the two of them, I was going to fade before Amelda got to rip out my throat. Nuts to her.

I laughed. So much for all that time Brennan had spent trying to teach me how not to piss people off. None of the above scenarios ran a bell curve. They were one big sucking pit of I was fucked.

The slivers of light had faded when the door opened again. Mica stood in its maw, outlined by a fire beyond. My breath clouded up between us. He crouched down and my eyes followed him.

"There we are, Pet. I told you I'd have a bed for you. Now, you and I are going to play a little game." He held out his hand to me. I hesitated until the growl started in his chest. Smiling, he helped me to my feet and brought me into a bedroom.

It smelled liked dirty socks and beef jerky. A fire roared in the hearth at the foot of a rumpled bed stacked with furs. He held out a thick green robe. I let him help me into it. I didn't know what was going on, but I sure as hell appreciated the warmth after that awful little room. I closed my eyes, trying to soak in the thick fabric's heat. God, I was frozen. He rubbed his hands over my shoulders, fixing the robe so it was close around that goddamned collar. It was so cold against my skin it burnt.

"Better?" His fingers pushed the hair back from my face, and I flinched. He sidled closer, liking that. "I can be a kind master, Pet. It's a pity you've been shorn. Shall I have an imp fix it?"

Huh? His smile at my confusion wasn't feral like Horatio's and lacked the sardonic warmth of Brennan's. It put me in the mind of something a fox might flash at a chicken before going for its throat. Right on cue, he raised up my chin.

"Mmm. I think so. I want to wrap it around my fist and pull when I'm behind you."

Asshole. It took everything I had not to spit at him. He grinned, having way too much fun lording over me. God, I hated men who got off on that shit.

"Now for our game. You're going to dress up to dine with me. If you're very good and please me, I'll allow you to sleep before the fire. If you're naughty, you'll go back in the closet after I strip you bare and flog you. Understood?"

I glowered at him.

His hand tightened on my shoulder. "What was that?"

I gasped. He liked that, too. "Yes, sir."

"Ah, it can be taught. You have five minutes." He closed the door behind him.

What Mica had left was laid out on the bed. He'd been serious about playing dress-up. I stood there for a moment, my eyes swimming as I looked at the ceiling. I'd made a bargain, and they were only clothes. Corset, fishnets, and shorty shorts with a sad cotton tail. I gritted my teeth and put it on, gagging when I noticed a spot of blood on one of the detached wrist cuffs. God. He hadn't just dressed me up as a sleazy cocktail waitress, he'd done it in a filthy, blood-spattered hand-me-down.

I wondered if the head of the previous owner was mounted on a wall somewhere.

The door opened while I was contemplating that and the battered, rabbit-eared headband. Mica stood there, grinning. "Well now, that's better. Come." He snapped his fingers and pointed to a spot on the floor in front of him.

He had to be—no. He wasn't. I knew he wasn't. Choking down my anger, I walked to where he'd indicated. He took the ears from me and slid them onto my head. They pinched, and one of the stupid things flopped down over my eyebrow.

I glowered at him, trying not to cry. He lowered his face to mine.

Have you ever gotten the feeling that an animal was about to attack? The small hairs on your body raise, and the air changes? Like, gets thick, and it all plays out in your mind so clearly you feel teeth sinking into you? Those slitted pupils of his expanded until I could see myself in them, and I knew I wasn't the only one imagining it happen.

I closed my eyes. Brennan's life for mine. I ran the words through my head like a mantra, but I'll be honest, they were already feelin' pretty hollow. I was having serious doubts as to whether I was wired for self-sacrifice. Mica's smug chuckle as he clipped a leash to the ring hanging from my throat didn't help. I was jerked forward.

"Come, Pet, it's time to eat."

He led me stumbling down to the dining room, never quite giving me enough slack to catch my balance. I hated him before we'd gone two steps. Like a visceral, burning hate I'd never felt before. I imagined killing him a thousand ways before we got to the table.

Mica had me sit at his right hand. There was a special hook on the table's side for him to loop the leash's slack around. Guess he'd done this before. Christ, all of it felt scripted.

A couple imps brought in a suckling pig and began carving. The juices didn't quite run clear, and I felt my gorge rise. Mica ignored them, watching my breasts rise and fall as he drank his cocktail. The stupid corset was beyond uncomfortably tight, my breaths mincing. If they'd given me utensils, I wouldn't have been able to resist the temptation to stab him for making me wear it. I imagined doing it with a dull spoon.

Mica sat there smirking at me like he knew it.

Then Horatio walked in. He smiled broadly as he sat himself across from me. How nice that everyone was in such a jolly mood. I scowled at them both, my back ramrod-straight trying to alleviate the corset's boning from digging into me. It wasn't working, and that damn collar was heavy. Like solid iron heavy. No wonder I felt sick.

It's a fact that fae can't abide the touch of iron. It was more of an issue way back when than now. Big Pharma's made a fortune on a vaccine. It doesn't actually cure a fae's aversion to iron, but I've heard it lessens the effects. Instead of sloughing off their skin and making them shit out their insides, it gives them symptoms that equate to a bad case of poison ivy with the stomach flu. They still avoid it whenever possible.

Halflings are a little more tolerant, think hives and persistent nausea, but who wants that? As a rule we keep our distance, too.

You know about my stomach, and the thing was already making me itch.

The imps finished loading up a platter of pig. The slices had an iridescent sheen to them. I bit the inside of my cheek so hard it bled. Mica put the apple from its mouth on my plate.

I stared at it, wanting to cry, my stomach churning, listening to them fill their own plates with that poor, disgusting dead beast, and chatting about some stupid battle. After several mind-numbing minutes of troop placement and politics as they ate, Horatio turned to me.

"Where's the anathema?"

I kept my mouth shut.

"I say we just take off her hand at the wrist. One nice clean cut, no more fae-band."

Horatio's eyes slid from me to Mica. "Unfortunately, it doesn't work like that. Shame Amelda's taken pity upon him. His death would solve more than one problem."

"It's not too late."

"Mmm." Horatio looked like he was considering it as he chewed. "Perhaps if the other had lived, but now… No, Brennan's serving a purpose. Until he was dropped back into her lap, she'd refused to accept Earth's wergild for the child. The Dowager threatened to recall Silas. Playing with the bastard is a poor substitute for war, but we should have a proper one at any moment." His eyes flicked to me with a little smile I didn't like. "The fools are a hairsbreadth from declaring another Cleansing."

"Silas's fixed it then... Will the Dowager intercede?"

I'd been trying not to act too interested, though I was dying to know what the hell they were talking about. I couldn't hide the way my ears perked up at the hint of fear in Mica's voice. I'd known the Dowager was powerful, but Brennan hadn't given me the impression he was afraid of her. Horatio's eyes had moved back to me, and I dropped my own to stare at the withered apple on my plate, its skin sloughing from the fetid brown flesh inside.

"She hasn't thus far, but it doesn't bode well." He sliced into his meat. I hoped he got worms. "What's the matter, Envy? Your agreement with Amelda make you lose your appetite? Shame. Now, where's the ember?"

I tried to school my face. Without that double thump in my chest, he must've thought I'd figured out how to stash it somewhere. Was it better to keep him guessing, or to tell him? Mica reached over and pinched my cheeks together with his thick fingers, squeezing until I looked at him. He hadn't shaved for dinner, and my eyes got hot. What would Brennan do?

"Speak, Pet." He pushed me backward in my chair, and I had to open and close my jaw a few times to make sure it still worked.

"I would bargain."

They looked at each other and laughed like Pesci and Liotta in *Goodfellas*.

I probably should've said this before, but there are certain rules to bargaining with the fae. Biggest one is neither party can lie. Now, that's not to say you can't misdirect the shit out of them, but to quote a T-shirt I once saw, I'm only responsible for what I say, not for what you understand. You also can't indebt anyone else with your bargain. That whole firstborn child thing is bullshit. I mean, come on. Nobody likes other people's kids unless they're pervs or into fringe cuisine. I hear we taste like veal but aren't as tender. Not really worth the effort, unless you're going for the yuck factor. Horatio didn't seem the type. Mica did.

So what was I doing?

I was going for a Hail Mary.

Horatio looked eminently amused. "You're in no position to bargain."

"I'm in the perfect position. You've completely ruined what's left of my very short life and I've nothing to lose. You've everything to gain, or not."

His eyes hardened, his smirk dripping malicious. "Very well. What do you desire?"

"To spend my last few days at Brennan's flat. I'll answer two questions, then you'll take me there and leave me alone until the ball. All of you will leave me alone."

His lips tightened as Mica looked between us.

"You can't honestly be con—"

Horatio held up his hand, cutting him off. "Six questions."

"Three and I want an imp there that can cook."

"The collar remains, and should you attempt to call flame, or step one toe off that spit of rock, you'll belong to me." He raised his eyebrows at me over the rim of his cocktail as he sipped. Damn, that looked good. I didn't even have a glass of water.

164

"Should the contract be broken in any way, you'll let me carve out your stigmata with a rusty knife and leave you to die in the Neither."

Horatio smiled at me like I'd just said I wanted to blow him. My stomach rose up into my throat.

"You are an exceptional little nugget, aren't you. Agreed. Where are the other anathema?"

"I don't know."

What? I didn't. Technically, they could be anywhere.

Mica's face twisted. "I wonder if Brennan would."

I shrugged, pretty sure that if they asked him, he wouldn't give a straight answer either. Like ninety, ninety-five percent. Mica must've thought so, too, because he sat back looking pissed. Horatio wasn't concerned at all.

"I have a feeling he will when Amelda compels him."

Crap. I tasted bile. That collar was doing a number on my stomach, and this entire dining experience wasn't helping. Mica had sliced back into the pig and pulled out some kind of innard. The air was spiked with an awful mineral funk, and he chewed it with his mouth open.

"Have you bargained with me in bad faith, Pet?"

I shook my head, swallowing the saliva pooling in my mouth. That only made it worse.

"No."

Horatio's expression became cagey, and he smacked his lips. "Very well then, I'll leave Mica to it." He pushed back his chair and got up to leave. He laughed at my expression. "You didn't really expect me to ask them all now, did you? You'll be much more forthcoming after a day or two of hunting."

Poof.

I stared at the space he'd occupied and fought not to hang my head. My fingernails gouged into my palms. Fucking fae. I'd damned both Brennan and me, Berk, and Kyle to boot. Amelda could compel him to spill all of it, and I didn't even wish the fallout from that on Morgana. I mean, maybe for an hour or two, but—God, I was so stupid!

My head did hang then. Midsummer's couldn't come fast enough.

"Eat, Pet. You'll need your strength for the hunt tomorrow."

My eyes flicked to Mica's, and he grinned. Hunt?

I didn't eat the apple, and I didn't get a blanket.

I did get flogged. Which sounds a lot more fun than it actually is. I cried. He laughed. I must've passed out, because the next thing I knew, I was in that freezing room, naked, face down on the pallet. My throat burned, and I felt like shit. The sound of someone snoring at a decibel range I'm pretty sure OSHA would flag sawed through the walls and into my pounding head.

Sure fingers were on my back, spreading something slimy over my wounds. A pleasant heat radiated from it down into my core. God, I was so cold… My eyes fluttered open to stare at the wall. It was lit by a dim flicker of light to the other side of me. Who was touching me? I tried to turn my head, and a sob escaped.

"Shh. You lie still."

Karen.

Tears pricked at my eyes, and I bit my lip to keep

from bawling. A soft blanket was laid over me, and her hands were in my hair, brushing it back between her fingers.

"This no good." She tapped my collar with a talon, and I heard her spit. "Tomorrow, do what he say. In woods, we find you."

My lemming heart leapt and promptly fell into the abyss. As much as I wanted to, I couldn't bail. It burnt my ass, but I'd made a bargain. It was a shit one, but I could suck it up for three more days.

I told Karen I had to stay, and then about Berk, Kyle, and even Morgana. None of them deserved to die just because of me and my bright ideas. If she was going to help anyone, I wanted it to be them. They deserved to become.

She listened, her clever fingers twisting out farther and farther from my head, the rhythmic motion lulling me. My eyes closed, and I drifted, her words following me up and out into sleep. Find me... How could anyone possibly find me when I was so very lost...

In my dreams, I roamed through a strange wilderness of howling beasts, everything I saw blighted by sorrow. It felt right. It matched my heart...but there was something else there, too. A quiet fury had begun to burn, and when I raised up my hand, a thread of fire wove itself between my fingers, like a serpent.

The next morning, whatever Karen had put on my back had sped my healing, and I could move without passing out. My throat was another story. It hurt to swallow and felt raw beneath the metal. Around the edges, the skin had blistered, and it was oozy. Between that and my stomach, I was a mess.

And yes, somehow Karen had grown my hair out. I

twisted it into a thick rope between my hands and wondered if I could hang myself with it.

Mica was in my room before the sun was up, dressed in head-to-toe camouflage. Like, serious hardcore stuff. He had stripes of it across his face and smelled like pee. I wasn't one hundred percent convinced that was hunting related. He came over to the pallet and ran his rough hand across what he'd done to me, then wrapped a hank of my hair around his fist and pulled. I couldn't help whimpering.

"Much better. Something to look forward to after the hunt."

Behind him, an imp shook out the bundle it was holding so I could see.

I laughed and not in a funny ha-ha way. Like in a despondent, my soul is being crushed and eaten by jackals kind of way. More dress-up. "You gotta be kidding me."

Mica grinned, and this time it was feral. He slapped my rear, and I screamed.

"Not at all, Pet. What did you expect, me to lock you in a room and have my way with you?"

I glared at him. That was exactly what I'd expected. Mica moued at me like he was disappointed. God, I hated him.

"Where's the fun in that?"

"You're right, what would we do after the first three minutes? You don't look like the canasta-playing type." Yeah, yeah, I know it was stupid to antagonize him, but I was really pissed, and he just made it so damn easy. That, and a part of me kind of hoped he'd kill me and get it over with.

No dice. He snatched the outfit from the imp and

threw it at me.

"Put it on."

I dashed a hand across my eyes. He left, and the imp followed, leaving the door open with the light streaming in. I was glad for the heat, but that also meant I could see the bright red and purple welts snaking over the tops of my shoulders and around my thighs. No wonder I was having trouble sitting. Whatever was oozing from my neck was a disgusting pink-tinged slime. I retched a bunch, but there wasn't anything in my stomach to come up.

What he wanted me to put on was one of those fuzzy sleepsuits that zipped up the front and had a hood. It was chocolate brown with a large white oval on the midsection. There were dopey ears, and little stuffed antlers on its hood. The back had a flap like long-johns and a fabric tail. It burnt my ass, but I stepped into the stupid thing and zipped it up.

Fuck my life. A daemon was going to hunt me while I was dressed in a Bambi onesie.

At least it was warm.

The imp came back and led me through the bedroom, downstairs. I had trouble navigating the steps. What Karen had put on me worked wonders, but I was far from healed. Mica watched me limp into the foyer, his lips twisting with cruel satisfaction as I jammed my feet into a pair of rubber boots. He came over and raised up the hood, then my chin.

"Does it hurt, Pet?" I didn't answer, and he smiled. "You know I watched. Every time you were with him. We all did. He's not what you think. Everything he told you was a lie. Sweet words to make you do what he wanted. If I cosset and flatter you, will you do the same for me?"

Part of me knew he was full of shit, but there was another part of me that was afraid he was right. That kicked dog part that gnawed on all my underpinnings. As miserable as I was right then, I couldn't tell which was bigger. Mica bit at his bottom lip and brushed away the track of tears on my cheek. I could see the resemblance between him and Brennan, and I choked back a sob.

"I can be kind. Kiss me like you kissed him, and it all goes away. I'll take off the collar, heal your back…" Mica's nose brushed against mine, and his lips lowered.

My knee raised. Right into his groin.

What the—

He jammed his tongue down my throat, then pushed me away, laughing in my face. I spat, trying to get the taste of him out of my mouth. The sack of shit was wearing a cup. He grabbed up the rifle an imp was holding ready. Racking it one-handed, he grinned, licking across his teeth.

"Run."

I ran.

Another imp had opened the front door, and I took off through it, into the woods.

It's worth mentioning that prior to this, I'd never actually been in a forest. I mean, I'd seen them on TV, but I was a desert gal, and between Vel City and the Priory, it wasn't like I'd had the opportunity or inclination to camp out under the saguaros.

In the event you're as naïve as I was, let me give you the skinny. First and foremost, forests are messy. Branches and sticks are all over the place, and leaves are a problem. What I wasn't snapping and crashing through looking like one of those floppy air people things at a used car dealership, I was skidding over, or plummeting through, into holes hidden beneath all of it.

Rocks and roots hidden by the aforementioned leaves didn't help. I swear to God, I was on my knees more than my feet, and by the time I put my back to a massive bole trying to catch my breath, the palms of my hands were raw and stinging, and I was filthy.

Fil-thy. There were bugs with too many legs in my hair. Bugs! I swear I could feel them going down the back of the onesie—ugh! God, it was gross. I brushed at them and swore, my eyes darting to the shadows.

Forests are also creepy as hell. You get in deep enough, and they're dark and still. Like, everything's muffled. The air doesn't move, and it feels all thick.

Sitting there, trying to shut up the sound of my own breathing so I could listen, I'll admit, I was freaking out. It didn't help that my breath was billowing up into one hell of a cloud. I needed to calm down. I called a trickle of flame to thread through my fingers.

And it wouldn't come.

The collar abruptly felt like it'd doubled in weight.

Mica's laugh sounded in the distance. It boomed off the landscape, and I couldn't tell what direction he was in. "That's a knuckle, Pet!"

I scrabbled at the pitted metal. How was it even possible? It had no keyhole, just two thin lines like the halves had been snapped together, and the ring for his leash.

I started hyperventilating.

"Pet…" The sing-song whisper almost made me piss myself it was so close. I jammed my fist in my mouth, keeping still. A twig snapped to my right, and I screwed my eyes shut.

A massive crash followed it, and I took off. In retrospect, that was my first mistake. I mean, my first mistake since I'd tried to knee him in the nuts. I was racking them up like student loans otherwise.

The forest floor quickly smoothed out and become easier to navigate, but the trees here were spiky, twisty things crowded close together. They didn't look, I don't know, earthly. I had a bad feeling that I'd somehow wandered into Fae.

It doesn't happen often, but there are some places where the veil is thin enough to walk right across. Usually it corrects itself, but I'd told you this whole thing with Mica felt scripted. It wouldn't surprise me if he was holding a way open, funneling me exactly where he wanted me to go. I thought about it, but stopping and waiting for him to show up with his rifle seemed worse.

I stayed on the stupid path. Through narrow gaps in the trees I could see patches of mire and bracken, some clusters of stone, but getting to them would be a bitch. Mica's howl in the not-so-distant distance took that off the table.

I kept running.

The path curved around, and my heart started going double-time. Cue second mistake. I took the first offshoot, and it dumped me out in a gully of thorns that immediately burst into freaking fire roses. Come on! There wasn't any place to hide. I couldn't go back. I scrambled across the scree. Maybe I'd get lucky and find a hole to die in.

"I smell your fear, Pet…"

How the hell had he gotten here so fast? Duh. He'd seen the freaking conflagration and materialized. He probably knew this place like the back of his hand. There was a sharp crack, and I cried out as something struck my thigh. I collapsed to the ground, agony stealing my breath. I pressed over the spot, expecting it to erupt red at any moment. The asshole had actually shot me! I scrunched up my eyes, jaw clenched. Christ, it fucking hurt!

I heard loose stones kick away from his boots as he approached, and something long and hard pressed into the base of my skull.

"Bam." Mica squatted down next to me with a shit-eating grin on his face. He flicked my hand away from my thigh. There was nothing there but horrible, lingering pain. "Rubber bullets, Pet. They hurt like hell but won't kill you. Now what shall we do for the rest of our time together?" He brought his lips close to my ear. "Maybe you can teach me how to play canasta."

I spat at him, and he smiled, wiping it off, and licking it from his fingers. I wanted to barf. Then I was on my back in the dirt with a knife up under my chin. I hadn't even seen him move. Blood dripped down my throat, the knife so sharp its bite had been painless. I swallowed, very sure that what was coming next wouldn't be.

His eyes flicked from me to the roses and back again. He laughed.

"No wonder she wants you dead. You owe me a knuckle first. Right hand or left?"

Why she—I met those snake eyes of his and was hit with the realization that I was playing a losing hand. He got off on this shit, and me fighting him just kept upping the ante. It was time to fold.

I started bawling.

Big, sloppy, wet sobs. I mean, let's be honest, I had a lot of angst and unresolved issues to pull from. His eyes narrowed for all of three seconds, and then he pushed off me in disgust. I curled into a ball, not having to try very hard to look pathetic. He kicked a rock across the gulley, muttering to himself. What is it with guys and tears? Not that I was complaining.

Swearing, Mica racked his rifle again. I let the snot drip down my lip and kept blubbering. He put the barrel to my temple.

"Get up and run."

Despite his assertion that rubber bullets wouldn't kill me, I had a feeling if he shot me point blank in the face, I wasn't just walking away. Sniffling, I got to my feet and staggered out of the gulley. I wasn't playing up my injury either. Where that thing had hit me it'd done some damage, and I was having trouble putting my full weight on it.

Once on the path, I turned back the way I'd come. That whole devil you know thing. Specifically, I was thinking about the cup-like outcropping of stone I'd seen in the mire at the beginning of the wood.

If I could pull it off, he'd have one hell of a time following me through those trees. Prying me out would be a whole 'nother issue, and he'd have to wade through some seriously questionable swampage to do it.

Hey, I wasn't going to kid myself that I could win at this. That being the case, I was going to do my damnedest to suck the joy out of his victory.

It was a tight squeeze between the trees, even for me, and I didn't realize until halfway across the rocks that my stupid tail had gotten caught on a branch and was waving like a flag. It was too late to do anything about it. I could hear Mica whistling as he came down the path. Asshole.

The rocks were slick, and I almost went ass over teakettle into the drink. My balance was way off between the collar and that stupid rubber bullet. Something burbled in the far corner of the pool as my foot disturbed the slime-covered water. Hello, mistake number three. A V began cutting through its surface toward me. Never a good sign.

I scrambled the rest of the way to the rocks and wedged myself into the gap just as a tentacle slapped upside the formation. It was close enough I could see the suckers blindly questing for purchase. I flinched away, something crunching beneath my feet. A horrific smell assailed my nostrils. My back hit the rocks behind me as I dry heaved, tasting its foulness. What the—

Eggs. I'd stepped on at least a dozen of the disgusting things, and was ankle deep in gelatinous, semi-formed squid things. I retched again, my eyes watering. The stones shifted around me, and I laughed. Jesus, when I stepped in shit—

Blinding agony.

A scream tore from my throat. Something had struck the back of my arm. My whole body spasmed from the burning pain. A line of round holes had melted through the cheap material, and beneath them, welts tracked across my triceps. A wave of dizziness crashed over me. I put out a hand to steady myself, falling to my knees and squelching down into the soupy mess.

I gagged again, and a tentacle whipped out, wrapping around my outstretched arm, pulsing itself up my wrist, and beneath my sleeve. The burn that accompanied it began to feel good.

The abrupt jerking motion that smashed my face into the stones around the gap didn't. From across the pool, Mica bellowed, and there were several rapid cracks from his rifle.

If he'd been hoping to distract it, that wasn't happening. The thing bludgeoned me against the rocks again, and I laughed, seeing stars. Of all the situations on my bell curve, being a swamp squid's dinner wasn't one of them. Way more dramatic than that hole I'd been looking for.

There was a whomp of flame, and the creature squealed. Its cries became a high-pitched shriek, and the air filled with scalding gouts of steam as it flailed, flinging me back. It hit the stones hard, and they shifted again, one of the larger ones falling over and to the side. I kind of rolled after it and came to a stop looking up into a churning cloud of whipping tentacles, vapor, and flame.

Smashed eggs trickled down the neck of my onesie. Not that I could do anything about it. I couldn't move at all. This was problematic. I was gathering that the squid wasn't doing so well, and its thrashing was kicking up all kinds of nastiness from the deep. Heavy slicks of mud and algae splattered over me, along with a peppering of surprisingly white bones.

Gradually, the kerfuffle subsided, and Mica splashed to me, tentacle over his shoulder, and a knife in his hand. He was absolutely covered in swamp and gore.

And really fucking pissed.

I wanted to laugh, but I just stared up at him, not able to blink, or breathe very well, come to think of it.

He swore, and we poofed.

3 Days

I hurt.

Like, there had to come a point when it all just stopped. I mean, other than stopped, stopped. Got easier before that, I guess. They say God only gives you as much as you can handle, but man, I must've pissed him off royal somewhere along the line. Maybe it was that only drinking on the weekends thing. Sunday is kind of his day, which I'm totally cool with, but, come on, if it was your day of rest, wouldn't you want a beer?

Sorry, I was rambling again, but when you wake up feeling like shit in a bed that smells like stale sweat and cured meat, these are the things that go through your mind. Talk about questioning my life choices. Somewhere along the line, I'd lost the deer onesie, and it felt like I was in gym shorts and a tank. I would've preferred another Bambi suit. I was freezing. It didn't make a lot of sense, considering the furs heaped on top of me, and the roaring fire. Whatever, I was too tired to expend much effort thinking about it.

I tried to curl up on my side, but everything was leaden. I managed to drag up a hand and flinched as it hit the marks from that thing on my arm. They'd gotten all puffy and oozed something that smelled horrible. They were also weirdly numb. That I wasn't going to complain about.

I was lying there against the yeasty pillows, feeling

like my stomach was digesting itself, when the door opened. I cracked an eye. Morgana came in carrying a tray. I must've made a noise, because the look she shot me was a big eye-slap of shut the hell up. Mica followed right behind her.

She set the tray by the bed, acting like she didn't hate me.

Mica's meaty hand swept across my forehead, and he frowned. "The imps said you could clear the poison."

"I can." Morgana bristled. "But if I did it all at once, she'd go into shock and die, and that, that thing around her neck—"

"Is not your concern. She dies, you die, fish." His lip curled up over a long canine. Morgana cowered back with a little cry, and he pushed past her, out of the room. Once she didn't look like she was about to piss herself, she closed the door. Returning to the bedside, she glared at me.

"You don't know me."

"Thank God."

I swear, she almost smiled. "You just go from zero to bitch, don't you." Her hands were on me, and that awful chill started to recede. "Karen brought us over and got me in here. It's a good thing you sent her when you did. After the Priory burned to the ground, the Feds started raids again, rounding us up… They're doing it everywhere, not just in Vel."

It took me a minute to wrap my head around what she was saying. The Priory was gone? "My mother?"

"All over the news, calling for our extermination. Cleansings have started, and everyone's blaming you. They say you murdered the Prioress. That the

Redemption was a mistake, and this proves out our evil nature. They're rioting in freaking Budapest over it."

I laughed. That was the grift my parents were pulling. Fae had gotten its war, and my mother had reinvented her celebrity in a single stroke. No wonder I felt like shit. That was one hell of a bus to be thrown under.

"Did you?"

"What? No, but I wish I had."

She made a face and kept doing whatever it was undines did. My arm started to itch, and I dragged a hand up to scratch.

"Stop. It's healing. Well, not that." Her eyes flicked to the collar. "I can't do anything about it unless he takes it off... I think... I think it's doing something to you. Like, maybe it's a collar, collar."

I just closed my eyes, having already figured that out. God, undines were stupid.

Oh, sorry. A collar is something normals came up with when fae first started making themselves known. They're super bad juju and feed off an elemental's power, which I think I mentioned is basically our soul. They were banned by the fifth Geneva Convention and were supposedly all destroyed. Kind of like all the Nazis were killed.

"Envy, I heard them downstairs, arguing. Who's Silas?"

"My father."

The look on her face was priceless. Stood to reason. I didn't know another halfling that could pick theirs out of a lineup. Morgana recovered quickly, her mouth pruning up as she flicked her hair over her shoulder. "Well, they seem pretty worried about him finding you."

I snorted. Yeah. Me too. I couldn't decide which would be worse, him or another couple days with Mica. My stomach flipped, and I dry heaved.

"God, you're a mess." She did something, and a wave of fatigue washed over me. "There, you're going to get really sleepy...like coma sleepy. Don't fight it." Morgana stood. Whatever she'd done had tamped down the nausea, but I could feel it lingering, just waiting for a reason—

The door flew open, and Mica stalked in like he expected to catch me halfway out the window. In fairness, if I hadn't been so beat to shit, it wasn't outside the realm of possibilities. He gave a satisfied grunt seeing me still in bed.

Morgana had picked up a bowl of something from the tray like she was about to feed me. He held out a hand for it, and she gave to him, then slipped into the hallway.

The mattress sagged beneath his weight, and I rolled. He settled me against him, then scraped up a spoonful of goop. I wanted to refuse it on principle, but I hadn't eaten since Brennan's peanut butter and jelly.

I didn't want to think about him. I opened my mouth, praying whatever it was wasn't meat-based. It was oatmeal, and I can't even tell you how good it tasted. My stomach wasn't as enthusiastic.

"We're going to have to find other ways to spend our time, Pet. Until you, I'd never heard of an animal stupid enough to crawl into a nadra's birthing creche. Were you trying to cheat our bargain?"

Was that what that thing was? I didn't respond, too tired to banter. He didn't appreciate it anyways. I mean, that was half the fun, but—look. I felt like shit, and it'd been hard enough keeping a front up with Morgana. I really wished I'd found that hole to die in. Short of that, I opened my mouth for another spoonful.

Mica grunted at my silence, scraping an errant oat from my lip with the spoon. He fed me another bite. Before I knew it, the bowl was empty, and my eyelids dragged.

"What else shall we do, Pet?" His fingers ran down my sternum, then over the rest of me. I steeled myself for the inevitable. At least I'd be asleep for most of it.

I know what you're thinking happened next, and you'd be wrong.

Yes, seriously.

That son of a bitch felt me up, got bored, and left.

Now hold on. Don't look at me like that. That's not where I'm going with this, I mean, Mica? Really? Ew. Give me some credit. I have standards, and they're a hell of a lot higher than his Neanderthal ass. Besides, I... Look, after Brennan...

I told you I didn't want to think about him.

I wasn't mad because Mica didn't press his advantage. I was mad because it suddenly dawned on me that I had it all wrong. Like, I thought we were playing Texas Hold'em, and he was betting on Razz. It's all poker, but trying to get the high score in his version was a losing hand.

Look, fae on the whole are stronger and faster than any human, or halfling for that matter. Mica had straight-up said it: "Where's the fun in that?" Their bread and butter was manipulation, and they'd come damn close to perfecting the art of the mind-fuck. Could he have raped me while I was lying there half dead? Well, duh. Then or any other time. Was it a hell of a lot more amusing to just make me think he was gonna do it, and turn me into a paranoid mess? You better believe it. It was part and parcel of that feeding-off-emotions thing, and he was milking me.

Whatever, you know what I mean.

Now, there wasn't a chance I was gonna be stupid enough to let him figure out I'd caught on to his game. I had zero doubts if I did, things would go bad, quick. But weirdly, the realization made me feel better. I drifted off feeling like I had more control over my life.

Sorry, I don't mean to laugh.

Waking up in one of those stupid catacomb cells cured me of that impression.

I mean, I didn't know that's where I was at first. It was dark. But between the rock slab beneath me, and the dank whisper of charred wood in the air, I had my suspicions. I lay there, under a threadbare blanket, listening to a rhythmic clicking, feeling a manic kind of laughter burbling up in my throat.

See, I'd had this bizarre dream that I'd been in the middle of a football game. Like, literally. I was the ball. The teams were made up of imps, and Silas and Mica were screaming out plays from the sidelines. Guess my father had won.

What can I say? I have a very active subconscious, and yeah, I wished it would pipe down, too.

I sat up and whacked my head against the low ceiling. Yup. I was definitely in the catacombs. Whatever Morgana had done made me feel a whole lot better, but there was still a leaden-ness to my limbs, and I was muzzy. I was sure it was that damn collar eating in around my neck, and it itched like hell on top of it.

I dropped to the floor, scooching over to the bars. This time my jailor wasn't at matins. That miserable bitch, Sister Reticence, sat in a straight-backed chair beneath one of the lamps, knitting one and purling two for the needy. Why the hell anyone needed a beanie or a scarf in the middle of the desert had always been a mystery to me, but she kept churning them out.

"Mother's blessings on you, Sister."

Her lips screwed up, and I couldn't help but smile as she grabbed her chalk. She'd taken a vow of silence early on. I'm positive she regretted that decision. In her defense, it was before my mother had decided to stick her with babysitting duties. She couldn't scrawl fast or small enough on that stupid paddle around her neck to say half the things she wanted to.

It was a fact I took advantage of, and I was eager to see which psalm she'd reprimand me with. I was on a standard rotation of damnation and censure. She finished her scritching and punctuated it with a sharp crack before holding it up.

Fuck you, whore!

I laughed. Like, a lot. She got all pissy and packed away her knitting, then shuffled down the hall. My stomach hurt by the time I'd sobered up. I rubbed at it, leaning my head back against the wall, closing my eyes, trying to pinpoint the exact moment that everything had gone to shit in my life.

I kept coming up with conception.

I'd read somewhere that we all choose which parents/life we're born to. It was some messed-up karma thing. Like, I was here in this moment because there was something that I needed to learn so I could move on. You know, to grow spiritually.

I won't lie. I did some serious soul searching in that cell, and the only thing I determined I really needed to learn was how to pick a lock. Screw the rest of it.

It was pointless, but I couldn't help myself. I tried to call flame.

Yeah, really bad idea.

The collar felt like it'd doubled in weight again.

My eyes burnt. Despite my unconventional, and at times penal upbringing, I'd never felt like a trapped rat before. There'd always been a way out. If this helpless feeling was what it meant to be human, it was no wonder everyone who sputtered offed themselves after.

I guess I should explain that whole choosing thing a little bit more. I can't tell you about fading. How it feels, I mean. Remember I said when the guys ate the anathema it was like a Technicolor moment? Fading's like that. It's this intenseness that comes over the person. Their eyes widen like they're seeing the best thing ever, and they kind of dissipate, going to it. Like, their skin can't hold them together anymore, and they become misty, and, well, fade. Sayonara. It's really creepy but doesn't look like it hurts. Watching someone do it is kind of a rite of passage, but trust me, once is enough.

Sputtering is just the opposite. When you give up the elemental half of your soul, you go all gray, and they say it's like being ripped in two. Barely anyone does it. I knew of a guy who did because he was stupid enough to have a kid, and the mom faded the year prior. He made it a couple months before he couldn't stand it. The murder-suicide was national news. Normals were horrified, but we all understood.

Anyways, for both, they say it's like a door in you

opens. You decide what comes in or out. That jived with what Brennan had said about being filled with flame, so I guessed it had to be true.

Crap. I was back to him.

I spun the fae-band on my finger. It just felt like a normal ring now, if a little tight. I hoped he was okay. It still wouldn't come off, and I still wasn't trying very hard. I'd decided that meant he wasn't dead. I mean, other than to me.

I wiped my face with that lousy blanket. Footsteps were coming down the tunnel, and they weren't the Sister Reticence shuffle.

Hello, shoe number two.

It was my mother with a brown paper bag. She stuffed it through the gap between the bars and it let it drop when I didn't take it. A squished sandwich and a carton of milk fell out. My traitorous stomach rumbled, and I glared at her, snatching it up from the floor.

Calista looked good. I mean, like the best she had since the casino good. Her cheeks were pink, and there was a brightness to her eyes again. She sure as hell didn't seem particularly contrite, despite her robes. I couldn't help but notice they were a great deal more tailored than the ones issued under the Prioress's stern eye, and a rich mauve. So much for bullshit brown.

I picked up the sandwich, peeking between the slices of bread for razor blades or mayonnaise. Either one would've improved it. Just a single slab of sad bologna, and that cheese that comes in the individual plastic wrappers. I knew because she'd forgotten to take it off. I started peeling.

"Last supper before you burn me at the stake?"

Her lips smiled, but the rest of her face was marble.

Had she gotten more of those stupid injections again? She pulled over the chair Sister Reticence had been in. Lovely. She wanted to chat.

"No, burning's all done. Just holding you for a friend."

I laughed. God, my father was a lazy son of a bitch. "How is Silas?"

"Quite well." Her smug smile made me want to vomit.

I flicked the staticky cheese-plastic off my hand. "Bummer about that whole Redemption thing."

She looked at me like I was an idiot. "Oh, please, Envy. Do you really think I believed for one moment you were going to go along with that? It's beyond tiresome how you always think you're just so much smarter than everyone else…"

And with that preamble, I tuned out. Not for nothing, but I usually was. I slapped the stupid sandwich back together and took a bite. It was disgusting, and I ate it anyways while she cataloged my extensive list of personal failings.

"…being saddled with you after just once—"

"Bullshit."

"Truth." She smirked, reaching through the bars to open my milk carton for me. "Silas and I spent one night together after *Rosina* opened. I didn't see him again until after you were born, to bargain. You really should've come with me to more Fae-A meetings. I'm afraid that's how it goes. One moment of weakness…" Her eyes slid down to my midsection.

I rolled mine at the insinuation.

"Yeah? What'd he want?" I took the carton back from her. The fact that I didn't have to slurp it from the hairy frayed mess I always made out of it didn't win her any points. I hated skim. It was freaking nasty.

Her lips pursed, not getting the reaction she'd been gunning for. The lines around them were notably missing. Yep. She'd definitely been hooking up with Dr. Freeze again. Bet his wife was thrilled.

What, you, too? Look, even if I was pregnant, which I'll admit was possible, why the hell should I care? I was dead in a couple days. If a soul had picked me, it'd bet on the wrong horse.

She rolled her tongue around in her mouth like she tasted, well, skim. "Silas wanted you."

That got a reaction.

She laughed. "Well, I suppose not you, but a daughter. If I'd known how desperately, I would've bargained for more than a retirement plan. Still, I'd say I got the better deal." She laughed again at my expression and stood. "Drink your milk, Envy. It helps build strong bones."

I glared at her as she sauntered back down the tunnel. All of what she'd had to say was par for the course. Calista wasn't stupid, and regardless of dropping enough bank on injections and surgery to put all the little Freezes through college, she wasn't getting any younger. Nobody wanted to see a trilling granny in lycra and feathers, but she'd sure as hell age right into Prioress v2.0. It was pretty cush as far as gigs went, and more importantly for her, she wouldn't fade into obscurity, especially if this whole dog and pony show really had kicked off another Cleansing.

Hmm? Oh, sorry. I told you halflings aren't real tolerated, and I think I mentioned at one point there being an open season on us. Every dozen years or so, normals get a hair across their asses about how many of us there are, then do something about it. I was a kid the last time the pitchforks came out, but then some guy started preaching tolerance, and for whatever reason, people actually listened. Anyways, he got offed by another normal, there was a ton of bad press, and instead of a full-scale Cleansing where they could let off some steam, things just got a lid slammed down on them.

We all know how that goes.

That's when the Priory hired that marketing firm to "freshen" their image. It was also right around the time Calista signed us up with them, and all that crap about my redemption was born. Who knew it was actually an insidious evil plot to wipe halflings from the face of the earth? I had to give her credit, it sure as hell was slick.

Until Fae invaded. I'd let Silas surprise her with that. Those dang bargains…

Hmm? Yeah, I guess I was ambivalent about it, but come on, I was locked in a freaking cell trying to suck bologna out of my molars. I had three days to go before none of it was my problem. Hell, none of it was my problem now, and even if it was, I couldn't do a damned thing about it.

I drank the skim. It was gross. Then I blew up the paper bag and popped it. I was going to chuck it into the tunnel, but restrained myself when I realized there was nada for toilet paper. I did have a bucket and practice using one, which was one thing going for me at least.

So that was it then. Sure solved that I-can't-be-in-two-places-at-once issue for Midsummer's conundrum. I bet it'd been Silas that fried the Priory. Lucky dog.

They left me there for a long time. I mean, it felt long. Long enough for me to start fantasizing about Sister Reticence and another bologna sandwich. Long enough to use up all that paper bag.

Right. So look. I'm not even gonna lie. I wasn't in the best place. Mentally, I mean. I told you the worst part of contemplation was being locked in my cell. This put that to shame. It was darker, damper, and a hell of a lot colder.

And I couldn't call flame.

If you haven't figure it out by now, that's kind of my security blanket. Whenever Calista had confined me, I'd call a thread. You know that Olympic sport where some chick in a leotard dances around with a ribbon on a stick? I can do that. Not the dancing part, but flipping flame around, swirling long ribbons of it, making it jump between my hands... I can even change the color. If there wasn't such a prejudice toward halflings, I bet I could've made serious bank on stage. I mean, fire eaters always draw a crowd.

Anyways, locking me away in the dark when I couldn't call flame wasn't doing me any favors. That collar was killing me. It felt like it was searing through my neck, and whatever was oozing past it was a lot more viscous than it had been. It itched like hell, and I'd swelled up so much I couldn't get a finger under it. I still wasn't a hundred percent from that squid thing, and the cold was leaching out what little strength I had. The lamp in the tunnel slowly gutted, and everything went black. I curled up in the corner, shivering under that crappy blanket, a sad piece of plastic-y cheese.

I tried to see the positive.

Karen had Kyle and Berk safe in Fae, and they

wouldn't fade. Morgana wouldn't either. Surprisingly, I was happy all of them would live. At least I'd die having done one good thing. Maybe it'd earn me brownie points in the here-after.

I snorted. Not likely. Halflings and souls were a thorny subject. Heaven was for normals and, honestly, sounded really freaking boring. All that celestial choir crap? Yeah, count me out.

Like way out.

Hell sounded more up my alley. I mean, come on, fire, brimstone…but I was pretty sure the writhing in eternal damnation portion of it was not intended to be a selling point.

So where did we go?

Back to our element. Yeah, it was super nebulous, but I guess the concept of Heaven kind of is, too. It was the not-knowing that got to me, shivering there in the dark.

I kept thinking about the way Berk's face had looked as the pebble sank into his chest, trying to hold on to that moment of joy. How it'd made him bloom. I smiled, tracing my fingers over my scar. They were like ice. You'd think having an ember in my—

Hold up. The pebble had absorbed right into Berk's chest.

Why did I have a scar?

I pondered that for a while, the bell jar pinging, but who the hell really knew?

Enter Silas.

His footsteps slapped down the tunnel, the lamps flaring before him. I shut my eyes against the sudden brightness. When I opened them again, he was sitting backward on the chair, arms folded across its top as he stared at me. He was in a tux with tails looking dapper.

I really did hate him.

"Why did I have to get sliced open to hide the ember?"

It wasn't the question he was expecting, which is probably why he answered. "You didn't."

"Sooo, you were trying to get it out?"

His eyes narrowed and went cagey. "What am I to do with you, Envy?"

Of all the turns of phrase… I laughed. "Let me die."

And then, I fell apart.

In case it hasn't been apparent, my mental state can be a bit dicey. I buried my face in my knees, and cried, like, for real. Why all of it? Why me? What had I done that was so bad to deserve this? Goddamn it, I was sorry already!

I didn't just want to not be me, I wanted not to be.

Silas watched. His face was totally dispassionate as I lay there, scrunched into the corner, feeling that hollowness and all the black seething awfulness inside me burbling up into it.

"Are you quite finished? There are matters we need to discuss…"

I stared blankly at the dust motes falling through the light, his voice attenuating out as he spoke, going all Charlie Brown's teacher, *waaawaa waaa…*

Reality grayed out, colors bleeding away, and I let it swallow me. This time there was no tranquilizer or hypodermic…no glamour to pull me back.

And for once, I didn't want it to.

I'm sure that's why it was so clear on the other side of the static.

That dreamscape of stone and ash. This time I didn't have to follow the path. I was just there, before the tree. It shimmered with heat, its stunted branches tipped scarlet with new growth as they stabbed into the sky. Behind the stone where my doppelgänger had sat, a door was carved into the bole. My door, the one that would open so I could escape. There were no hinges or latch, no knob to turn. Just a smooth pale slab, like the bark had been recently stripped away. Why couldn't it open now? I didn't want to wait.

Tendrils of sporadic flame leaked from around its edges, reflecting off the emerald scales of the serpent that had covered her lap. It came down from the branches, coiling upon her stone. I stared at it, remembering it in shades of gray... But we knew each other. Its head rose up as I drew near, weaving hypnotically until I was close enough to touch it. I held out a hand, and the serpent flicked its tongue, then fell back, slithering to the door and disappearing beneath it.

Falling to my knees, I slid my fingers under the slab after it. There was a sharp bite of flame, and then they licked at me, pulling me to them. The realization that I could fade washed over me. A smile flickered across my lips, imagining myself streaming off into nothingness...

Faint piano music teased my ears—

And a hand was up under my jaw, jacking me against the wall.

Silas swore. "You don't even know what you're doing, do you?" He made a noise of disgust, ripping the blanket from me. A vein in his forehead throbbed. His hand was at my chest, searingly hot...and familiar.

I laughed, arching against him, offering myself up.

My eyes rolled back into my head. God, the heat... I wanted to suck it from him into myself, push the dankness of the cell out of me. Go back to the tree and the door. He bellowed in pain, trying to pull away. I'd gripped his wrist, the sleeves of his tux turning to ash beneath my hands.

Silas screamed, and there was the sound of metal striking stone as the collar fell away.

The weight on me lifted, and there was nothing holding me together anymore.

Poof.

43 Hours

So, you know that whole spiel I gave about the inherent dangers of focusing on something, versus somewhere, when you're poofing?

Yeah, that again.

Believe it or not, my focus wasn't on Brennan. It was on the music, which I thought was the same thing.

It wasn't.

It was a breakfast piano concerto being given for the five great dae clans. Materializing under the piano, sucking the life force out of my father probably wasn't the best first impression. Or maybe it was. I mean, they were daemons. Either way, it was one hell of a conversation starter.

The music cut out. There were gasps. Someone screamed. Another laughed, and I swear I heard wagers begin to fly. All of it was just background noise as I held Silas's wrist in a death grip, trying to keep doing what I was doing, which was basically draining him dry. I was freaking pissed, and let me tell you, every ounce of strength I siphoned from him made me feel like a million bucks.

He was still more than a match for me, but I didn't care. I mean, I'd surprised him, but now he was rip shit. His skin started to turn that over-ripe cherry color as his stigmata flared. I called up a blast of plasma to send at his face. He wrestled me onto my back and was hauling back to slug me. The underside of the piano complicated that, as did someone grabbing his ankles and yanking him out. The motion made Silas slam down onto me, knocking the air from my lungs. My shot of plasma was messy and went wide. It splattered into the piano, incinerating a good portion of it, and blowing the rest into a bazillion pieces.

There were more screams, and the sounds of chairs scattering. I rolled to my knees sucking wind, then tore after Silas. I wasn't gonna let that son of a bitch get off so easy.

He obviously felt the same way, because he was struggling mightily against some seriously bad-ass looking daemons. Like, they made Horatio seem all little Miss Muffet. Coarse, spiked black hair, skin that looked like thick-grained leather, and muscles with muscles.

Everyone was on their feet shouting at once. I didn't care. I ran over and sucker-punched Silas in the stomach as hard as I could, then nailed him in the nuts. His eyeballs just about shot out of his head.

"You fucking fairy!"

Probably not the wisest thing to scream in a crowd of, uh…fae. It was like I'd punted a beehive. Not that it stopped me. I went at him again, cursing a blue streak even after someone grabbed me and was hauling me away. I kicked and spat, not even close to being finished. Whoever had me laughed.

"Meow! Whoa, whoa, cool it, Miss Kitty!"

Berk?

It wasn't, but the gravelly voice had shocked me out of my fury. I quit straining against the massive arm pinning back my shoulders. Tux-clad, a scalded pink, way hairy wrist poked out of the sleeve. It was owned by a close relation of the two bad-ass dae holding Silas. This one had tusks. I stood there panting and becoming painfully aware of my surroundings. I went limp as I looked around, my chest heaving.

Crap.

A room full of dae nobility stared back at me. Their expressions ran the gamut, everything from gleeful amusement to horrified disgust. I started laughing. So much for my introduction into society.

We were in someone's conservatory, amidst a circle of tables and bamboo chairs strewn from where they'd been only moments earlier. It smelled like pancakes and looked like a bomb had gone off. People were splattered with what was left of the breakfast buffet, and pieces of piano were everywhere. I think it'd been white. A woman was flicking bits of sausage from her hair. Outside, the sky was the lavender of very early morning, and stars were still populating the heavens. They were the same constellations as back home. Same sun, moon... I wondered how that worked. A mountain of muscles was at my back, and somewhere along the line I'd lost a toenail.

It's funny the things you notice when you're trying to avoid the reality of a situation.

I immediately picked Horatio and Amelda out from the crowd, but I didn't see Brennan anywhere... Amelda's eyes met mine, and she raised a supremely satisfied eyebrow.

"Oh, come on!"

Someone in the crowd laughed. Fuck him. I just knew that bitch was going to try and get me for breaking our bargain. There was no way she could blame me for Silas's bullshit abduction.

They started walking over. I tried to wriggle away from the behemoth that held me, but I wasn't going anywhere. It was a problem. Now that I'd stopped trying to kill Silas, whatever I'd sucked from him was making me twitchy. Okay, that sounded bad, but it was true. It was like a teeth-grinding, can't-stay-still type energy that usually came in a twisted-off baggie. I needed to go find a treadmill or do some laps.

I looked down around the meaty arm smooshing me, fiddling with the too-short hem of my tank, and laughed, feeling really underdressed, and abruptly aware of how bad I smelled. God, I was filthy, and couldn't stop bouncing. The guy that had me didn't seem to object. Like, had started breathing heavy didn't object. I tried to make a break for it again and felt more than heard the asshole chuckle. He put a hand on my hip, pressing me back into his bulk. I considered biting him. Low flames started to flicker over my skin.

"I said cool it, Kitty. Boss-lady's comin'."

Hah, easier said than done. The longer I stood there the more jittery I got. I didn't give a shit who was coming. In another minute or two it was gonna be flame on, with zero apologies to that dude in the comic. I gripped the dae's arm, my nails digging into him. Christ, he sounded like he liked it.

The murmur of the crowd was all around me, and Silas was pleading with a very tall, very thin, very old woman. I didn't see her move, but I sure as hell heard the crack of her hand across his face and saw his head snap back. It was savage, and totally would've dropped him if it hadn't been for those two dae holding him up.

"Come to deliver yourself, Pet?"

Crap. Amelda stood to the other side of me, smug. Horatio was right behind her.

"Yes."

It wasn't the answer she'd been expecting. It wasn't the answer I wanted to give, but what else could I say? "Silas interrupted before the terms of our agreement could be met. I didn't want you to think I was welching and thought coming to renegotiate best." My words came out too fast, and I couldn't stop biting at my lips.

Her eyes narrowed. Horatio just watched me bounce. Well, parts of me. She wasn't buying it, and I had nothing else in the till.

"Amelda, do you have business with this young lady?" The voice was low and smokey, like a jazz singer's, the kind that stops and resonates in your core instead of just tripping by your ears.

A shadow of emotion flickered across Amelda's face so quickly I couldn't catch it. She looked past me to smile at the woman who'd slapped Silas. It was so incredibly fake I don't know why she bothered. She should've just given her the finger.

It was obvious from the woman's expression she felt the same. Did I say she was old? Like, I was pretty sure she'd turned down Methuselah for the prom, old. I'd had no idea dae could get to that level of ancient, and I can't even describe the resting bitch face on her. She made Amelda look like one of those yappy little rat-fuck dogs.

You could tell Amelda knew it and wasn't a fan. She forced her smile wider. Even less convincing. I would've cringed if I wasn't wholeheartedly enjoying her squirm.

"Good morning, Dowager. I didn't think you'd be up so early."

"I find that difficult to believe. You know how much I enjoy a good concerto. Pity this wasn't one, but Brennan's still far too ill to play, and I doubt he would, were he able."

My face paled. What had I done? I twisted the band on my finger. Now that the stupid collar was gone I should've been able to feel him, but I was too hopped up to focus.

"I'm sure if I asked, he'd be happy to play for you."

"If I wanted to hear soulless drivel, I'd call on you more often for tea. Now answer the question."

Amelda bristled, her form wavering. "Yes, Pet and I have a bargain—"

"No longer." The Dowager raised her voice and held out a large gold coin between her fingers. "I claim this child by right of blood. All bargains satisfied. All debts paid."

From the expressions on everyone's faces, the Dowager was pulling some serious rank. The two of them glared at each other—well, that's not true. Amelda glared. She was beyond wavering. Her skin burbled mottled patches of bright magenta, and her pupils became hourglasses, like a goat's. Horatio's hand slipped around her arm, and she shrugged him off.

The Dowager just stood there with the coin in hand, and I totally got where Silas had pulled that "are you quite finished" shit from. She did it better. Weirdly, other than being super old, she looked about as vanilla as a fae got. I mean, like some normal's grandma. No tusks, or scales, or anything.

It was terrifying.

And I couldn't stop bouncing. Those little flames? Not so little anymore, and my control, hah, yeah, I know, right? It was sporadic at best. Not that I felt particularly bad about smoking my jailor's tux, but my clothes were getting crispy, too. I had zero desire to be up here buck naked against this guy pantomiming riding a pogo stick.

The room had gone silent. It lasted just long enough for Amelda to take possession of the coin and then a ferocious clamor ate up the space. Her eyes met mine, and there was no question that regardless of what had just changed hands, come July, I was still dead.

The Dowager looked me up and down, and I had an urge to show off my fetlocks and let her see my teeth. "Jonas is going to let you go. When he does, you'll do as you're told, now won't you?"

I readily agreed, but if she asked me to sit still, I was screwed.

Her mouth pursed, but she nodded over my head to the dae restraining me. "Come." He let me go, and she turned away, sweeping out of the room way quicker than an old lady should be able to move. Jonas gave me a nudge.

"Better catch up."

He didn't have to tell me twice.

The Dowager was already at the end of a long monochrome hall. I ran across the checkerboard tiles and down an arched hallway of statuary and urns. An ornately carved balustrade flanked me, the second floor open from a balcony. To the right were sitting areas in front of large windows overlooking an expansive lawn. It was like being back at the casino's convention space.

Pops of color were reserved for the greenery erupting to either side of doorways large enough to drive a semi through.

She went out one of them into a garden. Pretty soon, it started looking familiar. Well, the bones did. I followed her through the twisting paths, flame blossoming from the thorns as I passed. No matter how fast I ran, she was always just turning the next corner.

Until we got to that super creepy skull fountain, and yeah, it was still looking at me.

The Dowager was sitting on its lip as I burst out into the little plaza, panting. She wasn't winded a smidgen, and there was nary a wrinkle in her peach chiffon gown. It was all mother of the bride and had a little matching jacket, bedazzled with sprays of what I can promise you were not rhinestones. I'd never seen anyone with skin as white as mine, but hers was, and her chignon the same, shot with silver strands glittering like spider's silk.

It sounds weird, but she was beautiful.

I'd been standing there way too long, and from her expression, was expected to do something. Crap. I gave a little wave and bobbed my head. Her wispy eyebrow rose.

"Brennan assured me you'd been taught manners."

She'd talked to him about me? I tried to stop wiggling like a puppy and attempted a curtsey.

"Now I see why you waved." Man, she had a sultry voice. It softened the smirk she didn't bother to hide. Her slim hand motioned for me to sit beside her. I tried, but couldn't. I was still too keyed up and bouncing again.

"The nature of a succubus is that of an amplifier.

We evoke strong emotion and derive pleasure from it. Energy vampires, if you will. However, unlike a vampire, we're able to store that energy and set it to other tasks."

She'd pulled a long jade stick from her skirts and affixed a cigarette to the tip. My brow furrowed as she did. Something about it was, I don't know, familiar. And not in a good way. She held the end between her lips, looking me over again as it began to smolder.

"You've taken far too much and need to divest yourself of the excess. Humor me, won't you? Push some into the fountain."

Push it— I floundered for half a moment and then sent out my aura. Everything else started like that, right? That tingly, teeth grinding buzz flowed with it, jumping at the chance to do something. Relief almost distracted me from the fact that the bones weren't dead. They had the same kind of thick resistance to them as a living being.

They caught me up, dragging me out of me.

I freaked.

"Calm yourself."

Did telling someone that ever work? Not that I had a choice. Whatever had me wasn't letting go, and was pulling me farther out. It wasn't anything like poofing. It was more like… you know that fake spiderweb stuff at Halloween? How it starts as a cottony blob, and then gets thin as it spreads out, catching on everything it passes?

Yeah, that was me.

It was not an enjoyable experience. It didn't exactly hurt, but it was way too reminiscent of the one and only time I'd tried peyote. I am not a one-with-the-universe-type gal. The teensy part of me that wasn't paralyzed with fear was pissed that Brennan hadn't given me a heads-up that something could just spin me out all over the place.

Because that's what'd happened. When that pulling sensation stopped, it was like my consciousness had been webbed between all of those stupid thorns lining the paths, and I was everywhere…

Then it got weird, because obviously, that wasn't strange enough.

I wasn't alone. There were people, conversations…

"…her now. She's not willing to accept it's over."

Horatio. A sense of him became clearer as I focused on it. The rest was still there, but it was, I don't know, like hearing it through a closed door. For this conversation, it was like I was standing in the room.

Silas laughed, and he sounded like shit. "If Amelda won't step down, she'll be thrown."

"Don't be so sure. If the Reincarnation works—"

"Whether her fertility returns or not, she'll still be dangerously incompetent. Make no mistake, brother, as long as Amelda's deposed, I care very little who's pulling the girl's strings. I offer you this chance, once. Walk away lest you fall with her."

Several moments of loaded silence passed between them.

"I can't do that."

"Then we are at quits."

There was an abrupt sensation of release, and I flew back into myself like I was a retractable cord. It knocked me for a loop. I kneeled, panting in front of the fountain. It had become filled with a viscous blue flame that burbled over the bones like a caress. I was shaking, but this time, it wasn't from energy. What the hell? I looked at the Dowager, still smoking from her jade stick, not a doubt in my mind it'd been her mandibles I'd been carried along in. Looking me over, she had one hell of a poker face. I started sweating at what it covered.

"Not all the way awake, but farther along than you've any business being. Tell me, child, do you know who I am?"

I wiped my palms on my thighs, and it didn't help. "The Dowager."

The corners of her eyes crinkled like glass shattering. She stood and extended a hand to help me up, looping my arm through hers when I was beside her. It was a weird gesture, possessive. My arm made a damp smear on her sleeve, and I swallowed.

We strolled down the path. It was a very different garden than the one I'd just run through. No longer dead, but alive with flame and shadow, alternately flickering and eating at each other. There was a weird harmony to it, a familiarity—

"At the apex of the Midsummer's moon, you will be required to elect a Guardian as you become."

I nodded, distracted by a murder of goblins that had swarmed around a stunted tree studded with flaring cadmium blossoms. My brow furrowed. All lit up, everything was... God. I was having the worst case of déjà vu.

"If given the choice, whom would you choose?"

I was not distracted enough to miss the "if." "Uh, does it have to be a daemon?"

Her eyebrow raised a fraction. "Traditionally."

So no. "Karen."

The Dowager laughed, and it was so rusty, I swear cobwebs blew from her lips. It was absolutely terrifying. The goblins scattered. Chuckling, she patted my arm looped through hers.

"I can understand Brennan's attraction. A feast for the eyes the least of it..." She'd stopped to stare at me intently. Her hand reached up to caress my cheek, and I blushed, my heart rate jumping. "What would you say if I told you that the imps all answered to me?"

"I'd wonder why I hadn't met you a lot sooner."

That smirk of hers was back. "Silas thought to hide you. I chose to let him think that he had. You were in good hands until Amelda got her panties in a twist." Her face went hard, and I felt like I might wet myself. Making an enemy of this woman would be a very, very bad idea.

"Afterward, I was just curious what you would do. I must say, you've provided me with the most entertainment I've had in a quite a long time. I don't know that I've ever encountered a creature with more dumb luck. I'm assuming that's the anathema's influence...but who can tell?"

"Can you get it out?"

"Why ever would I want to?"

I just kind of stared at her.

Why... I don't—hadn't... What the hell?

"Come, child, we've little time as it is."

My feet raised obediently, and she led me through the garden and back inside, dazed.

Checkerboard floor, people passed. Steps and thick gray carpet. Through a door and more steps. Here the carpet was worn. All I could smell was fried eggs. Fingers on my face with long tapered nails. Beige polish. Eyes of the palest pale blue searching mine.

"All these cracks in you I see...and into the crucible you go."

A door opened, and the Dowager pushed me through it.

42 Hours

I'm embarrassed to say as soon as the door opened and I saw Brennan, I burst into tears. Stupid, right? I know, you'd think I was an undine, but cut me some slack. I had a lot on my plate, and considering the last hour? Please.

"After he regained consciousness, Amelda made a series of rather unfortunate requests. As soon as she left the room, he in turn made liberal use of her sword. Peter got him to that fish of yours before he bled out, but he's hellbent on fading."

I crossed the room, rethinking my stance on undines. Well, one of them at least. Maybe.

Brennan was in a narrow bed that stuck out from the wall, into the middle of the severe room. It had metal rails, and he was hooked up to something that beeped. He looked awful. His cheeks were sunken, and his skin was yellow instead of that golden bronze. Dark bruises pitted beneath his eyes. That damn watch hung on him like a shackle.

My legs gave out, and I collapsed into the chair by his side. A television was on a rolling cart in the corner, volume low as CNN scrolled across the screen. Same stars, same cable channels. How did that work? As for the rest of it, the floor was tan, walls off-white. There was a suspended ceiling and vertical blinds on the window to the left. A chair with a small table beside it, and that damned fried egg smell.

I'd been here before.

I've said my earliest memory is of the hospital after my surgery. I was four. They say you can't remember pain, and they're right, but fear's another story. So is loneliness. That's when that kicked dog moved in, and I'd never lost the gnawing sense of abandonment from my mother leaving me there. Sitting in that room next to him fading, it was waiting for me.

What? Yeah, I'll add finding a therapist to my to-do list.

Anyways, an imp came in with a tea service. The Dowager sat, smoking. She offered me a cup, and I shook my head.

"Why does it smell like eggs?"

"Imps have a fondness for them. This is their corner of the Manse."

I took Brennan's hand in mine, tracing one of the pale pink scars running up the inside of his forearm. God, this was all my fault.

"You were the one who tried to get it out?"

The Dowager didn't mince words or try to misunderstand. I liked that about her.

"The anathema had already rooted in you. It was all I could do to slow the assimilation. Silas has the unfortunate tendency to think he's smarter than everyone else. The Proscriptions regarding their keeping are there for a very specific reason." She took another drag. As she did, my vision doubled, and for a split second she was much younger. I pinched the bridge of my nose, wishing that imp had brought a bottle instead of a teapot. I wouldn't sneeze at a couple of aspirins, either.

"Which is?"

"To prevent the reincarnation of the beings they hold."

I laughed. Like, really laughed. Every one of them this side of the veil was batshit crazy.

She kept going. "The anathema were originally created as prisons. In our infinite wisdom, we decided we didn't need kings and queens of Fae. They cursed us in return, weakening the Neither. The realms contaminated each other, birth rates plummeted... We cut ourselves off from that which feeds us and have found humans too weak a mead to sustain our needs. There are those of us who would bend the knee and see our borders restored."

I thought of that place of silence and ash. The other me had called it the labyrinth...and where else would she be but at the heart? Christ, if I heard one more twisted phrase or play on words...

"Do your knees do that anymore?"

Yeah, that was flip and not particularly well advised, but seeing Brennan like this along with the shit she was laying on me—God, I hated fae.

Her eyes glinted from behind her jade stick like I'd said something awfully clever. It didn't give me warm fuzzies. "The better question is, did they ever?" Her gaze flicked to the TV. "Between Silas's rashness, and your Blessed Lady of the Inferno, we've come to our tipping point. Allowances need to be made."

"It's not my blessed anything," I muttered, brushing back Brennan's hair. Someone, Peter, probably, had recently given him a shave, and there was a drip of foam on his lobe. I wiped it off, my fingers lingering as I looked at him. "How long has he been like this?"

The Dowager tapped off a bit of ash into a bed pan. "They moved him here last night. That fish of yours is very good. How did you choose them for the anathema?"

"Proximity. Otherwise I wouldn't have chosen her at all. I just didn't want Silas to have them. They're safe?" I'd found a remote in Brennan's bedsheets and was surfing channels. The news was so depressing. Maybe cartoons or PBS... My thumb froze at my mother's voice. Footage was playing of the Priory engulfed in flames. Our Lady of the Blessed Inferno was an inferno. Hah. Ironic that they've been preaching the rest of the world was gonna go up like that.

The Dowager chuckled. "Spoken like a true Malten. They're as safe as they can be. The imps have them in a secure location, and aside from yourself, Brennan, and I, no others know they exist. I've made arrangements for them to be at the ceremony to become."

I looked at her in surprise, and she smirked around that damned jade stick.

"I tend to take the long view on matters such as these. Their return was inevitable, and if managed properly, my knees shouldn't have to bend at all."

The way she was looking at me made it very apparent that she wanted something. Whatever it was, I was pretty sure I didn't want to oblige. I was just as certain I wasn't going to be able to opt out.

Across the room, my mother was on the screen again, soot streaking her tragic beauty, decrying the Priory's destruction as an Act of Terror and lamenting the loss of the Prioress. The news anchors came on calling the gassy old bag Saint Benevolence, then the shot went to rioting in some foreign city. People held up signs with my picture, screaming horrible things at the camera.

What the f—

The Dowager took the remote from my hand and clicked the TV off.

I licked my lips. They were very dry. The rest of me was soaked in sweat. "And all of that?"

"Appalling. So much so, the Council has finally agreed to intervene. They'll have their war. The humans will bring iron to bear against us, and after an acceptable amount of losses, they'll come to the same conclusions that I have. Fae needs to step in and shepherd the chattel as the primordials once did."

How she kept a straight face...

"Is that why Earth keeps trying to kill me?"

"They've declined to share their reasons, but are united in their opposition to the Reincarnation. Someone tipped them off one of Silas's offspring had become a vessel. I can only assume incinerating that assassin before your stigmata came in made certain individuals more cautious than is their wont. They pointed Earth in your direction before understanding the long-term implications of their actions. Unfortunate, but not unsurprising."

She didn't say it'd been Amelda, but her face had gotten the same expression as the last time she'd been mentioned. It made my toes curl up. My fingertips found the smooth slice of scar down my sternum, that feeling of familiarity when Silas's hand was burning into my chest... God, that hadn't been a perv trying to molest me, he'd been trying to rip out the ember. I

211

didn't know if the realization made it more or less traumatic. First the hospital, now this… Not being able to trust my memories was definitely screwing with me. When I spoke again, my voice was very small.

"Why me?"

"Perhaps it was just dumb luck. You seem to have an abundance of it."

She was full of shit, but I wasn't calling shenanigans.

"As to how you survived after, you'll have to thank your mother for making you disappear so effectively. Even after that horrific interview, we couldn't pin down your exact location, and now here you are." She smiled at me, and I hoped to hell that "we" wasn't a Freudian slip lumping her in with everyone else who wanted me dead.

I dropped my eyes to Brennan and felt them well up. I had no illusions that if I crossed her, I'd be very sorry. The Dowager had brought me here to see him like this for a reason, and her threat was implicit.

"What do you need me to do?"

"You will name me your Guardian when you become. In turn, I will name you clan Malten's heir. Upon your majority, you will rule at my discretion. Should you fail to name me, the primordial fae imprisoned within the ember will strip you of your will and wear your body like a meat-suit as it rampages through the realms."

Well, that sounded less than ideal. I licked my lips.

"Amelda?"

"Will be dealt with." Her face softened watching mine. "The Proscriptions require a fertile female of our line to head the clan. Thanks to her hubris, no others remain. I'm keenly aware of your lack of suitability to act in that capacity. You will do so in name only. As long as you meet your societal obligations, I've no issues with you holing up on that rock of Brennan's. In fact, I prefer it. I've had enough of incompetent children seeing to clan affairs."

You'd think that would've pissed me off, but I was pretty numb. I just nodded, then collapsed, sobbing onto Brennan's chest. The Dowager left, and I couldn't blame her. Who wants to stick around for that? I didn't even want to be around me.

After a while, I sat up and found something to blow my nose in. The room was a horrible kind of quiet. I'd never been around anyone who was really sick, and it was, I don't know, awkward. I'd already told him my life story, and I wasn't going to be one of those lame chicks that just whines about how badly they need someone. Boo frickin' who.

Boo frickin' me.

God. It was totally hypocritical. I mean, whatever the Dowager was thinking was gonna happen, mmm, not so much. I was still pretty set on fading. So what if some primordial fae wanted to use my body? It's not like they were going to ruin my image. My mother had beaten them to the punch.

Nah, I was checking out. How could I ask him to stay?

Ugh, then why did I feel like such a douche? I mean, it wasn't like I owed him anything, but… Christ. He deserved better. He should have someone with him that—I don't know. I couldn't just let him—Look, it all just pissed me off.

Shut up.

It didn't help that all I could think of was that damn record I pulled out the first day at the flat. I mean, I wasn't going there, but the casino had done *Chicago* a year or two before the whole stigmata debacle. I wasn't part of the show, but I'd filled in Roxy's parts when Calista had practiced…and sung Velma's when she wasn't around.

Anyways, the score seemed strangely appropriate. My mouth opened a bunch, and nothing came out. Then when it did, man I sucked.

Oh my God, what did you expect? I hadn't even hummed in like, a decade. No way I was busting out all "Amazing Grace," and I sure as hell didn't expect a revival. I squawked and cracked. Broke on the highs. Gutted on the lows. Ugh. It was embarrassing. Brennan didn't seem to mind, but the man was comatose. I warbled until my throat was sore and then kept going.

It felt good…and bad. I cried more.

Yeah. Like a lot.

Whatever.

So this next part was totally stupid, and I'll be honest, creepy, but I just wanted to feel him. Yeah, yeah, it was a little necro, but whatever. I'd pushed my aura out to him after the Dowager had left. That was a lot of the reason I cried. There was this whole resonance of the shit storm Silas had inflicted on him, but Amelda… Christ, the compulsions he was wrapped in—

I'm not going to get into it, but I would've sliced my wrists, too. I'll admit to being a little emotional, and it totally bled out all over him. The last of that fidgety energy was more than happy to hitch a ride over.

At some point, I lifted up his wrist with that

goddamned watch. He'd never really let me look at it before. It was a solid piece. Heavy. Wicked expensive, with little diamond chips on the hours, and like the skulls, it had a kind of life.

Huh.

So, you know I couldn't leave it alone. I put my hand on the clasp and started sucking that bitch dry.

It was disgusting. I can't even tell you the foul funk that poured off that thing. I started gagging, then puking bile. I mean, I could actually taste it. My insides twisted, and I was afraid I was gonna shit myself. Seriously bad mojo. I don't know how long I was there gripping that stupid thing. I did hear yelling at one point, then someone pounding on the door.

None of it registered as clearly as that click of the watch clasp falling open.

Nor the wail of absolute desolation and rage from the hall. Oooh. Now that just warmed the cockles of my withered little heart. I flung it off his wrist and incinerated the damn thing mid-air. Suck it, you dirty bitch.

Then, narrow bed or not, regardless of the fuckery going on outside the door, I squeezed in beside him, all that nastiness dragging me down into the same oblivion.

Right, we've had this conversation. You know, the one about people knowing better laughing at you? Apparently, when a succubus feeds off energy, it's not just energy they suck up. Like, there needs to be a memory filter on it.

I had some seriously wanked dreams.

I mean, they weren't like memory, memories, more like a flickering montage of some seriously filthy, hardcore sexcapades, and a smattering of violence. They came with a flavor all their own that tainted everything. I'll give you a hint. It wasn't pineapple.

All of it was Silas. The man was straight-up ambition and lust. Normally, I would be totally into that, but sucking it off my father was just gross.

Sorry, I don't mean to laugh, and yes, it's super skeevey, but I'm a freaking succubus. It's kind of what I do. I probably should've had a clue from the get. I mean, I'm a polarizing kind of gal, and I'll admit, I get off on screwing with people. That one shrink Calista took me to called it "attention-seeking behavior." Some crap about any being better than none. Whatever. He stared at my boobs the whole time.

Anyways, I wasn't the only one who got to experience Silas's considerable kink. My aura was still all over Brennan, and that energy and emotion fed right into him. The pervy vitality from my father jumpstarted him enough to swim back up to the land of the living. I guess saturating someone's subconscious in triple-X porn will do that.

I will also give them one hell of a hard on.

Hmm? Oh yeah. You better believe I got bent over. I'm not going to try to psychoanalyze any of it, but it was intense. Afterwards, all I could do was lie there panting, wondering what the hell just happened, and what round two was going to be like.

Well duh, there was a round two. There was always round two. What do you think I spent so much time in bed with him doing? Reading the Bible? Fae are way more virile than normals, and the man had been seriously pent up. Teenaged boys had nothin' on him, and I sure as hell wasn't complaining.

His hand brushed through my hair as I nestled against him, listening to his heartbeat mellow and realizing I was happy. I'm aware of how ridiculous that sounds. I'd just spent the past I don't even know how long getting threatened and the shit kicked out of me. Now here I was in a crappy twin bed, with my love, completely, stupidly, and unrealistically happy.

Yeah, I said it.

But in my defense, I also expected flying monkeys to raid the room at any moment.

Brennan couldn't stop staring at his bare wrist. "Tell me."

I did. All of it.

His form wavered, and so did the shadows in the room. They thickened and moved toward us as I spilled the last of it. I was seriously freaked and sat up, thinking about those monkeys. They…I don't know…shambled. All the little hairs on my body stood up, and the air was like ice. My breath came out in a freaking cloud. I pressed closer to him, and Brennan's whisper was low and ragged in my ear.

"They won't hurt you, Lovely. They're mine."

"Yours?" My brow crinkled at his nod, running all of the subsets of dae I knew through my head, and coming up blank. He sat up and stretched like he'd been constrained, somehow bulkier than he had been, and mussed his hair. His hand trailed over his jaw.

"Yes, give me a moment. My case isn't around here, is it?"

I snagged it from the bedside table, and he lit up. I waited, watching the darkness send out tendrils toward the bed and shivering. Totally unconcerned with the encroaching darkness, he finished his cigarette, then calmly lit another. A smile began teasing his lips. Not like an I'm-so-happy-smile. It was more of a someone's-going-to-bleed-smile. Two drags in, he gave a sharp laugh, and the shadows melted away. The sunlight streaming in the window seemed way brighter than it had.

What the hell!

He hugged me to him. "You know, I heard you...in the pavilion, now."

I just kind of blinked at him. What—? I... That was not where I thought this conversation was going, and not for nothing, but the only reason I'd said half of it was because I'd thought he'd been out cold. I licked my lips.

"Yeah?" My voice was calm.

My insides were screaming.

"Mmm." He took another drag and frowned like it didn't taste very good. Go figure. "Bits and pieces...enough. Your mother and mine would fancy each other."

I wasn't sure about that, but I could sure as hell see them as frenemies.

"And our fathers? Did you know yours?"

Brennan nodded with a funny little smile. "They hate each other."

"Wise man. Your father, that is."

"Kennet's brilliant. Amelda chose him for his military prowess...and because he's a bloodthirsty bastard. He rides with the wild hunt. I spent a great deal of my childhood with him."

He had to be a murderous son of a bitch if he'd been accepted into the hunt, but that wasn't what got my attention. "You said it was a woman's duty to raise

218

her child."

"Did I?" His eyes laughed at me, and he shrugged. Asshole had been messing with me. "It was like going to boarding school. I learned a lot from him… We were close until I was banded." Brennan's fingertips brushed across my abdomen. "I would be the same for our child. I'd ask you to become, if you haven't already decided to. Stay with me."

I lay down against him, the room going blurry. His lips were soft on the top of my head. I couldn't even begin to entertain…it was too much to process.

"Why did you say those shadows were yours?"

He took another long drag. "Because they are. I'm a fiend, Lovely."

My breath caught right before I called him a liar. There was no way—

Look. Fiends were ridiculously dangerous and notoriously unbalanced. When one lost it, it was a safe bet there was going to be extensive destruction, and collateral damage of the fleshy sort…and they lost it a lot. Like, more than they kept it. They could do all sorts of crazy stuff regular dae couldn't because they were freaking nuts. How could he—It didn't make sense. Amelda, the club, the way Horatio and Mica spoke to him… I rubbed my wrist remembering that stupid limp-dick comment I'd made. His reaction was nothing compared to how it should've set him off. All of it should have.

"How…?" I think that's what I said. It might have come out squeakier.

"I've been so wrapped up in compulsion, I haven't been myself for a long time. But even prior to that, we're not all psychopaths. Though I'll admit, I've had my moments. My vengeance tends to run cold, as opposed to hot." He tilted my chin up so he could see my face. "Are you afraid?"

I'd be stupid not to be. But let's face it, on the bell curve of brilliance, I was closer to moron than Mensa. I took his hand and placed it over the scar on my breast. He trailed his fingers down the waxy slice.

"Are you?"

"I'm afraid you'll choose to fade, not of what you'll become."

"Do you know what that is?"

A smile quirked up his lips. "I'm still under contract, Lovely."

I glared at him, and he laughed. Mother f—

"Amelda will kill me if I do."

"The Dowager's interceded on your behalf. With her protection, no one in their right mind will touch you." So having my throat sliced open by his mother was still on the table.

He met my eye. "I've been thinking about what I'd do with my freedom for a very long time, and I personally guarantee she won't draw breath much longer...nor will several others."

His eyes were very hard, and I didn't doubt his sincerity.

"Can you really control it?"

"The woman I love just told me my brother hunted her down like an animal, almost got her killed by a nadra, then molested her while she was semi-comatose. You were then abducted by the man that flayed me, locked in one of those fucking cells, and then he tried to rip out your heart. They're both downstairs, still smiling and breathing the same air as Amelda. I think I've got a handle on it."

I supposed he did at that. Christ, I needed a drink or three after hearing it laid out. I scrubbed at my face. Being terrified I was going to die was old hat at this point. The prospect of living freaked me out more, and my latest source of anxiety was what the Dowager had spilled. I wasn't going to kid myself that things would be as cut-and-dried as she'd said. There was a catch somewhere, and it felt like a doozy.

A knock came from across the room, and Peter poked his head in, rattling off something with a seriously toothy grin as he came to the bedside. They chatted back and forth for a time, then Brennan laughed, and Peter left.

"He's got my suite ready. Shall we go see?"

I nodded, and he poofed.

We materialized in the center of a much larger bed. Other than that, it wasn't anything special. Firmer mattress than at the flat. Lots of blue. Door leading to a bathroom, also blue. A large picture window overlooking that extensive lawn, that creepy wood beyond it. There was a haze above it now, like it was smoldering, and the sun was a funky orange, low in the western sky.

We'd slept most of the day away. No wonder I was starving.

Brennan was staring out the window at the sun, too. His color had come back, and he didn't look like he was on death's door, just tired.

"There's a feast tonight. We're expected to attend." He didn't seem particularly excited by the prospect. I was down for the food, but assumed the same people I'd imploded a piano all over would be there. I laughed.

Not my first walk of shame.

There was a knock on the door, and this time Karen stuck her head in with another one of those too-toothy smiles. She came in yammering, handed him a small box, then left.

When he flipped it open, there was a wide, plain man's ring inside. He held it out to me on his palm. "I need you to band me."

33 Hours

He had to be kidding, but he wasn't.

"Lovely, please. Serena has enough of my name to make things difficult for me, and dangerous for everyone else if you don't. She has in the past, and I can guarantee that won't change should I remain un-banded. That's the only reason I agreed to wear Amelda's. While I did, no one could glamour or compel me…not even by my true name."

I spun the fae-band on my finger, staring at the one on his palm. "You'd trust me?" It was a seriously bizarre concept. Like I said, dae aren't exactly considered on the up-and-up. I mean, no one had ever even let me hold their beer…with good reason. I'd totally drink that shit.

"If given the same assurances I gave you. You'll not compel me, and release me should I ask thrice."

It sounded legit, except for one niggling detail.

"You know my true name." That'd been one of the things I told him when I thought he was passed out, back in Amelda's tent. So stupid. If he remembered—

"I do."

Crap. "I want yours."

"If I told you, would you speak it back to me?" He blew out a long stream of smoke, that sardonic smile playing over his lips.

I just looked at him, and he laughed. Asshole.

Me and my big—damn it. I'd broken out in a sweat, and I suppose I should explain why.

Exchanging names is a big deal to fae. They only do it for important stuff, you know, like ending blood feuds and pledging vassals. Taking a fae's name and speaking it aloud binds them. I told you at the beginning of this thing that names hold power. They can be used to compel you, mess with your nature…it's like giving someone access to your code. They can go in and totally change the program. And once someone knows your shit, they know it. I could absolutely see why Brennan had been so desperate for Amelda's help. No way would I want that chick from the bathroom with her fingers on my keyboard. He already had full access to me. So why was I balking at the chance to get mine on his?

Because he'd freaking one-upped me again, and he knew what that did to me.

Look, exchanging names and speaking them back is also how fae wed, or their equivalent to it. I mean, it's kind of more serious because you can't just get a quickie divorce. Instead of rings and vows, they hold a sword to each other's throats in perpetuity. Romantic, right? I felt like I was going to throw up, and my head had gone all funny and light, like it wasn't attached to what my body was doing.

I needed a drink.

He stubbed out his cigarette and moved closer to me. "Shhh, here now, Lovely. I didn't mean to upset you. I was teasing. You can't be bound while banded."

Brennan, teasing? Since when? I wanted to cry, right after I punched him in his stupid, handsome face. Goddamn it. I hated him. No, I didn't. I—I grabbed the ring. I didn't have to speak his name, but if he knew mine I sure as hell was gonna know his.

"I want it in exchange for banding you, and I want it now, not when I'm eighty." Ugh, I hated the way my voice caught.

"All right." It made me feel better that he looked as nervous as I sounded. "Push a bit of your aura into the ring to key it." I did, and it gained that alive feeling, like it'd somehow become an extension of me. My stomach churned thinking of what I'd siphoned off the watch. That'd been Amelda? I was abruptly glad all of it had gone right through me.

He held out his hand, and mine shook. Jesus freaking Christ. I...fuck it. It took a couple tries, but I jammed the damn thing on him. His eyes caught mine. "As agreed?"

The terms. I laughed. God, I hated fae. "Yeah...uh, yes. As agreed."

A weird latching sensation washed over me, the small hairs on my arms standing up. Then he kissed me, and it was the kind of kiss that makes you forget about everything except where it's going next.

Brennan wrapped me in wings of carmine and candlelight. Flames surrounded me, searing the dross from my body, heating the depths of my core. The residual burn of frost from the collar was licked away, his mouth heavy and insistent, mine more so. I moved above him.

Round one had been primal. This was, I don't know how to explain it.

I needed to feel. To make it real again. To remind myself that it had been.

That it still was.

His breath hot in my ear when he spoke his true name. It was strong, beautiful, complex, and…him. His forehead pressed against mine, his eyes trapping my own as his hips worked. Taut of breath, I met them, and he groaned.

"Say it, Lovely, I swear it won't bind you, I just want to hear it when I—please…"

I could feel the hunger for it in his voice, because I felt it too. That need to hear your name pass over another being's tongue, slide through their lips…to tell you who you are and complete you…

I wasn't doing it.

I bit him instead, and he laughed. Then his lips were on mine, and nothing else mattered.

When I was capable of rational thought again, I didn't do much of it. I stared up at the ceiling watching the smoke from Brennan's cigarette curl, enjoying that after-sex lassitude.

The imps shocked me out of it by coming in with a bottle of champagne like something momentous had happened. A flute was pressed into my hands, and I wasn't going to argue. Brennan smiled a lot as they yammered, that dimple of his showing. I was seriously gonna have to learn Impese.

He turned to me with a laugh and polished off his drink. "Sorry, they're very excited I'm not dead. I wish we didn't have to go do this, but the Dowager wants us both at the feast. It's going to be uncomfortable, but I suppose there's no help for it, now is there? Let Karen help you dress, Lovely. It starts before long, and the Dowager's asked to see us first. I'll be back to collect you."

He kissed my cheek and left Karen to it.

So, personal hygiene wise, I was gross. I mean, my sessions with Brennan had seared anything really offensive off me, but I couldn't remember the last time I'd actually bathed. Like, I was pretty sure I kept catching whiffs of swamp squid in my hair.

Karen cleaned me up, made me presentable. I had fewer injuries than you would've thought. She said all that life force I sucked from Silas went a long way toward healing me. Something about freebasing adrenochrome. I believed it after jumpstarting Brennan from that coma. So much for undines cornering the miraculous market. I couldn't wait to rub Morgana's face in it, because I did feel amazing.

Well, physically.

The rest of me was as strung out as Sunday's washing. The Dowager, knowing Brennan's name, man, all that touchy-feely stuff had knocked me for a loop. I mean, my emotional range doesn't go much past lust and shades of anger. Everything burbling inside me right now…my anxiety was on a major uptick. Luckily, the rum and coke Karen had brought was leveling me out, and I almost felt like I could deal. You know, pretend none of it had happened. I was usually pretty good at that, but it would've been easier if I didn't have a visual reminder of the past couple days.

A bevy of red scars banded around my neck where the collar had been. They were ugly and puffed out in ridges. Karen put something on them and told me not to worry. I worried. They looked super gross, and I hated scarves.

She gave me one anyways. It matched the slinky, sparkly evening gown she'd pulled out of her rear. Hah. She hadn't, really. Brennan had commissioned a bunch of fancy stuff weeks ago for the Midsummer's festivities. I vaguely recalled him saying that the night before all the hoopla each clan had a huge feast.

Yeah. I was getting ready to go have dinner with his family and already on the verge of a panic attack.

Fuck my life.

But on a positive note, between the stress and being beaten on a regular basis, a super model would've killed for the way my hip bones were popping. I would've rather done keto to get them, but Brennan's expression when he came back into the room made it seem worth it. So much for working on sit-ups along with my sobriety. With that out of the way...

I tipped back the last of what was in my glass.

Brennan offered me his arm with a goofy smile on his face. Damn, he cleaned up nice. He was in a charcoal suit, which wasn't anything new, but this one had a smokey waistcoat beneath it, and a matching cravat wrapped up high around his throat. They were the same shade as my gown.

He led me down a monochrome hallway and back through that foyer with the checkerboard floor. It was bizarre. Like I'd somehow stepped into a black and white version of the real world. I laughed, thinking of my complexion. I fit right in. We went to one of the smaller archways. You could probably only get a VW bus through it, if the doors had been opened. Only one of them was cracked. Brennan pushed it wide for me, and I walked into a formal sitting room. There was a fire burning in an alabaster hearth, and the room was ridiculously hot.

Yeah, even for me. Not that I was complaining.

A pair of salamanders slinked from behind the

Dowager's black and white striped skirts. The big wicker chair she was sitting in flared out behind her like a throne. Brennan's bow to her was super deep. I tried to curtsey again, and she failed to hide her smirk again. Whatever.

She motioned to the flocked loveseat on the other side of the hearth. Brennan sat beside me and reached down to pet one of the salamanders. The beautiful creatures radiated heat like tiny reactors and were roughly the size of a terrier. The one he was scritching was a deep ruby with an apricot belly. The other was solid maroon and had stayed at the Dowager's feet.

"Congratulations are in order," she said, putting a cigarette into her jade stick.

Something about that stupid thing still bothered me, but I'd be damned if I knew what. He beamed at me, and I just kind of ducked my head.

"I'd wondered if you'd be smart enough to apply your earlier lesson, and I must say you did so with aplomb. I can't tell you how delighted I am you managed to get that gaudy piece of trash off his wrist. It'll be quite a thumb in Amelda's eye, especially at this stage."

"Why didn't you just tell me what to do?"

She smirked from around her stick. "You don't tell metal to melt when you put it into a crucible. It reacts according to its nature. Yours is decidedly contrary."

I couldn't argue with her there, though I wanted to. Shut up.

The ruby salamander had curled up beside me and was making me drowsy with heat. It was delicious, and I was having a hard time resisting the urge to pull it into my lap and snuggle it like a teddy bear. I wondered if

Brennan would let me keep one at the flat.

The thought slapped me right upside the head with a big ol' what the hell is wrong with me.

Look, you gotta understand that good things don't happen to me. I mean, sometimes, yeah, but they didn't last. When it did come around, I'd kinda been conditioned to ride that horse hard before it dropped dead beneath me. Imagining being back at the flat with Brennan, and a salamander sleeping at the foot of the bed... I was just setting myself up to get hurt.

I pushed it away from me. Stupid thing was making my eyes water.

"Amelda is less than pleased at how things have progressed. Bringing the dead garden to life and removing Brennan's band has forced her to officially recognize your challenge for the throne..."

I just stared at my lap as she talked. Would've been nice to know that'd been what was going on. I'd have made it a point to stay in bed. Not that I'd really thought much about it since the Dowager unloaded all of it on me earlier, but it didn't sound any better this time around. In fact, I was pretty certain I was not okay with being her puppet and becoming any more than I'd been okay with being Calista's and sputtering. Unfortunately, I had a feeling that making the Dowager's nostrils flare out would be quite a bit more hazardous to my person...and Brennan's.

What in the ever-loving fuck was I going to do?

Brennan's arm slid around my shoulders. "Don't worry, Lovely. The Dowager will take everything in hand."

That was exactly what I was afraid of. My heart was in my throat, and I was having trouble breathing.

Karen came into the room with a tray of drinks, and my nails bit into my palms to keep from diving for them. The Dowager noticed, her eyes intent on us. They honed in on our fae-bands.

"You've had her bind your daemon form?"

"Envy is in control."

"Wise of you. When do you plan on removing hers?"

"Once we're back here. It shouldn't interfere with her naming you. Silas was a bit too keen to have me release her earlier."

Her eyes narrowed a fraction. "I've spoken to him about his methods of persuasion. Whereas I can't fault him, I would've been rather vexed had you imploded. I'm assuming you'll act as her consort?"

"We haven't discussed it."

"I suggest you do." She tapped the ash from her stick and turned her attention back to me. "As long as you're within the Manse and remain upon its grounds, your person is sacrosanct. To cause harm and break my guest rights is to forfeit your own. The ball is another story. Play for the anathema continues right up until the apex of the moon and carries on after. However, my favor will afford you a not-inconsequential amount of protection upon the mesa."

"Earth will still be an issue."

"As will your mother." The Dowager stood. "They're beginning to gather in the great hall. I suggest you make your entrance sooner than not. Again, the Manse is neutral ground. Break my peace at your peril."

Brennan rose with her, and I followed suit after a moment's hesitation. He kissed her papery cheek, and I heard him thank her. The salamanders trotted obediently at her heels as she left the room.

I fell back onto the loveseat as soon as she was gone, grabbing up my drink from the table. I wished Karen had left the bottle. Brennan gave me a quick hug, a cigarette already dangling from his lip. I couldn't help but note he'd used his Zippo.

"That's what you meant by 'among other things' when I asked why Silas flayed your stigmata? Why didn't you tell me he wanted the band off?"

"You would've asked to be released, and it's critical it remains on your finger, especially now."

I thought about how the Dowager had been looking at it and shivered, trying to wrap my head around the big barrel of what-the-fuck I'd been presented with. Look, I still wasn't cool with the idea that I wasn't getting rid of this thing inside me. I mean, I'd been under that assumption since the word go. All that shit about some prehistoric fae... What was it gonna do if it stayed in? I had this vision of that other me clawing her way out of my chest like in *Alien*.

But it didn't seem to bother anyone else, and they all had plenty of plans for me after. Well, they had plans if by some miracle I got through the gauntlet of people wanting to kill me. Then the icing on the crap-cake was I got to be a figurehead.

Cue more people wanting me dead.

None of them had bothered to ask what I wanted, which was actually a good thing, because I didn't have a clue. I mean, the easy answer was I wanted to fade...but did I? My eyes drifted to Brennan, that consort comment making my stomach drop. Jesus Christ. What was I going to do?

Believe it or not, I had a plan. For the immediate

future at least.

I was gonna get wasted and worry about it later.

I slapped the empty glass down and wiped my palms on my thighs. They were uncomfortably moist, again. Brennan handed me his cocktail. I did love him.

"Have you seen it? The anathema being reconsecrated, I mean."

"A thousand years ago?" He looked insulted. "How old do you think I am?" I didn't say anything, and he snorted. "Not that old. From what I understand, they're placed where the realms intersect on the mesa. There's an inset circle of silver. When the moon is directly overhead, it's filled, and the anathema become...other. That I can't explain, nor can anyone else. I hear you have to experience it to understand, whatever that means."

I had to ask the next question, even though I was pretty sure I knew the answer, especially after he'd totally misled her about me having control over his daemon form.

"Do you trust her?"

He blew out a long stream of smoke, and that sardonic smile was on his lips. "I'd be a fool to, but I'd be a bigger one to cross her."

None of it gave me warm fuzzies. Luckily my drink was, and Karen had brought me another. Brennan watched her go back out with her tray.

"Why did you pick Karen? The Dowager's claimed you. You'd be mad not to name her as Guardian. You'll have her protection for the next century, and you'd share in her status."

"For the next—what?"

Brennan blew out another long stream of smoke,

and he got that look that meant he was choosing his words carefully. "When you name a Guardian, you give them, ah, prerogative over your ability. Speaking from experience, having full access to it can be…overwhelming. A Guardian is named to make sure you use what you have responsibly. Think of it like applying a governor to your fire."

For a hundred years.

I stared at him deadpan, and he returned it, cigarette crackling. We both knew there wasn't a freaking chance I was down with that happening, but he played it off better than I expected and didn't miss a beat.

"I can only imagine you'd benefit from having the Dowager's experience to guide you, Lovely. She is after all, a succubus, and as I said, you'd be mad not to name her. Why would you even consider anyone else?"

He steadily returned my gaze, and I tried to read between the lines. He'd been contracted as a neutral party between Amelda and Silas, but I wondered if either of them knew the Dowager was who he was shilling for. Or supposed to be. I had a sinking suspicion that deal wasn't on the up-and-up either. As much as I wanted to know what the hell he was doing, now wasn't the time to ask. I smiled and tried to look coy.

"You gonna bargain with me for the answer?"

"No, you still owe me two."

I shrugged. "Karen's crepes are to die for."

He laughed, pulling me close. "So are you. You're going to make a delicious daemon."

I was glad he kissed me, because my smirk had faltered. Did I want to? I tried to push the question away, sipping at my drink, but the thought of allowing anyone to use me as a puppet rankled.

Hmm? Why not name Brennan?

Hanging out with me had already almost killed him. Twice. You know what they say about the third time. Fiend or not, if something happened to him because of me—

"Well, if it isn't Romeo and Juliet," Mica sneered, coming into the room. He flopped down into a chair across from us, and it cracked beneath his weight. "Weren't you both supposed to die at the end of Act 5?" He grinned as Brennan's form wavered. "Good evening, little brother. I need to congratulate you on a fine coup, running to hide in the old bat's skirts, then stealing away the prize from under everyone's nose. Has Pet told you all about our time together? She's a tasty little thing." He licked one of his fingers, and I felt ill.

Brennan's lip curled up into a snarl, his canines elongating. I glanced at the shadows, but they didn't waver. "You even think about touching her again, and I will kill you."

"I think about it all the time. How does pistols at dawn sound?"

"There will be no challenging or accepting within my home, Mica," the Dowager said sweeping back into the room and collecting her jade stick from the table. She tapped her palm with it and raised an eyebrow at him. "Did you search them out just to antagonize? But of course you have. Come, Amelda wants to begin the feast. Calm yourself, Brennan. You know he just wants to get a rise out of you."

Growling, Brennan stood and offered me his hand.

Maybe he really did have a handle on the fiend. The chair Mica had been in smacked against the wall as he pushed up from it. He leered at me and followed her out.

I held Brennan back as he started forward.

"Why doesn't she do it? Take power from Amelda, I mean."

"She can't. The strength of the clan is tied to its queen's fertility and Amelda's wanes. She's no longer able to bring a pregnancy to term. My sister, Genevieve, should have taken over a century ago. She'd begun making plans to forcibly take the throne, which is why Amelda had her killed. That's also when Silas hid the ember in your chest."

"I thought he—"

He shook his head. "My mother suffers no rivals. You need to name the Dowager as your Guardian tomorrow."

I stared into his frank gray eyes, trying to read what was there. "Why not you?"

He laughed. "I couldn't give a rat's ass about any of it, and because of that, I don't have the political clout to protect you. As soon as I'm done with this damned contract, I'll tell you all about it. My interests lie in a very different direction."

"Is that anywhere near consort?"

"I wouldn't want to push my luck, but perhaps something a bit more dignified sounding than boyfriend." I laughed, and he smiled. "Come, we're going to make quite an entrance as it is."

He looped my arm through his, and we went out across the checkerboard tiles and down the arched hallway of statuary and urns. Music and the murmur of voices became louder as we walked. Just before the door, he pulled me to the side of a marble column and kissed me breathless.

"I'm the biggest fool, Lovely. I haven't told you how incredible you look. You're going to knock them dead. Chin up, and trust me. Everything we talked about, yes?"

I tried to smile and gave a little nod, knowing fae doublespeak when I heard it. What else could I do?

31 Hours

The great hall was massive, its ceiling disappearing into shadow, and the parquet floor hidden beneath rows of trestle tables. They were spread with snowy cloths and bedecked with crystal and china. Their centers were studded with elaborate candelabras that twisted and branched like thorn bushes.

I took a sharp breath. Not for nothing, but everything they say about the beauty of fae is true. They roll out of bed that way and when they put in some effort? Psh. Fugeddaboutit.

A bead of sweat tracked down my spine as we moved farther into the hall. Behind us, I heard one dae bet another that it would hit the edge of my gown before we made the dais. Asshole. Brennan flexed his bicep beneath my hand and raised an expectant eyebrow.

Crap. It was go time.

I let Calista's megawatt smile bloom over my face with a new appreciation for the poisonous bitch's stage presence. My stomach churned. Once I'd been able to do the same. Granted, my thirteen-year-old self had a hell of a lot less swagger than I needed at the moment, but at least it was something. I called up what I could.

And just about lost it as the first centerpiece we passed burst into flame. Goddamn it, why did they keep doing that? The others caught like the burners on a gas grill and the entire room went silent, staring at us.

Brennan laughed with a feral smile. "I told you we'd make an entrance."

The sound broke the hush. Wagers and whispers started up fast and furious. I tried not to bristle at some of them, or the snatches of conversation I overheard. Bets and predictions, more unflattering comparisons than you would think, and some downright catty jabs that had me grinding my teeth. I looked like a pencil hanging between two grapes, did I? The one beside her opined that they were implants, and a bad job at that. I'd show her a f—

Brennan's hand came up to cover mine, and my teeth popped as I ground them. We were almost to the table at the head of the room. Raised up and set crosswise to the others, Amelda was front and center, ensconced behind it on a throne.

I'm not talking evocative of, like that wicker deal the Dowager was in. I'm talking full-blown, gilded Louis the whatever with ermine cushions. Considering the rest of the place, I was gonna bet Amelda had brought it with her. She wasn't wearing a crown but had enough jewelry on to compensate. If she'd been a man, I would've wondered what else she was trying to make up for.

And whoo boy, did she hate me. As we got closer, her skin began to darken. I'm sure my smile didn't help with that. It'd become genuine somewhere between the center of the room and the lip of the dais. She should have chosen a different gown. The bright red Frederick's of Hollywood number looked like shit with her mottling magenta complexion.

Brennan had gotten increasingly tense the closer

we got, but it wasn't like the club. Then he'd been dreading it. Here... Call me crazy, but it was like right before he gave me a present. He had that crooked little smile on his face when he stopped before her, lighting a cigarette sans Zippo. It didn't flare. Her eyes narrowed, and he barely tilted his head toward her in a mocking bow.

"Mother."

Amelda was less than amused. She completely ignored me, fixated on him...his bare wrist specifically, and then the ring.

She laughed, and it was damn near a cackle. "Talked her into shackling the beast, have you? Well, I suppose she looks better holding your leash than Silas." The room tittered politely as my father glowered at her from the far end of the table. What he looked like was shit, and now that we were closer, Amelda didn't look so hot either. Like, aged. It was too bad I didn't have a card for Calista's plastic surgeon, I totally would've given him a referral.

Amelda raised up a jeweled goblet, and the room went silent. That fake smile plastered itself across her face. "A toast to my son and his pet! I wish you both ever-fleeting joy."

She emptied the goblet onto the floor beside her, and the whispers started up again. Amelda kept smiling. I'm not sure how many people saw what happened next, but I sure as hell did. The shadow cast by the goblet moved to stroke her wrist. Her eyes widened, and she drew in a sharp breath through her ivory veneers. I had to give her credit though. That grin of hers didn't so much as flicker as she tossed the goblet from her with ill-feigned contempt. I mean, it probably

240

fooled the rest of the room, but I was close enough to see her eyes.

She was scared shitless.

Brennan took a lazy drag. "You're a fucking cunt."

There was a collective intake of breath, and I failed to swallow a laugh.

"I suggest you apologize to your mother," Horatio snarled.

To either side of her, he and Mica had leaned forward, low growls in their throats. Amelda's hands snaked out, landing on their shoulders as she stood. Whatever fear I'd seen had been replaced by rage. The tension in the room thrummed. I would've taken a step back if it hadn't been for Brennan's hand at the base of my spine. He calmly took another drag as Amelda addressed the room.

"Now is not the time, nor the place for discord. Brennan has made his allegiance clear, and I've wished him the joy of it." She snatched Horatio's goblet from his hand and held it up. "Tomorrow we'll settle our differences upon the board, as is right. Tonight, we feast!"

Her announcement was met with a few half-hearted cheers, and a smattering of applause. I looked at Brennan, and he flashed me a grin, then steered me toward the far end of the table, closest to the chamber orchestra and farthest from my father.

He was deep in discussion with a dae that looked like the Crypt Keeper and hadn't bothered to acknowledge my existence. That was fine by me. The rest of the table had a smattering of dae I didn't know, and then the Dowager. She gave Brennan a hint of a sly smile.

"Well done."

He gave her a much deeper bow than he had Amelda and pulled out a chair for me. I sat down in kind of a daze. He kissed my temple and took the last empty seat.

"Was that really wise?" Yeah, I actually asked that question. I couldn't believe it either.

"More so than you would think and extremely satisfying." He flicked his napkin out and placed it in his lap. I did the same, my eyes running over him. What kind of man had all of those compulsions bound?

Imps promptly came out with a salad of frisée, bacon lardons, and cherry tomatoes. It was like it'd been designed purposely to make a mess all over your shirt or grease up your cleavage. I took a sip of my drink. Implants my ass.

Brennan and the Dowager were way too chummy for comfort, chatting away about one thing or another I couldn't care less about. If he hadn't made that cryptic comment, I'd totally believe he was in her pocket. Christ, maybe he was, and I'd just read into the whole thing wrong. Gah, I hated all of it. Daemon games sucked.

The more I thought about the mess I was in, the pissier I got. I mean, I was used to being up to my ass in alligators, but they were my alligators. All this bullshit… Nah. I had the worst urge to engage in some drama of my own making. Because that would make things better.

Silas sat at his end of the table passing on the salad as well. I took an unhealthy amount of pleasure in his sallow complexion and sunken cheeks. He glowered at me over the rim of his cocktail like I'd pissed in his cornflakes. I was pretty sure he hated me as much, if not more than Amelda, but his hate wasn't all rabid batshit. It was cold, and that was a hell of a lot scarier.

I blew him a kiss.

He looked like he wanted to come at me over the table, and I laughed.

"You do like to keep things interesting, don't you," the Dowager remarked as an imp collected dishes. I shrugged. I think I told you I'm not real good with knowing when to quit, but I do know when to take a hint. I more or less kept my eyes on my plate for the rest of the meal.

I should say plates. And bowls. Some of them you didn't even eat out of, you just wet your fingers in. I sat through course, after course, after course. It was extravagant, indulgent, and a waste.

It was also mind-numbingly boring.

At least the imps were keeping me well-lubricated. I raised up another empty glass, way past buzzed, and well into blotto.

Amelda was eating all of it up. No, no, I'm not talking about the food. I'm talking about the constant stream of sycophants that stopped by to kiss her ass. I didn't pay too much attention after the first few, and trust me, it was better that way. Still, it pissed me off I wasn't able to use any of the zingers I was coming up with in response to all of the brown-nosing that was going on.

Around the time the swan was served swimming in a brandied plum sauce and re-feathered in its plumage, a soloist stepped up beside the orchestra and began an aria. She was a svelte little red-headed thing in a Grecian gown. Now, I'm not big on opera, but Jesus

Christ, I know a hack when I hear one. You'd think they could've skipped a couple courses and sprung for a professional. I closed my eyes and waited for the migraine.

Brennan laughed, kissing my cheek. He'd pulled his chair close when he caught me flicking peas at some woman. What? Her braids were wrapped around her head to make this coronet, cuppy—Whatever. He was seriously no fun sometimes.

"Wretched, isn't she?"

I would've used a stronger adjective. "How much longer do we have to stay?" I leaned against his shoulder, so done with all of it. That, and I could feel myself flirting with a blackout. Trust me when I say nothing good ever happened when I reached that point. If he thought peas were bad... The soloist mangled a sharp, and I winced. Blacking out might not be the worst thing if I stayed pointed in her direction.

"No one can leave until Amelda declares us sated. Don't you remember your lessons?" That smile was tugging at his lips. Asshole knew full well I was struggling to remember I was even at a table.

Oh wait, yeah, I did. This was the whole if you have to pee you get drawn and quartered thing. Crap. Now I had to go. The opening notes of "I Dreamed a Dream" killed the inclination, and a portion of my soul. Of all the show tunes... I felt the blood drain from my face, and that blackness in me start to burble. The door we'd come in through telescoped about two football fields farther away than it had been.

"I need to go." I meeped, trying not to hyperventilate. He frowned, his eyes flicking over my shoulder to the soloist. Guess that was one of the bits he remembered. She warbled out the opening lines, and a full-body shudder went through me.

"I need to go." My eyes were hot and very wide.

"Lovely, calm down, there's not a chance she'll let you, especially seeing you like this. You need to breathe, if you bolt, Amelda will kill you." He put his napkin on the table. "I'll handle it."

I whimpered, but he was right about leaving. Amelda was far too interested in seeing what was going on play out. She and the rest of the table were eating it up, but it wasn't her doing. I could tell she didn't understand why I was a mess.

Silas knew exactly what was going on.

Right. So, we kind of know each other now. I can tell you things.

Like, I had zero doubt Calista had clued Silas into my worst-case scenario. There's no other way he'd know about that song—Don't know it? YouTube the damned thing. I hear Anne Hathaway did a bang-up job. Whatever. Look, my point is, I didn't have any illusions that my mother had any use for me, I mean, other than selling me out, but she'd never gone out of her way to be cruel just for the sake of being cruel.

She'd opened my milk for me.

I know. Stupid, right?

I didn't think she could hurt me anymore, but her spilling my crazy did.

A lot.

And that son of a bitch was using it to punish me, positively gleeful I was about to have a mental break. A wave of panic started to crest just as the soloist was really getting into it. Like, the lyrics were spot on. It was all going really wrong, and I'm not just talking

245

about her pitch.

"It has indeed!" Brennan said loudly with a laugh, after she'd botched the line. He stood and went over to the soloist, taking one last drag off his cigarette. "Have a seat, darling. That really is quite enough. Here, take this with you." She stared at him open-mouthed and then went crimson, snatching the butt from his hand. He turned to the rest of the room, every one of them focused on him to the exclusion of all else. Damn, he had swagger. Where had that come from? My anxiety receded beneath the shock of it.

He rubbed his hands together, massaging his fingers and shaking them out as he spoke. "My apologies, but I'm afraid I couldn't sit idle through that. It's been some time, but if you'll all humor me, I've an urge to play." The room erupted into whistles and fervent applause. He gave a little bow, going to the piano. The woman sitting on the bench beat a hasty retreat. He said something to her and the rest of the orchestra, and they laughed as he sat.

He settled himself, then his eyes met mine, and his fingers met the keys.

It wasn't music.

Whatever he was manipulating those notes to do was nothing less than raw emotion, and I abruptly understood why Amelda had glommed onto him so tightly. What he could do was one of those things the fae coveted, and she had hoarded him away. To say he was talented… He wasn't a half-dozen bars into it, and there wasn't a dry eye in the room, mine included.

I don't know how you deal with "emotions," but I tend to ball them all up, eat them, wash 'em down with a shit ton of booze, then alternately beat the hell out of or cozy up to someone. I was already blitzed, but this time…

I'm not gonna say I ugly-cried, but it came close. Surprisingly, I wasn't the only one. Amelda was not on the list. She sat there expressionless, staring at Brennan playing, and I swear I could see the crow's feet etching out from the corners of her eyes.

What he was pumping through those keys… Man, I'd never heard anything like it. Then the song came to an end, and he segued right into some wickedly upbeat jazz piece. I laughed, and he smiled at me, jerking his head for me to come sit next to him. People had gotten up, pushing the tables back to dance, and some of the braver musicians had joined in. I wiped my eyes and just for the hell of it, tried pulling flame to sober myself up a bit.

Score. Not gonna lie, that was handy.

He grinned as I slid onto the bench beside him. "Light me a smoke, will you, Lovely?"

I laughed. Asshole. "That's why you wanted me over here?"

"Not just that." His eyes flicked back to the table.

Whatever. Amelda could kiss my ass. I reached into his jacket and pulled out his case and Zippo. It was weird. Sitting at that piano had changed Brennan… I don't know, lit him up somehow. He was so animated and more at ease than I'd ever seen him, like all this time he'd been holding a chunk of himself back. I lit his stupid cigarette and held it up to his lips.

"No, you first. Come on, let's see if you can make me drop a note."

I liked it. A lot.

Laughing again, I tried my damnedest, but the best

I could do was make him flub a few.

"Now I'll take that cigarette," he said, with a devilish grin as I pulled away. He started up another dance number, even more energetic than the first. Just about everyone was on their feet, and the entire feel of the room had changed. Suddenly people actually wanted to be there. Even my toe was tapping. The soloist had retreated to the edge of the room and was speaking with Silas. He didn't look particularly happy. I frowned, turning back to Brennan.

"Thank you."

He shook his head, reaching way down the keyboard, then back up again. "No. Thank you. I can't tell you how much I've missed this. Be patient with me. I'm a bit rusty. It'll get better once I'm warmed up."

"Get better?" He had to be kidding.

"Mmm, and what would you say if I told you that you sounded like an absolute angel upstairs, my divine diva?"

"I'd say you were full of shit."

Brennan laughed. "Fair enough, but false. Tell me, with your register, do you know 'Candy'?"

I did. "No."

He didn't bother to hide his smile as he rolled into it. I don't know if you're familiar, but it's one hell of a song, especially the Big Maybelle version. She was like the original Janis Joplin. Whatever. Look, I knew it, and you needed that kind of a voice to do it justice.

I wasn't biting.

"No?" He shrugged and segued back to a dance number slow enough for him to flick his ash. Damn, he was slick. He must've played with this orchestra before, because they were following his lead and jumping in after the first few bars of every song. I looked around the room. It had become a party.

Well, unless you were still sitting at the head table.

After that first song, Amelda had stood up all crocodile gracious and declared the clan sated. They'd completely ignored her. As you can imagine, that went over poorly. She and Horatio were deep in conference, arguing, and trying very hard to look like they weren't.

Epic fail.

The Dowager sat within earshot, her eyes half closed, fingers tapping lightly against the edge of the table. A smile was on her face. I wasn't sure if that was in response to Amelda's drama or the music. I didn't see Mica, and Silas had disappeared with that soloist.

"Mmm, just like old times, isn't it?"

My head snapped around.

The two dae from the bathroom had come up and were leaning against the piano on the other side of Brennan. His ex, Serena, toyed with the piano's key cover thingy. Bubble-butt watched her all slitty-eyed like a cat. He flicked his ash in their general direction, and she scowled at him, brushing at her skirts.

"If you're referring to you irritating the shit out of me by fucking around with my fall board, then yes."

Whoa. I was liking this new and improved Brennan more and more.

Serena slammed the cover thingy back with a nasty glare, and Bubble-butt smiled, licking her lush lips. She was way too smug about something. "Don't be like that. We just wanted to put in a request, play something by that composer… What was his name?"

"Mickael something," Serena supplied, watching his face.

Mine went livid. I couldn't believe she'd just dropped part of his true name like that.

He glanced up at her. "Fuck off. I don't do requests."

"Perhaps not tonight... I'll check back after the ball."

They laughed and melted into the crowd.

"God, they're miserable twats."

"You weren't kidding about her."

"No. Five, Kelly," he called over his shoulder as the song wrapped up. The conductor nodded and took the next piece. "Serena's relentless. I know this has all been a bit much, but things will calm down after tomorrow. We'll go back to the flat. You'd like that, wouldn't you? Spend a day down at the beach. We can take some time to figure things out, just the two of us."

I thought about that stupid salamander, and my chest got tight. I couldn't meet his eye.

He kissed my forehead with a sigh and stood, taking off his jacket and rolling up his sleeves. I looked up at his laugh. He smiled past me, and a huge dae came up and shook his hand, then pulled him in for a hug.

"Good to have you back, bro. Heard it got dicey. You make it all the way, or leave some behind?"

"Feels good to be back, and it was at that, but I've come through intact."

"Nice. Keep it wrapped until you need it." The dae turned to look at me. It was Jonas, the one who had pinned me after the whole Silas piano debacle. "Shit, I'd come back from the dead for that, too. Power of pussy, man."

"Asshole."

Jonas's grin stretched across his face, showing the ridiculously sharp teeth behind his tusks. He had to be part piranha. "Meow. S'a compliment, little Kitty, you bounce real nice. Boss-lady's put me and the other Riders on your detail tomorrow. Thought you might sleep better knowing."

Brennan clasped him on the shoulder. "I certainly will. I'll look forward to seeing you in the motorcade." Jonas grunted through his tusks and winked at me as he left. I raised an eyebrow at Brennan. What the hell was that about? He shook his head at me.

"You weren't listening at all during dinner, were you? The Dowager has arranged for our entourage. Every fae noble has one. The Riders usually escort her. It's a great honor that she's lending them to you for this, and it will remove any doubts she's adopting you into her household. No dae are more feared. It will give many pause."

But not all. Amelda had finished up her tête-à-tête with Horatio and was very busy getting drunk. Understandable, given the circumstances. Brennan had seriously pissed on her parade, and if she was anything like Calista, it was time to cue the retribution.

I grabbed a flute of champagne from a passing imp's tray and swallowed it down.

Nothing good had ever come of that.

18 Hours

The next morning at the breakfast table, I stared at the front page of Brennan's paper. It was taken up by a huge shot of protesters burning me in effigy. I was pretty certain the irony of that was lost on them, but their intent wasn't on me. I pushed Karen's crepes around my plate. For whatever reason, they weren't doing it for me this morning, and my stomach was a mess again.

But it was finally Midsummer's Eve, so at least I had that going for me.

The sitting room in the blue suite had a little nook with a table and two chairs. I missed the flat, especially after last night. I'd had no idea Brennan was some kind of celebrity on this side of the veil. Apparently, Amelda had compelled him into retirement for the past couple centuries, and the clan was over-freaking-joyed to attend his comeback concert. It was like Kurt Cobain had risen from the dead mid-Seattle. I think every dae in the room had stopped by at one point or another to gush over him. It was stupid, but I hated sharing him with freaking groupies and fan-boys. I think he knew it, which made it worse.

I was totally Courtney Love.

"Feeling all right, Lovely?"

See.

I was, at least from what he was referring to. That

flame thing? Worked on hangovers, too.

"Why didn't you tell me I could sober myself up?"

"Perhaps I thought it unwise for you to prematurely discover you could act like an ass with absolutely no repercussions or incentive to mend your ways."

I snorted. "Like I have incentive now?"

His eyes dropped down to my abdomen. "The thorns wouldn't bloom otherwise." He snapped his paper back up, and it was like a slap.

Wait, that was why—

Goddamn it. I felt like I was going to puke. I mean, you know what he was alluding to, right? The same bullshit Calista had tried to dig at me with, and look, I get it, the law of averages wasn't on my side with this. I'd pretty much spent the last solid month in bed with him and taken zero precautions…and yes, I was late, but he would've had to—

You know what, just no. I wasn't thinking about that or any—

Come on! I was supposed to be dead tomorrow!

God help me, I was running out of time, and I still didn't know what I was going to do… what I could do.

What could I do?

I had a really bad feeling whatever was going to happen, I had zero say in.

I started sweating, and my pulse thudded in my ears.

Brennan chucked his paper onto the table and lit a cigarette. This new him was throwing me for a loop. All that careful control was, not gone, but, I don't know, messier. It made me think about that first day at the flat and how everything was so pristine until you got to his office. I grasped at the chance to change the subject.

"What were all those books on your desk about, that first day I was at the flat?"

His head jerked up. "Hmm?"

"After you left, I went into your office and there were books all over the desk. Like weird religious stuff." I rubbed at my chest. My esophagus had started to burn. Something new to add to my panic attacks. Maybe I needed to cut back on the blueberries.

He exhaled with a little shrug. "I was trying to figure out more about what I'd signed up for. I've never seen a reconsecration and wanted to know more about what the ember held."

Well, that made two of us.

"Anything interesting?"

His smile was indulgent. "Lovely, I've told—are you sure you're feeling all right?"

I wasn't. My throat had started to close up, and I was having trouble breathing. That burn was just getting worse. I coughed, and his eyes went wide at the crimson spatter that landed on the table. His chair fell back as he tore around it to get to me.

"What did you—Peter! *Karen!*"

When no one answered, Brennan swore, grabbed me up, and poofed.

The next thing I saw was Kyle's bare ass pumping away at Morgana. Then he was flying across the room and she was screaming.

Things get fuzzy after that.

I was in agony. Like, something was scraping out my insides, then rubbing what was left down with rock salt. I could hear Brennan arguing with Morgana, and then with Kyle. The shadows in the room began to writhe, and the temperature dropped. Morgana was over me, yelling at everyone, and her hands were all fishy and cold.

You've probably figured it out already, but I'd been poisoned. Yeah. It'd come super close to killing me. Long story short, both Peter and Karen were missing, and her crepes really were to die for. So much for the Dowager's guest rights.

Brennan was beyond pissed. His form had bulked up to something easily in Horatio's ballpark, and he was having trouble reining the rest of it in. He was definitely a grower and not a shower. He paced the floor looking like he was going to rip something apart, and everyone that could make themselves scarce, had.

I was in bed. No, not that one. They'd brought me into a different room that didn't smell like a porn set. It did smell like fried eggs, and that was making me nauseous.

"I feel like I'm gonna puke."

Morgana handed me a trashcan. "Get used to it. You're pregnant."

She didn't have to sound so freaking smug about it.

Brennan stopped short. "Is it—"

"Fine, but if you hadn't gotten to me when you did, they'd both be dead. You owe me, twice."

He ran a shaky hand through his hair and came to sit beside me. "What do you desire?"

"I'll let you know." She tossed her hair over her shoulder, just pleased as freakin' punch as she left. God, she was a bitch. An imp passed her on his way in and yammered something at Brennan. His face got hard again, and he put an arm around me. I was digging the extra bulk. It was too bad I felt like shit.

"We're to stay here until the Riders come to collect

us for the ball. The Dowager feels it safer while she cleans house."

"Cleans house?"

He clucked his tongue, pulling out his case. "Breaking the Manse's peace is no small thing. When she finds out who's responsible, both they, and their associates, will be expunged very painfully and very publicly. The last time it happened was well before my time. Those who witnessed it describe the experience as…medieval."

I lay there against him, remembering that one glimpse I'd gotten of her face and didn't doubt it. Brennan's hand had come to rest on my abdomen, and I bit at my lip.

So, I kind of avoided delving into the subject earlier, but stupid Morgana just blurting it out like that…it was another freaking slap of reality. I was getting really sick of those, but look, there was another reason I hadn't reacted to Calista's assertion I was knocked up. Her "first time every time" theory was flawed, though I could see how normals would take it at face value. I'll just lay it out. Male fae have control over when they decide to get someone in the family way. How do I know? Half-fae guys can do it, too. We didn't correct their impression, because quite honestly, it was another F you, and until I'd been clued in on the whole right side of the veil thing, it made zero sense why halflings existed at all if fae were just coming over to get their rocks off.

All right, it still didn't make a whole lot of sense, unless they were a bunch of freaking sadists, which wasn't outside the realm of possibilities. I didn't think that explained why Brennan hadn't been shooting blanks though, and that bitch Morgana had just thrown it out on the table where I had to look at it. Now I couldn't stop.

"When... Why?"

The tip of Brennan's cigarette flared as he lit it. He blew out a long stream of smoke with a little shrug. "Since the beginning. I don't give a rat's ass about any of their politics, but when given the opportunity to throw a wrench into all of it, I couldn't resist. Still, it shocked the hell out of me when the thorns bloomed. Halflings are largely resistant to being bred. But I'd do it again, if only to deny Mica the pleasure. Be very certain that's the only reason things didn't go any further when he had you."

I laughed. What a fucking asshole.

My eyes got hot, and I rolled away, curling around my stupid stomach. And there it was. The reality of the situation. Like I'd said, good things didn't happen to me. Nothing had changed. The horse I'd been riding was dead. I was his goddamned assignment, and he'd fucking used me. It wasn't real, and I didn't want it to be. None of it. He brushed back my hair, spooning behind me. It felt good, and I hated him.

He didn't say anything, didn't apologize. Just held me.

I cried.

God, I was a pathetic mess. You'd think I'd be over myself by now. I wasn't even sure why I was crying. His arms tightened around me. I don't know why he bothered. I couldn't stand myself. Neither could anyone else. I kept seeing those people with my face on placards...the hate in their eyes. It was the Faith Hour all over again, except now normals wanted me dead, too. Was there anyone who didn't?

I just wanted to go back to that door and stream through it into the fire.

I'd be doing them all a favor.

Brennan stroked my hair, and that hurt more than any of it. He kissed the top of my head, and then he started saying stuff.

God, I didn't even know what to do with half of it. When he'd said he loved me it was terrifying enough when it was just sex, but now he said he wanted what regular people had, you know, like a life with that stupid salamander at the foot of the bed, and he said he wanted it with me, our kid—

Look, it's not important what he said.

It was stupid and lies like always, so why did it bother me so much? I'd said it myself. Fae had perfected the art of the mind-fuck. It was my own damned fault for pretending it was something else. God, I hated myself. A horrible ache had started in my chest, bad enough for me to break out in a sweat again. I needed to buy some stock in deodorant. I pushed him away, feeling sick.

I ran. I don't know where. Just out. Into that wood.

Every one of them wanted to use me, then throw me to the wolves like Calista had. People wanted me fucking dead because of her spun up narrative, and she just smiled and waved, no regrets. This wasn't any different. I fell down onto my knees in the bracken, panting, feeling things close in on me.

Christ, that was a lie. It was worse. He'd made me think he'd cared. Made me feel. Not even Calista had done that. A sob escaped my lips, and I gagged, feeling like I was going to throw up. I pulled my knees to my chest and started rocking. But it'd been real. Hadn't it? I raised my fists up to my temples and bit back another sob.

Berk found me.

I cried then too, but it was different. Berk had never wanted anything from me. Didn't expect things. He pulled me into in his lap and held me. There was something just safe about him. Steady. Platonic.

And he had a hip flask.

I told him about all of it. He listened and then was silent for a time.

"I have thought a lot on the nature of things this past year. What it means to be in this body. The soul that fills it. There are pieces of me that I can prune away and grow to be more pleasing. Others that I cannot change. I think… What has happened to you is the nature of fae, and of daemons. A conscience is a uniquely human facet, and even with the benefit of one, if you were in his stead, would you have done differently?"

I played with the cap on his flask, not wanting to answer. Berk knew anyways. If I'd been Brennan, I would've crawled through broken glass for the chance to screw Amelda over, never mind the rest of them. I wouldn't have given a shit about anything or anyone to do it, either. Even sadder, I'd totally be into the fuck-all-y'all he'd slapped down on the table if I didn't have to bear the brunt of it. For whatever reason, that made me feel worse.

"The Dowager said you've been put in a crucible, and I think she's right. You're very strong, Vy, but you're brittle. If you don't let yourself soften, you'll shatter. This dae… For better or worse, he has your heart along with your name. Perhaps the same is true of him. You want what he's offering you. There's no shame in admitting it or striving for happiness. I think you need to let yourself do both."

"But what if it's all a lie? What if—"

"I will kill him."

I looked up at that and his expression was stone, eyes fixed on a point past me. Brennan stood there, meeting Berk's stare, his hands jammed into his pockets. After a moment, he held one out to me, his eyes beseeching. Berk hugged me, and I let that loamy scent of him fill my lungs before I stood. He walked with me to Brennan.

"She is a sister to me. Hurt her, and I will spill your blood, dae."

Some unspoken man-thing passed between them, and Brennan grunted. Berk turned and disappeared into the wood. It was creepy. I mean, I'd heard Earth elementals could do that, but had never seen it.

Brennan tipped up my chin, making me meet his eyes again. They looked as broken as I felt. I hadn't thought about what me running out like that must've been like for him. Nice going, Vy. Man bares his soul, and you run screaming. God, I was an asshole.

"I'm sorry." I actually meant it. First time for everything.

"No, I am. I didn't think about... You've no idea how long I've been—" He dropped to his knees and pressed his face against my waist. I ran my fingers through his hair. His eyes when he looked up at me... "I swear I'm not playing you false. Say it, please. Speak my name and see the truth of me, who I am. Who you are to me."

I was terrified, but there wasn't anywhere else for me to run, and I was out of time.

Before I chose, I had to know.

I kneeled in front of him, leaning in close so I could whisper in his ear. He shivered as my lips brushed his lobe, and he let out a moan as I spoke his name.

His arms came up around me, and I was assailed with images and emotion…

But not before I heard him whisper mine back to me.

I'd never heard it spoken by another, and it laid me open, stripping away everything but my soul…and we knew one another. Intensely, intimately…all of it.

That son of a bitch.

Yeah, it sucked. He basically got to play fetch with my kicked dog, but he had one too, and his made Cujo look sweet. No bond formed between us, other than we'd seen each other exactly as we were without artifice.

Somehow, I'd ended up in the bracken, and he was looking down at me. We stared at each other, breath coming fast. I was pissed…and terrified…and vulnerable. My voice grated out in a husky whisper.

"Asshole."

I went to slap him, and he caught my hand, kissing its palm, unrepentant. "There's nothing I won't do to finish what I've started. If I'm going to keep us both alive, you have to trust me. Now you've no reason to doubt my intentions and have seen how I feel about you."

I had, and the depth of them terrified me. I mean, I didn't know his plans, but I knew exactly the kind of man he was. It wasn't the nice guy I'd pegged him for. I mean he was, but there was a bigger part of him that was way more vindictive than my petty ass. I also knew that my misconception of his nature wasn't his fault, but Amelda's. The layers of compulsion that she'd laid on him...she'd softened everything about his being until he was as worn down as midterm eraser. He was meant to be razor sharp and ruthless. God, it was no wonder he played piano the way he did. It was the only outlet he'd been allowed, and then she'd taken that from him, too.

I also cannot overstate the importance of the fact that he'd just been subjected to all my crazy and wasn't halfway to Mexico.

He let my hand go, and I touched his cheek. Ran my fingers over his jaw.

"Still mad?"

"Less."

"I love you, Vy." He smiled and kissed me like he meant it. My legs wrapped around his waist, and his hips pressed into mine.

What? Oh my God, shut up. Evil Brennan was like different dinner and just as delicious. Who doesn't want to bang hot twins? I'd be lying if I said I didn't get off on the personality shift. You're just gonna have to go with me on this one when I say it was all good.

God, was it good.

I almost took a drag of his cigarette afterward.

"Will you change what you're called now?"

"Not until this is finished. That would give the game away. Pick one for me?"

"I already have." I went to whisper it in his ear, and he pulled away with a little growl, kissing me. The blue in his eyes had become threads of silver.

"No. Tell me after you become."

I sighed and snuggled down against his shoulder. Don't get me wrong. I was still terrified, but I wasn't terrified of him, per se, though there was plenty that should scare me.

Look, Brennan wasn't kidding about being a fiend, and he was old. Older than I'd thought. Old enough to have seen some shit and to have caused a lot more of it. Very little regret went along with that, and what there was could be only attributed to being caught. Fae were different from normals like that. They were big on might making right.

But then there was the noble stuff. He was loyal to a fault, and his word his bond. I didn't have to worry about him sneaking around with any of those stupid groupies or fan-boys behind my back, and he'd lay his life down for mine. Driving all of it was an iron freaking will. He was utterly implacable in his goals, and after seeing that in him, I could understand how he kept the fiend under wraps.

I wasn't afraid of him, but I was kind of afraid of what he would do. Like, the kind of afraid you get at the beginning of a slasher flick. I was pretty sure it was going to be a horrible freaking mess, but at the same time, I couldn't tear my eyes away, and I was totally bringing popcorn.

He propped himself up on one elbow. I smiled and picked a leaf out of his hair. I didn't even want to know what mine looked like. From his grin, it must've been pretty bad… Then he got all serious.

"Will you, Lovely? Tell me you'll become and give this, us, a chance?"

He brushed the backs of his fingers across my cheek, waiting.

I couldn't tell him no, and I didn't want to. I tried to ignore that little voice screaming inside me, tensing for the blow when it all came crashing down...

I did more than just not say no. I said yes.

Shut up. I... Just shut up.

The smile that broke across his face... He kissed me, and then we were back in the room, and I didn't have to talk anymore.

I spent the majority of that last day asleep against Brennan's chest, worn out from all of it. He didn't object. A knock on the door woke me up, and Peter poked his head in. I guess he and Karen had been waylaid and locked in a closet. They'd found them pretty quickly after everything happened, but still hadn't any idea who was responsible for it, or for poisoning my crepes.

Karen helped me get ready and brought in my gown. It hung on me, but it was beautiful. High necked and an opalescent gray, artful tatters of iridescent cloth framed my chin, then clung close, flowing down into a fitted bodice. A satin sash encircled my hips and an offset profusion of ribbons and pearls trailed to the floor. The skirts billowed out in a cloud of gossamer, scattered with the tiny gemstones. More were in my hair, with combs to match. Earrings were in my ears.

Karen took the dress in the best she could. I was handed long gloves and slid them on. She fastened the tiny buttons inside the wrists and added the cuff Brennan had given me. I stared at the lump my fae-band made beneath the fabric, biting at my lips. I was still terrified, but maybe... I don't know. I was just

264

going to leave it at maybe.

After tonight everything would be different.

I could be, too.

Karen stepped away, evidently satisfied. She should be. Somehow she'd turned me into a decidedly non-PG fae-tale princess. I stared into the mirror...

Mirror, mirror... What the hell had I agreed to?

Brennan laughed in the other room and came in, his tailed-tux so black it ate the light. He was smiling ear to ear. God, he was too damned handsome, too good to be true—

No. Tonight I wasn't listening. It was real. If I said it enough, maybe I'd convince myself. Fake it 'til you make it, right? I could do that. I'd been doing it all my life. His eyes took me in with a sweeping glance of delight. I went to him without a word, and he kissed me.

"My God, Lovely... Pardon the phrasing, but you truly are the fairest of them all." I blushed. For whatever reason, when he said it, it didn't sound like a cheesy pickup line. All right, maybe it did, but I didn't mind. I took his arm when he offered it.

We went down a short hall and into a stone foyer. Berk and Kyle were there in tuxes, and Morgana was in a sea-foam green gown. My pearls were bigger than hers, and she sniffed. I smirked. Brennan looked them all over.

"You know what you're doing?"

"Yeah, man, the imps have been drilling us," Kyle said, pulling at his cravat. He'd gotten a haircut, and it looked bizarre all slicked back and tamed. Guarantee that wasn't going to last. He ran a hand through it, proving me right.

"As soon as the mists close around the mesa, it's cut off from the realms. You need to be with your element, preferably on the board, when that happens. If you're not in your territory, they'll throw you into the strath. We won't be able to help you if that happens."

Morgana rolled her eyes. "Yes, we know. Interference of play is punishable by death. We've been warned a hundred times."

Brennan frowned, taking a top hat and gloves from Peter, and glowering at her as he put them on. "Well, then I've nothing more to do with you. Good luck. Envy?"

I'd just given Berk a hug and Kyle a peck on the cheek. Morgana and I eyed each other and left it at that. I totally looked better. I could tell Kyle thought so, too. Not that I cared. I took Brennan's arm, and Peter held the door for us.

A long black limousine was waiting outside, flanked by Jonas and his brothers on Harleys. Brennan went over to shake his hand. The gas tank was a brilliant white with scrolling script that read "Conquest." The one on the far side of the limo that I could see was blood-red and stamped with "War." I had a sinking suspicion the other two were "Pestilence" and "Death." I laughed, and they looked at me funny.

"Riders, like, of the Apocalypse?"

Jonas's lips split into a wide grin. "Hey, yeah. You heard of us?"

He asked me like they were a garage band or something. I laughed again and let Brennan help me into the limo. I slid into the seat and sat back, thinking tonight wouldn't be so bad, and that I could handle it. Maybe even what would come after.

Sorry; I'm laughing again.

Silas was at the other end of the limo with a cocktail.

7 Hours

Brennan closed the door and sat next to me. He saw Silas and growled, his form wavering again. My father laughed, and it didn't sound particularly robust. The LEDs lining the roof of the limo's interior weren't doing him any favors, either.

"Did you really think you'd be able to avoid me completely?"

Brennan pulled out his case, glaring at him. "Can't imagine why I'd want to do that."

"I can," I muttered.

Silas's lips curdled at me before his attention returned to Brennan. "Our agreement was for you to keep Envy secure."

"Being flayed precluded my ability to deliver on that arrangement."

Silas rolled his eyes, his expression clearly "but did you die?" What a prick.

"You know my intent was to keep her from garnering the Dowager's attention. Whatever possessed you—"

"We didn't discuss motive." Brennan blew out a long stream of smoke, clouding the air. "If we had, I'd have told you she was already aware of the situation in its entirety."

I kind of had to laugh at that, considering Silas had screwed Brennan over with the same dick line. My father was less than amused. Like, about as much as I cared that he wasn't.

"And impregnating her?"

Brennan smirked around his cigarette. "I didn't hear any stipulations to the contrary, and with a temporary stay from Amelda's proscription, I felt it my patriotic duty."

Wait, what?

"It's complicated things considerably."

Brennan's grin was massive. "Yes, it has, hasn't it?"

I wanted to know why, but now wasn't the time to ask.

My father looked like he was ready to give that flaying another go, but I was pretty positive Brennan could take him now. So was Silas. He settled back in his seat. "We still have a contract." He eyed Brennan's ring. "Despite some provisions becoming moot."

"I'm aware, and here I am, fulfilling it, though my incentive to act on your behalf has become rather lackluster. What are you prepared to do about that?"

"No more than I already have."

"Oh?"

My father smirked, rolling a mouthful of liquor around before he swallowed, then smacking his lips. "If it's quite all right with you, I prefer to keep the details closeted, but the end result should suit both our needs."

Brennan's knuckles on his free hand went white, and his form wavered. Silas had that "but did you die" look on his face again, and after a moment, Brennan grunted and sat back. I swear, fae innuendo was its own goddamned language, and it pissed me the hell off. What just happened?

Silas poured himself another drink. "Are you prepared to move forward?"

"There's nothing left preventing me from doing so."

"Ah, then as I see it, we're still in the position to help one another."

They went back and forth with more cryptic references, but honestly I was less annoyed about being in the dark after that first exchange than you would think. I was just kind of sitting there watching Brennan, trying to keep my jaw shut.

He was a freaking shark.

I told you fae live to bargain and are totally cutthroat, but I hadn't actually experienced—What? Well, yeah, I'd bargained, but that was like them playing checkers with a three-year-old. This was a whole 'nother level.

Brennan had always gotten this kind of intensity to him when we'd make a deal, but holy crap. Him and Silas? All I could do was just sit back and listen to them twist words as they haggled. You could tell they were both getting off on it, and I'll be honest, I was too. Seeing Brennan like that was freaking hot.

Taking that shackle of Amelda's off his wrist had definitely unleashed something.

"Agreed. Once she's deposed and Envy names me warlord, we can proceed."

And again. Wait—what?

They shook, and Brennan sat back, putting his arm around me. He lit another cigarette, the air in the limo already dense, and smiled at my confusion. "The Cleansings, Lovely. They have to stop. Fae's lost too many generations as it is. This recent spate has torn it.

270

The Council has decided to intervene, and war is dae business…in particular, clan Malten's. Holding the title of warlord will effectively make Silas second in command to our queen."

I swallowed at Brennan's expression. He meant me.

"Yes, and who better than your loving father? I've already begun rounding up those inciting the violence," Silas said with a funny smile.

God, I hated him.

"What do you mean you've lost too many generations?"

Brennan flicked his ash to the floor. "The female fae fertility rate has been close to zero for well on nigh a millennium. Bringing halflings across is the only way we've sustained our population. Male fae are required to breed humans and encouraged to do so frequently."

"Pity so few of our get show the necessary qualities to become. But that is a self-limiting problem, now, isn't it?" The smug asshole smirked into his drink again.

I was floored. My parents were two peas in a goddamned pod.

Sorry, but you see what Silas did right there, don't you? This latest Cleansing had been triggered by all that bullshit with Calista and the Priory. Like, he'd literally instigated a halfling genocide so he could rationalize going to war with normals for carrying it out, making himself big man on campus.

And if his fingers were in that pie, I was pretty positive the Dowager had baked it to drum up support for her whole reincarnation thing. Talk about wheels within freaking wheels, and I was the goddamned hamster.

I did kind of have to snicker about him playing Calista so hard. It was too bad she'd just had her face done, but I was sure her lack of expression would still be—

Hmm? Oh, the breeding thing. Well, yeah, it was super sketchy using normals as hosts for their spawn, but it wasn't like we were bursting out of their abdomens and eating them. Anyways, I wasn't exactly in the position to decry the practice. I did wonder what that necessary quality quip was about, but honestly, Silas was a dick, and he'd probably said it to piss me off.

I mean, it did, but more on principle than anything else. Look, I couldn't get all teary and say I'd lost plenty of friends, because I didn't have friends. Well, okay, Berk, but that was only because Berk's, well, Berk. But in general, halflings don't get real cozy with anyone. You can't, and after the whole abandonment thing, most of us have some serious trust issues.

I had them even without being abandoned. Christ, I probably would've been better off.

Whatever.

So I was in this smokey limo, and the two of them were just tickled about the deal they'd made. Each of them sitting back smug, thinking about how they'd gotten the better end of the deal. It definitely gave me more perspective on the whole impregnating thing. I mean, Silas had literally gouged out Brennan's stigmata with the intent of him imploding like a supernova to start his war, and the both of them were sitting not six feet apart like it was no big deal.

I guessed I was going to have to stop taking people

wanting to kill me so personally. Talk about cultural differences. Anyways, we'd slowed down and had been moving forward incrementally, like we were in a line.

The glass partition at the front of the limo dropped down, and I could see a crowd through the windshield. "We're coming up to the carpet, sir."

Brennan stubbed out his cigarette and straightened his lapels. Silas brushed off a sleeve. I drummed my fingers on my knee. What? I was as good as I was gonna get. Well, I'd thought so. Brennan fussed with a stray lock of my hair, then kissed me.

"You ready? This is what we've been working towards. Let's nail it, shall we?"

I smiled at him, envisioning the lid of my coffin.

The door opened, and Jonas stuck his bristly head in, giving us a nod. Brennan got out, and there was a volley of flashbulbs. My stomach was eating itself again. A literal red carpet stretched up a wide, tiered staircase. I couldn't see what was at the top. Hell, I couldn't see how far up it actually went. My feet hurt just looking at it.

I took Brennan's hand and let him help me out. A crowd of press had been roped off. Jonas's presence shadowing us ensured they stayed well back from the velvet swag. We were peppered with questions as we started up the steps. Brennan didn't stop, and I sure as hell wasn't going to.

The first tier leveled off, and there was a wide landing. More stairs headed upward. A glowing pearlescent fog hedged in the staircase, occluding everything beyond. It cut off sharply around us, roiling as if behind panes of plexiglass. Above was an inky black sky, studded with stars. I couldn't see the moon.

The landing and the steps were that worn, ancient-looking marble. You know, Parthenon type stuff. The edges were all like melty butter. The carpet was definitely new and cut across it all in a swath of scarlet. Fae were standing in small groups, most of them scary as hell. Christ, one leviathan-looking dude had a spiked crest. My fingers tightened on Brennan's arm, and he put it around me.

"This is where we pick up the rest of our security detail."

Right on cue, three of the more intimidating dae separated themselves out and flanked us. Even the guy with the crest gave them a wide birth. I glanced at Brennan, and he shot me a brilliant smile.

"The Riders have a bit of a reputation, even for fiends."

Jonas winked at me.

Fiends. My escort was four—no, five—fiends. I laughed, and we began to move toward the second staircase, fae splitting for us like a pair of aces on a blackjack table.

Surprisingly, I recognized the Riders. Two were the big guys that'd held Silas during the piano debacle. The third was the Crypt Keeper that he'd been talking to at the feast. Guess I knew who was riding the bike named "Death."

And speaking of Silas, I've no idea where he went. I didn't think he'd gotten out of the limo. Maybe he was pissy about those dae, or just couldn't handle all the stairs. I was having doubts that I could, and wondered if the mesa was handicapped accessible. The ACLU would have a bird if someone dropped a dime.

Whatever, the rest of the detail fell in, flanking us,

with Jonas bring up the rear. We continued upward.

I'm not gonna lie. It was a lot of freaking steps, and doing them in four-inch heels? I was in no goddamned mood by the time we hit the next landing. I was even in less of one when I saw another staircase.

Mother f—

Brennan laughed at my expression and led me over to a bar that'd been set up. "Bit of an inconvenience, isn't it?"

I glared at him, about this far away from taking one of the damn stilettos off and stabbing him with it. He ordered us a round, the Riders staking out a bubble of space around us. There were other parties like ours up here, and some couches. I plunked down on a barstool, my skirts foofing around me.

The bartender slid a martini in front of me. Looking around, I noted that seemed to be en vogue. And before you get on me about the whole drinking while pregnant thing, it's not the same for fae. One of the benefits of having a metabolism that will let you live for several millennia is you can get away with stuff like that. Same deal with Brennan's lack of emphysema.

Whatever. I had a martini and checked my posture, resigned to playing the part. It wasn't just dae up here, and I tried to unobtrusively check out the crowd as I sipped my drink.

So in case I haven't spelled it out, you can tell a fae's affinity just by looking at them. Like, Earth elementals are, well, earthy. They're all some kind of green or brown. None of them here was that same rich loam color as Berk, but they all trended big like him, or willowy, with not much in between.

Air was just straight-up Aryan. Sylphs ranged every shade of blonde, blue eyes, and I don't know, were sunny. They also were congregating as far from Earth as possible.

I didn't see any Water elementals, which are probably just as well, because there were a lot of dae. You know our rundown. Dark hair, gray eyes, look like they're about to steal your lunch money—

Water? I don't know, lank blondes gone chlorine-green or greasy brunettes. Fish are all limp and soggy looking. Think over-cooked noodles. They're all just kind of sad like that.

Anyways, a few had come up to talk with Brennan. Not fish—some of the other fae. Word of his comeback must've spread fast and furious. I told you, he was like some kind of popstar, but with actual talent. I tuned out, chomping on an olive as he schmoozed.

"—my fiancée, Envy."

I inhaled the olive, coughing like I was gonna die. The bartender brought me over a glass of water, and Brennan patted me on the back all concerned, but his eyes were laughing at me. The group he'd been speaking to watched with varying degrees of curiosity…and suspicion. Shit. I pulled it together and tried to recover with Calista-esque bravata. As soon as I could breathe, I giggled like one of those party girls I hated.

"Oh! I still can't believe my luck, and every time I hear that—" I simpered at him. He was trying not to laugh as I fanned at my eyes. Asshole. "I'm just so blessed."

Yeah, I know. Cue the vomit.

But it won me plenty of murmurs of approval

amidst the eye rolls. More importantly, no one seemed inclined to split me open and root around in my chest. I took it as a win. Brennan wrapped things up, then helped me off the stool, and we made our exit.

He didn't start chuckling until we were on those damn stairs. I wanted to kill him.

"Your fiancée—"

"Do you know what I love about you?"

Whatever I'd been about to spit at him died on my tongue. He pulled me to him.

"I love how you're so completely oblivious to your effect on everyone around you, unless you're trying to manipulate them. Every man in that bar, and more than one of the women, was absolutely drooling over you. I don't share well and thought that a better deterrent than tearing them asunder. Shall I go back and correct their impression that you're my intended?"

My breath caught. He'd just called me a self-absorbed bitch and threatened to murder a bunch of people for looking at me.

Christ, it made my panties drop.

We've already established I have issues. "What do you intend to do with me?"

"Dirty, filthy things." He gave me that crooked smile of his, and I was game. "Tonight may go smoother than I'd envisioned if you're able to continue pulling that off."

I snorted. "You really want me to keep pretending I'm some ditzy bimbo?"

His fingers trailed down the side of my cheek, to my neck. "The less they think of you, the less they'll expect you to slit their throats when they're not looking."

Then he kissed me, slow and deep.

Yeah, I know. Holy who is this guy and what did you do with Brennan? But I gotta tell you, the whole best-served-cold vindictive vibe he was rocking was a serious turn on. I mean, don't get me wrong, I dug the nice-guy thing, but this…

God, he got me hot. Like he was my cake, and I was going to eat him, too.

One of the Riders cleared his throat, and Brennan pulled away with a little growl. I laughed, stealing another kiss and putting my hand on him. His chest rumbled as he removed it and kissed my knuckles.

"That's not going to help me climb these steps, Lovely."

"Why can't we just poof?"

"Part of the Proscriptions. The mesa is used for rituals and can only be accessed or exited by foot. This is the last staircase. Then we go through the trials."

"Trials?"

He gave a sour grunt. "You'll see. Each element has control over certain aspects of the strath. In order to pass through, each must be submitted to in turn. They're not difficult, in and of themselves… But we all do our best to make it as unpleasant for the other elementals as possible."

Sounded fan-freaking-tastic. He offered me his arm again. I took it.

The last of the steps had brought us up onto a landing that extended out for about ten feet and then dropped abruptly. Kind of like my jaw as I tried to wrap my head around what I was seeing.

Brennan laughed, lighting a cigarette. "Not what you were expecting?"

Uh, no. Stay with me now, 'cause this was weird.

Apparently the four realms of Fae intersect in the center of a massive caldera. If I'd known I was hoofing it up the side of a freaking volcano, I'd have rented a sherpa. Those steps must've been built where some ancient flow had broken loose and cut down the side into the daemon realm.

And they'd turned it into a seriously fucked-up arena.

The caldera below was roughly circular and easily a couple miles across. The outer perimeter was set up like a steeplechase course. It had been segmented into distinct quadrants. One was a pastoral field, then it looked like some kind of a wetland, a pretty painted canyon shrouded in mists, and a stretch of desert. Lamp posts were sprinkled throughout, and the four sections were separated by ornate metal gates. They were that harsh black that only comes with wrought iron. What the hell would iron be doing in the heart of Fae?

That wasn't my only question.

Smack-dab in the middle of all that was basically Ayer's rock. Well, maybe not that tall. The thing stood around three or four stories. A fae probably wouldn't die if they fell off, but they'd be messed up.

Whatever, same concept. It was a ginormous rock in the middle of a pit, and it had a massive chessboard set on top of it. Yes, seriously. I could just make out faint orchestra music and see ant-sized twirling forms on the center of it. Carpenter, not sugar. The board was lit by those tall lamp posts and strewn with colorful tents and pavilions laid out like a painter's palette. Right at the board's edge, platforms and bleachers looked out over the rest of the valley.

"That's the mesa," Brennan said coming up behind me. "The strath is the portion around it where the scrum will be." He pointed down at the steeplechase part below.

"Is it a game?"

Brennan laughed, a mischievous glint in his eyes I hadn't seen before. "You'll see."

Fine. I could wait, but what I did not see was how to get from point A to point B.

I told you the landing we'd climbed to went for maybe another ten feet, and then ended like it'd been sliced off. One of the Riders had edged up and peered over the side. The other two waited by us, and Jonas was still bringing up the rear. Brennan flicked his butt over the edge.

"The lift takes a bit, Lovely. Be patient."

Lift?

A minute or two later, a construct of brass rose up from below, and one of the Riders opened a little gate when it came to a stop. It was a freaking elevator. Why couldn't he just say that? Brennan motioned for me to get in. I did but wasn't thrilled about it. I'm not particularly squeamish about heights, but we were high. Like high, high. I hadn't been kidding about the ant thing, and dropping down to the strath in what equated to a gilded bird cage with three seriously stacked Dae, and two more that weren't anything to sneeze at, had me looking for that little "do not exceed this weight" tag.

There wasn't one, and I couldn't help but notice there weren't any cables or pulleys either. My stomach burbled, and I got a little dizzy. I stumbled against Jonas.

"Easy there, Kitty. You'll make your old man jealous."

"You bothered by heights?" Brennan asked, gathering me in his arms.

"No, by the lack of anything holding us up." I closed my eyes and pressed closer into him. He kissed my forehead.

"Air operates the lift. It will be over soon."

I was too busy feeling sick to really pay attention. The whole making-things-unpleasant what's-it he'd been talking about? Air had definitely checked off that box. I skipped oohing and ahhing over the view.

It was way too long before I felt the gentle bounce of the elevator touching down. We exited onto a wide stone pier. At the end were several gondolas floating at the ready. My knees buckled, and Brennan caught me up against him.

Oh, please God, no.

So, I mentioned earlier that dae don't have an issue with water. We do have massive issues with boats. I could literally freebase that motion-sickness stuff, and just thinking about being in one will still make me puke. I regretted eating. Like, ever.

I'm not going to detail what happened next, other than to say I was ill. Violently so and had to be hauled out of that goddamned dinghy and carried the rest of the way to the mesa. I've no idea what the dae contribution was to all of it, other than hot. Earth's trial was dark and close before it brought us up onto the chessboard, and I didn't get a good look at that, either. My face was buried in Brennan's neck for all of it, and I felt awful.

When he finally put me down, it was in a big tent with wide couches and a lot of scattered pillows. I wasn't the only one in there looking worse for wear, which made me feel better—well, my ego at least. Jonas brought me a glass of water and some crackers, then went back to stand perimeter. I nibbled on them, feeling miserable. Brennan and the Riders were completely unfazed.

"I'm sorry."

"Don't be. You're the epitome of an expectant fae lady." He put a hand on my stomach and warmth spread out from it. "Does that help any?"

It did, and I said so. "I decided I'm not mad about it anymore."

His eyebrow raised. "No?"

I crunched on my cracker and shrugged. Berk had made a valid point, and it was stupid to be pissed at him for something I totally would've done. Hell, I'd been glad when I saw Silas's face in the limo.

"Why did it mess up everything?"

Brennan pulled out a cigarette and tapped it on his knee. "Because while you carry my child, no other can be named your consort. I've locked up any potential betrothals your Guardian could make upon your behalf, stopping them from making political alliances, and gotten a claim on clan Malten's heir, should it be female. It also forced the Dowager to prematurely play her hand and involve herself overtly, something both Amelda and Silas were hoping to avoid. She's reclusive, but when she does exert her prerogative, it's more often than not unpleasant to be on the receiving end."

I blinked a lot at all of that. "I thought you said you didn't give a rat's ass about politics."

He flashed me that crooked smile, his cheek

dimpling. "I don't. Screwing all of them over is another thing entirely."

That I could totally understand, except for one thing. "I got the impression you and the Dowager were close."

"We get on quite well when it suits her. She's pleased that I'm able to play for her again." He lit his cigarette and gave me a look. I sighed. He wasn't going to give me any more than that. "Now that we're here, we have to make an appearance on the board, then check in at the main pavilion. Until the mists close in, everything stands at detente, but once the scrum starts, things will become hectic. Anyone who has a feud is free to settle it tonight. I want you on my arm the entire time. It's very easy to get lost in the chaos."

"You keep saying that word, scrum. What does it mean?"

He grinned and kissed me. "I won't spoil the surprise, but I think you'll like it."

I didn't push the issue. He'd given me enough to think about and had that golden ticket look. I was content to let him have his fun. His thumb skated over my abdomen, and he grinned again. My cheeks warmed, and I had to look away. An imp was called over to freshen my makeup, and then we exited the tent, the Riders keeping us within that bubble between them.

I wasn't prepared for what was outside. It was something out of, well, Fae.

I mean, I'd seen the checkerboard floor from up high, but hadn't been able to tell it was massive squares of quartz interlocking with obsidian. The sheer size... We were standing on a black square that probably equaled two football fields. Brennan told me there were sixty-four of them when I asked.

I supposed it needed to be that large, because literally every elemental, with or without a solid form, was in attendance. Fae strolled and drifted about, congregated in groups and in pairs, flew solo and in formation. They came in every shape and size, ranging from circus-style freak to plain vanilla normal. I had no idea what half of them were, and more than one looked like it wanted to eat me. I held onto Brennan's arm and tried not to act like a complete tourist, but it was super hard. He had a smirk on his face that I probably would've found irritating if I wasn't so busy shaking the weird little pod things out of my skirts. They'd gotten entangled as they bounced past.

At the very edge of the board stood those tall gas lampposts and then aluminum bleachers. Wooden platforms were between them, overlooking the strath. There wasn't a guardrail or anything else before the floor just dropped off. I made a mental note not to stand close enough for Amelda to push me off.

Erected behind the seating was an elaborate rainbow of pavilions in every color you could imagine. Beyond the white one we'd been in, they were ocher and olive, leaf green, and loam. The ones I could see to the east trended toward sea-foam and cerulean. Brennan put a hand on my arm laced through his, moving us through the crowd and leaving the edge of the board behind us.

Above, the heavens unfurled across the expanse, an ombre velvet of midnight and purple. The moon was a sickle, its tips sharp reaching talons, punching the stars from the fabric of the sky. The night was still young, and it hung low in the southeast, the mists still teasing it as they parted just so. Here, they drifted low upon the ground, spiraling up as we came to the edge of the dance floor. Fae glided and swept across the squares, each couple a microcosm of beautifully cultured cruelty.

I had no illusions as to what becoming meant.

Brennan and I joined the dance.

The music... It was teasing and low. Like secrets overheard. The whisper of perfume in an empty room. A flavor that lingers after the kiss. All of these filled my senses on its haunting refrains, and we were caught up.

The moon had risen a handsbreadth when the currents of song brought us to the far side of the floor. Brennan pulled me close, his hands trailing down my back, that smile on his lips as he kissed me.

"You are divine. Ready to check in?"

I nodded, muzzy and soft, all of it a dream. I was glad when he took my hand, tethering me to him, else I was sure I'd float away.

We threaded in and out of tents of scarlet and carmine, burgeoning with dae. Some passed, others paused. There were conversations and laughter. A flute of something was pressed into my hands, and I forgot to drink it. Then it was gone, and we stood in front of a towering pavilion, this one pomegranate. Tiny gold bells dripped and ting'ed from the awning above its entrance and on scarves swathing its sides.

Brennan was brushing my hair back from my forehead, his lips moving like he was speaking to me, but I couldn't... He tried again, patting at my cheek.

"Lovely, you need to call a bit of flame to clear your head. Ah, yes, that's right. Better?"

No. Everything was abruptly jarring, I pressed my

face against his shoulder. His hand came up to cradle the back of my neck.

"One more time. The Lethe swings in close to this edge of the mesa, and there's a fog tonight. I'm afraid it's the real deal, not that bosh at the club. You need to burn it away if you feel yourself slipping, else you'll forget. That's a girl. We've made it half through, and you've done brilliantly. Just this bit, then onto the scrum. You remember what I told you?"

"Stay close to you." I'd called enough flame to steady myself, that weird dream-like state receding into the background. I could taste it on the breeze now, the sweetness of oblivion dusting across my skin. I licked my lips, liking it.

"Yes, that's right. Come on then."

He steered me into the tent's maw, arm around my waist. I couldn't help but notice the Riders seemed a lot tenser, and one of them had a cut above his eye, still in the process of healing.

My pulse sped up. What had I missed?

Brennan followed my gaze and gave me a smile that I was sure he meant to be reassuring. "Nothing to worry about."

I called more flame to steady myself, very much doubting that.

5 Hours

Inside the pomegranate pavilion was a clamorous mass of dae. I recognized a few of them from the feast, but the vast majority were unknowns.

The Riders were not.

They cut through the crowd in a wedge, and we followed in their wake to a long table at the back of the room. Three male dae sat behind it, scribbling in thick ledgers. Behind them were a wall of screens with constantly updating numbers beside lines of unfamiliar characters. A ticker with more of the same scrolled along the top.

One of the men with sweeping ram's horns curving back from his shock of gray hair looked up over his glasses as we approached. He smiled broadly at Brennan and stood to shake his hand.

"Good to see you, my boy, good to see you! I can't tell you how happy I am the rumors are true. Back to yourself, are you? Tell me you've a concert in the works."

"Ah, not as of yet…" Brennan's eyes were glued to the screens as he pulled out a billfold thick with cash. "How are we looking in the second quad this year?" He leafed through it, listening to what boiled down to odds. Hey, I didn't know a lot about a lot, but I knew a bet being placed when I heard one.

It was another conversation I tuned out. Brennan

asked me to pick a number at one point, and then to choose between black and white. I almost asked if I could blow on his dice but figured that wasn't something a lady would say.

See, I could behave when I wanted to.

Ok, let me amend that. When I needed to. More than a few of the dae in here were taking an unhealthy amount of interest in us, and the whispering was easily ten times worse than it had been at the feast. Like, enough where I couldn't ignore it. I thought it best to avoid contentious behavior.

Look at me all grown up. Hah.

Whatever, I stood there channeling doting party girl as I hung on Brennan's arm. I wasn't particularly thrilled with the role I'd been given but figured I'd treat this whole thing as one big satirical social commentary cosplay.

Say that five times fast.

All right, look. I was taking that throat slitting comment of Brennan's to heart. There were more than a couple bitches giving us both the up and down that were begging to be added to my list. I struggled to keep my expression vapid.

Brennan tucked away his billfold and watched the screens for a moment more before giving a little grunt. Something there had made his brow furrow. He did a double take at my expression and laughed, kissing me, then pressed his forehead to mine.

"Is it that bad already?" My eyes flicked to a dae in a slinky black dress before I could help myself, and his grin widened. "The jealous type, are you? I have to say, I rather like that, but you've no cause to worry. None of them holds a candle to you."

"Kiss me like you mean that." I pouted, playing with his lapels.

He obliged, and my knees went weak. "Does that suit?" His lips teased mine again, and I wanted to jump him. Stupid ball. He laughed with that crooked smile. "Let's get our obligations out of the way. You don't want to miss the start of the scrum." He was absolutely gleeful at the prospect, and I had to smile, regardless of whatever obligations he was talking about.

To either side of the betting table there were curtains, and beyond them, the pavilion kept going. The Riders cut ahead of us into a large reception area. A buffet was to one side, and imps bearing silvered trays of hors d'oeuvres and champagne moved around the space. The farther we got into the room, the tenser Brennan became.

"What's the matter?"

"I don't see Amelda's throne."

I didn't either, though there were four considerably more tasteful ones on a dais toward the back. The women sitting in them were a lot classier, too. They had to be the queens of the other great dae houses. A line of supplicants stretched out before each of them, but there was no mistaking the shift of attention as we came closer. Somehow I didn't think it wise to engage with them, and if forced into it, the party girl schtick wasn't gonna work.

"We need to find the Dowager," Brennan murmured. He sounded nervous. I couldn't imagine that boded well.

Couches had been set up creating islands of calm within the shifting currents of dae. They all kept a respectful distance from us, whispering. The Crypt

Keeper flanking our left was fingering the bone pommel of his knife. There were other security details in the room that looked just as jumpy.

It wasn't hard to tell that nobody here liked each other. I was pretty sure the only reason there wasn't open bloodshed was that everyone had a knife on everyone else. I was abruptly very thankful I was with five fiends, but even though they were the badasses of the bunch, there were a lot more of everybody else.

Our group made for the couches in the center, where the Dowager sat holding court amidst a circle of older fae, though none so old as her. She presented her cheek for Brennan to kiss. I did not attempt a curtsey. She still smirked at me, and then her expression went hard. The mood in the tent shifted with it. Conversations dropped out, and heads swiveled toward us. I started to sweat. Even the queens had paused to hear what she was going to say.

Crap.

The Dowager's voice carried to every corner, low and resonant.

"I'm pleased to see you well and fear I owe you both a debt. I promised you sanctuary, and it was compromised. You'll be pleased that the offending parties have been apprehended, and as a result, I've formally acknowledged Envy as a Malten. Tonight, she not only becomes full daemon, but Heir Presumptive. I shall see to clan matters for the foreseeable future as her Guardian." Her eyes drilled into me. I met them and swallowed with a quick nod, not even gonna play. The Dowager was done being amused with me, and I wasn't even close to being in her league.

Brennan blanched. "Amelda's—"

"Last living child was you. Even before her treachery, the clan chafed at pandering to her ego. Especially when a more than suitable replacement, already ripe with life, stands before us. Your mother's attempt to rob Fae of a child while under my roof goes beyond the pale. That my own son aided and abetted her cuts me to the core. I'm unable to remain passive any longer." There were angry murmurs of agreement from those seated around her and throughout the pavilion.

Wait, it had been Amelda who'd mickied my crepes? For whatever reason, I had a hard time wrapping my head around that. She'd been pretty hot to slit my throat, and poison seemed a bit subtle for a woman who wielded a flaming sword.

"Brennan, I shall leave it to you to determine the manner of their deaths, but if you're feeling merciful, I suggest you do so soon." She made a motion, and an imp pulled a cloth from what I'd thought was a low table.

I recognized the throne first, then had to make a concerted effort not to throw up.

It had been bent and melted into something roughly rectangular and fitted with glass panes. Inside its confines was a mass of oozing, pulsing flesh, still very much alive. I could pick out bits of teeth and long strands of golden hair amidst the chunks of muscle and globules of yellowed fat. It all seethed within a slurry of horrid crimson goo. A silver ring rose up from it to glint in the pavilion's light before it was sucked back down.

The last time I'd seen it had been on Horatio's chest.

Bile stung the back of my throat, and I hid my face

against Brennan's shoulder. It was like she'd put them in a blender and poured them in there. How was that medieval? My God, that was... I don't even know what that was.

Brennan gave a curt nod, his face a careful blank. "As you wish."

Christ, that comment about her attentions rarely being pleasant... I swallowed the acrid saliva that'd filled my mouth, not looking up until I heard the cloth settle back over that abomination. If I had any lingering doubts who I was naming, they'd vanished. She smirked at us past her jade stick.

"The two of you should run along and enjoy yourselves. The scrum will be starting soon. Mind the mist."

Dismissed, Brennan whisked me away before I could draw a breath. His brow had furrowed, and he didn't seem pleased. We exited the tent, and he lit a cigarette with his Zippo. I puked to one side of the pavilion. The Riders looked grim, talking amongst themselves, not happy about what had just gone down, either.

"What was that?" I tried to spit the taste of vomit from my mouth.

"Fae justice leans heavily toward corporal punishment, and I'm afraid the Dowager is a big proponent of providing cautionary tales."

An imp had followed us out and offered me a tray with a hotel toothbrush and a little bottle of mouthwash like it was a routine thing. Christ, they had an after-audience protocol. That was who was going to be ruling the clan? Who was going to be governing my ability? I brushed, swished, and spat, feeling beyond screwed.

"She's horrible."

Brennan blew out a long stream of smoke with a sad laugh. "Without question. However, I'm more concerned about the why of it than her character."

I went to go stand against him, and he kissed the top of my head, holding me close.

"You don't think Amelda did it either."

"I'm very certain the details on what really happened will remain closeted."

Silas.

What he'd said in the limo... The garden—that asshole had almost killed me! My stigmata flared, drawing eyes.

"Shh, Lovely. Time enough to deal with that later. We've enough fallout now. Bastard's pushed her to move. The dynamics of the game have changed considerably. By removing my mother and inserting herself using you as proxy, she's issued a formal challenge to Earth and any other fae that would oppose her politics. It makes you even more of a target."

I stared at him not understanding.

He drew on his cigarette so hard it crackled. "I'd hoped for more time to get you clear of her, but she's kicked the damn hornet's nest, and you'll be at your most vulnerable after the moon's apex. God, she's a cunning bitch."

"Tonight's the night for settling scores, my man." Jonas laughed, popping his knuckles. "She's got your number and is gonna use it to take out her opposition. They come for your sweet young thing. We put 'em down. Boss-lady's hands are clean, and she walks over their corpses to her throne. Buttons up nice. You run cover. Me an' the boys'll get Kitty out."

Brennan's expression had become calculating. "No… Do you remember what we talked about after Leipzig? It's time."

· The three larger Riders tensed, and the Crypt Keeper glanced between them. Jonas started laughing. "Yeah? Shit, I'm in, and I know these three ain't got nothin' better to do. You think you can pull it off?"

"Not alone, but I'm not without resources." Brennan brushed a stray lock of hair from my face. "Stay with the Riders for a moment."

He flicked away his cigarette and went to speak with the imp cleaning up the mess I'd made beside the tent. They yammered at each other for several minutes with an intensity that made me pretty positive they were negotiating some kind of a deal. Then Brennan was back. He smiled at me and threaded my arm through his.

"Right. Step lively, my love. We'll miss the opening play." He didn't give me a lot of opportunity to ask questions as we headed toward the edge of the board. I'm sure that was by design. All of them had gained that anticipatory tension. It had to be a fiend thing.

"Shouldn't we be hiding?"

"No, looking weak right now would be very bad. If you don't act like a predator, you become prey. After the second quad we can bow out for a bit. Until then, we need to be seen, but mind the crowd. As soon as the mists close in, they'll start coming for us openly. Envy, I need you to trust me and should anything happen to me, listen to Jonas or go with the imps."

"But the Dowager said the imps work for her."

A smile tugged at his lips. "They take her coin, but

loyalty is bought with more than that. If all goes to plan, this time tomorrow we'll be out on the balcony with a board game, and Fae will be a distant memory. You'd like that, wouldn't you?"

I just kind of nodded. I mean, what else could I do? We'd come to the large stadium seats overlooking the landscape below. The mists had thickened and were rolling down over the edges of the caldera. Where we'd come in, the gap had almost been filled. I wondered if Berk and the others had made the mesa, or if they were still down there somewhere, lost.

We sat on the hard metal seats, and Brennan put his arm around me, grinning ear to ear. He was pretty chipper for a guy who knew people were about to try and kill us. That, and the whole double-crossing the Dowager thing, which was completely insane. I'd lost any doubt he was a fiend. I told you, they were nuts. The anticipation in the air was thick, and other fae crowded in close Well, as close as the Riders would let them.

"Remember, Lovely, keep hold of my arm."

An air horn blew, and the stands exploded into cheers. Even Brennan added his voice to them, whooping like some kind of reprobate at the pub. I laughed, not believing it, but loving it.

Below, the strath had gone strangely quiet. Everyone leaned forward, waiting.

Someone appeared below within a cleared circle of earth. I couldn't tell much about them, other than they were nervous. They wore a white football helmet with a black line, and a padded black and white striped tunic and trews. In their hands was an oblong golden ball. They kept worrying at it between their palms.

A hush fell upon the crowd as the figure surveyed their position, looking out over the landscape, being careful not to break the confines of the circle. Brennan was watching with a peculiar predatory intensity that was more than a little disturbing.

"What are they—"

The figure made a quick break from the circle, and the crowd roared. As it did, great gouts of earth blasted up, then were blown away half a second later. Lesser elementals appeared, wrestling and beating the hell out of each other as they tried to either protect or get to the runner.

The fae in the stands went crazy, cheering. I've no idea what happened to the guy with the ball. I was completely absorbed by the free-for-all his bolting had kicked off between Earth and Fire. Water and Air were gleefully adding to the mayhem, respectively fanning the flames and muddying the field. It was absolute chaos, and the crowd was loving it.

Brennan glanced over with a feral smile. "That's the scrum, Lovely, and the normal's gone east. They'll be up against the wrong side of the paling in the third quad. Not a chance they'll get it over that to the spires."

Yeah... So, I'm not super big on sports outside of beer cozies and cute team shirts. All of this was beyond Greek to me. I mean, don't get me wrong. I enjoy watching men beat the hell out of each other as much as the next gal, but I kind of get bogged down on the play-by-play. Brennan was super into it. I watched for a while, but honestly, how long can you pay attention to that kind of thing? My wavering interest wasn't necessarily a detriment, because instead of having my eyes glued to the action, I caught the first of the fae being chucked over the side.

I know, right? What the hell!

I pulled on Brennan's sleeve, trying to get his attention. When he finally looked, he shrugged it off.

"Yes, that's why I said to stay close, else the pinchers will toss you in to ransom. After the Dowager's announcement, I don't know that I've enough available funds, and the bidding for you would be vicious."

I just kind of stared at him, not particularly liking the gleam the prospect brought to his eye. He gave me a smile and a peck on the cheek before focusing back on the game.

All right. So let me give you a rundown on what was going on. Apparently, every year on Midsummer's, they had the whole snooty dancing business up on the mesa itself, but below in the strath, they glamoured a poor, unsuspecting normal, gave them an actual ball, and told them to run like hell.

It really was a seriously fucked-up steeplechase. Ideally, the goal was for the normal to make a complete circuit of the mesa, which I think Brennan said was not quite four miles, through the strath, and then deliver the ball back into the circle they'd started in, ending the game.

But that never actually happened.

While this poor sap was running, elementals were doing their damnedest to either stop him or aid him, depending on what straws they'd drawn. This year was Fire and Air vs. Earth and Water. Even I had to admit, it was an epic matchup. The field below reflected it. That pretty park we'd come in through? Now it looked like Stalingrad, littered with fae bleeding out into the muck. A contingent of undines poofed in and patched up whoever couldn't do it themselves, then the combatants jumped right back into the fray.

Hmm? Oh, game-related poofing was sanctioned. Look, don't ask me. I didn't get it either. Everything in Fae has its own weird rules. Anyways, all that was happening down in the strath. Above on the mesa, pinchers skulked through the crowd, shanghaiing seemingly random fae and chucking them down into the melee.

This served two purposes. First and foremost, it's all in good fun. A fae noble goes over, has a rough and tumble with the lesser fae below, they ransom them back to their clan or whomever is willing to pay the asking price, and improve their financial prospects for the coming year. Meanwhile, the noble has to shine shoes if their clan doesn't get them back. Win-win and chuckles all around.

The second reason, and more applicable to my particular situation, is it's used to get rid of rivals. You pay a pincher, they snag whomever you've got a beef with, and over they go. Once down there, something unfortunate happens, and the undine doesn't quite get to them in time. A handful of fae bite it every year. It's expected. Aw, shucks.

Either way, it didn't sound like a lot of fun.

The air horn sounded, and Brennan laughed along with the rest of the crowd, clapping as they stood.

"Ah! That was brilliant! We almost got the little bastard by the nines. What do you think so far, Lovely?"

"It's…like nothing I've ever seen."

I guess that was the right answer because the smile

he gave me was dazzling. He took my arm in his, and we descended the bleachers. As soon as we were on the ground, the Riders were there. Jonas pulled Brennan aside to say something in his ear. His smile faded, and I couldn't help but notice the dae who rode War had a hand pressed to his ribs.

Brennan turned back to me. "Right. Let's get you a drink." His arm tightened on mine, and we started walking. I sure as hell wasn't going to argue but wanted an explanation.

"What happened?"

I could tell he was about to give me some bullshit line, but he must've thought better of it. "There was an attempt to get to you. We need to be seen through this next stretch, then Jonas has secured an area for us to wait for the apex."

Honestly, that sounded amazing. Between all those stairs and the hard stone floor, my feet were killing me. I could also really use the bathroom, but hadn't seen any port-o-potties. I swallowed a giggle, imagining trying to stuff myself into one of those wearing a ball gown. Christ, the entire back of my dress would end up sani-blue, which was ironically not in the least bit sanitary. I had an abrupt longing for Karen and a handicapped stall.

A booming voice filled the air, and I jumped. Brennan laughed and pointed behind us, toward the ballroom floor. Above it was an enormous projection of a screen. One side had those weird characters and flashing numbers. The other had a headshot of a sylph, absolutely caked in mud. I had to laugh at how miserable she was. Below a ticker was scrolling furiously.

"First ransom. Earth got ahold of her. Must be from a lesser house. What do you think, Lovely? Would you like her to do your laundry for the next year?"

I just kind of looked at him until his fingers raised up my jaw. He laughed.

"Ah, too late. Looks like her clan's bought her back." The next shot was of an absolutely livid dae. Everyone in the immediate vicinity started hooting and hollering. "Serves the bastard right. I hope an undine picks him up," Brennan said, chuckling.

"So what? They just let themselves get captured and then go to the highest bidder?"

"No one lets themselves get captured, but it's harder to get to your element's quad than you would think. If you can, your clan can bring you back up to the board. Otherwise you're on your own. That asshole Chaz probably paid to have himself thrown in thinking he'd win the pot." Brennan looked back up at the screen and grinned. "Haha, clan Gormast has got him. That's almost as bad."

I just shook my head. I'd rather be playing a board game with the imps. Fae games were as twisted as their politics and just as tempting to dabble in. Whatever. We'd gotten to a long promenade that'd been set up behind another row of bleachers. Black and white tents lined the sides, selling food and drink. Another had ribbons and one toward the end, flowers. It reminded me of a carnival, but without kids underfoot. My hand ghosted to my abdomen before I could stop it.

"Are there really no fae children?"

Brennan handed me a cup of something and shrugged, lighting a cigarette. We started walking again. "God willing, ours will be the first during my lifetime. I think I can count on two hands the halflings born the same century as me in the daemon realm. They mostly bring them from across the veil. Some years more than others. Not all of them last on this side, even after they become. Earth has the biggest numbers, then the fish. Air's a bit ahead of us population wise. As Silas mentioned, not many have what it takes."

I sipped on my drink, not wanting to think about him. "He did, but I thought he was just being a dick."

Brennan laughed, sending out a fitful stream of smoke. "He is, but not about that. Being dae is more than playing with fire, Lovely. You have to be flame."

It sounds stupid, but I knew exactly what he was talking about, and no, I can't explain it. It was just something I felt the truth of. I wasn't worried I fit the criteria. Like I told you way back when, I'm really good at fire.

"Do you believe the Dowager?"

"About?"

"That whatever happens tonight is going to fix that whole fertility thing."

He shrugged, taking another drag. "Maybe. It certainly dropped off after the primordials were imprisoned. Amelda was convinced it'd restore hers. That's the only reason she agreed to stop trying to kill you."

"You know it's not gonna work, right?" He stopped to give me his full attention, and I rolled my eyes. "The Dowager's gone to all this trouble to use Silas and this war of his with the normals to drum up support to bring those primordial fae back. But if I was one of them, there's not a freaking chance I'd be all babies and rainbows when I got—"

Son of a bitch.

Technically, I was one of those primordial fae. I mean, I was housing one. I wasn't sure what that would mean after I became, but I was pretty sure that was why she wanted me to name her Guardian. I'd be under her thumb for a century, along with my ability, and whatever came out of the ember. Christ, she'd freaking laid it out with that whole rampage spiel, and I bet she'd said the same thing to the others, too. Yeah, I was positive she was pulling a Pokémon and had to get 'em all. She'd have us name her Guardian, and then wheel and deal to get what she wanted from us, quid pro quo.

No way was I putting lotion in the basket.

My eyes narrowed, and I wish I could describe to you the look on Brennan's face. It was a frightening combination of his someone's-going-to-bleed-smile and a fierce anticipatory hunger.

"I'm contractually obliged to remind you of the importance of naming a suitable Guardian."

I literally hissed, and he gave a shiver of pleasure, then pulled me to him and kissed me like he wanted to eat me.

"You've no idea how turned on I am right now."

Oh, I had a pretty good idea. "Are you going to kill her?"

He smiled, his lips teasing mine. "Ah, Lovely, that would be telling, and the night's still young. Let's see how things progress, shall we?"

I glanced up at the moon, halfway to its peak. I had to tell the others before the apex. When my eyes came back to earth, my stomach plummeted with them. Mica was coming down the promenade toward us, and he wasn't alone.

3 Hours

Mica looked like a gorilla in a really expensive tux, and Serena was doing her best Fae Wray impression hanging off his arm.

Hah. Fae Wray. Sorry. Couldn't help myself.

Anyways, they were all match-y, the cravat at his neck the same shade of bruised plum as the gown clinging to her curves. I never would've imagined that slightly terrifying pairing, but they had that weird ease between them long-term couples get. Glancing at Brennan's expression, I had to wonder how long-term.

Serena turned, saying something to Mica as they neared. He smiled broadly, showing off those wickedly sharp canines of his. It didn't give me or anyone else warm fuzzies. The Riders went on guard, subtly shifting around us. My hand tightened on Brennan's arm.

"Little brother! I've just heard the news. I'd congratulate you on ridding us of the hag, but I know you don't have the balls to have framed her."

Brennan snapped his Zippo closed as Mica and Serena laughed. "Moving quickly with her out of the way, aren't you? Shall I gift the two of them to you as a wedding present? A little something for your entry hall. Seems like your taste in decor."

"Perhaps, but I don't like having to feed things. I'd much rather kill them."

Brennan shrugged like he'd expected that. The

crowd around us had slowed to a crawl, with plenty of fae not bothering to hide their interest in the conversation. The tent selling popcorn had to be making a fortune.

"I'm assuming you're threatening me?"

"Oh, yes."

"Fair enough." Brennan tipped his hat to them both. "If you'll excuse us, I don't want to miss the start of the second quad."

"I'm coming for you, little brother, and I'm planning to start on those fine fingers of yours."

"Here's one of them now." He shot Mica the bird, and I laughed as we left them.

"They're a couple?"

"Mmm. Before, during, and after I was with her. It was quite the joke, though I didn't know it at the time. I owe Mica for a great many things. Amelda prevented us from settling up. His death is overdue, and Serena's with it. Stay sharp. He'll strike tonight."

I cringed, feeling that damn gun barrel on the back of my neck again. "Why now?"

"My brother's impatient. With Amelda out of the way, he'll see no need to wait until next Midsummer. Recent history suggests I won't come out ahead against him. He'll continue to bank on his brute strength to finish it this time, but I believe he'll find that quite a bit more difficult than he anticipates."

"Why? Have you been taking Aikido or something?"

The Riders laughed, and Brennan's grin went feral. "Or something."

"They all think you've got his nuts in a vise, Kitty. Gonna be one hell of a shock when he brings the pain."

I glanced between Jonas and Brennan.

"My daemon form's been bound for so long I doubt they remember."

War snorted. "You don't forget that shit."

I thought about the fear in Amelda's eyes at the feast and had to agree.

"Don't worry, Stewie, we ain't kicking you out," Pestilence said, clasping the Crypt Keeper on the shoulder. "But he's probably gonna want his bike back."

Brennan pinched one last drag off his cigarette. "I do at that."

His bike? I glanced at him askance. What had taking off that watch set free? We settled into the bleachers overlooking the second quad, and I tried to take it all in.

If the last portion of the strath was Earth's, this was Water's. I mean, there were spits of land, but they were few and far between, and made up a labyrinthine path between thorns and sketchy stretches of open water. From up here, I could see a clear path through, but I doubted it would be so easy on the ground. The whole thing made me shiver. It was way too reminiscent of my swamp squid experience. Some poor fae went over the edge, and I heard a splash several moments later. At least it was a softer landing than the last quad had been.

Brennan put his arm around me and smiled. "After this, we'll find that tent."

"Good. You can tell me all about your bike."

His grin went feral again, and my stomach flip-flopped.

An air horn sounded, and my eyes moved over the crowd. They were wholly engaged by what was going on below. That figure in black and white, now completely spattered with mud, sat in another one of those circles. Boos started up when it became obvious they didn't seem inclined to move. Well, not until the ground began sinking. Then a whipping tentacle gave them some added incentive. I shivered again, watching them take off, but after the first few moments, it was hard to make out anything.

Gouts of water sprayed up, and a moment later, there was a horrific screaming that was way too familiar, but from a much larger creature. Like, I'm talking foe-of-Godzilla larger. Brennan and the rest of the fae in the stands went silent, then shot to their feet. A hand snaked around my ankle from under the bleachers the instant Brennan stood, taking his arm from my shoulders.

"Nadra queens aren't within regula—"

Poof.

Yep. I'd been pinched. Some sketchy fae poofed me to the edge of the mesa before I could blink and pitched me in. Then I was falling through the air, into the strath, and it was weird.

Time seemed to slow down, and I saw every leering smile and belly laugh at my plight. The fury on Brennan's face as I picked him out from the crowd. Then the lip of the mesa hid all of it and just wrapping my head around the fact that I was plummeting was a lot harder than you'd think. It didn't even occur to me to scream, and by the time it did, it was too late.

I hit that water hard and all the air slammed out of me. My skirts dragged me down, and I couldn't get out of them. Then fishy hands were on me, and my vision started to prick gray. A trail of bubbles erupted from my mouth. Through them, I saw the knife coming toward my chest.

Oh, hell no. There wasn't a fucking chance a fish was taking me out.

I called flame.

A lot of flame. It was like an underwater bomb went off, pushing the water back and propelling me upward. I slammed onto the bank and got a mouthful of mud. Above me, I could hear the crowd screaming, and I hoped the assholes were enjoying themselves. The air was thick with steam, and the water level had dropped by a good three feet. I clawed up the side of the pool onto a spit of rock, searing off my skirts into a tutu as I did, one of those stiletto pumps in my hand. Worst case, I figured I could stab someone with the damned thing.

I stood and tried to orientate myself. It was super murky down here, the lamp posts haloed points of distant light. I'd fallen at about the half-way point and was in a dead end. A bevy of wisps had swooped in, congregating around me. Crap. So much for hiding.

Wisps are like golf ball size, glowing, I don't know, foofy things. They'd be awesome at a rave. Anyways, they fall into the Fire elemental category and are only marginally sentient. They're also fantastic at leading people places. Most often to their doom, but we were on the same side, right? That and I figured I was already there.

"Please, can you get me to the next gate?" They paused, then gave halting bobs. I took it as a yes, running after them, absurdly grateful.

The cloud of them screeched to a halt, like they were confused, then took off in a different direction. I told you. Marginally sentient, but what were my choices?

Look, I was kind of screwed. Until that stupid normal made it around the strath or the moon hit its apex, the game kept going. I couldn't wait for their dumb ass to finish. I had to be up in that circle to stop the others from naming the Dowager. No one had implicitly spelled out what would happen to me if I wasn't with them, but I was thinking the outcome wouldn't be ideal. Neither would being ransomed or murdered down here.

The ground beneath me started to soften. After a few steps, I was up to my ankles and sinking fast. Goddamn it… Earth getting hold of me was a worse proposition than the fish. I fell onto my hands and knees, wrist deep in the sucking stuff. The wisps bobbed, and a bunch of them peeled off. I heard squelching footsteps behind me and wasn't going to wait to find out what they belonged to.

I sent flame into the ground, baking it cake-y. More than one blobby jack-off of mud fought me as I did, and that just pissed me off. I mean, what the hell was with these assholes ganging up on a girl? It was bullshit! My stigmata flared, turning them crispy, and I ripped myself out of the mire, shooting out plasma at whatever was behind me. I don't know what it'd been other than big and brown, but the top half slid off the bottom half, and both fell into the drink.

I ran in the opposite direction, following the wisps that were left. That horrific screeching sounded again, and let me tell you, down here, it was so much worse. I fell to my knees, hands clasped over my ears, no longer having to pee. The sound reverberated off the mesa thingy, amplifying painfully, and shaking the ground.

I didn't have a real clear concept of what a nadra queen was, but considering what the lesser one had done to me, I was certain I didn't want to engage in any more squid-scapades.

I splashed onto another path. The thorns lining it bursting into flame, setting off a chain reaction that lit up the entire landscape. Goddamn it! I stamped my foot, splattering mud. When the hell was I going to catch a break? The cries from above were manic. What fucking assholes! I stood there, not sobbing, in the center of a four-way intersection. That screaming came again. It sounded pissed, and a lot closer. Something ridiculously heavy crashed through the thorn hedge to my right, spraying me with broken branches and foul water. I fell to my knees, gripping that stupid shoe like a teddy bear.

The wisps swirled around me, urging me to move. I started running again, but wasn't particularly confident they were taking me in the right—

They weren't. They'd been taking me to where the normal was on the ground, cowering around that stupid ball. They bobbed above him like lightbulbs, and I abruptly had an idea.

It wasn't particularly bright, but just the fact that it didn't involve alcohol was pretty revolutionary. Baby steps here, people. Anyways, if I could manage to get this guy through the strath in the next three hours, the game ended, and I'd be able to make that freaking circle. Not only that, the Fire and Air elementals down here would help me do it.

Sorry, I'm laughing again. Every damn time I think I've got a handle on shit...

That stupid helmet tipped up, and my mother

looked at me.

I laughed, and probably would've kept on laughing if that scream didn't come again, accompanied by another crunching spray of thorns way too close for comfort. I snatched her arm and hauled her up.

"Run!"

For a woman who'd just turned thirty at least a dozen times, my mother was surprisingly fit. I wondered if the Priory had a gym I didn't know about. It was probably down in the catacombs with all the rest of the illicit shit they had going on. I laughed, imagining Sister Reticence giving a Jazzercise class.

"Can we stop with the inappropriate laughter, Envy? This situation is intolerable as it is without your chortling."

Yeah, that didn't help, and she shot me a glare. I tried to rein it in. "How are you even here?"

"God, crawl out of a bottle once in a while, maybe pick up a newspaper. We're at war with Fae. That son of a bitch Silas double-crossed me—"

That set me off again. How could it not? This was why you don't make deals with fae. I wondered if she still thought she got the better end of the deal.

A massive tentacle whipped over our heads, and a burst of ribbon-y Air elementals streamed past us. Guess the cavalry had finally gotten off their asses. The flames blooming from the thorns burst forth exponentially, and that thing screamed again. The wisps led us down a different path, and then my mother was the one that was screaming.

Her foot had gone into a hole I was positive hadn't been there before. It closed around her ankle, then morphed to stone, proving me right. Well, this wasn't looking good, I mean, at least not for her.

So, remember when I was explaining how this whole game worked? The goal was to make a complete circuit of the course to get the ball back to the first circle, blah, blah, blah. Fast forward to the "it never ended that way" part. Ideally, you wanted to get the normal to the end, something about extra points on the spread, but, eh. Things happened. The important part was the ball.

I grabbed it up and kept running.

My mother screamed. I laughed some more.

What? Like she wouldn't have left my ass in the dust. If someone had thought I'd be weighed down trying to save her, they were sadly mistaken. I mean, I did feel a little pang when the steady tirade of obscenities she was throwing at me splatted off rather abruptly, but for the most part, I was cool with it.

That made me laugh, too. I was pretty sure hearing your mother squished by some monstrous beast wasn't supposed to be cathartic.

Oh well.

So I was running through the mire, dressed like a demented ice-skater, gripping a shoe and a golden football. Fire elementals had come up to flank me, taking out Earth every time it tried to rise up. Whatever Air was doing behind me was pissing off that thing something fierce, and it kept slamming itself onto the ground making my footing dicey. I tore around a corner, and a massive arched gate was just beyond the next flooded section of path. Out of the corner of my eye, I caught movement and flattened myself into the muck.

It wasn't a moment too soon. One of those

tentacles whipped overhead. Unfortunately, a lot of smaller ones shot out of the water to either side of me. They held me down and ground my face into the mire.

I don't know if you've ever tried breathing mud, but it's not real feasible, and I started to panic. Those tentacles were all over me and in my hair. Like, messing it up and pulling out my combs. Another ripped off a glove to get at the ring on my finger.

The sons of bitches were mugging me!

I mean, at least wait until the freaking corpse is cool. My stigmata flared, and wings burst out from my back, frying all of those tentacles and anywhere my dress wasn't submerged. I clambered back onto my feet and ran like hell.

I was literally two steps from the gate when a massive fleshy tube snapped around my waist. It wrenched me backward, and I dropped the ball, my stigmata fizzling. This time there was no searing pain from the suckers, which I was super grateful for. Where it was gripping me, they were as big a dinner plates. If there had been those needle things like last time, they'd have skewered me like an Envy-kabob. It lifted me way up in the air, I could've seen into the stands again if I wasn't so busy looking down at the gray-mottled horror that had me.

I couldn't fathom how the hell it'd gotten in here. I mean, it was coming out of one of those pools, but no way was it was deep enough for it to have just been chillin' in there until someone came along. No wonder it was pissed. It was some deep-sea thing marinating in a kiddie pool. It had at least a dozen tentacles, and a massive beak in the middle of them. Huge gooey eyes were to either side. I've no idea what it looked like past them, but I had a feeling I'd be finding out from the inside. It whipped me through the air, and I dry heaved. Air elementals zipped around the thing like gnats. Below, Fire was doing its damnedest, but same deal. I didn't think one of the lords could put a dent in this thing, never mind a lesser fae.

I was gonna be a midnight snack.

The tentacle snapped me down toward its body, and I hovered in front of one of those nasty fish eyes, the pupil wangling like it was trying to focus on what it had.

Huh? Why didn't I call fire? Seriously? Fire wasn't gonna do squat. This whole time I'd been trying to summon plasma, but being whipped around like the end of a rat-tail made that kind of difficult. Let me tell you, it pissed me off, and knowing I was gonna get eaten by a stupid fish just made me madder.

I stabbed it with that goddamned stiletto.

So, I don't know if you've ever popped a fish's eye, but it's super disgusting. Like, it's got all this liquid-y grit inside. How do I know? It gushed out over me in this horrible slimy burst of ooze. The reek of it was so much worse than when I stomped on those eggs. But as nasty as it was for me, it must've been hella painful for the squid, because that thing went wild, flailing and screeching like nothing I've ever heard before. If it hadn't been squeezing me so hard, the whiplash would've killed me. As it was, I thought my eyes were gonna pop. A rib definitely did, and then it chucked me clear across the strath.

1 Hour

So I feel the need to make a small clarification here about stigmata and a dae's wings, because I can hear the question already. Why didn't I just fly?

Uh, because I didn't have my daemon form yet, duh. I told you Brennan's wings were like flame made flesh. Mine were, I don't know, insubstantial, and they definitely couldn't support the hundred some-odd pounds of the rest of me. In order for a dae, or a sylph, to fly, they had to be purely elemental. Gnomes and fish don't do wings. They get gills and some crap that lets them breathe dirt or something.

Whatever. It boiled down to me being shit out of luck, careening over the gate into the third quad, through a group of Air elementals. They did their damnedest to slow me down, then tried to cushion my fall. Crashing onto bare rock still hurt. I skidded away from a fence made of nasty metal spikes lining a ridge, not even wanting to think about how close I'd just come to being impaled...or splattered on the ground...or eaten by a squid...

How the ever-loving fuck was I still alive?

I lay there on my back, laughing manically, and it hurt. Oh my God, did it hurt.

I put a hand to my ribs and winced. Did I get a reprieve now? Like five minutes before something else tried to kill me? My fingers glopped at the thick coating of slime all over me.

Somehow, I managed to call flame and burn it off. It'd started to tingle, and that rarely led to good things. I mean, unless club music was involved. The only thing I could hear was the squid screaming and flailing around back the way I'd flown. Been pitched. Whatever. I wondered what Brennan was doing right now. I mean, other than smoking. Those stupid fucking fae rules would keep him or anyone else from poofing over here to rescue me until I reached Fire's quad. Christ, didn't I qualify as a damsel in distress? I lamented the death of chivalry. Why the hell did I have to be all liberated? Some prince on his faithful steed sounded mint right about now.

Fae-tale princesses had all the luck.

I pushed myself up against a low bit of ledge and almost died. That thing had definitely busted a rib or seven. I looked out over the last third of Air's quad and just kind of went numb.

Fuck my life.

Brennan had called them spires. They were these really tall outcroppings of stone with nothing between them. Or below. Well, nothing I could see. Just gray mist. As far as I knew, there could be punji sticks down there. Snakes. Shit, there could be a multi-colored ball pit, or it could go on forever. Maybe I'd jump down and join Alice for tea.

Sorry. I was rapidly reaching the end of my rope and losing my shit a little.

Yeah, all right, a lot.

Because speaking of rope, that was the only thing tangible between those fingers of stone. It crazed around them like some drunken asshole had tp'd the place with it. Maybe a dozen car lengths away, the next gate stood open, mocking me.

That stupid gold ball rolled over and hit my thigh. Where the hell had—

A sprite ginned at me with sharp-tipped teeth and vanished.

Then I felt the first drop of rain.

I didn't cry.

They had to be kidding. You and I both know they weren't. I could just see the moon through the clouds that'd snuck in overhead. I still had time. I could do this.

But not carrying a damn ball. Wincing, I shoved the thing into the remaining bodice of my dress. It came to rest at my gut, and I looked down, laughing. I regretted it. The laughing, I mean. Well, maybe all of it. My ribs were a serious issue and if an undine hadn't come to heal me by now, one wasn't going to.

I tried to heave myself up using those stupid spikes on the fence behind me and couldn't. I ended up flailing around and kind of wedging myself between them, trying not to pass out. The pain from my ribs was really bad. Every time I moved, there was one spot that felt like I was being stabbed, and my head went all light. The odds of me doing a ropes course were basically zero.

The ridge below me started to tremble. I could feel the Earth elementals coming up from below for me, which was weird. Like, the stone was alive—

Hey now.

I laughed again. Seriously, I couldn't help it. There's got to be some berserker swinging in my family tree, because no matter how much it hurt, and it did, the fact that I was able to suck those fuckers dry like I had Brennan's watch was hysterical. Then I was feeling pretty good, and that was even funnier.

I may have gotten a little carried away. It happens. You know, that whole lack-of-control thing we talked about at the beginning of all this? I'd gotten better at it, but let's face it. Right then I wasn't exactly at my best.

And I wanted to make them bleed.

So, the thing about taking another elemental's energy. I told you Amelda's and Silas's had "tasted" like them, for lack of a better term, and it had, but it was all, I don't know, Tex-Mex. Amelda might've been a shitty food-truck taco to Silas's carne asada, but the spices were all basically the same, and I'd been raised eating them.

Earth elementals were like biting into schnitzel. Totally freaking bizarre, and I hate veal. What do you even do with that? Well, I mean, I know what I did with it. I glutted myself on the stuff, but it didn't sit very well, and it was hea-v-y. It also made the base of the rock I was sitting on crumble once I'd sucked it dry of energy.

I'll admit it. I freaked when the ridge started tipping forward into the abyss, and I did scream that time. It was a good thing I'd wedged myself between those fence thingies, because there wasn't anything else to hold on to.

So, fun fact. I hold on to extra energy about as well as I hold my bladder when I'm terrified, and it all just kind of...went. That Earth energy I'd sucked up shot out of me like a massive wrecking ball, and those other fingers of rock? Yeah, think bowling pins.

I totally broke Air's quad. Whoops.

When the dust settled, those spits of rock were all kind of lying propped up against each other making a sort of busted up ladder to the gate.

I blinked, a lot.

The Dowager having control of our abilities abruptly took on a whole new meaning. She was a succubus. She'd not only be able to limit our power, she'd be able to draw on it, and use it, just like I had, and we wouldn't be able to stop her.

The four of us would be like her own personal batteries. She wasn't going to cajole us into working with her. She was just going to take what she wanted. Restore fertility, subjugate the human race...worse, she'd probably be able to put us right back into our prisons when our century ran out...unless we wanted to bargain.

You know how I feel about bargaining with fae.

I had to get through that goddamned gate and back on the board. I snapped my jaw shut and made for it.

The rain at that point was coming down in earnest, and everything was slick as hell. Elementals were trying to bash me off the spires, but those wisps were keeping the worst of them at bay. They went at the mistlings, and it was all exploding kittens. Think shrieking, hissing fluffy M-80's going off mid-air. Yeah, it was pretty epic, and I was giggling my ass off, the freaking "Star Spangled Banner" running through my head.

Until I slipped.

Air had my back, bolstering me until I was steady, but it was enough to slap the serious back into me. After that, I scampered across the busted spires pretty quick. It wasn't much different from going across the

Priory's roof…I mean, if semi-corporeal entities were fighting over a ball I had shoved down my shirt while I did it.

I crossed over the threshold and collapsed into the circle just past—

Poof.

I knew it was Brennan that'd grabbed me without him saying a word. The shape of his arms, the smell of tobacco, his aftershave… I ditched that stupid ball and buried my face in his neck, totally falling apart. He wasn't much better.

"My God, Lovely—"

"We ain't got time for this, bro. Take her with."

I caught sight of Jonas and the other Riders looking grim as Brennan picked me up. We started moving at just below a jog. There was yelling, the smell of burning textiles, and something briny and metallic. The snick and clash of steel. A lot of screaming. Brennan laughed.

"That was absolutely amazing. If we weren't in the middle of battle—"

Something beside us exploded, and he turned to shield me from the debris, then kept moving. "Getting you to the circle is going to be more difficult than anticipated. I'd hoped to have you on the central board—" There was a loud crack, and War grunted beside us. No one broke stride. "We're coming in from the edge. I'm afraid Earth has made their move, and it's rather impressive." I peeked around Brennan's neck.

Impressive? It was complete pandemonium.

Tents and pavilions were listing or in the process of burning to the ground. The bleachers looked like a Mack truck had hit them, and as I watched, one of those platforms teetered and crashed into the strath. Something big picked itself up from where it had stood, flinging itself at a similarly sized behemoth. Lesser fae were squaring off against each other in smaller battles, and on the central part of the board, an all-out war was being fought. There were freaking berms and explosions. Fae sprawled over the ground like it was the beach at Normandy.

"Is this supposed to happen?"

A blast to our right made Brennan stumble. He gripped me tighter, laughing. Guess he had some berserker, too. "No... This is strictly for your benefit, Lovely. We need to get behind our lines. Jonas thinks we can skirt the main battle. Can you run?"

Can I run.

He set me on my feet, and that's what we did. The Crypt Keeper (I couldn't think of him as Stewie) cut down anyone who got in our way. The other Riders did the same on our flanks, and Jonas had our back. The few who slipped by them didn't get past Brennan.

Then Earth ambushed us.

We'd gotten maybe halfway through the ring of pavilions when figures materialized up out of the ground, surrounding us. Not like those Earth elementals had done in the strath. This was some crazy ninja shit. I hadn't felt them at all. Well, I mean, I hadn't been really looking for them either, but you gotta trust me, it was scary slick, and there were a dozen of them, easy.

Did I say they were scary? Because they were scary. Every one of them were these melty manikin things of waxy tan-veined stone. They only had the suggestion of features, but I felt them hating on me. I'd never seen a sentinel before, but that was the only thing they could be, and that was bad. Like, really bad. Sentinels were Earth's hitmen and got sent out to take care of their, uh, problems. Permanently.

The Riders moved closer to us, and a morning star dropped out of Jonas's sleeve. It took a chunk out of the floor when it hit. One of the sentinels came forward, and its face rippled.

"Our quarrel's not with you. We just want the vessel."

"Sorry, bro, ain't happenin'."

The sentinel didn't seem displeased by the prospect. But then again, neither did the Riders. Brennan was more pragmatic. He looked up through the smoke at the moon and swore. We didn't have much time.

War followed his gaze, then let out a terrifying howl.

And it was answered.

Everything on that board paused for a heartbeat, and then it was like someone hit fast forward. I screamed as a sentinel took a swing at me. War took the thing's head off with a freaking scimitar as long as I was tall, and then the dogs tore the rest of its body to shreds.

Yeah, dogs. What dogs? The dogs of freaking War. I don't know where the hell they came from either, but they were there, a massive snapping, seething, drooling pack. Nightmare-inducing red brindled things, and ones black as night. I stood there agape, watching them rend the sentinels to bits.

And just for the record, you can get blood from a stone. A shit ton of it, as a matter of fact.

"Hurry, Lovely. They won't stay down long."

What? They came back? Brennan took my hand and advantage of the confusion. We ran past War, him and his slavering, snapping pack keeping the other sentinels at bay. Jonas, the Crypt Keeper, and Pestilence were at our sides.

You'll note I haven't really said much about him. There's a reason for that. I mean, he didn't look much different from War and Jonas, but he radiated this like, funk. Whenever he got too close, I felt like I was gonna puke. I mean, I'm sure he was a nice guy and all, but my stomach wasn't going to let me get too friendly.

Which was okay, because he wasn't letting anyone get too friendly with us, either.

As soon as we were past the sentinels, more of Earth's troops were waiting, and they weren't alone. Water had decided that it wasn't going to sit this one out. Undines are such assholes. The vast majority of what came at us was a mix of boggarts and freaking nixies.

Nixies are basically freshwater sirens…ah, mermaids, I guess. You know, the kind that lure sailors to their death.

Boggarts are like brownies gone bad. Not like the fun Girl Scout Brownies, or the delicious chocolate ones that I could really go for at the moment. These were bloodthirsty, evil little bastards. They stood about waist high and were all armed with nefarious looking kitchen implements. Don't get it twisted; they were nothing to laugh at. In particular, I was scared shitless of the guy with the corkscrew. He looked like he knew how to use it.

The nixies started to sing, and I'm sure their plan was to enchant the lot of us, then have the boggarts chop us up for stew.

Pestilence had other ideas. He ripped open his shirt and went all lord of the flies. A swarm poured from him, blackening out the moon. Brennan tried to keep moving me forward through the disgusting cloud of fleshy buzzing bodies, but I balked hardcore. They were everywhere, littering the ground and tangling in my hair... They popped under my bare feet, and I screamed, getting them in my mouth. In my freaking mouth!

Brennan picked me up, extending his aura over me like a shield. Yeah, I felt stupid for not thinking of it, but he'd been at this dae stuff a lot longer than I had, and at this point?

Jesus, take the wheel.

I'm not ashamed to say I sobbed against him like a little girl, letting him carry me through it. Shut up. I hate bugs. They're freaking gross! And I'd like to see how well you do midway through your own customized plague.

Whatever. So, you might be wondering where our reinforcements were. I mean, I sure as hell was. The Dowager had a lot of pull, and my stupid father was supposed to be warlord of the dae army or some crap. This thought became especially poignant when Brennan started to sink into the floor.

Yeah, we still hadn't gotten through the freaking blowflies, and Earth was doing that rock-softening crap. Something skittered across the stones, and then there was this horrific clacking surrounding us. Not being able to see what it was through the bug cloud made it worse. Brennan threw out a blast of heat like I had in the strath. It got us up out of the stone, but it slowed us way down. Which really was all they had to do, now wasn't it? As long as I didn't make that freaking circle for the apex, they won.

Looking up at the moon, I was pretty certain they'd achieved that.

Well, I was until Jonas ran forward and slammed his morning star onto the ground. A wide road of bones materialized leading to the center of the board. He clasped Brennan on the shoulder.

"Been savin' this one. Path to glory, bro. Let them fuckers suck on that. Stay on it. We'll catch up."

And that's why we didn't have any back up.

Brennan nodded, and we took off, following the Crypt Keeper. I don't know if you've ever run for your life down a path of bones shadowing Death, but it's pretty surreal. Not that I had much time to think. I did have some time to look around, though. To either side of us were some seriously pissed-off fae. For whatever reason, they couldn't touch us here, but I didn't kid myself that was gonna last. The edges were already beginning to turn to dust. I guess Patton was right. Glory really was fleeting.

Whatever. It got us through the worst of the fighting, and the center of the board was in sight. The path ended maybe a hundred yards before an inset ring of silver set into the floor. I was as thick as my thigh and split into quadrants by the floor tiles.

Berk, Kyle, and Morgana stood in three of them, and the moon was just shy of dead nuts above. A throng of armed dae was between us and them, the Dowager front and center.

As I stepped off the path, a smile sliced across her face. She had dimples, and I stumbled.

Brennan caught me up and kissed me. "Go, Lovely. Become."

The Dowager held out a hand to me, her gaze drawing me across the last of the expanse. Her fingers closed on mine, and a bellow of absolute anguish cut through the air. I spun around.

Brennan!

When I tried to pull away, the Dowager whipped me into the circle, almost ripping my arm out of its socket. I fell through a tangible barrier of light and scrambled to my feet, screaming and beating against it. The damned thing had solidified, trapping me in there. I struggled to make out what'd just happened as the barrier slowly clouded over like dirty ice.

Apex

I could barely see the crowd I'd passed through, but between them and me, a mangled body was bleeding out in a heap. I recognized the dress and not much else from this angle. Serena had been disemboweled, and her guts were splayed across the ballroom floor. Above her, two massive dae were ripping each other apart. One of them was a big bruiser of a daemon, all pumped up and a vibrant scarlet. He wore the remains of a bruised plum cravat, and the other—

"Damn, yo…" I shot Kyle a glare, but that about summed it up.

The other was tenebrous, shadow with form, a shade or two darker than midnight, clothed in black flame. Massive horns curved toward his chest, and wings of carmine and candlelight splayed from his back.

Half of his face had been ripped away.

Oh my fucking God. Brennan.

They didn't fight like men, they fought like beasts, slashing and tearing at each other—

And were gone.

I screamed in frustration, that stupid barrier had completely clouded over, and I couldn't see them anymore. I kicked it, then swore, looking around, frantic. I needed to—

"Envy. Calm down. The circle's closed. For good or ill, we are here for the duration." Berk's words were like being doused with cold water. He opened his arms, and I fell into them, my eyes hot.

Right on cue, Morgana made a noise like she'd stepped in something and started bitching.

"Great. So how long is this supposed to take?"

Kyle blew a curl from his eyes as he rolled them. "Chill, babe."

"It will take as long as it takes. Fighting amongst ourselves won't speed the process."

"No, but it kills time," she shot back.

I gritted my teeth and started to pull away from Berk, totally wanting to kill something.

"You guys can't name the Dowager—"

"We know," Morgana scoffed. "Karen told us and after this she's getting us out of Fae."

"Yeah, this place blows, and I'm dyin' for a Big Mac."

I just kind of looked at Kyle and blinked a bunch. I'd been doing that a lot lately.

Berk went to say something, and the moon hit its apex.

Heat caught me up, holding me rigid. Like lizard-basking, baby-oil-on-the-beach heat. That pervasive chill I'd had since falling into the strath sizzled away. The others were caught up in it, too.

My stigmata began to itch.

When they'd first come in, I'd thought I'd gotten poison ivy. Because casinos were loaded with the stuff. Look, googling your symptoms is always hit or miss. It was either that or terminal cancer. Anyways, this was that same horrible feeling, and I knew the routine. I fought not to scratch, my fingers balling up into fists. I backed against that solid wall of light, scritching up and down and wishing it wasn't so freaking smooth. Kyle was doing the same thing, and Morgana clawed at the sides of her throat where gross seaweed-y lines had started to ooze, then split open. She shrieked like she'd been stabbed. Berk just froze.

There was a pang in my chest, and I knew things were about to go downhill, fast.

The itch of my stigmata became a burn and then a sharp tearing sensation. I cried out and fell to my knees, putting a hand to my breast. A godawful ripping went through me. I coughed, blood filling my mouth.

My death felt very close.

That wrenching in my chest came again, and I screamed as the ember pushed out from my rib cage.

I was back in that place of flame and shadow, on my knees, panting before the tree.

It had leafed out and was studded with blossoms. The outsides were a delicate pink blush, and the insides as white as snow. Their light, sweet scent drifted against the haze of charring wood. The door in the bole had blackened, and flame flickered through the spaces eaten away by heat, edges glowing as they smoldered.

I rocked onto my heels and took my hand from my chest, looking down. A smear of gray and a bit of ash clung to my palm, like an afterthought. I stood and walked to the tree, my bare feet scattering cinders. When I placed the flat of my hand against the char, the door fell away in a shower of embers.

Beyond it was the inferno.

"You can still walk through." The voice from behind me tickled the small hairs at the nape of my neck.

I stood there frozen, my hand stretched out before me, Brennan's fae-band on my finger like an accusation. An anchor. A promise. I mean, pearls were just something that irritated the shit out of an oyster. I wondered if they were glad to be rid of them. My other hand brushed at the scar bisecting my chest, then fell to my abdomen. Would I?

"Will you take care of them?"

She came around me to sit beneath the tree. This time she wasn't quite me. For one, she was a lot cleaner. "I'm not much for kids, but I won't kick him out of bed."

Bitch. Not that I could disagree with the kid thing.

She laughed, picking up the snake that'd slithered into her lap and rubbing its muzzle against her nose. She gave it a kiss. "Brennan is your love. I know better. So would he... Pretty quickly I'd imagine. If you check out, first thing I'm doing is some backtracking with that sylph."

I rolled my eyes. Seeing him with Morgana had kind of killed it for me.

"And if I become?"

"If. You're already practically there. You wouldn't have needed this ceremony if the Dowager hadn't wrapped you up in one of her webs." The other me reached forward. Her finger sank into my chest and hooked out a clump of... I don't even know what it was, other than gross.

I took a massive gasping breath as she flicked it to the ground, and my skin bloomed the way Berk's had. Not super brown like him, but that perfect shade of golden. Everything got blurry, and I rubbed at my eyes.

The other me wiped her fingers off on her skirt with a frown.

"That's how she slowed our assimilation. When she couldn't remove the ember, she wound it up like a bug she'd planned on sucking dry and tied my hands. It threw us out of sync, and you couldn't finish taking what I had to give you. Silas getting Calista to put you under so deep when she drugged you circumvented the Dowager's meddling." There was a tremor, and the stones around us groaned. What the hell was that?

"Why did the Dowager want to slow it?"

"To keep me out of the way, and you in the dark, duh. She knows if you figured out making her your Guardian would let her feed on your ability, you'd never go along with it. With that kind of power, she'd rule Fae uncontested."

See, I freaking knew it, and I was pretty positive having a supreme ruler that put people in a blender was a bad idea. Still, I wasn't totally sold.

"What about all that running rampant stuff?"

She rolled her eyes. "Seriously? Do you really believe that meat-suit crap? Through the apple, you took enough of me in when you were a child for my consciousness to meld with yours. Granted, the others won't have it so easy." She seemed pretty tickled about that, and I wondered why. "All that's really left for you to assimilate are my memories, and I won't thrust them upon you unless you need them. With that said, there's a few choice ones you'll be reliving right away."

I didn't particularly like how hard her voice had just gotten. A violent tremor shook the ground, and I had trouble retaining my footing. One of the standing stones crashed down behind me, and she frowned.

"Look, you need to hurry up. I can't hold this place together with the ember gone. It's not like it's a secret what you're gonna do, but our Heavenly Father is big on free will and all that… You need to clearly state your intentions, so just shut up and choose all ready."

My fingers worried at Brennan's pearl, but she was right.

I didn't need to choose. I already had.

And that terrified me for more than one reason.

I did it anyways and named myself as Guardian. Screw all of them.

She laughed as the inferno filled me.

And I was reborn.

Light flared behind my eyes, and a tumble of, I don't know, everything, poured into my mind, burying me beneath it. I tried to focus on the little pieces of gravel digging into my palms, my knees. Something, anything to ground me.

Flames rushed into me, and my stigmata flared, wings exploding from my back and extending far out into the night. They were heavier and lighter than before. I stretched them, feeling parts unkink and furl out that hadn't been there before. It hurt and felt good, like working out a cramp. They created a nimbus of light, and the stone beneath me softened. I rose up and hovered, spreading my arms wide, rising on the thermals I was creating. My hair whipped violently, and the fire licked at me, but this time it came from my core, filling my chest, my lungs—

My memories.

I faltered, falling back to earth.

I don't know if you've ever had an ocular migraine, but it's basically a light show from hell that you can't not see. Eyes closed or open, it doesn't stop. The damn thing plays out, forcing you to witness what looks like a writhing, jagged hole in the space-time continuum.

The inside of my head felt like that.

All the snippets of that other me's memories realigned and slotted themselves somewhere in that ninety percent of gray matter I hadn't previously been using. It was seriously bizarre. Like I'd forgotten, oh, I don't know, several dozen millennia and suddenly been reminded of it all.

Boom. There ya go.

I closed my eyes, not that it helped, and waited for the Wayback Machine to stop at my floor.

All in all, it took less time than you'd think. I kept my promise to tease stuff out as needed. I mean, I still get the odd tumble of impressions now and again, but until I see a figurine of King Ur-Nammu, I don't remember having brunch with the guy. It's like when someone starts telling you about that one time at band camp, and that cues the flute, but you don't think of it otherwise.

Thank God.

The first thing that came in clear was how to poof. I would have laughed if I didn't feel like there was an icepick in my skull. The second was that it wasn't going to help me get out of here. This stupid volcanic pit was way shielded and if I tried to force past it, I would fry myself on it like a bug zapper. How did I know? Somewhere in the dawn of time, that'd been my bright idea.

I told you, my judgment wasn't always stellar.

That memory led to the next montage.

Crap.

So, back in the day, there were four fae courts, realms, whatever. Remember when I opined that fae had nothing better to do than sit around and think up ways to screw with each other? I'd hit the nail on the head. Most fae aren't immortal, but their lifespan's so long it might as well be. Deals, games, bargains… All of it's to alleviate a creeping ennui by drumming up some excitement with ever-increasing stakes.

And those freaking Proscriptions? Yeah, I'd decreed a bunch of them solely to mess with people. They were kind of a tit-for-tat joke between us primordials. It was probably why they'd finally decided to overthrow us. I mean, that and what could possibly be more exciting than screwing over the assholes making your life miserable with dumb rules?

Anywho, none of us saw it coming, and by the time we did, it was too late. There was a total uprising. Think French Revolution. Yeah. Those things never end well. They couldn't kill us, but figured out how to bench us for way longer than I would've guessed.

It was a good thing I'd gotten off that curse.

Hmm? You better believe that whole fae sterility thing was me. I might've been down for the count, but I wasn't out, and I sure as hell was sucking the joy out of their victory. The Earth Mother was the one that weakened the veil. I was pissed when she did it, but in retrospect, I guess I'm glad, though it added time to our sentence. Fae would've caved and let us go way sooner if they'd been trapped in the realms like rats.

I had the worst desire to return the favor.

Whatever. That wasn't the crap portion of the memory. The pertinent piece was what I had failed to see back then. You know, hindsight being 20/20 and all that.

It was the Dowager. Or as I'd known her then, Eris.

I'd trusted the bitch implicitly, and she'd been the one to plant the seeds of discord, hoping to reap the harvest, as she was doing now. She wouldn't have told Silas to stick the damn ember in my chest, but I'd bet good money that was where he'd gotten the idea from. As far as me giving the others to Berk, Kyle, and Morgana? I don't know. Maybe at some subconscious level I knew what I was doing.

Or it could've just been dumb luck. I seemed to have an abundance of that.

Anyways, I had zero doubt that she'd been more than happy to take advantage of the situation. If nothing else, dae are total opportunists. Hopefully Kyle and Berk were smart enough to name themselves, or at least someone trustworthy.

Morgana? Please.

Anyways, when my trip down memory lane faded, I was back on the floor, my wings cocooned around me. I trailed my fingers across them. Fire made flesh. They looked like they had back in the labyrinth. The tops were so dark red they flirted with black, fading to scarlet.

Then I noticed my skin.

It really had become that perfect shade of tan I'd always dreamed of. I sat there turning over my hands and looking at my legs in the light flickering from my wings. I couldn't believe it. I was so taken with all of it, the fighting took a while to register.

Not like a battle, this was people arguing, and their voices were familiar.

I dropped a wing and almost pissed myself.

So, becoming had physically changed me. My wings had come all the way in, and I'd lost the whole monochrome look I'd been rockin'. I mean, my hair was still black, but my skin had gone insta-bronze. Kyle's wings had come in too, and his curls were now as close to spun-gold as you could get. Think angel, and let me tell you, he was way dreamy. But like me, not all that different from where he'd started.

Berk had boobs.

Like, *boobs*.

Big ones, and hips to match.

All of it jiggled and swung as he and Kyle were trying to calm down Morgana.

Morgana...ah, haha...you gotta give me a second.

Sorry. It still kills me. She was screaming, ripping at the full beard dropping to her skinny, way-flat chest, and fighting to get them off her...him. I didn't know what was going on over there.

I made the mistake of laughing and the next thing I knew, she was on me, her hands around my throat. They were a lot bigger and a lot stronger than they had been, but she was clumsy with her new proportions.

She couldn't get a good enough grip to shut me up.

Man hands. Morgana had literal man hands—

"You fucking bitch! You did this to me!" Christ, even her voice had deepened.

Kyle grabbed her arms, hauling her back. "Chill. How could she have known? If you're gonna get all pissy at someone, be mad at Eris."

Eris. He remembered.

So did I.

Brennan.

I spun around to where I'd last seen them. That stupid barrier was still there, hiding what was beyond it. I stood, trying to pierce its depths. Maybe it was clearing? If it was, it was doing it way too slowly. I pressed an ear against it, but other than the idiots bickering at my back, it was eerily silent.

"Oh, my God, will you shut up!" I snarled back at them. They cut off mid-protest. I swallowed and tried to act like it hadn't shocked me, too. My voice had a weird resonance it hadn't before. I don't know how to describe it. Let's just call it authoritative.

My toes came to the edge of the circle, and I stared down at my chippy silver polish. It looked bizarre, lighter than my skin. Like I was a negative, but in color. I turned back to the others.

"Who did you name?"

Berk sighed, making her, his, prodigious chest heave. Think nipples the size of Lender's bagels. "Each other. It seemed safest. Did you name your dae?" His...her voice had gone all falsetto. Yeah, more blinking.

"Uh, no. I named myself."

They all glowered at me deadpan.

"Look, it's not like I planned it—"

"You never do." Berk went to cross his arm over his chest and looked down, shaking his head. "How do you get anything done with these?"

"Psh. I could ask the same thing."

Kyle and Berk snorted at Morgana man-spreading, and I couldn't blame them. It wasn't particularly impressive. I pulled my hair back and twisted it into a rope, trying to ignore Kyle eye-fucking me. All right, maybe I arched a little bit.

"Do any of you remember before?"

"Some, but it's jumbled. When the Earth Mother spoke to me, she said I was to wear her form, and she would come to me in dreams to ease our internal transition."

"Samesies," Kyle said, licking his lips at me before looking up at the moon. I was surprised to see it hadn't moved much past the apex. It felt like hours had passed. "All-Father went all Spiderman on me with some 'great power comes great responsibility' yada, yada. He's not letting me play with lightning 'til I learn some shit. Unless we see Eris. He wants to fry that bitch." He made a weird kung-fu noise, and I couldn't believe we used to date.

All right, yeah, I could. He was freakin' hot, and I'd never been interested in his brains.

Whatever. So much for preventing those primordial fae from wearing us like meat suits. Eris just wanted to stop them from making her a greasy smear in the pavement. It sucked that I wasn't going to be able to count on them for help getting out of here, though. Well, not the immortal badass kind at least. I briefly considered ditching them by flying up and out but scotched that thought pretty quick.

Even if I could, I wasn't willing to leave them. Shocking, I know. Fae weren't supposed to have consciences. Why I'd suddenly decided to develop whatever the hell I was rockin' was baffling. Well, unless you bought into it all that "self-sabotaging" bullshit Calista's boob-ogling therapist had rambled on about. He didn't have a very high opinion of me beyond my cleavage, but I have to admit, it is rather impressive. I glanced at Berk's.

Whatever.

Giving a shit was still really inconvenient. I looked at the barrier, biting my lip. What the hell was out there? My fingers went to my fae-band. I could feel Brennan, but it didn't give me any more insight than that.

"What about you?" Morgana asked. Her mouth was all thin-lipped and tight. She was totally about to have a mental break. How did I know? Please. I was kind of an expert. "He made me take his form and won't give me any of his power, and you're over there stupid gorgeous with your spray tan and big green eyes, looking like you know something. So yeah, what about you, bitch?"

"My eyes are green?" I already knew I was gorgeous.

"Yeah, it's sexy as hell." We all shot Kyle a dirty look.

Don't ask me why, but I decided to be honest with them. "I don't remember everything, but I remember enough. I've had the ember since I was a kid, it's always been kind of bleeding into me…she…she's me. There isn't any difference."

Morgana's lips peeled back from her teeth, and a growl started in her throat. Berk's arm wrapped around her shoulders.

"Don't, Morgana. We need to conserve our strength for whatever's out there." A moment passed, and she collapsed against him, sobbing. I kind of couldn't blame her. Waking up a dude must suck. My eyes flicked to her lap. Especially packin' that.

"Did Karen say what was supposed to happen next?" I asked.

Kyle shrugged. "This thing is supposed to fade, and someone's supposed to come get us."

Great. Nothing to do but wait.

It seemed like forever, but probably was only a couple of minutes. Slowly, the barrier became more transparent, and as it did, sound filtered back. Or lack of it, I should say. We all moved to the center, back to back. Outside of the odd scream in the distance, it was eerily quiet, and totally black, like the moonlight wasn't hitting outside of our circle.

Everything lay in shadow.

Tendrils licked right up to that silver ring inset into the floor but wouldn't pass over. The cold did. My breath began to cloud, and I rubbed at my arms, furling my wings tight around me, but I recognized the darkness.

It was Brennan's.

I crawled forward, and Kyle made a kind of strangled noise behind me. Like he hadn't seen my bare ass before. I was tired of waiting, and we couldn't stay here all night.

"Snow, I don't think that's a—"

I ignored him and reached past the ring, into the tendrils.

The entire circle dissipated with a blinding flash of light and a rush of freezing air. I heard a sharp crack, and something struck my shoulder, knocking me back. I had just enough time to realize I'd been shot before I was plowed down, and another bullet whizzed past. I landed on my back with someone holding me prone. A scream came from the direction of the shots.

"Your old man's one lucky son of a bitch, Kitty."

Jonas.

"Where is he?" The last visual I had of Brennan flitted across my mind's eye, and I felt sick.

The big dae gave a grunt that had nothing to do with my question and pushed up off me slow enough to make it awkward. "Damn, you look good cold."

I glared at him, and he grinned, showing me those piranha teeth behind his tusks. Shivering, I slapped his hand off my bare hip, and he chuckled, taking off his shirt. He threw it to me, the dog tags around his neck chiming.

"Better snuff those wings and put that on. The other Riders ain't all gentlemanly like me. You hear that, Gabriel? Kill the glow."

Kyle's wings faded a second after mine, and an awful kind of twilight rushed in, smelling of blood and viscera. Worse, it was tinged with the sweetness of oblivion. I licked my lips and looked around.

Forgetting would be bad.

The landscape resolved out of the gloom as my eyes adjusted to it. Shredded corpses littered the surrounding vista, and grotesque figures loped in the darkness. The air was thick with shadow and smoke, intermittent fires illuminating small pockets of desolation. The Riders crouched around us, looking out into the murk.

I focused on the gory hole in my shoulder until it pushed out a jagged stone, sizzling as the wounds closed. God, it had been a long time since I'd done that, but I was grateful for the refresher. Among other things, it'd given me a heads-up that this body was definitely not immortal.

Fun times.

I shrugged into Jonas's battered button-down. The

340

shirt hung to my knees, and I started rolling up the sleeves. "Thank you. Is Brennan ok?"

"He took a hit but has 'em pinned." Jonas picked up the rock that'd I'd been shot with and frowned, flicking it away. "We gotta move if we're gonna make the rendezvous." He stood, and everyone else did with him. Well, almost everyone.

"I'm not going anywhere—"

War decked Morgana and knocked her ass out. "Guess again, fish." He threw her over his shoulder like the catch of the day, then shrugged at Berk's shock. "We ain't got time for drama."

The Riders set a quick pace with a definite goal in mind. War had to call his dogs once, but all in all, there was less opposition than we'd run into on the way in. The Crypt Keeper kicked a severed arm out of his way, and I was pretty sure that was because there were a lot less alive to oppose. The pomegranate pavilion loomed up out of the smoke, and my steps slowed. Jonas came up beside me and waved the others past.

"Come on, Kitty, imps are inside waitin' to get you clear."

"Tell me the rest."

The big dae scratched the back of his neck and made a face. "That bitch Serena caught him with a sucker punch when he was watchin' you go in. Ripped him up bad, and he couldn't hold back the fiend. Gutted her. Mica lost it. Shithead jumped him. Brennan put him down pretty fast, but then Earth made for our lines… Man called shadow, pushed 'em back."

I shivered and rubbed at my arms. "Where is he now?"

"Hunting."

"And the Dowager?"

"Prey."

My stomach twisted. "Do you know where she is?"

"Nah. Shit started goin' sideways, and she disappeared, but last I saw, she ain't happy."

No. I couldn't imagine she would be. Spoiler, neither was I. Closing my eyes, I threw out my aura like a net. She wasn't far, and neither was Brennan. Taking a deep breath, I faced Jonas.

"Get the others across the veil. I need to finish something."

He started to laugh, then saw the look on my face.

"You for real?"

"You heard me."

"Against the Dowager? Just who the hell do you think you are, Kitty?"

All I could think of was that effigy that'd hung behind my mother's desk at the Priory.

I smiled at him. "I'm the Apocalypse."

After

I ran through shadow, Jonas and Stewie at my back. I'm pretty sure that looked a lot more impressive than it sounded. At least, in my head it did. I'd be lying if I said I didn't feel better having them there, and Jonas had made a very valid point. If Brennan was messed up, there was no way in hell I'd be able to carry him out.

Been there. Failed miserably trying to do that.

Besides, who doesn't feel ten times more badass with muscle behind them? For all my big talk, I needed the psychological boost. Especially since wearing a grubby button-down, like thirteen sizes too big, wasn't exactly dressing for success. God, wasn't this the part where I got to wear slick armor, or wield a magic sword or something? I stubbed my toe on some rubble and bit back a yelp.

Jonas put a hand on my shoulder, and we crouched down behind a collapsed pavilion. He pointed in the distance. The Dowager was out there, a man-shaped lump at her feet. Fog from the Lethe drifted between us, and the taste of oblivion was heavy on my tongue. I called a steady trickle of flame, keeping my senses sharp.

"What did Brennan mean when he brought up Leipzig?"

"It was a stupid idea. Just drunken bullshit—" Jonas snorted, giving me the side-eye. "Freedom, Kitty.

We was gonna defect to the other side. Set ourselves up with a harem of honeys and patrol the veil to keep the rest of them from our plunder. Fuck 'em over real good for all the shit—don't matter. Brennan went and screwed the pooch with that slut Serena. He's the only one of us that could've taken the Dowager back then, and now the man's out of practice. I shoulda known this would go sideways when that fuckin' stone got by him and tagged you…"

It was scary close to what I'd been planning. Great minds and all that.

"I can take her."

Yeah, he looked at me the way you are, but I was a goddamned goddess now, and pretty sure I wasn't full of shit. I tried to look like I believed it and was surprised to find I did.

"Look, you'll get your harem if you get him out with the others while I deal with her."

"We're with you, regardless. Gettin' the others clear played our hand. Either you're what Brennan says you are, or we're soup. But even if you get her under wraps, what about the rest of 'em out there?"

This one time, at band camp…

"They're right where I want them."

He didn't look convinced, and I didn't care. I took a deep breath and stood, sending whispers of my aura out around me, mapping the terrain and finding the fae hidden amongst the rubble. Eris had done the same, leaving the sticky residue of her being all over everything, like a seriously gooey sneeze. She'd never had a particularly refined touch, and age hadn't improved it. I slid in and around her threads, creating an intangible web of my own.

I stopped several yards in front of her. Brennan was out cold, but otherwise seemed unharmed. The way he was lying, I couldn't see his face. I quested out a tendril of energy and came up short. She had him completely encased in her webs.

"Touch him, and he dies."

My gaze rose to meet hers. "If I don't, the Lethe will kill him anyways."

"Bit of a pickle, isn't it?"

I rolled my eyes at her smirk. "What do you desire, Eris?"

A shiver ran through her as I spoke her name. It wasn't enough of it to bind her, but it would put her hackles up. "I can't tell you the last time I've heard that... Shall I return the favor, for old times' sake, Lilith?"

I shrugged, and her nostrils flared.

God, that was satisfying.

Hmm? Well, yeah, that was my name, the oldest of them, actually, but it wasn't who I was anymore. Her sidelining me and then the whole being-reborn thing had subtly altered my being. You gotta love unforeseen consequences, I mean, when they're not screwing me over.

Anywho... There we were, surrounded by mists on a desolate plain, with the father of my unborn child prone on the ground between us. The moon had begun to break through the shadows, and wreckage smoldered around us. Eris stood untouched by it all, her ivory gown pristine amidst the destruction. Her lips pursed, and she took out her jade stick.

"His life for three boons."

"And they are?"

I crossed my arms under my breasts. She noticed. That was the point. Her eyes roamed over me as she affixed a cigarette. Someone hadn't gotten any in a while.

"You'll act as my protector against all threats, be they mortal or immortal. You'll swear eternal fealty to me, and not interfere with my rule, either by direct or indirect means. Lastly, you will lift your curse of infertility."

Wording was pretty solid. Sounded like she'd thought a lot about it. Hmm? Why didn't she just ask to band me? Same reason I was able to get out of the collar. If I didn't want it to hold me, it wouldn't. They were designed for elementals. I was the freaking element.

"You really think he's worth all that?"

Eris met my eye with the same shrug I'd just given her. Bitch. She had me against the ropes and knew it.

"Answer me a question first, without evasion. Why this body?"

A massive smile bloomed across her face, and those dimples of hers were about a mile deep. I wasn't up for mental gymnastics, so I'll spare you the long, overblown, muah haha evil villain explanation she gave. It was super convoluted, and her rationale was tenuous at best. Whatever, I totally tuned it out. Hmm? Because I didn't care, and it wasn't important. What was, was her focusing on her own brilliance, to the exclusion of all else.

Let me explain.

Say you won a competition, and the grand prize is, oh, I don't know, a coffee mug. World's Best Hotdog Gargler. You drink out of your mug every day. Show it off to people who visit. Tell the story repeatedly of just how many wieners tickled your tonsils to earn you that title. After a couple millennia, it's old hat, and the mug is just a mug. You forget where it came from. It's something you take for granted.

Except to the person who lost, because you cheated.

What? I don't know how you'd cheat at—maybe one was a freaking kielbasa. I'm not real versed in tubed-meat contests. Let's focus, people.

Anyways, I tried to look suitably shocked and appalled as she wrapped up her diabolical monologue. Finally getting the reaction out of me she'd been gunning for, she grinned, raising up her jade stick to light her cigarette, and as she slid it between her lips, I broke the enchantment on it.

I wish I could adequately describe for you the look on her face as my snake reanimated and forced itself through her open jaws and down her throat. I mean, I'd been stuck in an ember for I don't know how long, but my snake'd had a like a bajillion cigarettes shoved up its ass and been forced to play kissy-face with the hag.

It was super pissed and really hungry.

Eris keeled over, clawing at her throat and grasping feebly at the length of tail lashing against her face. I threw out my aura, shielding Brennan and severing her webbing, then filling him with flame, burning the Lethe from his body. The Crypt Keeper and Jonas were at my side before Eris hit the ground. Jonas didn't lose any time hefting Brennan up in one of those firemen's lifts.

His face lolled toward me.

I'd kind of known what to expect, but seeing something for yourself is always worse than just knowing. I took a good long look, steeling my resolve for what was coming next.

A battery of stones smashed around us, deflecting off my aura.

"You sure you got this, Kitty?"

I just looked at Jonas. He grunted, then they took off. The imps would be waiting.

I had other plans.

Brennan had said after the apex I'd be at my weakest. You know, vulnerable, new. And in his defense, there is a period after becoming when a half-dae typically struggles with Fire. When they tried to reconcile the vindictive hunger of the flames and the total lack of control, or remorse as they raged, consuming with completely unsympathetic abandon—

You see where I'm going with this, right?

Fire and I were on exactly the same page.

Another barrage of stones slammed down around me, some as big as cannon balls.

I placed my palms flat on the board and called to those tendrils I'd sent out earlier. They lashed around the elementals firing on me, and I drained them of their power, then sent it back at them in violent torrents of rage. My serpent coiled up around me, nestling itself around my neck and draping beneath my hair as the ground shook and fractured. From far below, flame answered my call, and rock became molten. My form fell away, and I was free.

Enduring and ancient.

I was the inferno.

And my desires were divine.

I rose up, a perfect being of light at the heart of a maelstrom of flame. Below me, the ground churned liquid, eating away at an ever-widening portion of the strath. The stone of the mesa's wall softened and crumbled apart like a glacier falling into the sea. The chess board tipped.

Fae screamed, and a rush of Air elementals went past me. Laughing, I drank in their power and sent it out again, amplifying the intensity of the conflagration into a firestorm. I hovered, watching it burn...until I felt Brennan's presence attenuate. They'd left the realms of Fae. I turned my attention to that bug zapper over the caldera. It had taken all four of us to create a weaving complex enough to stymie each other's power, and like I said, I didn't have a chance of breaking through it.

I could, however, relocate it.

I pulled the energy into myself. It was too much to hold for more than a heartbeat, but that's all I needed. I poofed to the Neither, chucked it, and ran.

You've already had the concept of the Neither explained to you. Remember, that whole gross in-between onion skin that's not a skin, a boundary between planes of existence thing? Right. Setting loose all of that energy from the caldera was basically the equivalent to Brennan imploding, and as he predicted, it was absorbed.

But it wasn't like an explosion where it's one and done. The weave I tossed dispersed out and thickened. It was kind of like using that crazy expandable foam, and trust me, you don't want that shit on your hands. I poofed out before I got stuck. For better or worse, I'd just sealed off earth from Fae, until the four of us agreed to lift it. Seriously, it was better that way. If the others didn't get a handle on their abilities first, they'd be easy pickings for those douchebag fairies.

Yeah, I said it.

With one threat mitigated, I turned my attention to the next. The stained-glass window from the Priory's chapel flooded my mind, and I was there.

The building was a shell, the charred skeleton of it baked hard and dry from the desert sun. I went through its desiccated corpse to where the supply room had stood. A concealed hole in the ground led down into blackness.

I brought the light.

The dedicates of the Lady scurried away, cowering from me. They searched for shadows to hide in where none could be. My outstretched wings scraped along the close tunnel walls, shedding long ribbons of flame. They writhed in my wake, becoming serpents of Fire. I sent them forth, herding the nuns into the skep where the anathema had been.

There was no piety in their eyes, nor in their hearts. That ancient part of me that'd once known priestly adoration raged. Their blasphemy could not be borne. Shrouded within coils of my serpents, the women bore witness to the retribution of flame. The sound of Sister Reticence's screams were all the prayers I needed.

I brought the catacombs down in on them, leaving their ashes entombed in melted stone, the desert above sinking down to settle into a shallow valley. The adobe walls cracked and fell, and there was the screech of metal twisting as the highway running to the city fragmented with the shifting land.

I stumbled, and I sat on what had been the roof of the Priory, buck naked with my snake, looking past the crumbled soot-stained and blackened adobe wall. Don't let anyone kid you. Divine retribution is freaking hard work. There'd be time enough to hunt down the rest of the assholes killing halflings. With the four of us back, they'd be the last generation, and I was going to personally guarantee all of them became.

Yeah, even the stupid fish.

The sun was just starting to pink up behind the mountains, and Vel City still slept in the distance. I didn't wish I wasn't me. That'd come true.

But I did want a drink.

Footfalls sounded on the gravel behind me, and tobacco was in the wind. My stomach flipped. When I thought back to all those books on his desk now, I knew what they'd been about. All of them, the very oldest accounts of the world's creation, and the garden, before it'd been thorn and bone...

Whatever. I petted my snake.

Faint birdsong began around us as the sky turned the landscape a rose gold.

Brennan's cigarette crackled, then he exhaled, low and long. When he spoke, his voice was thick. "Was the lobotomy a success?"

My lips tipped up. "An epic failure, I'm afraid."

"Hmm. Can't say I'm disappointed. Are you ready to come home, Lovely? I'm rather fond of snakes."

Home. I closed my eyes, and my wings faded. His footsteps came closer, the weight of his jacket settling around my shoulders.

"I'm not above bribing you." His breath was soft on my ear as he handed me an open bottle of cognac. I laughed, turning as I took it, and even though I'd been expecting it, I couldn't stop my cry of dismay.

He grimaced. "Ghastly, isn't it?"

It was, even in the weak morning light. The right side of his face was a ruin of gouged flesh beneath his tousled hair. I ran my fingertips over the ridges. He winced but let me. Clawed furrows ran from his brow to his jawline, one of them slicing across the bridge of his nose. The socket beneath his eyelid was sunken and puckered. I threw my arms around his neck. He winced like he was injured elsewhere.

"Careful. The fish could only do so much."

"I wish I'd seen you kill them."

"Serena's death was quicker than she deserved, but one of the imps has a video of Mica's demise on his phone. We're going to have to figure out where to put them all. Right now Berk's got them in the catacombs, but that's hardly—"

"Wait—the imps are all here? Like all, all of them?"

"Well, yes, that was part of our deal. They help get us out of Fae, we relocate them... Think of it as a witness protection program." He took another drag and grinned at me. "Quite a few of the lesser fae jumped ship. Honestly, most of them preferred living on this side of the veil, anyway. I don't know if you noticed, but every elemental lord I've ever met is a pretentious dick."

I laughed. "Yourself included?"

"Especially me."

"Will it heal?"

"In time. Regenerating an organ is a bit of a process."

My hand trailed over his cheek, and I sent energy out to him. The ridges smoothed as some of the damage faded, but he was right. It would take time. He pressed

352

his forehead to mine, and I breathed him in.

"You haven't said no, but I need to hear yes, Lovely."

"Tell me first. You're not under contract anymore."

"It began as my chance to be free of Amelda. The Dowager needed a front man to keep tabs on Silas, and to ensure his plans progressed to suit her. But then…" He laughed low in his throat. "You opened up so many possibilities. Forgive me for taking advantage of them…of you. Will you let me spend eternity making it up to you?"

I let him kiss me. It was teasing and sweet, leaving me wanting more. God help me, but I did want more. He kissed me again, and for a time I didn't think about much else…but something niggled, and I couldn't let it go.

"Why all those books on the beginning?"

"Will you bargain for the answer?"

"Only if you promise to grow your stubble. I don't think you can be a proper pirate without it." He'd make one hell of a rogue with that and an eye patch.

Brennan scratched at his unmarred cheek. "You negotiate like a fae already." I laughed at his expression, and he smiled, giving a little shrug. "You'll think I'm mad, but at the pub, that first time I glamoured you…I saw her. You. Neither version was what I was led to believe. I spent that first night trying to figure out what I'd gotten myself into."

"And what did you find?"

He tucked a lock of hair behind my ear. "That from the beginning, you'd been as trapped as I, and they wanted me to help them do it again. Then that look on your face when you slammed my trousers onto my desk… I couldn't. I swear to you, Lovely, I'll not make the same mistake Adam did, nor will I ever supplant you with another. I don't want your submission. I want to feel your fire—"

I won't tell you the name he whispered before he kissed me. Not Envy, or Lilith, but something of them both, those halves of me creating a greater whole. My stigmata flared, and my wings extended out, bathing the desert in scarlet and a red so dark it was ebony. His fingers trailed through them, and it was bliss. How could I say no?

Things were good after that.

Well, until the kid was born. But that's another story.